The Archangel Drones

By

Joe Nobody

Edited by:

E. T. Ivester
D. Allen
www.joenobodybooks.com

Other Books by Joe Nobody:

Holding Your Ground: Preparing for Defense if it All Falls Apart
The TEOTWAWKI Tuxedo: Formal Survival Attire
Without Rule of Law: Advanced Skills to Help You Survive
Holding Their Own: A Story of Survival
Holding Their Own II: The Independents
Holding Their Own III: Pedestals of Ash
Holding Their Own IV: The Ascent
Holding Their Own V: The Alpha Chronicles
Holding Their Own VI: Bishop's Song
Holding Their Own VII: Phoenix Star
Holding Their Own IX: The Salt War
The Home Schooled Shootist: Training to Fight with a Carbine
Apocalypse Drift
The Little River Otter
The Olympus Device: Book One
The Olympus Device: Book Two
Secession: The Storm
The Ebola Wall

Foreword by Joe Nobody

The drone technology depicted in this work is real. It exists today and is commercially available through the internet, a local hobby store, or your favorite big box gadget dealer. For no more than the price of a top-tier hunting rifle and optic, any American can purchase the equipment depicted within the pages of this manuscript.

It is common knowledge that unmanned aerial vehicles are being utilized over American soil by government agencies ranging from the U.S. Border Patrol to rural police departments. Many citizens feel their privacy is already threatened by such devices. Private ownership of these machines can only compound that issue, especially if the sky becomes pudding-thick with cameras, microphones, and memory cards.

But what if that technology were turned around and used to curb abusive authority? What if the average citizen could protect his family or business against overstepping agencies or those guilty of government corruption? In this work, I use an example out of today's headlines, the excessive use of force by law enforcement. In reality, I could have penned the IRS or the Bureau of Land Management or ATF as the antagonist. There is no shortage of potential villains that could be inserted into the story line – our world seems to produce a target rich environment of agencies who have been caught blurring the lines of the law.

Which brings me to the police.

The law enforcement tactics and methods described herein, as well as the information pertaining to the legal system, are based on fact and actual events. While it may seem I have a bone to pick with Harris County, Texas, that isn't the case. The same can be said of the Houston Police Department. I selected my hometown as a basis for this fictional work due to the availability of experts and the proximity to resources required for background research. No reference to any living individual is intended. If you are ever pulled over by HPD, I'm sure you'll find the officers are as professional as those serving in any law enforcement department in the country.

LAISSEZ LE BONTON ROULET

I am not anti-police or a cop hater. In fact, the opposite is true. Throughout my professional career, I have worked with, trained beside, instructed, and generally supported law enforcement professionals at local, state, and federal levels. I have no ax to grind. I've never been arrested - not even a single traffic ticket in the last 20 years. Not one member of my immediate family has spent a single night in the gulag.

Like many Americans, I have relatives who patrol the streets. They are good, honorable people, the kind you want alongside if trouble comes your way. As I wrote this book, I often thought of them, and other dear friends who carry a badge and gun.

But within law enforcement, there are always the rare few who take authority too far, abusing the public trust. These predators infuriate me, deserve community wrath, and should be prosecuted to the fullest extent of the law. While typically a small percentage of any policing organization, they can destroy the reputation of entire departments, eroding the people's faith and generating widespread ill will. The bad apple can indeed rot the whole barrel, especially with the advent of cell phone cameras, internet video, and security monitor systems on practically every street corner.

For this title, I conducted extensive research to create fiction within a structure of reality. This effort included interviews with numerous law enforcement personnel, an in-depth study of three different Department of Justice investigations, a review of court documents from no less than a dozen individual cases, and hours of online fact finding.

I read hundreds of newspaper articles, watched countless videos posted on the internet, and struggled through piles of FBI and DOJ reports.

As an author who pens fiction, it would be easy to dwell on the negative side of any organization, group, or department, including peace officers. I could hype the evil, monstrous examples and paint a picture of draconian doom. Doing so would be dishonest and result in bad storytelling.

But it would be just as deceitful if I ignored the truth, no matter how distasteful or troubling. Abusive law enforcement personnel do exist. They always have and probably always will. The primary difference today is that video technology exposes their presence more than ever before, and it's not pretty.

The reader will find characters on both sides of the good/bad cop equation in this book, because that is reality, which in my opinion, leads to better storytelling.

It is my greatest wish that this tale engender new awareness and understanding by citizens and peace officers alike. But more importantly, I hope it entertains as a story. From the beginning, that's all it was ever meant to be.

Enjoy,

Joe

Chapter 1

Peelian Principle
The police are the public, and the public are the police.

The game was a real barn-burner. On practically every play, one side or the other of the packed gymnasium erupted, the rabid fans surging to their feet, screaming to the rafters. It was the city championship, two of the best high school teams in the country locked in a desperate contest.

Officer Marwick stood with his back to the wall, maintaining a courtside position that would have been denied anyone not in uniform or part of the athletic staff. He was a peace officer, and a large, mean-looking one at that. He could stand anywhere he wanted.

Broadcasting such an unapproachable demeanor was as much a defense mechanism as a marker of aloof authority. Such a social barrier was necessary because citizens were constantly approaching policemen and saying stupid shit, often at the worst possible times.

Marwick could remember a time not long ago when he was trying to coax a belligerent drunk out of his pickup, the inebriated citizen stopping in the center lane of a busy expressway and causing a traffic hazard. A new vehicle stopped, blocking yet another lane while the middle-aged driver rolled down his window and inquired, "Excuse me, Officer, but can you tell me where Portway Avenue is?"

Anyone who wore the uniform could cite similar experiences. Folks who didn't seem to be able to follow mobile telephone turn-by-turn instructions often saw cops as the human version of Google Maps. People approached while officers were eating, attending church, or sitting in the middle of a dark lot, filling out paperwork. A few years ago, Jim was rousted from bed in the midst of the night, a complete stranger seeing his squad car in the driveway and wanting to report an obnoxious barking dog. Social fences had to be erected, if for no other reason than maintaining even a modest amount of sanity.

While his dark eyes never left the on-court action, it would have been impossible to tell which team the policeman was rooting for. The emotionless expression, so often worn by men in authority, remained firmly painted on his face. It was a façade, covering the frustration boiling inside the 300-pound muscle mass wearing the shield. Still, he had to maintain a cool and stoic expression, removing all evidence of personal interest from his presence and demeanor. After all, he was a peace officer in a public forum.

Big Jim, as his brother officers called him, wasn't anxious about the crowd, traffic, or any potential law breaking. His son was in the game, and it wasn't one of Junior's best efforts.

Marwick could care less about basketball, the typical parental frustrations accented by his oldest boy's devotion to the sport. Football was a real man's game, and despite his fatherly guidance, Jim Jr. never seemed to connect with his dad's legacy and love of the gridiron.

Big Jim had graduated from this very high school over 20 years ago, his team pictures still adorning one of the large institution's halls. No doubt there were trophies somewhere, dusty relics citing J.T. Marwick's athletic prowess for everything from "All City" to "All County," and "Defensive Player of the Year."

Marwick relished football, the only sport socially sanctioned where a man could establish himself in a physical manner and dominate others without fear of disdain or retribution. People actually cheered when he inflicted pain on opposing players, patting him on the back, and expressing support for the internal rage he could unleash during the contests.

But high school football was a completely different game than its college sibling. In the post-secondary school environment, Big Jim found himself competing against men his own size. He no longer was physically intimidating, and he quickly discovered that he wasn't athletic enough to dish out pain to others without suffering himself.

Only then did he realize that it wasn't the competition that drew him to the sport – it was the gratification of controlling others, of physically imposing his will. College linemen didn't bend and break like his opponents in high school, and that reality slowly drained Big Jim's enthusiasm for the sport. His performance, both on and off the field, faltered, and by the end of his freshman year, he dropped out.

The referee's whistle, followed by an explosion of both booing and cheering, summoned J.T. back to his son's game. Until the boy's senior year, Jim hadn't even bothered attending the contests. But dinner table talk of a potential basketball scholarship had piqued the father's interest, renewing an opportunity for him to exercise some influence on his "misguided teenager's" life.

Despite rising to the rank of sergeant in one of the largest police departments in the country, Jimmy and his wife hadn't saved much money for their son's college expenses. On two different occasions, some scumbag citizen had filed a lawsuit against the officer, the police union covering only part of the expenses necessary to clear his name. Junior's college fund, as well as Marwick's reserve to purchase a saltwater fishing boat, had been reallocated to defend his livelihood.

He continued watching the game, silently, stoically evaluating Junior's performance. The simmering storm of rage brewed to a boiling point inside the officer, his mental tirade alternating salvos of fury that targeted his son, the referee, the coach, and the opposing players.

It would have taken an extremely skilled observer to note even the slightest variation in the cop's bearing. Years of interacting with an often-hostile citizenry had created a deadpan mask to replace his true emotions, fashioning an on-the-job poker face void of any tells. Like most police officers, Big Jim had become a refined thespian, achieving the high art of robotic, detached presence on the public stage.

The referee's whistle signaled a time-out, both teams hustling to their respective benches to gather around tense coaching staffs, awaiting final words of athletic wisdom. There were only a few seconds left before half time, the final play critical given the tied score.

Jim watched the coach draw up a play, the squad huddled around his clipboard. The burly cop considered what he'd be instructing the players to do if he were issuing the orders. His guidance would involve singling out the best man on the opponent's team and knocking the asshole into the third row of seats. *What's a little collateral damage?* the public servant smirked. *It would be so easy to make it look like an accident.*

With the teams now ready and back on the court, a referee handed the ball to one of Junior's squad to inbound. A flurry of movement, a couple of clever picks, and then the ball was sailing toward Jim's son.

Four seconds on the clock and a head fake.

Three seconds left, Junior dribbling once, trying desperately to shake his opponent.

Two seconds left, and Jim was sure his son wasn't going to get off the shot.

Uncoiling his legs, Junior launched skyward as the clock read 01 remaining. The defensive player was right with him, both boys' arms extending as their bodies continued to rise into the air.

The ball left the shooter's hand just before the buzzer droned. Out of nowhere came a new defender, like a missile streaking to intercept an airborne target.

The soaring opponent's hand swatted the basketball, picking it out of midair and redirecting its flight path. The ball smacked Big Jim in the shoulder, bouncing off his uniform sleeve before he could react. On both sides of the court, the crowd leapt to its feet in a screaming frenzy.

For a just a brief moment, Jim thought the bleachers were applauding the sight of the errant basketball smacking a police officer. *No respect for law and order*, the officer instantly surmised, his dander rising. With a stare icy and blank, he watched the teams sprint off the court, heading to the locker room for the halftime pep talk.

Jim's ire wasn't fueled by the fact that the opposing player had blocked his son's shot. No, what really pissed him off was that about 3,500 people had just witnessed the humiliation of a cop. That was a bad image to propagate.

Peace officers had to establish command and control over any encounter, any situation. They had to appear invincible, unquestionable, and wholly confident in their authority. Jim knew good and well that even the slightest, innocent breach of that façade would serve to erode a department's efficiency. If the public viewed law enforcers as soft, people would take advantage. If citizens perceived their local officers as forgiving or benevolent, word would get around, and criminals would be emboldened in their illicit pursuits. Lawlessness would have the leg up on the guys in the white hats.

Scrutinizing the throng of fans filing out the gym's exit doors, Jim studied every pair of eyes heading for the concession stand and restrooms. He was somewhat relieved that no one cracked a stupid joke or made any comment about the basketball's assault. It was just as well that few people made eye contact with him.

Before long, the teams were back out on the court, running layup drills and preparing for the third quarter. Junior's team would now have the basket closest to Jim's perch.

He observed the warmup, standing absolutely statue still. After judging the rotation and cycle, he stepped closer to the court and without warning, reached out and pulled Junior aside.

"You better get your ass in fucking gear, dipshit. That blonde-headed kid on the other team is making you look like a fool," Jim growled in a low, harsh voice.

"Dad, he's one of the best players in the state. He makes everyone look like crap."

"I don't give a shit if he plays for the Houston Rockets. Put him on his ass... or elbow his nose... take out his knee... do something, or you're not going to see any scholarship money. You will end up flipping fucking burgers while you attend some second-rate school surrounded by ghetto freaks and crack heads."

Junior knew better than to respond; he'd lived under Jimmy's roof for 18 years and could sense when his father was "in a state." He had his own bumps and bruises as evidence of his father's efforts to toughen him up and make him a man. Simply nodding, he tried to return to his team, but Jim maintained his grip, balling up the jersey's material even tighter. "I'm not fucking around, son. This is your chance. If you don't get your shit in one bag right now, your whole life is going to be a mess."

Jimmy released the boy, turning calmly and moving back to his spot. When his gaze returned to the court, he noticed Junior's coach staring back. He didn't look happy.

The big cop gave the guy every chance to look away, ignoring the obvious displeasure the team's skipper was displaying. After five seconds, the coach's unwavering gaze had become rude. At 10 seconds, it was downright challenging.

Again, Big Jim approached the court, walking directly toward the coach. "What's your problem?" the cop asked, spreading his hands wide in show of readiness.

"I don't like fathers messing with my players' heads during the games," responded the older man.

"I was just trying to motivate the boy; that's all," Jimmy replied innocently. "Motivation seems to be a problem with your team," he baited.

But the coach ignored the insult, choosing instead to break eye contact while shouting a quick criticism to one of his players.

He's a coward, Jimmy thought, returning to his spot along the wall. *I just insulted the shit out of him, and he played that little diversion card as if he never heard me. Bullshit. What a pussy. No wonder they're going to lose.*

The second half proved to be a disappointment for Junior and his team. At the final buzzer, the opponents claimed the title of city champion, winning by a safe margin.

After shaking hands at mid-court, Jim watched his dejected son shuffle off to the showers with his teammates, the boy not even having enough balls to look at this father. *Serves him right,* Jimmy thought. *He didn't follow my advice. Damned kid lacks the killer instinct it takes to win. Too much like his mother.*

The big cop's gaze then returned to the court, taking in the trophy ceremony with his usual statuesque pose. He watched the blond headed star receive his prize, wondering if the kid's father liked to fish. *At least somebody will be able to get a new boat,* he thought. After it was all said and done, the victorious coach hooked elbows with his best player and led him over to two men waiting at the edge of the gym.

Jim could guess that the two visitors were the college scouts. He watched with building frustration as their conversation was all smiles, nods, and back pats, finally concluding with an exuberant round of handshakes. The star then bounced over to his mother and father, the proud parents beaming with joy as the three of them shared a close embrace.

I'd be happy, too, Jim thought. *If my kid had just saved me tens of thousands of dollars, I'd be a bucket of smiles and shit-eating grins.*

It was time to go, the stands practically empty, Jimmy having had enough. He knew Junior would ride home with a friend.

As he pivoted to exit the gym, Marwick took one last glance at the celebrating family. They had been joined by a young female, the kind whose looks might land her on the cover of a fashion magazine, her actions identifying her as the ball player's girlfriend. "That's just sickening," he muttered. "So... so... so damned yuppie and suburban. I think I'm going to puke."

Chapter 2

Peelian Principle
The degree of public cooperation that can be secured diminishes proportionately to the necessity of the use of physical force by the police.

Jacob bounded down the stairs, his bright mood reflecting the crisp, late-morning sunlight. Invigorated by the extra hours of sleep afforded by the Saturday, no-school, non-alarm morning, the teen immediately made for the kitchen, his thoughts consumed by the refrigerator.

He paused at the dining room's threshold, glancing up at the high ceiling like he had a thousand times before. There was a smoke detector up there, the safety device now discolored and smudged from years of fingerprints. His fingerprints.

Briefly ignoring his teenage body's need for substance, Jacob reflected back on the first time he'd been able to jump up and touch the detector. It had been a dream when he was 12, a frustration when he was 14, and just out of reach for what seemed like an eternity. He'd just received his learner's permit in the mail on the day his finger finally brushed the 10-foot high device. The excitement of learning to drive a car was immediately superseded by the realization that he could finally touch a basketball goal's rim.

That had been a memorable day, he reflected, glancing right and left to make sure his mother wasn't anywhere around.

Reassured the coast was clear, Jacob bent slightly at the knees and effortlessly launched into the air. The top of his hair rubbed the detector.

Landing gracefully, he peered up and smiled at the once unachievable benchmark. What had been impossible just a few years ago was now easy. He wondered if the rest of his life would be the same.

Deciding it was too early for such introspection, the ravenous teen pivoted for the kitchen, only to bump into his father.

Gabriel Chase stood with his arms crossed, trying desperately to maintain a fake frown. It was a difficult feat, quickly turning into a hopeless cause by his son's sheepish reaction at getting caught. "You better not let your mother see you doing that, young man," he warned with a sly grin. "She had me up on that ladder for an entire Sunday afternoon trying to clean off your finger smudges, and I don't like heights."

"Yes, sir," the guilty son muttered, sensing he wasn't in any real trouble, but not wanting to ruin his amazing mood. "But think about this, Dad. The next time that sensor needs a new battery, you won't have to drag the ladder out of the garage. I'll just use my hang-time and replace it for you. No charge."

Gabe nodded just as his wife appeared around the corner. "What are you two boys up to?" she teased, rubbing her chin in mock apprehension. "I sense a male conspiracy."

"Nothing, Mother," Mr. Chase responded with an equal amount of feigned innocence. "I was just on my way upstairs to roust our sleepy son and talk to him about his college fund."

Maneuvering around his father, Jacob steered for the kitchen while replying, "Oh, Dad, do we have to discuss that right now? It's such a great day, and Manny is supposed to meet me at the park in a little bit."

"Girls, food, and basketball," Mr. Chase said to his wife with a chuckle. "That's all that boy ever thinks about."

The parents followed, watching as the always-hungry teen bent to rummage through the fridge.

"Seriously, Jacob, your mom and I have been saving up for your education," Gabe began with his typical matter-of-fact voice. "But since you've been awarded a full scholarship, we decided we can spend some of the money now."

"Yeah?" the teen responded, instantly intrigued at the prospect. "What did you have in mind?" he quizzed, looking up from the crisper drawer and sounding like a 5-year-old working to discover the contents of a Christmas present.

Then an odd expression soiled the moment, the teen suddenly worried his parents were going to force him to go along on some weird family vacation or trip. The thought of being away from Manny and his teammates was enough to ruin a guy's Saturday. *Don't they know I'm a little old for Disneyland*, he vexed.

"Your mother and I have been discussing a few possibilities. How would you feel about a new smartphone? Or maybe a more robust laptop for all that college homework?"

The stated prospects returned a smile to Jacob's face. Seeing the mental wheels begin to whir and spin inside his son's head, Gabe realized the bait had been taken. Knowing that timing was everything, the crafty father set the hook. "But we'll talk about that later. Right now, could you please take out the garbage?"

Jacob started to protest, glancing down at the sandwich makings in his hand. Sandy timed her intervention perfectly, reaching to take the ingredients and saying, "Go on, son. Do as your father asks. I'll make you something to eat while you pull the cans to the curb."

Handing over the lunchmeat and mustard, Jacob muttered, "Yes, ma'am," and headed toward the back door. He didn't notice the knowing glance exchanged between his parents, nor did he detect their stealthy movements to follow him out the door.

The new Honda completely commanded the ordinarily mundane driveway, its freshly detailed paint accessorized with a big, red bow covering the hood. A five-foot banner, flanked by oversized clusters of helium balloons, announced his success to the world, "Congratulations, Jay-man!"

The unexpected gift of a new ride stunned the teenager, his body freezing mid-stride while his mouth moved with a soundless flapping. "Mom! Dad! When did…. It's beautiful…. How?"

Both of the Chases had their cell phones snapping and recording away, the proud parents glowing almost as much as their offspring.

Gabe finally stopped taking pictures and moved to his son's side. "She's three years old, Jay. Like I always say, we may share the same last name as the big bank, but they've got all the money."

"Dad, it's perfect," Jacob beamed, moving to open the passenger door and look inside.

"It was a good deal. She's got low miles and had a single owner. She's got brand new tires, and I had a mechanic check out everything under the hood. If you take care of her, she should last you quite a few years."

"And it had a good safety rating," Sandy chimed in.

Abandoning his examination of the interior, Jacob closed the door and darted toward his mother with open arms. "Thank you so much! I can't think of a better surprise!"

After a quick walk-through of the auto's features, Jacob was soon backing out the driveway for the first test drive. "I'm going to head over and show Manny," he announced. "I already texted her pictures, and she's dying to see my new wheels."

"Be careful, son," Gabe advised. "Take your time and get used to it."

But he was already pulling away, honking and waving as he motored off.

Gabe turned to his wife and said, "Do you ever feel like chopped liver?"

"Now, Gabe… you know how it was when we were his age. Besides, Manny is a sweetheart. I think they're cute together."

After a moment, his smile returned, along with an agreeing nod. "Yes, they are a nice match, and I do remember when seeing you was all I could think about. I still feel the same way, just so you know."

Sandy stood on her tiptoes, kissing him on the cheek. "Come back inside, you flirtatious young man, and I'll make you that sandwich I promised your son. That'll teach him to rush off and leave us old folks in his dust."

It was with no small amount of relief that the Chases met their son at the door after his first journey in the new car. Realizing their apprehension was a little too obvious, they tried to recover. "So how did Manny like the new wheels?" Sandy asked.

"She loved it just as much as I do," Jacob replied with a huge grin. "The radio sounds great, and she helped me program in the best stations. We're going to skip the movie tonight and just relax to some good music while we drive around."

Gabe was about to make a comment regarding the wisdom of his son's dating plan when his cell phone rang.

Frowning at the unusual number displayed on the screen, he answered with a neutral tone. "This is Gabriel Chase."

"Mr. Chase, this is Bob Covington, the basketball coach up at State. I've had a last minute trip to Houston come up, and I'd love to take your family out to dinner tonight. I'm anxious to meet Jacob and welcome him to the team."

Gabe's smile filled the room as he glanced up at a curious Sandy and Jacob. "Why sure, Coach Covington, we'd be honored to meet with you. What time is your flight arriving?"

"I'm supposed to land at 7:15 this evening. If you want to go ahead and make reservations, I can probably meet any time after 8:30... given the rental car counter isn't too backed up."

"What kind of restaurant would be a good fit?" Gabe asked.

"I'm a steak and potatoes type of guy, Mr. Chase. If you've got a pencil nearby, I can give you the name of my favorite H-Town steakhouse."

The call was disconnected a few moments later, Gabe smiling widely at his son and wife. "That was your new college coach, Jacob. He wants to take us all out to dinner... at one of the most expensive restaurants in the city."

The young basketball star surprised his father, a look of disappointment crossing his face. "But, Dad... I had a date with Manny tonight. She's so excited about the car."

Rolling his eyes, Gabe wrapped an arm around his son's shoulders, pulling him tight. "Well, why don't you invite her along? I'm sure the coach would like to meet Manny as well, and if there's any problem with his expense account, I'll splurge for her steak. Besides, she's such a little thing... she can't eat that much."

Jacob struggled to stifle the yawn, the combination of a satiated stomach and the late hour impacting his body more than his still-racing mind.

His attention had remained fixated on Manny most of the night, the young girl's reaction to the glamor and ritz of the fine eatery enhancing what had already been an enchanted evening.

Like Jacob, a middleclass upbringing had never exposed her to such a highbrow establishment. It was as if the dim, candlelit ambiance and well-heeled clientele had cast a magical spell.

Shy at first, not wanting to make any social errors that would demonstrate bad manners or a lack of sophistication, Manny had approached every course of the meal with an air of dainty reserve. She had fussed over which fork to use, waiting until the adults had proceeded and following their example.

Her appreciation of each dish's presentation had been charming, Mrs. Chase and she exchanging comments of awe and amazement over what the chefs had prepared.

Jacob, on the other hand, had simply dug in with the gusto of a famished 6'5" teenager who was being fed well past the normal hour. The coach's flight had been late, the fancy restaurant's lobby full of diners cued up for a limited number of tables. While very tasty, the full-course meal certainly did not qualify as *fast* food either. And then the conversation among the adults had dragged on... and on... and on.

His parent's reaction to the shindig had been predictable.

Mr. Chase had immediately bonded with Coach Covington, the two men discussing everything from UCLA's famous winning streak, to Bobby Knight's legendary, chair-throwing temper.

Jacob's mother, on the other hand, had tried to steer the conversation in the direction of academic requirements and the expected behavior of her soon-to-be freshman son. Sandy had eventually given up, letting the men go on while Manny and she dissected everything from the other diners to the artwork adorning the walls that surrounded their table.

Manny had remained fascinated by it all, the upscale atmosphere and mood lighting triggering a twinkle as her eyes bounced around the lavish steakhouse. Despite the nearly constant stream of food leaving his plate, his girlfriend's reaction wasn't lost on Jacob.

"You know if I make it into the pros, I'll be able to take you to places like this all the time," Jacob offered, wanting to be part of her experience.

Manny smiled at her boyfriend's ever-present optimism. "That would be great, but you promised your parents and me that making good grades would come first. I don't need places like this to be happy, Jacob. It's really great, but I'll be just as proud of you earning a good degree as a basketball contract."

"I can do both," he replied, a slight defensive tone entering his voice. "But I guess you're right… and Dad keeps reminding me that not many guys make it into the pros. I should always keep that in mind, I suppose."

Manny covered his hand with hers, a knowing smile brightening her face. "I'm sorry, Jay. I don't mean to rain on your parade. What you've accomplished so far is amazing, and I don't want you to lose sight of that. But I like you just the way you are, and I worry sometimes that all this fame is going to fatten that cute head of yours. Yes, going places like this is super-cool, but we were just fine before. I can live without it."

"I dunno," he responded. "Being here… in a place like this… is just so exciting… I feel like we're important or something."

"We are important," she responded with a perky tilt of her head. Then, leaning in closer to whisper in his ear, she added, "Don't tell anybody, but I would have been just as happy with our usual Saturday night popcorn and three-star movie."

As usual, Manny's perspective on life confused Jacob. She always seemed so… so grounded and mature, seldom reacting in any way he could predict. All the while, she was constantly cutting jokes and acting like nothing really mattered all that much. Her behavior bewildered and intrigued him.

Jacob had approached his father with the dilemma, finally coming to the conclusion that he wasn't going to figure it out on his own.

"Welcome to the real world, son," had come his pop's response, complete with a knowing smirk. "Men are from Mars, and women from some other galaxy. We're wired differently, use completely opposite methods of logic, and have biological differences that would make you question our sharing of the same DNA. The term, 'opposite sex,' wasn't an accident."

Frowning, Jacob wasn't satisfied with the answer. "Then why do people date… and marry… and have kids and stuff? Why do I want to be around Manny so much? And why does she confuse me with the way she acts?"

"Well, son, because sharing your life with someone is often like that. Each sex provides a balance for the opposite. Your mother bolsters my weaknesses, and hopefully I shore up hers. Life is difficult, a constant string of challenges, problems, and issues that never stop popping up in front of you. Having someone at your side who looks at things from another perspective can make all the difference in the world. And then you have the biological attraction, but that's a conversation we should probably hold off on."

Waving off his father's conservative attitude, Jacob said, "Oh, I know all about the birds and the bees, Dad. They teach you that stuff in school before you're even interested. You don't have to worry about having the 'the talk,' with me. Still, beyond any physical attraction, I want to be around her… yet she drives me crazy sometimes with how she looks at things."

Nodding sagely, Gabe said, "Like I said, welcome to the real world. You'll never completely understand this mystery, so take my advice and don't even try. Just enjoy it and make each other happy. That's all you need to know."

Looking deep into Manny's eyes, Jacob concluded that she was indeed happy, and that his father had been right. He would just run with that.

Finally, the adults were pushing back from the table. As the valets hustled off to retrieve the Honda, Gabe took his son aside and issued a warning, "Drive carefully, and get that young lady home safely." He added that at such an hour, drunks would be leaving the bars and to watch out for the other guy on the road.

As they left the lot, Manny called her father for the third time. After their short conversation, Jacob threw her an inquiring look. "Are you in trouble for being so late?"

"Naw, Dad's fine. He knows this was a special occasion. Even he's excited over your good news."

Despite the wee hour, Jacob didn't have any problem staying awake on the drive home. His mind was still busy, reviewing and processing the events of the last few days. Truth be told, he probably wouldn't have been able to sleep, even if he'd been home and in bed by his usual eleven o'clock curfew.

Glancing over at his attractive companion, he gushed, "I still can't believe all of this is happening to me. Only three days ago, I was just another kid about to graduate… worried about keeping my grades up and getting into a reputable university. I'm still a little dizzy over everything happening so quickly. It's almost like a high from some drug."

Through a genuine, warm smile, Manny replied from the passenger seat, "You earned it Jacob. You worked harder than anybody else on the team. You spent more hours in the weight room, jogged halfway across town at

5 AM every morning, and stayed after practice almost every day to perfect your game. An insecure person could've easily thought you were trying to avoid them."

He laughed, slowing for a traffic light about to turn red. "Now you know better than that, Manny. In the off-season, you were complaining I wouldn't leave you alone… that I was being a pest. You can't have it both ways, you know."

"Sure I can," she teased. "I'm a girl, and it's my God-given right to have my cake and eat it, too. Besides, you asked me out four times before I finally gave in. Apparently, you find me attractive for some reason, so I'm going to take advantage of that every chance I get."

Jacob breathed deeply and exhaled a smooth sigh of satisfaction with his life. His eyes shifted briefly from the traffic signal to the petite sweetheart seated beside him… the contact just long enough for his companion to notice his adoring gaze. Manny made him laugh, and that's what he liked about her the most. "I suppose," he breathed. "Well, *that*… and the fact that you *are* the hottest girl in the entire school."

She reached across and playfully smacked his arm, "Flattery will get you nowhere with me, Jacob Chase, especially at 1 AM in the morning. Now stop this shameless flirting, and get me home. I've got a big biology final tomorrow, and with only a few hours' sleep, I'll be lucky to prop my eyelids open long enough to finish the exam. If I mess up my GPA, you're going to be in trouble, Mister. Not everybody gets a free ride to college, you know."

Nodding without comment, he carefully accelerated through the now-green light.

His cautious driving wasn't due to road congestion, their headlights the only pair visible on the entire street at the late hour. Nor was the smitten lad trying to extend their time together.

Jacob was driving like an old man, exercising great caution with his "new baby." Earlier in the evening, he'd asked the valet if he could straddle two parking spots at the restaurant, wanting to avoid dings from the doors of neighboring cars. While the conservative Honda sedan was three years old, it was the most magnificent gift the young basketball star could have imagined.

Manny's yawn increased his urgency, but he didn't dare exceed the speed limit. According to his mother, insurance for a teenage driver was outrageous. "If you get a ticket, we're going to have to get a second mortgage," she had warned.

"It won't be long now," he informed Manny. "Just a few more miles, and you'll be snug in your bed. Promise you won't hate me when the alarm goes off?"

"No," she giggled. "No promises," she added with a defiant look.

The radar gun's digits read "34," one mile per hour below the posted speed limit. "I wonder what they're doing wrong," Jim speculated as he watched the headlights approach. A seasoned veteran, he realized that folks who made incredible efforts to stay within the rules of the road in the wee hours of the morning often had something to hide. *Even law-abiding citizens who see empty pavement ahead of them take a few liberties,* he told himself. He quickly dismissed the thought, returning to a combination of boredom and apprehension as he deliberated over the entire graveyard shift being a snoozer.

As he watched the vehicle's low beams approach his hidden position, a wave of frustration began to build, his thoughts returning to Junior's basketball game. In order to attend the contest, the only taker he could find was a trade for the midnight shift. Despite being a weekend night, it was slow as hell. The game obviously hadn't been worth the price he was paying now.

More than two hours had passed since he'd signed in, and now the streets were nearly deserted. The small car heading his way carried the first citizen he'd seen in almost ten minutes.

Marwick watched as the non-speeder passed by his position, a streetlight's pool of illumination making the driver's profile surprisingly clear.

Big Jim did a double take, something familiar about the kid passing by. His eyes immediately spotted the license plate, a temporary paper tag indicating the operator hadn't owned the recent model two-door very long.

Inhaling sharply, Big Jim realized who the driver was. His hand immediately reached for the gearshift.

He pulled out behind the little sedan, not entirely sure why. The operator was the player who had bested Junior during the game, and now the little shit was driving around in a recently acquired vehicle. That just rubbed the cop in a wrong way.

"Let's see how cool you are off the basketball court," he whispered. "Bet you aren't as calm with *my* full court press," he added.

He accelerated rapidly, taking his squad car up to 50 mph, quickly closing the gap. Just when it appeared that the front bumper's safety cage was going to slam directly into the temporary tag, he braked hard.

He could see the outline of two heads through the back glass, the shorter figure in the passenger side appearing to be female. "You've had your girlfriend out awfully late, young man. I wonder if there's a date rape involved. A party to celebrate your new trophy? Underage drinking?"

But the three-year old Honda Civic didn't flinch or react, the driver's only response being to slow down.

In a way, Jim was disappointed, but not discouraged. He keyed the cruiser's microphone, "Edward 40."

The female dispatcher's voice acknowledged immediately, "Go Edward 40."

"Traffic, temporary tag, 17 Adam 7331 George 1," Jim reported, "Suspicious vehicle. Cypress Road, one mile west of Jester."

It was less than a minute before the dispatcher responded, "No WW, no reports. Registered to one Gabriel William Chase, Green Forest Avenue, Houston."

Marwick hadn't expected any "wants" or "warrants," satisfied that little Mr. Goodie Two Shoes and his Barbie and Ken family wouldn't dare put an illegal car on the road.

"Clear," Big Jim replied, his eyes never leaving the taillights ahead.

After another half mile, the Honda slowed even further and then signaled a right-hand turn. Jim followed, entering a residential neighborhood of middle-class homes. He noted the speed limit dropped to 20 mph.

But the kid kept his foot off the pedal, the large red digits of the laser gun never topping 19. "You know I'm back here, you little shit," Jim hissed. "No matter."

At the next stop sign, Jim watched eagerly. Having a cop car right up their ass tended to make most drivers a little nervous. The kid didn't roll the stop, but he still violated the traffic code.

Jim smiled, concluding that the Honda's front tires had exceeded the white crossing-line by a least a foot. Glancing at the dash cam mounted behind the cruiser's rearview mirror, he grunted. There was no way the video could clearly record where the driver had stopped.

He reached for the lights and siren.

Like most civilians, the driver's first reaction was to tap the brakes. That response told Jim the teen had spotted the flashers, proved on the video camera that the operator was aware that a peace officer was initiating a traffic stop.

Instead of pulling over immediately, the Honda kept on driving. Despite it being less than a block since he'd flipped on the lights, Jim keyed the microphone. "Edward 40... Edward 40.... Possible evasion, late model Honda Civic, blue, previous temporary tag, 3800 block of Santa Fe Drive. Requesting additional units."

"All units, all units, proceed to general vicinity of Santa Fe Drive, three thousand, eight hundred block to assist the officer. Possible evasion."

The sleepy demeanor vanished immediately from Manny's face as she cast a quick, frightened glance at Jacob. "What did you do?" she asked without thinking.

"Nothing! At least not that I know of," he answered, his response equally concerned as he glanced back at the lights in the mirror. "He's probably just checking us out because of the temporary tag," Jacob tried to reassure his date. "This may take a bit, but don't worry, your house is right up here."

"You better pull over, right now," she countered. "Isn't that what they taught us in Driver's Ed?"

"It's only a block or so," he replied, glancing at the strobe of lights behind them. "He will understand. I mean it is so late; there are no other drivers on the road, and I am driving below the speed limit. We can safely park once we get to your house. That way, you can get to bed. Your mom and dad are probably still waiting up. We're almost there anyway."

"I dunno, Jacob," Manny argued.

"Look. I already switched on the hazard lights and slowed down so he knows I am looking for a place to pull over. The officer will understand. You'll see."

Another block passed before the little Honda switched off its emergency flashers and signaled its intent to stop.

Pulling to the curb, Jim rolled up behind, switching on the spotlight, reaching for the door handle, and exiting the squad car as fast as his large frame could pour out the opening.

He unsnapped the safety strap on his sidearm and then drew his flashlight, flipping on the beam and moving it to his off-pistol hand.

All the while, he was stepping toward the Honda. Halfway, he started screaming at the top of his lungs, "Get out of the car! Get out of the car!"

As expected, the driver hesitated, his sensory input completely overloaded by the sudden sequence of unexpected events. Even if the kid had anticipated the command, the officer didn't give him enough time to respond. The harsh light, barking orders, and aggressive movements all served to freeze the human body while it's brain tried to digest its environment. The tactic was implemented by design, a commonly used method with which law enforcement used to establish dominance over any suspect.

Officially, as recorded by the dash cam, the citizen had not followed a legal order by a law enforcement officer. It didn't matter that the command was humanly impossible to execute, and Jim now had reasonable cause to draw his service pistol.

For a split second, Marwick pined for a body camera. The expression on the kid's face, staring into the barrel of his Smith & Wesson .40 automatic, was a classic. It was a bouquet of uncertainty, confusion, and outright terror, sure to generate a good round of chuckles from his coworkers back at the station.

Still yelling for the nearly-paralyzed driver to exit, Big Jim was a little disappointed when the door popped open, the young man having enough wherewithal to push the opening wider with his leg while his hands remained in the classic, "Don't shoot" position.

The kid managed to stand with his hands still in the air, evidence of his athletic abilities and coordination.

Jim immediately changed his command and tempo, "Against the vehicle! Turn around! Get against the vehicle!" The staggered, contradicting orders were intentionally delivered in a way to confuse suspects and keep them from initiating any offensive action against the officer. That is exactly what was accomplished. The driver was bewildered, unable to decide which of the officer's orders to follow.

There was another factor in play, Marwick's extensive years on the force providing the experience to set his first "tiger trap."

With the driver's hands in the air, the motion of turning to face the car as ordered forced his elbow to swing in an arc as he spun. Marwick knew it was coming and stepped into it on purpose, jerking his head back at the last instant to avoid being brushed.

On the squad's video camera, the "assault" on a police officer was clearly documented. It gave Big Jim all the justification he needed to escalate the encounter and teach the cocky little shit a lesson about life's true authority.

For a fraction of a second, the cop was disappointed. Some people would drop their hands in order to execute the turn, certain body types unable to spin with their hands in the air. The movement of lowering once-raised hands could easily be interpreted as "making an aggressive move," or "trying to reach his waistline," the location where the vast majority of felons stashed weapons. Marwick would have been completely within his rights to shoot the driver right on the spot if he'd made such a gesture.

He let the kid make three quarters of the turn toward the car, and then shoved him hard against the sheet metal. Again, uncontrollable reflexes took over, the young man's hands dropping to the surface of the hood, attempting to protect his face from the impact of smashing into the solid surface. It wasn't conscious thought, but on camera, it looked like he was moving his arms to resist.

At that same moment, the first backup car screeched onto the scene, the officer pulling his cruiser up directly behind Jim's, blocking the middle of the road.

So far, Marwick had the kid on an improper stop, evading a police officer, assault, and resisting arrest. Now that other officers were arriving, it was time to initiate a "pig pile."

When the driver's hands moved to prevent the face plant, Jim took a step back and redrew his weapon, screaming, "On the ground! Get on the ground!""

The newly arriving patrolman, completely unaware of what had really just transpired, doubled his pace to assist. He accelerated rapidly, slamming his shoulder into the small of the suspect's back and taking Jacob to the pavement. From the recent arrival's perspective, it looked like a brother officer was in danger from a punk kid.

Again, the driver's survival instinct took over, both of his palms coming forward to break his fall while he turned his face to avoid a nose-crushing impact.

Now there were two voices shouting at the top of their lungs at the utterly bewildered teenager, soon joined by a third and then a fourth officer as responding units poured in, their urgency prompted by the broadcast of an evasion. The fact that it was the shift supervisor involved in the arrest made it all the more urgent.

There is an unwritten law invoked by every police force in the nation – "Run from us, and we have an open license." Fleeing suspects, especially in motor vehicles, were a nightmare. Multiple cars racing through the streets endangered civilians, police, and property. High-speed chases generated massive adrenaline dumps, frayed nerves, and most importantly, showed a blatant disregard for the officers' authority. There were few more visible markers of guilt. When the pursuit finally ended, the result was a recipe for disaster – a bunch of edgy cops handling a disrespectful suspect who had broken numerous laws and threatened the police.

The newly arriving officers had no way of knowing if the driver "fighting" with their supervisor had fled for one block or ten miles. They merely recognized that a suspect involved in an altercation with one of their own, and that was enough.

A swarm of blue uniforms rushed to subdue the suspect and make sure none of their brothers was hurt. It was a full-on assault, little different from a charged-up infantry squad taking a hill.

Within seconds, most of the experienced officers sensed that the Honda's driver was most likely not resisting, the telltale signs obvious to their trained eyes. They were also reasonably sure that the kid lying face down on the pavement wasn't a threat. Those indicators, however, made little difference as a carefully choreographed sequence of events began to unfold. The suspect had ran, and everybody knew that if the police had to come and get you, they were bringing an ass beating with them.

Policemen were famous for their "gotcha" questions, typically snarled inquiries that offered no good answer. "Do you know why I pulled you over?" was one of the more commonly known gotchas. If the driver responded that he didn't understand why he had been stopped, then he had little, if any, basis to deny the infraction. After all, if a driver weren't paying attention, how could he say with certainty that he was not speeding? If the hapless citizen answered, "Yes," to the officer's query, then he admitted guilt.

There were also physical "gotchas" that could be implemented during an arrest. The Honda's driver was about to experience a sequence of these tiger traps.

The first action was often referred to as "the huddle." Hard lessons had been learned from the advent of internet videos decrying police brutality and abuse, an education hammered home to all cops. The commonality of dash cams, bystander cell phones, and security cameras mounted who-knew-where, were countered by the group of officers surrounding the suspect as if they were a football team calling a play on the field.

With the driver on the ground in the middle of the formation, it was nearly impossible for any video recorder to get a clear view of the proceedings.

The "quarterback" held the most critical position, blocking the one known and most important camera of all – the dashboard video system in the facing cruiser.

Once the picket line of fast-moving, blue-uniformed bodies was established, the kid was subjected to his first body-gotcha. The police wanted the young man's hands at his lower spine so they could apply handcuffs, but with over 900 pounds of officers on his body, there was no way Jacob could move his arms to comply with their shouted commands.

This led to one of the officers initiating an Academy Award-worthy performance, shouting, "Stop resisting! Stop resisting!" – the command issued more for the benefit of the in-cruiser camera's audio system than any anticipated response from the suspect.

Finally, the man with his knee in the small of Jacob's back raised just enough to allow the kid to free his pinned arms, an event which immediately resulted in the second body-gotcha.

Fully anticipated, the kid's arms wriggled out from under his body, but the liberated limbs couldn't move to his back. Despite his desperate attempt to comply with the orders screamed at him from all directions, there was a burly cop's knee on both sides of his rib cage, pinning his appendages tightly to his side.

Of course, the cops knew this would happen, ready with the second round of lines from their theatrical script created for the benefit of the dash cam. "Stop reaching for my weapon! He's reaching for my weapon!"

Now things were getting serious, the real fun about to begin.

With ear-piercing screams coming from all sides, hundreds of pounds of weight on his ribcage and legs, the completely overwhelmed Jacob tried to lift his body in order to move his arms as commanded. This resulted in the first kick.

In legitimate academy training, instructors harped on not allowing a suspect to regain the initiative. The well-meaning cadre would drill in a grim reality – If the criminal had a gun in his belt and managed to draw the weapon while his arms were under his body, then that weapon could be aimed and discharged once those limbs broke free.

Foot strikes aimed at the arms were an approved method to keep the prone suspect from lifting himself off the ground. The goal was to knock the weight-bearing limb out from underneath the apprehended person, much like removing the leg of a stool. If the occasional kick missed, impacting the head, ribs, or neck, the blame rested squarely on the civilian who shouldn't have been resisting.

The driver started screaming in pain as heavy-duty boots struck his head and trunk. After a half-dozen vicious blows, the cops let him move one arm to the small of his back. But only one.

On the opposite side of the dash cam, out of clear view, one of the policemen pressed his boot on the still-free wrist, pinning it to the pavement. Again, a perverse moan of agony sounded through the neighborhood.

At this point, the girl passenger interrupted the carefully orchestrated blue-payback. Hearing her boyfriend's moans and screams, the terrified Manny gathered herself and exited the car. She was, after all, parked in front of her own home.

Her only thought was to reach the comfort of her parents and the security of her childhood home. With the riot-like backdrop of sound, she didn't hear the officer who ordered her to stop, instead moving in a hurried rush across the yard. The cop pursued.

Manny's parents had been drawn by the sirens and sea of flashing blue lights in front of their home. Her father, peeking through the living room blinds, recognized Jacob's new car just as it had stopped out front.

Chip liked Jacob, finding the kid respectful and honest. Given the parade of young boys that had sought Manny's company over the years, the keen-eyed father had considered the young Master Chase as one of the top-tier candidates for his daughter's long-term affections.

Seeing an opportunity to exercise his often ill-timed sense of humor, Chip had snatched up his cell phone, thinking to record Jacob's first traffic ticket and leverage the embarrassing event for future, good-natured harassment. The threat of social annihilation could be a powerful tool, should the need ever arise.

After less than a minute of recording, Chip knew something was horribly wrong.

The anxious father dashed through the front door and darted for the street just as the armada of police cars rolled up. Like the paralyzed teens in the car, Chip froze in the middle of his driveway, cell still recording the drama a short distance away.

When he spied Manny exiting the car, he moved to rescue his clearly frightened girl. They embraced just as the pursuing officer caught up with her.

Yanking her forcefully from the hug, the cop began shouting orders for her to return to the car. All along, the police in the street continued to roar at Jacob while the youth was subjected to a catalog of painful restraining techniques.

Realizing things were completely out of control, Chip refocused on the video recording, now carefully aiming his smartphone, moving here and there for a better vantage while his daughter was being pushed back toward the Honda.

He continued recording, Jacob's disturbing howls of agony combining with Manny's desperate cries for the police to stop abusing her boyfriend filling the air. Chip didn't know what else to do, the aggressive, weapon-wielding cops making it clear his presence was unwelcome. Somehow, his phone remained focused on the action in the street.

After both of his arms were finally allowed to the small of his back, Jacob prayed the worst was over. His head and left side were throbbing with knife-like pains, his forehead bleeding so profusely he couldn't open one eye due to the sticky crimson rolling down his face.

But the cops weren't done.

With his wrists finally handcuffed, one of the more sadistic officers decided to show off for the shift commander. Raising the boy's bound arms into the air, Jacob felt like his limbs were being detached from his shoulders. Involuntary body defenses took over, the lad lifting his hips to reduce the angle and torque being applied to his limbs.

A renewed chorus of commands emerged from the huddle, one officer stepping away so the dash cam could capture the suspect's hips coming off the pavement. This time, rather than push down, one of the junior cops grabbed Jacob's ankle and applied what was known as a "hot foot."

The technique was simple enough in practice – lift and pull the suspect's leg so it couldn't be leveraged for resistance. The academy instructors had been very specific when teaching the hold, informing the class that any twisting or pulling on the limb could cause damage to the knee. In extreme cases, the torn tendons and ligaments might be traumatized beyond repair.

Jacob's incredible leaping ability, courtesy of basketball toned limbs, worked against him. The foot-cop, having never applied the technique in real life, encountered more resistance than anticipated. His training with the maneuver had included an expectation of a deep moan of pain from the victim after twisting the joint slightly right and left. But the guy they had on the ground wasn't making any noise, apparently not feeling the effect.

Applying even more pressure, the cop was surprised when a loud pop sounded from the kid's leg, all resistance to the twisting vanishing in an instant, the foot going limp in his grasp. A howl of agony overrode the continued screaming of police commands.

Jacob's body started convulsing involuntarily, fueled by the streaks of hot lightening shooting from his knee. He didn't even feel the additional blows to his head and arms.

One of the officers raised up, his need for post-evasion retribution satisfied by the level of the kid's wailing. Mumbling, "He'll have some respect for the law now," he stood and stretched his back. That's when he noticed Chip in the driveway filming the episode.

The cop's attention had been on the suspect at his feet, not the occupants of the house. The lawman had no idea how long he had been on camera.

With as much urgency as he could manage in a low tone, he warned his comrades, hissing the word, "Camera."

In less than a second, Marwick was moving up the driveway, his voice carrying as much authority as the big cop could muster. "What are you doing, sir? Please step back for your own safety. Is that a video camera, sir?"

By then he was within arm's length of Chip, the homeowner lowering the phone to address the onslaught. But Jim didn't give him a chance.

"I need that camera, sir," the officer growled, reaching for the smartphone.

"No, you don't," came Chip's harsh reply as he backed away. "What did Jacob do? Why are you kicking the shit out of him like that?"

"Police matter, sir. Now I need that phone and video. Right now!"

Chip turned away just as the cop reached for his phone. "You have no right to take my phone. I'm on private property... my property."

"Resisting suspect!" Jim yelled back to his co-workers, grabbing Chip in an arm bar and twisting him to the ground.

Manny was still standing by the car when the cop standing next to her moved to help Big Jim with the new troublemaker - her father. Realizing the officer's wrath was now focusing to her dad, she pulled her cell phone out of her purse, hit the video recording button, and then tucked it back into her front shirt pocket, the lenses exposed and pointing at the assault of her father.

About then, the ambulance arrived, the attitude of the police changing immediately as the red and white strobe lights of the paramedics appeared on the street.

But the police weren't done with Chip. Clutching the camera with both hands while lying flat on his face, he refused to give the evidence to the cops, screaming and yelling back for them to get off his property. By now, there were dozens of sleepy, pajama-clad residents watching the proceedings from the manicured lawns of suburbia. Jim noting several of them with cell phones in their hands.

Signaling his men to back off, Jim lifted Chip to his feet and tried to be reasonable. "Your recording may have important evidence, sir. I promise to return the device after we've made a copy of the video."

The irate homeowner was now beyond caring about his own safety, his sole intent to deny the bullying cops standing around him. "Tell you what," he barked, "I'll email you a copy. How's that?"

"I'm sorry, sir, but that won't do. The chain of evidence requires that we extract the video from your device. Now please hand it over, or I'll be forced to arrest you for obstructing justice and interfering with a law enforcement officer."

"How long will you have my phone?" Chip asked.

"No more than a few days, sir."

"Okay, tell you what. Let me back up my calendar and contacts, and then you can have it."

Jim wasn't ready for that. It was impossible to keep up with the damn technology, and he had no idea what the man in front of him was implying. Not knowing what else to say, he finally asked, "How long will it take you to copy that information?"

"Here," replied Chip, holding up the device. "It's just a couple of buttons and…. Boom… there goes a copy of everything, straight up to the cloud."

Jim, realizing he'd been had, lunged for the phone, but again, Chip pulled away. In the scuffle, the device plummeted to the ground and then was crushed under the boot of a policeman as he helped subdue the homeowner.

A few minutes later, in front of his neighbors, friends, and horrified wife, Chip was escorted to a squad car in handcuffs, charged with resisting, hindering an investigation, disobeying a police officer, and a laundry list of lesser charges. All of those paled in comparison to what would end up on Jacob's arrest record and police report.

He was trying to stay awake until Jacob made it home. Heady evening aside, Gabe wasn't accustomed to late night excursions. The rush associated with a fancy restaurant accompanied by conversation with the nationally known, college coach had worn off, and now he wanted nothing more than to hear the hum of Jacob's car as it pulled into the driveway.

He'd decided to go ahead and get ready for bed, performing his usual teeth brushing and washing routine in preparation for a short night's rest. *It was all worth it*, he mused, sitting on the edge of the bed. *All of Jacob's hard work has paid in spades, and I'm so proud of him I could almost burst.*

Gabe's heart jumped when his cell phone rang, his fatherly concerns immediately overriding his daydream of Jacob's NBA debut. The need for Jacob to drive Manny home at such a late hour initiated ten different parental nightmares to stream through his sleep-deprived mind before he answered.

After exchanging a worried look with his wife, he glanced at the number on the smartphone's display. The caller ID allowed him to exhale for a moment. It was Manny's mother, probably a courtesy call advising him that Jacob had just dropped off their daughter.

"Hello."

The voice on the other end was in a panic. "Mr. Chase, this is Amanda. Something's gone very wrong over here... the police... Chip has been arrested... Jacob, too... I don't know what...."

Gabe shot off the edge of the bed, spinning to throw a look of concern at his wife. "Settle down, Amanda, please. Go slow. Take a couple of deep breaths. Tell me what's wrong."

Amanda started crying again, blurting out the sentences between sobbing inhalations. "The police were here, a lot of them. They were pulling Jacob over and must have thought he was a robber or something. They had their guns out and your son on the ground. Chip went out to see what was going on, and got into a fight with one of the cops. They took my husband and your son to jail."

"Okay… it will be okay, Amanda. Walk me through this; everything will be fine. Which police? Do you know what kind of cops they were?" While Gabe had never been in any trouble with the law, he knew there were several different departments with jurisdiction over the surrounding area.

"I don't know!" she cried. "They threw Chip down on the driveway, and there is blood on the concrete where he landed. I could hear Jacob screaming in pain… like they were torturing him or something."

None of it made any sense to Gabe; his first conclusion was that Amanda was near a breakdown and not rational. He knew Chip, and the man wasn't a hothead by any measure. He couldn't envision a scenario that would escalate as described with such a calm guy. And why would the cops arrest Jacob? Why would they hurt his son?

He tried a few more times to get a clearer picture from the distraught wife and mother, but she just repeated the same basic information over and over again.

"Is Manny there?"

"Yes. She's on the internet, trying to figure out where the officers would take Jacob and Chip."

"May I speak to her?"

There was a slight hesitation, and then, "Sure… she's very upset, but I'll get her."

It was a few moments before Manny's shaken voice came on the line. "Hello, Mr. Chase… I'm so… so sorry."

"What happened, Manny? Tell it to me from the beginning."

"We were almost home, and this cop came up behind us. He followed Jacob for a while, and then when we turned on my street, he switched on the lights. I told Jay to pull over, but because we were almost to my house, he drove another block before stopping."

"And then what happened?"

"The cop started walking toward the driver's side window with his gun drawn. He shouted for Jacob to get out of the car... yelling like those guys do on TV. He shoved Jay up against the Honda... and then I don't know what happened... but all of a sudden there were police everywhere. They threw Jay down on the ground, and he started crying out as if they were hurting him. I tried to run and get my dad, but a policeman pulled me back. And then everyone was fighting. I couldn't see very well, but I think Jacob is hurt. He was moaning and screaming and... I've never heard anyone make noises like that, Mr. Chase."

All of the rage, fear, puzzlement, and apprehension in Gabriel Chase vanished after absorbing the girl's last statement, replaced by a solitary, compelling need – he had to find his son.

"They didn't say where they were taking him?"

"No. They put my dad in one car, Jacob in another. The cops stood around laughing and smiling for a few minutes, and then left."

Gabe tried to put it all together, but didn't waste much mental firepower on the brainteaser. There was simply no scenario that made sense out of the account he was being given. Jacob was not one to be disrespectful to the authorities. Chip was a sensible man. In the end, it didn't matter. What he needed was to get to his son.

"Is your mom still there?"

"Yeah. Hold on, let me get her for you."

Gabe could hear the muffled sound of someone blowing her nose, explaining the brief delay before the distraught woman took the receiver. More settled this time, Amanda's voice came back on the line. "Hello?"

"Amanda, I'm going down to the local police station and see what I can find out about both Chip and Jacob. Let's keep each other informed. I'll call you the minute I know anything. Please do the same."

"Okay, Gabe… and thank you. I'm sorry I was such a mess before."

He chuckled politely, "Don't worry about it. I'm not far from joining you. I'll be in touch."

He disconnected the call. Glancing up into the pale countenance of his wife, he realized she had obviously been hanging on every word. "Tell me," she insisted, her motherly instincts bristling from hearing one side of the conversation and arriving at the worst place as her mind filled in the gaps. "Is he alive?"

"Yes, Mother, he's alive. There was an incident with the police, but neither Manny nor Amanda could tell me why. Chip got involved, and apparently, he was arrested, too. Other than that, I just got a bunch of gibberish that didn't make much sense."

"Thank, God," she said, having to sit back on the edge of the bed. "As long as he's alive, everything will be okay."

With his wife following closely behind, he perched at his desk in his home office and was soon combing through an old telephone book for the local constable's office number. The call was answered on the third ring. "Precinct Four, is this an emergency?"

"No, no emergency."

"How may I assist you?"

"I just received a call from a friend that my son had been arrested. How do I find him?"

The less than interested voice on the other end replied, "He will be allowed a phone call after the booking process is completed, sir. At that time, he'll be able to inform you of his location. Is there anything else?"

"How long does that take?"

The woman on the other end exhaled loudly, annoyance evident in her response. "That depends on quite a few factors, sir. It could take several hours, depending on the number of suspects being processed."

"Can you tell me where he is being booked?"

"No, sir. Depending on where he was apprehended, the charges and circumstances, he could be at any one of three facilities. Is there anything else?"

A thought occurred to Gabe. "He's a minor; he's only 17. Does that make any difference?"

Again, the impatient voice exhaled before launching her retort. "In Texas, sir, suspects 17 years of age and older are treated as adults. Most likely, he's being processed at the main Harris County Jail, downtown at 701 San Jacinto Avenue. But he might also be taken here, or to the hospital. I advise you to wait until your son calls with specific information, sir."

The woman's uncaring attitude, curt responses, and partial information had the desired effect – Gabe wanted to end the call despite not knowing much more than he had before dialing. "Thank you," he responded, shaking his head.

Turning to Sandy, he explained, "I have a really bad feeling about this. If that phone call was any indication of what Jacob is facing, we're in for a rough ride."

"What are we going to do?"

"I'm going to try and find out where he is. They said we should wait for a phone call with further information, but I'm not going to be able to do that. I want to be wherever Jacob is or as close as they'll let me get to him. I'm going to start looking up phone numbers and making calls."

Sandy nodded, bending to kiss the top of her husband's head. "We'll get through this; we always do. Jacob is smart and strong," she reassured him. "He'll be fine."

Gabe nodded blankly, a victim of cognitive overload, the chaotic barrage of thoughts tangling as each message competed for the forefront of his attention. "You're probably right, but I won't be able to just sit here and wait. Our son has been gobbled up by a very large, very uncaring machine that is designed to deal with the absolute worst society can produce. I just pray they don't chew him up and spit out a damaged young man."

"Do we need to call a lawyer?"

"I thought about that, but I don't know one. We've used attorneys at the office before, but they do contracts and business things. I don't even know a criminal lawyer. Besides, it's nearly 3 AM in the morning. I'm sure they don't list their home phone numbers in the yellow pages."

Sandy took a bit to digest her husband's words, her own nervous energy suppressing the need to do something... anything. "How about I make some coffee? It sounds like we're going to have a long night."

Gabe stood, pulling his wife close, the parents drawing comfort from the embrace. "The java sounds like a great idea. We'll be fine. I bet we have this all cleared up by tomorrow evening."

The now-motivated father hit the internet with a vengeance, dialing a long list of often contradicting phone numbers displayed on overlapping law enforcement websites. A few lines were disconnected, some rang on for eternity without answer by human or machine, and the remainder led him into a bottomless abyss of automated attendant menus boasting vague descriptions and dead ends. Within an hour, the frustration was driving him to thoughts of committing his own criminal activity.

"I can't believe this," he spouted to Sandy in frustration. "Our son, a minor, has basically been kidnapped by the police. There is no way to locate his whereabouts or know his status. It's maddening."

The mother's face was drawn, her eyes becoming as desperate as her husband's voice. "Do we need to go down there? Find someone to talk to in person? Make them locate our son?"

At one point in his fruitless barrage of telephoning, Gabe had come to the same conclusion, but then reconsidered. His web travels had made him realize the Harris County law enforcement infrastructure was gargantuan, with stations, sub-stations, incarceration facilities, and offices all over the vast area known as metropolitan Houston. In addition, if the detained individual required medical care, there was no specific hospital where he/she might be sent.

Manny had said Jacob was hurt. Had they driven the boy to an emergency room instead of a jail? There was no way to know.

"I hate to say this… the thought of doing this is about to drive me nuts, but I think we have to wait until our son calls, or the day-shift people start arriving at their desks and answer the phone. I think our driving around downtown is a waste of energy and time. Waiting seems to be our only option."

Sandy didn't like it either but realized she had to trust her mate's judgment. Sipping their coffee, the distraught couple sat, their eyes shifting between the wall clock and Gabe's cell phone charging beside the computer.

Jacob's 6'5" frame was beyond the design of the squad car's tiny back seat. When the tried and true Ford Crown Victoria police model had been retired a few years before, law enforcement agencies hadn't had any choice but to go with the newer, smaller sedans offered from Detroit. Being handcuffed didn't help the young man's ergonomics.

He had no choice but to sit nearly doubled over, his head resting on the wire cage that separated potentially dangerous prisoners from the driver's compartment. The officer transporting Jacob could only see the top of the boy's head.

After several blows to the head and torso, loss of blood, and overwhelming waves of pain from his knee, the teenager was going into shock. While the arresting officers had attempted to clean his wounds at the site, they had completely misjudged the severity of his injuries, both internal and external.

The transporting constable arrived at the main jail's unloading area, met there by the guards charged with assisting officers with their often-unruly passengers. They found Jacob unresponsive and unmoving.

"Look at that fucking mess in my backseat," complained the officer. "This son of a bitch has bled and puked all over the place. Now I'll be stuck here waiting on maintenance to hose this shit out."

"He's playing possum," remarked one of the burly guards, trying to get Jacob to respond. "There's not enough blood on the floor for him to be out. He's faking it."

"You sure?"

"Yeah, we see them do it all the time. They think if they act as if they're out cold, they'll get a ride to the ER instead of our 5-star facility. Let's yank his ass out of there. If he keeps it up, we'll just carry him into the holding area. I'll bet a cup of coffee he snaps out of it as soon as he realizes we're onto him."

The guard reached into the backseat and grabbed Jacob by the ear, pulling and twisting the boy's head with the painful technique. But Jacob didn't react, his body slumping sideways in the seat.

"Did this dude take a blow to the head or something?" the now second-guessing guard asked. "Twisting a handful of cartilage normally brings them right out of their little act."

"I don't know," replied the deputy. "I arrived late to the scene, and since I was the junior man, I was given transport duty. He looks damn pale though."

They lifted Jacob out of the car, a muscular jailer on each arm.

With feet dragging and head flopping, they carried him into the building via his handcuffed upper arms.

The Harris County Jail's staging room looked more like the waiting area at an airport gate than a lockup. Rows of plastic chairs filled the space, televisions hanging from ceiling mounts.

As soon as Jacob was arranged in one of the plastic seats, the officer removed the handcuffs. They tried three times to prop the unresponsive kid in a chair, each attempt resulting with the prisoner's lanky body sliding to the floor. Finally, they pulled him to a corner and left him prone.

"I'll call the medical people to come down here and check him out," said the jailer. "I don't think he's faking it."

"Should I load him up and take him to the ER?" the young deputy asked, now worried he might be held responsible somehow.

"Naw. He might be drunk, passed out from drugs… any number of things. Scalp wounds always bleed like crazy, but no way has he lost enough red corpuscles to be in danger. The nurse will be down to check him out in a bit. Give me his packet, and you can go have your car cleaned out."

Shrugging, the officer handed over the envelope and then returned the handcuffs to his duty belt.

It would be difficult to find a position in the medical field more troubling than that of the admission review staff at a big city jail.

Exposed daily to the most troubled examples of the human race, the tainted, mind-numb registered nurse and aides were witness to a constant parade of drug users, prostitutes, alcoholics, lice-infested homeless, and hardened criminals.

Often, the incoming detainees were belligerent, fighting, spitting, and kicking balls of filthy humanity, either unwilling, or unable to respond to the medical questionnaires or attempts at examination. Exposure to blood, vomit, urine, and feces were as common as the foul language, combative attitudes, and hostile profile displayed toward anyone who worked for "the man."

It was a thankless, low-paying, exceedingly dangerous job that created calloused individuals who basically operated with one cardinal rule -

nobody was to die while in custody. Beyond that, the examination process was haphazard at best, often at the benevolence of the individual healthcare worker's mood at the time.

In this regard, Jacob was lucky. The nurse aide who was called to the staging area was in a reasonable frame of mind, having just spent 20 minutes with a business executive hauled in for a DUI. The man had made her laugh and had been cooperative, a rarity for the graveyard shift.

Escorted by two massive jailers, the aide had recognized immediately Jacob was in trouble. Rushing to the prone teen's side, her first check was the lividity of his arm. After watching the flaccid limb flop uncontrollably to the floor, she then pulled back his eyelid. She found him cold and clammy, his diaphoretic state coinciding with all of the other symptoms.

"Get him out of here – stat," she turned and instructed the idling hulks. "He's in trouble, and I don't want him dying on my shift. Get an ambulance here… now."

"Are you sure?" asked the guard who had helped drag Jacob in.

"Don't fuck with me, Bluto…. Get him to Central right now."

Rising from Jacob's side, she heaved the radio from her belt, lifting to speak into the black box's grill. "I need the RN and a cart to the staging area, stat," she said.

She then returned to Jacob and started patting down his body, searching for other injuries. With her patient's shirt soaked in blood, her first inclination was that he was suffering from a gunshot wound that had somehow been overlooked, but that was rare.

As she worked down his right leg, she suddenly stopped, pulling a pair of sheers from her breast pocket. After a few snips on Jacob's pants leg, she pulled apart the denim material and inhaled sharply. "Holy shit… look at this kid's knee."

Stretching to gawk over her shoulder, the two jailers were impressed as well. Purple and red, the tortured joint was the size of a mature grapefruit. "That's why he's out," one of them commented. "That has to hurt like hell."

About then the registered nurse arrived with another aide and a toolbox-sized container of basic medical supplies. The team quickly set about its business, cleaning and bandaging the head wound and elevating Jacob's upper body.

It took longer than usual for the EMTs to arrive, a major accident on I-10 involving two semis and a car full of vacationers had pulled several ambulances to the scene.

And then there was the delay waiting for a deputy to accompany the prisoner.

Over 90 minutes after being delivered to the jail, Jacob Chase was on his way to the emergency room, IV in his arm, ice pack on his knee, and bandages wrapping his head.

The ambulance was less than three blocks away when the jailer strolled back to the booking area and noticed Jacob's packet sitting on the counter. "Shit," he hissed, picking up the thin folder, "This should have gone with that kid."

Central Hospital ER was one of the few left open in the entire area. One by one, the major facilities in the nation's fourth largest city had closed their emergency rooms, the deluge of uninsured patients making such accommodations unprofitable.

Much like the jail, the massive facility was always functioning at near capacity... in a state of barely controlled chaos.

The Houston Fire and Rescue ambulance that had responded to the jail's call had to wait in line, the six unloading bays all occupied by other emergency vehicles. Despite the fact that this was a weekday and not even the chickens were yet awake, the facility was running with a shortage of emergency beds. The weekend shifts were marked by total ER gridlock.

Finally able to pull forward and unload their patient, the two fireman wheeled Jacob's stretcher into one of the few empty waiting rooms. Leaving the bored cop to sit in a lonely looking, plastic chair, the two EMTs returned to the main nurse's station, both dreading the upcoming paperwork.

"Where's the patient's packet?"

"I thought you had it?"

"Shit! I guess we'll just have to register him as a John Doe until his file catches up with him," shrugged the team's senior member.

Chapter 3

Peelian Principle

Police headquarters should be centrally located and easily accessible by the public.

"We have no one at this facility by the name of Jacob Chase," came the annoyed response. "I suggest you try the local precinct's lockup."

"I've already contacted them, the Northside facility, and everyone else I can dial, ma'am. No one can find my son. Did the arresting officers just take him out to an empty field and dump his body?" resonated the frustrated voice of a desperate father.

"Sir, are you making a criminal accusation against a law enforcement officer? If so, I can transfer you to the public affairs office."

"I just want to know where my son is, ma'am. Pardon me for being a little over the top, but wouldn't you be acting the same way if your child were missing?"

"My computer screen says he's not here, sir. That's the only information I can access."

"Thank you," Gabe replied, even though he didn't mean it.

After the call was disconnected, the jail operator glared at her co-worker. "Why do white people always think their children are innocent and being abused by the big, bad county jail? I get so tired of it. It's as if they think their pale, little asses never commit any crime or do anything wrong. Like they should be treated special or something just because of their color."

The co-worker laughed. "Guess what," she said mimicking a game show host delivering the big prize, "Your suburban, middle-class teenager is a criminal! You are about to enter a whole new world called the criminal justice system. Soon you'll discover what half of the black and Latino parents already understand. Jail sucks, and the system doesn't care about anybody's race or income level or how many half-baths are in your fucking home."

They exchanged looks before moving to answer the next incoming call. "Oh shit," the operator announced, covering the mouthpiece. "I've got a Latino grandmother trying to find her daughter. These are the worst."

It was the blowtorch someone was holding against his leg that made Jacob stir. Forcing himself to climb through the grey, swirling void of fog, he blinked his eyes and tried to move his screaming limb away from the fire.

The effort induced more agony, streaks of electric fire climbing up his thigh, boiling into his head. He howled, and then started to vomit.

The cop-sentry had fallen asleep, rousted from his upright nap by the animal-like clamor. Rubbing the fog from his eyes, he noted his prisoner's reaction and understood something serious was going on. He pressed the call button and immediately rushed into the hall to secure assistance.

Again, some luck was on Jacob's side. The nighttime avalanche of patients and emergencies had subsided somewhat, and soon a team of medical professionals surrounded Jacob's bed.

If anyone had cared, it quickly became obvious to the gathered staff that somebody had made a horrible mistake. The John Doe now experiencing dry heaves into a plastic pan had somehow gotten lost in the shuffle. He should have received medical care long ago.

The attending ER physician took one look at Jacob's knee and asked the policeman what sort of automobile accident had caused the injuries sustained by the patient.

"I don't know anything about this detainee," replied the cop. "I was just sent down here to make sure he doesn't escape or cause any problems."

Grunting, the doctor pointed at the ugly joint and said, "He's not going anywhere, and I doubt he's going to beat us all up. Please do your best to find out who this child belongs to, I have a feeling we are going to have to make some difficult decisions in the next few hours."

The cop nodded and started to pivot away to seek a telephone. The doctor stopped him. "And remove these handcuffs, please."

Almost embarrassed at having forgotten the patient was still chained to the bed's metal rail, the policeman did as ordered. "I'll find out who he is," he promised the doc.

After watching the policeman leave, the physician returned to Jacob's side and asked, "What is your name? Can you tell me your name?"

"Jacob," came the dry response. "Jacob Chase."

"And where do you live, Jacob Chase?"

The teen managed to give the fuzzy, distant voice his address.

"How old are you, Jacob?"

"Seventeen."

"Is there someone I can call? I need to know your medical history and allergies before I can give you anything for the pain."

"Call my dad, please, sir. Gabriel Chase. His phone number is in my cell contacts."

The doctor turned to a nearby nurse and said, "See if you can find me a phone number. Given our illustrious police department, I'm sure this child's parents have no idea where he is or his condition. It wouldn't surprise me if Mr. and Mrs. Chase will probably end up with coronaries themselves."

"Yes, Doctor. I'm on it."

"I want every inch of this young man's body x-rayed, high priority," commanded the physician. "I'll order something for his pain as soon as we get some information. That knee has got to be tearing this kid apart."

Gabe called Amanda, letting her know the bad news. They had yet to locate Jacob.

"Chip finally called just ten minutes ago. We're on our way down to post my husband's bail.... I never thought I'd be saying that."

"Where is he?" Gabe asked, his voice growing hopeful.

"He's at the local precinct, but I asked him about Jacob, and he said he hasn't seen him since they were being loaded into the squad cars. He's pretty sure Jay isn't at the same jail."

The two parents agreed to keep in touch and disconnected the call.

After contacting his supervisor and being granted a last minute request for a vacation day, Gabe began getting dressed.

"Where are you going?" asked Sandy.

"I've got to do something. I'm going down to the local precinct and find some sort of supervisor."

"Be nice," came the quick reply. "We've already got enough family members in trouble with the law. I don't know what I'd do if they locked you up, too."

"Don't worry. I'll be as warm as a pair of fuzzy, bunny slippers."

It wasn't a long drive to the combination police station and courthouse. Finding a parking spot, however, was a completely different matter.

Gabe entered the surprisingly small complex, realizing he'd never been inside the building and had no idea what to expect. After following several signs, he wound his way to the police section of the facility.

Half expecting some burly, no-nonsense sergeant behind thick, bulletproof glass, Gabe was surprised to find a middle-aged woman in civilian clothing sitting at a reception desk.

"How can I help you?" she asked in a neutral tone.

"My son was arrested about 2 AM this morning by officers from this station, and now no one seems to know where he is. I've called every jail and phone number listed on the web, and there's no record of him anywhere."

"Hold on one moment, Mister..."

"Chase, Gabriel Chase. My son's name is Jacob Chase."

She reached for the phone, punching in three numbers from memory. After a brief pause, she said, "Do you have an arrest record from this morning for one Jacob Chase?"

She listened for a few moments, scratching a series of numbers on a pad of paper. "Thank you," she said, ending the call.

"Your son was taken to the Harris County Jail downtown, Mr. Chase. I have his file ID number, and you should be able to track his progress through the system via the online interface."

Gabe reached to take the scrap of paper from the helpful woman, but wasn't satisfied. "I've called and talked to them, and they say he isn't in their facility. Could there be some mistake?"

The woman smiled, trying to reassure the obviously stressed parent. "Sometimes it can take several hours for them to process incoming prisoners. I've seen six to ten hours go by before they have his information uploaded into the computer system. Relax, Mr. Chase; we're in the business of catching people, not losing them."

"But he's only 17," Gabe pleaded. "He's never been in any trouble before, and this is all quite a shock."

"Take that number and go home, sir. I wrote down the web address for the jail's public information system. As soon as they have your son processed, he'll be allowed to call you."

"Thank you," he said, pivoting to exit the area.

His next stop was to see Chip, and find out what the hell had happened the night before.

Manny answered the front door, her bleary-eyed, disheveled appearance making it obvious no one had gotten any sleep in the Denton household. After a brief hug, she invited Gabe in. "Dad's in the shower, mumbling something about never being able to wash all the pig shit off his body," she said, trying to maintain a smile.

Amanda appeared, the two sharing a quick embrace, the question on her face requiring no words.

"We still don't know where Jacob is," he announced. "I do have his file number and was just told it might take a few hours before he is processed into the system. Not knowing what else to do, I decided to come over here and see if I could figure out what the hell happened last night."

"I'll tell you what happened," an angry voice boomed from the doorway, "Jacob smarted off or said something wrong to one of those cops, and they beat the shit out of him. That's what happened."

Everybody looked up to see Chip standing with a towel around his waist. Purple splotches were already appearing on his arms and wrists.

"Jacob would never do that," Gabe instantly replied. "I've always told him to respect the police and be polite to them."

"He didn't say a word, Daddy," Manny defended. "He never got a chance. They were pointing their guns at him and screaming before he could even roll down the window."

"Something set them off," Chip said, "I've never seen anything like it. How's Jacob doing, by the way?"

"I don't know. We haven't found him yet."

"He's got to be in the hospital," came the dreaded response. "He was badly injured, bleeding all over the place. He couldn't even walk...." Chip paused, realizing the effect his words were having on the boy's father. "I'm sorry... but you need to know. He's got to be at a hospital."

"I've called all the major facilities," Gabe replied. "No one has his name on any list."

Gabe's cell phone rang, stopping his report mid-sentence. Glancing hopefully at the caller ID, he was only slightly disappointed to see it was his own home number.

"He's at Central Hospital," came his wife's excited voice. "I just spoke to a nurse, and she was asking all kinds of questions about his medical history and stuff. They need us down there right away."

"Did they say how he is?"

"No. She wouldn't tell me anything until we showed up and proved we were his guardians. She said we should hurry."

"I'll be right there to pick you up," Gabe replied. "Please be ready."

"I'll be waiting by the curb," Sandy came back. "You won't even have to come to a complete stop."

The anxious father managed to tell Manny and her parents what he had just heard before he reached their front door. "I'll call you when I know more," he yelled, hurrying for his car.

The vending machine sandwich sat nearby, mostly uneaten. Keeping it company on the waiting room's end table were the almost full container of juice, half-eaten bag of potato chips, and a light dusting of salted pretzel crumbs. All were residual evidence of the Chases' lunch. Only the coffee cups, one with Sandy's lipstick, the other unmarked, had been worthy of constant attention.

After having provided insurance information, signing a seemingly endless stack of consent for treatment forms, and being told someone would be with them shortly, they had been idling for four hours in a corner of the main waiting room.

Finally a nurse appeared, holding a clipboard and shouting out the name, "Chase?"

"Now we get to see our son," Sandy hissed, her frustrations nearing the boiling point.

But it wasn't to be. Instead, the couple was shown into a small cubicle where a harried-looking physician sat examining a stack of documents.

He didn't waste any time. "Mr. and Mrs. Chase, your son has two broken ribs, a slight concussion, and numerous lacerations, three of which required staples. But what is the most troubling, is his right knee. Jacob tells me he played in the city championship basketball game just a few days ago. Was he, per chance, injured in that contest?"

"No," they both responded instantly. "As a matter of fact, he was showing off for his girlfriend yesterday morning, dunking the ball on our home goal."

The doctor frowned. "This is most troubling. His other injuries are non-threatening and quite common for people who fight with the police. But this knee is unusual. He has suffered what is called an 'unhappy triad,' which basically is simultaneous trauma to the anterior cruciate ligament and medial collateral ligament, in addition to a tear of the medial meniscus. It is extremely rare to see such damage outside of an automobile collision, or vicious football accident."

"We left him only an hour before he was arrested," Sandy spoke up. "He was walking fine."

"I just saw his car," Gabe added, "There was no damage or any other sign of an accident. A witness did tell me that the cops beat my son badly."

The doctor nodded, looking up at the two stressed parents sitting across from him. "Eventually, the knee can be repaired so that he has full use, but I must warn you – that could take several operations, and perhaps years of recovery."

"What? Are you sure? He just signed a scholarship to play college basketball…. What are you saying, Doctor?"

"I'm not a surgeon, nor am I a specialist in sports medicine, but I'm reasonably sure Jacob isn't going to be playing basketball for a very, very long time. I'm sorry, Mr. and Mrs. Chase, but that is the truth."

Waves of despair rolled over Gabe Chase. He flushed angry, some far recess of his mind screaming for revenge while a disabling current of remorse and helplessness flowed through his mind.

The guilt was the worst.

Gabe had talked his wife into purchasing the Honda. It had been his decision to let Jacob take Manny home despite the late hour. He had extended the dinner conversation, and thus the hour, blathering on and on.

If only he'd told Jacob he needed to talk to Chip and would take Manny home. If only he hadn't droned on and on with the coach. Things would be different. Jacob would be fine – if only....

Sandy seemed relieved that her son wasn't in danger of losing his life, her reaction seemingly mild compared to her husband's. "Can we see him now?" she asked softly.

The physician shook his head, "No, I'm afraid he's not allowed visitors at this time."

"What?" replied the confused mother. "I thought he wasn't in any danger?"

"Oh, it's not the hospital that is restricting his visitors; it's the police. They have some foolish policy that forbids visitation until the suspect has been processed."

That was it. That was the final straw for Gabriel William Chase. Rising suddenly from his chair, the irate man hissed, "Thank you, Doctor," and then pivoted toward the door with the intent of finding the closest law enforcement officer.

Sandy rushed to follow, determined to cool her husband's jets. She caught up with him in the hall, "Gabe... Gabe! Wait! Stop right here and talk to me."

"I've had enough of this nonsense. They beat the crap out of a helpless, good kid. They have ruined the only thing important in his life, and now we can't even visit our son because of some stupid rule? This is beyond unreasonable, Sandy, and I'm not just going to stand by and let Jacob be abused."

"Wait," she again commanded, "don't go rushing in all bullheaded and out of control. I know you and that temper, Gabriel Chase, and that tactic is not going to help Jacob right this minute. Let's get another cup of coffee and talk this through. Be smart. Be calm. Do this the right way."

Something in his wife's voice allowed her logic to penetrate the curtain of emotions obstructing his common sense. He pulled up short, exhaled loudly, and nodded. "You're right. Of course, you're right."

After a struggle with the change machine, both had fresh cups of java and were calming down. "Tell you what," Gabe finally spoke. "Let me work on getting a lawyer on this right away. That will keep me busy and out of trouble. We'll let someone who knows the system deal with this. How's that sound?"

Sandy smiled, relieved that her partner had come around to logical thinking. "Let's get started. How can I help?"

Gabe walked to a nearby phone booth and lifted the thick yellow pages for his wife to see. "Got a pencil and paper in that suitcase you call a purse?" he teased.

"You got it. Start reading off the numbers. I want to kick some police ass."

The first surprise for the Chases was the lack of criminal attorneys listed in the yellow pages. There were volumes of mediators, civil litigators, ambulance chasers, divorce attorneys, and other specialists, but the section for those dealing with accused lawbreakers was the least populated.

Even those firms who budgeted for the more expensive, box-shaped ads seemed to specialize in one form of crime, such as DUI or illegal narcotics. Gabe struggled to identify those legal eagles who were best able and willing to assist them. He quickly noticed that no listings advertised, "Did a cop beat the shit out of your kid? Well, then call us."

Still, Sandy managed to write down a page full of options. Gabe began dialing.

Many of the listed numbers connected to answering services, promising a return call as soon as so-and-so was available. A few more were answered by receptionists, but an actual lawyer wasn't able to take a call at that moment.

When Gabe finally reached a real attorney on the line, the man seemed disinterested. "What is he charged with, Mr. Chase?"

"We don't know. We're at the hospital, and they haven't booked him yet, so there's no way to know the charges."

"I see. What exactly was he doing when arrested?"

"Driving his car. According to his girlfriend, he wasn't speeding or breaking any laws. There are even witnesses that saw the police beating the hell out of Jacob."

"Mr. Chase, I speak with parents every day who swear their child would never break a law. To be honest, I've never had a single case where that ended up being accurate. I'll be happy to represent your son, as I work with the prosecutor all the time, and we can normally plead the charges down to something acceptable. I require a $5,000 retainer and a signed letter of representation before we get started. Would you like to make an appointment?"

Three hours later, after talking to a handful of lawyers, Gabe was ready to explode.

His frustrations were many, but none seemed more egregious than the fact that every, single attorney assumed Jacob was guilty and had to be proven innocent. "That's not the way I thought it was supposed to be," he informed Sandy. "I've always believed we lived under a system that presumed innocence. Clearly, that's not the case."

"Maybe they're all so jaded they don't believe that anymore," she responded, shaking her head. "It seems like everybody but us thinks

Jacob's arrest and injuries are par for the course, run of the mill, and business as usual. What has this world come to?"

Before Gabe could respond, he noticed two police officers strolling through the reception area, one of them carrying a large metallic case. He was approaching the lawmen when he heard one of them ask the attending nurse where they could find one Jacob Chase.

"We're here to do an off-site processing," announced the officer. "Our understanding is that the suspect is going to be incapacitated for some time."

Gabe didn't know what to do and halted his approach. The nurse finally found Jacob's location, giving the two cops directions to his room.

Turning to tell Sandy what he had just heard, Gabe again was interrupted by the ringing of his cell. He recognized Chip's number.

"Have you found a lawyer yet?"

"No, we've been working for hours on just that, and let me tell you, it's about as frustrating a thing as I've ever seen."

Chip's tone sounded like he was a man on a mission. "My brother-in-law is a civil attorney, but he knows some of the better criminal people. Here, write down this number, and give Adam Barlow a call. I signed up with him just a few minutes ago."

"Thanks, Chip. You don't know what this means to us."

Then the caller's voice became sad, almost as if he were reliving the incident. "I can't get the visions of those cops beating the crap out of Jacob to go away. What they did just wasn't right. I also got a replacement cell phone this afternoon. I can show you the video now."

Gabe didn't believe he heard the last statement correctly. "The what?"

"I took video of those guys kicking the shit out of Jacob. That's why I was arrested. The big cop wanted my phone, and I wouldn't give it to him until I got the video uploaded to the cloud. They crushed my phone during the struggle, but the data-backup worked. You might not want to let Sandy see it though. Amanda started crying and couldn't watch. It's pretty bad, Gabe."

Surprisingly, Chip's announcement was the only positive thing Gabe Chase had heard all day. He actually smiled. "We won't be leaving the hospital for a while, but I can't wait to see it. Do you think it will clear Jacob's name?"

There was a pause before the answer came through the phone's tiny speaker. "I don't know about that. I didn't record the beginning of the encounter. By the time I got outside, they already had Jacob pinned to the ground, so what happened before that isn't on my video."

"I see," Gabe said, clearly disappointed.

"But I will tell you this, there's not a reasonable person in the world who can watch what is on my film and say the cops were justified. It's... it's... it's painful to watch. It's just not right what they did."

"Thanks, Chip. I'll call you when we leave here. I'll come by and see it."

Officer Dole Kirkpatrick rested the clipboard against the steering wheel of his cruiser, re-reading his notes from last night's takedown. While it was unlikely he'd be asked to submit a report or testify at any trial, his training and personal habits dictated a quick documentation of every call. Now, as he prepared for his shift, he regretted looking at the words.

It was good to be back in the familiar surroundings of his regular patrol car. Sergeant Marwick's seniority and last minute scheduling change had forced Dole to surrender his newer squad car and move into one of the reserve units the previous evening. The switch had marked a harbinger of what would be the worst ten hours of his short career.

Kirkpatrick sighed, glancing at his scribbles, recalling the sensation and sound of that kid's knee giving way in his hands. He would never forget the wail of agony escaping from the young suspect's throat.

Despite two years on the nation's fourth largest police force, Dole was still trying to find a comfort zone within his chosen profession. Teased since the academy about his insistent note taking, he would never admit to anyone the real reason behind the routine. The habit wasn't indicative of any lack of mental capacity, nor did he harbor retentive tendencies. Dole kept his record because he wasn't sure he was really cut out for a career as a cop, and he knew that one day soon his pseudo-journal would help him make a difficult decision.

His grandfather had been a decorated New York City officer, his father still on the blue line with the Dallas Police Department. It had been assumed after graduating with a bachelor's degree in criminal justice that the youngest male member of the Irish family would follow in the tradition.

But Dole hadn't developed into what his father considered to be law enforcement raw material. At least not his mindset. "You're too nice, too caring, too liberal, and for sure too big hearted. You will have only an instant to make most of your decisions, and you can't go home and second-guess them. No room for backseat drivers or Monday quarterbacks on the front lines. Do something else with your life, son. Being a cop isn't a match for you."

The pronouncement had been devastating, crushing Dole's sense of belonging and family custom.

His father's prophecy hadn't developed overnight, nor was it attributable to any one incident. He'd grown up watching the two most important men in his life struggle with their chosen professions, witnessing the family hardships triggered by living with a badge. Heavy drinking, double shifts, constant stress, and a highly competitive political environment inside of the force had taken a toll on both the youngest Kirkpatrick and his older male role models. Dole had often rebelled, regularly questioning his father's management of life and family.

While Dole was sure he wanted to be a peace officer, he definitely didn't want to follow in his dad's footsteps. The younger Kirkpatrick often found himself at odds with his old man, constantly questioning the methods, tactics, and results of the local precinct. More often than not, the son found himself on the opposite side of the issues discussed around the Kirkpatrick dinner table.

Always an astute child, he'd watched his father struggle with checking the "my way or the hard way," attitude at the door after arriving home. If he made it home at all. There had been countless nights sitting up with his mother, waiting for either the dreaded phone call or the old man's footfalls climbing the tiny apartment's stairs. As Dole grew and matured, there was a string of black marks in the follow-in-the-footsteps side of the ledger. Yet, pinning on a badge seemed part of his destiny.

Then everything had changed without warning or discussion. In his early teens, Dole had come home one day and received urgent orders. "Pack your room; we're moving."

He'd never found out why his father suddenly had to leave the NYPD. He'd overheard only partial conversations and half-baked rumors indicating father and son legacies were no longer vogue within the politically charged department. Other stories delved further into a dark innuendo of corruption and skullduggery where Dole didn't want to explore… didn't want to know.

Seemingly unaware of the trauma they were invoking on their son, Officer Kirkpatrick and his high school sweetheart of 18 years had loaded the contents of their small Brooklyn apartment and headed west in a rented U-Haul. But they could only pack the physical things. There wasn't room in the moving van for their son's social circles, friends, and the comfort of familiar surroundings.

The upheaval in Dole's teenage life had been painful, his previous existence simply vanishing in the rearview mirror with the image of New York's largest borough. Absent were his buddies, teachers, grandfather, and streets of his childhood. Soon those were replaced with a completely different cadence of living including tap water that harbored a foul taste, and strangers who ridiculed his accent.

Still, he tried to make the best of it, focusing his energies on making a fresh start in Dallas, Texas. That glimmer of a brighter future included visions of a closer, more open and honest relationship with his dad. Maybe the slower pace of the country would offer the two more time together. He envisioned baseball games, county fairs, hayrides, and rodeos that they might share.

For a time, the Lone Star state had given Dole hope of a normal family life. The young Kirkpatrick's dream was quickly dashed, however, his father immediately falling into the old routine of picking up as much overtime as possible. "We have to make ends meet," his dad had explained after one especially late evening. "Money doesn't grow on trees, son."

"Then why do you do it? You're smart. You could get a job anywhere that pays more."

"What? And not be a cop? I can't think of anything else I'd want to do with my life. Being a police officer is honorable. It's the high ground. It represents the gratification of accepting a moral calling," his dad had refuted.

With age, Dole became more conservative in his politics, more in line with his father's view of the world and law enforcement. But his dad had changed since leaving the NYPD, some chip constantly parked on the old man's shoulder. Although it was due to a completely different reason, the senior Kirkpatrick was still firmly against his son following in the linage of law enforcement. "It's not for you. I want you to do something better... have a happier life. Things aren't the same for a cop anymore. The whole ball of wax has turned to shit, and I'd hate to see you neck deep in it like I am every day."

Dole had moved to Houston after graduation, following a classmate's prediction that the Bayou City would be hiring another group of officers in the next few weeks. Sure enough, the youngest Kirkpatrick had applied for academy admission and then been offered a position. However, neither his college degree in criminology, nor his lifetime spent living with police officers prepared him for a career in law enforcement. The "job" wasn't anything like he'd expected.

Last night's episode had represented the pinnacle of his discomfort, the summit of his regret.

Why had he torqued on that kid's leg so hard? Why had he been so eager to please the sergeant? The only answer Dole could ferret out involved proving himself to his father, honoring the family name. Last night, he'd seen an opportunity to demonstrate he was as tough as anybody. His part of the pig pile had provided a chance to show he was as hardnosed as his old man, and let his brother officers know he had their backs. Besides, the kid had been running from the cops, and everybody knew there was a price to pay for that stupidity.

His reasoning helped him rationalize his actions and feel a little better. "I've learned from my mistake. The next time, I'll know better. Chalk it up to a learning experience and stop dwelling on the negatives. No one but you will ever know."

That admittance, combined with the notes in his hand, prompted Dole to think of the dash-cam video storage in the truck. "You can't let one little thing ruin your life," he whispered. "Move on. Learn, but move on."

He shredded the paper notes, tearing them into unreadable scraps. After reaching for the trunk release, he exited the vehicle and scanned the sub-station's lot to make sure no one was paying him any heed.

The cruiser's trunk was equipped with a metal vault of a sort, the hardened, bolted storage box used to store an AR15 patrol rifle, spare ammunition, and critical radio equipment. The camera's memory card was housed within as well.

He punched in the code, relieved the bolting mechanism clicked open. Marwick might have messed with the driver's seat, but he hadn't changed the number sequence on the lock.

Pulling open a drawer-like shelf, he was surprised to discover that the memory card had already been removed.

"Now why would he have removed that video?" he wondered, his mind immediately traveling to a suspicious place. "Maybe Marwick is feeling the same regret that I am and wanted to destroy the evidence."

Shaking his head, Dole replaced the missing card with a spare and then proceeded to secure the unit. The sound of someone clearing his throat caused the rookie to startle.

Dole pivoted to see Big Jim standing less than five feet away, an inquisitive look on the senior officer's face. "How are ya doing?" he asked, and then nodded toward the trunk. "I was just coming to tell you I removed the memory card last night."

"Oh, thanks for letting me know. I always check before signing in for my shift."

"I'm going to make a copy for my file, and then I'll return the original to the unit," Jim explained. "I don't quite get all this fancy technology and think most of this shit is a waste of time… but policy is policy."

The younger cop started to inform the sergeant that a copy of the video was automatically uploaded to the department's cloud storage unit, but decided not to risk embarrassing the senior man. Quite a few experienced officers seemed to struggle with the latest gadgets, and he'd learned a long time ago that egos ran frail among the older badges.

As the two officers exchanged a few rounds of casual conversation, Dole found the sergeant's attitude puzzling. It was odd for Marwick to spend the time with a rookie, but the weirdness extended beyond that. The older cop had never spoken a word to him before, and yet now the sergeant was chatting with him as if they were close friends. It was peculiar… and uncomfortable.

Finally, the sergeant warned Dole, "Be careful out there," and sauntered off. The entire episode left the younger officer wondering what the hell was going on.

Shaking off the disconcerting sensation, he realized there was no time for extensive analysis. His shift was starting, and he needed to have the dispatcher sign him in. After making the final adjustments to the driver's seat, Patrolman Kirkpatrick was rolling out of the station's lot, whispering a quiet prayer that tonight would be a better night.

"Barlow Law Offices," the pleasant female voice announced. "How may I direct your call?"

"Hi, my name is Gabriel Chase. Mr. Barlow was recommended to me to represent my son."

"Hold on one moment please."

Gabe glanced at his wife, holding up crossed fingers. It was less than a minute before a gravelly sounding male voice came on the line. "Adam Barlow here."

Gabe introduced himself and was pleased when the lawyer said, "I've been waiting for your call, Mr. Chase. Where are you?"

"We are still at the hospital, sir. We would like very much to see our son, but they won't let us," Gabe replied in a voice more sad than frustrated.

"Why not?"

"The hospital staff said that the police wouldn't allow visitors until our son was booked."

There was a brief silence, then, "Which hospital?"

"Central... in the ER."

"That's not very far from my office, Mr. Chase. If you don't mind meeting with me in the waiting room, I can stop by in a few minutes."

Gabe smiled for the first time that day, flashing Sandy a thumbs-up signal. "I can't tell you how much that would mean to us, sir. We don't want to leave until we see how Jacob is doing, and who knows how long that will be."

Twenty minutes later, a man wearing a tweed sports coat and nice shoes approached the still-waiting couple. Setting down his briefcase as if he already knew the answer, he offered his right hand and said, "Mr. and Mrs. Chase, I presume."

They sat for 30 minutes, Adam asking seemingly unrelated questions about their home, marriage, and Jacob's childhood as well as his recent successes on the basketball court.

"I talked to Chip on the way over here, and he backs up your story 100%. That says a lot to me… the girlfriend's father giving a recommendation to the teenage boyfriend goes a long way. Jacob sounds like a pretty good kid to me."

"We still don't know why or how this all occurred," Sandy added. "I just can't imagine Jacob being anything but polite to any adult, let alone a policeman."

Nodding, the attorney looked at the worried mother with a sincere gaze. "We'll find out, Mrs. Chase. The truth almost always comes to light."

Gabe noticed the two police officers, the large silver case in tow, moving toward the nurse's station. "Those are the two cops I was telling you about."

"Excuse me," Adam said, rising to intercept the officers.

The Chases watched a longer than anticipated exchange between the attorney and the policemen, the hand gestures and body language making it all seem like a casual, friendly conversation initially. Then one of the cops reached into this pocket and produced a cell phone, appearing as though he was slightly annoyed.

Gabe readjusted his body in the uncomfortable chair in hopes of hearing part of the conversation. Soon, heads were nodding, hands were shaken, and one of the cops turned and said a few words to the nurse, who immediately scratched something down with her ink pen.

"Come on, let's go see your son," Adam announced after returning from across the room.

Gabe had never seen Sandy walk so fast, pure motherly love pumping her legs, propelling her toward her only child. They identified the right room number, and a few seconds later, they were staring down at a patient both parents barely recognized as their son.

Jacob was still pale, half of his head wrapped in bandages. One arm was in a sling, numerous scrapes and cuts thick with some sort of salve. The kid opened his eyes, focused, tried to smile, and then grimaced in pain. "Mom! Dad!" he whispered in a hoarse voice. "Oh God, am I glad to see you."

Sandy wanted to hug her offspring, but couldn't seem to figure out where to apply the embrace without inflicting pain. She bent and kissed his cheek, rubbing the unbandaged side of his head. Gabe took his turn next.

After the reunion was completed, Gabe introduced Mr. Barlow, who up until that point had been observing the family's exchange with a keen eye.

"Hello, son," the lawyer said. "I'd offer you my hand, but I don't think that's a good idea right now."

A few minutes later, they got down to the nitty-gritty. "I need to know what happened, Jacob," the lawyer prompted, pulling a pencil and pad of paper from his briefcase. "Tell me everything you can remember."

Jacob recounted the drive home, joking with Manny, and then the appearance of the policeman in their rearview mirror. "I thought he was going to ram into my bumper," the kid confided. "Then he backed off and just followed us."

"Did he have on his emergency lights?"

"No, not until we turned into Manny's neighborhood and came to the first stop sign. After I pulled through, his blue and red lights came on."

The lawyer scratched away at his pad, suddenly changing the tempo of his questions. "Why didn't you stop?"

"I did... well... I went another block or so because Manny was late getting home. I thought the police just wanted to check my temporary tags. Wasn't any big deal."

Again, the lawyer scribbled before asking his next question, "How far was it between the moment when the policeman turned on his lights and when you stopped? Really, Jacob, this is important. I need to know the truth, exactly how far?"

"Less than two blocks," the kid said honestly. "Just over a block, maybe?"

Adam nodded, "Okay, so then what happened?"

"I asked Manny to get my insurance card out of the glove box. The policeman turned on some extra-bright light, and then the next thing I know, he's screaming for me to get out of the car. He's pointing a gun at me."

"Was Manny in the glove compartment when he walked up?"

"No, she never had time to open it. She was just sitting there, trying to shield her eyes from the blinding lights."

On and on the questions continued, Sandy and Gabe standing, then sitting, but always trying to stay close to Jacob's side. Gabe knew enough to realize Adam was testing his son, several of his inquires repeated with a slightly different wording.

After thirty minutes of grilling, the lawyer returned his pad and pencil to the briefcase, and then looked up. Drawing the interview to a close, there was only one rhetorical question left to ask Jacob. "So you have no idea why this officer pulled you over?"

Jacob managed to turn his head slightly and then replied, "Yes, sir. I think I *do* know why he stopped me."

All three of the adults in the room perked with attention, the boy's revelation catching them by surprise. "I accidentally hit him with a basketball during the city championship game just a few days ago. I didn't mean to... but I blocked a shot, and it bounced off the guy's shoulder. I thought for a minute he was going to stomp onto the court and scream at me."

"What?" Adam said, coming upright in his chair. "You've seen this officer before? You couldn't have been paying attention to him for more than a second at the game. Are you sure?"

"Yeah, pretty sure it was the same guy. After halftime, he marched out onto the court and grabbed one of the other team's players. I was watching, scared he was going to say something to me next. Anyway, he grabbed this kid's shirt, and I thought he was going to arrest that player."

"Did he?"

"No, he talked to the kid for a minute and then let him go. Kind of freaked us all out, but then I forgot about it until I saw him walking up to my car last night."

Out came the pad of paper again, the attorney frantically scribbling another paragraph's worth of notes. After he had finished, he peered up and said, "I'll let you rest now, Jacob. Thank you for answering my questions. One last thing – if the police come back and try to talk to you, tell them you want to have me present for any questioning. Here's one of my cards. I want you to keep it on your bedside. Don't say a word to anybody except your parents or me about all of this. Not the nurses, doctors, police, or anybody. Clear?"

"Yes, sir. Am I going to go to jail?"

"No, Jacob. You're not going to jail. You just worry about healing. Your parents and I will take care of the rest."

Adam rose to leave, Gabe automatically following the attorney out into the hall.

"Well? What do you think?" the anxious father asked.

"Your son was given what the cops commonly call a 'tune up.' Why, I'm still not sure, but I can't help but think it might have had something to do with the basketball game, or something that happened that night. In the real world, the police operate under the premise that if you run from them, they can do whatever they want and get away with it. Clearly, with your son's injuries, their retribution got out of hand. I don't believe Jacob was trying to evade them, but like so many things involving law enforcement, the cops are given a lot of latitude when it comes to making that judgment call. I can't tell you much more without reading the police report."

"Have you seen the video?" Gabe asked.

"Video? This is the first I've heard of any video."

"Chip filmed the cops beating Jacob in the street. I've not seen it yet, but I'm told it's very disturbing."

"Email me a copy of the video as soon as possible, please. In the meantime, I'll let the district attorney know I'm representing your son. They'll most likely schedule an arraignment soon. I'll go in front of the judge, plead Jacob not guilty, and see if I can get him released on his own recognizance."

Gabe watched his new ally exit down the hall, his confidence returning. The check they'd written for a retainer was going to hurt, as were the hospital bills. For a moment, he wondered if the county was going to foot the bill for Jacob's medical costs, but quickly dismissed the notion. So far, the local government hadn't exactly performed like a well-oiled machine, and he doubted they'd ever see a penny.

The nurse soon shooed them away, having given the parents an extra 30 minutes after normal visiting hours to remain with their son. The gesture wasn't lost on a thankful Gabe and Sandy.

They drove home in silence, both of them processing and reprocessing recent events in hopes of organizing their thoughts and implementing a plan. When the passing landscape began to look familiar, Gabe announced, "After I drop you off, I'm going to head over to Chip's house and watch that video. I think I can handle it now that we know Jacob is going to be okay."

"I want to go," his wife responded sternly. "He's my son, too."

"I don't know if that's a good idea, hon. Chip said it was pretty rough, and the last 24 hours haven't been a picnic. Are you sure you want to do this?"

"I'll be okay. I want to go."

Gabe knew enough not to attempt further discouragement, his 20 years of marriage having taught him that Sandy was a kind, big hearted person. But, when the woman made up her mind, she was a stone pillar of resolve, and any attempt to change that was wasted energy.

After calling Chip to make sure it wasn't too late for a visit, they bypassed their own neighborhood and proceeded to Manny's house. Seeing the still-parked Honda in the street initiated an unsettling bout of cold chills in both parents. Despite Chip having hosed it down twice, the street still contained dark splotches that both parents believed were their son's blood.

Amanda met them at the door, all smiles and warm welcomes. After refusing a cup of anything to drink and a quick update on Jacob's status, the exhausted parents waited while Chip left to retrieve his laptop.

Manny and Amanda couldn't watch. Out of necessity, they'd watched the video once before, and that was enough. Each of them tried to convince Sandy it was a bad idea, but Jacob's mother wouldn't budge.

"It's a little shaky at first. I was freaking out and not paying much attention to what I was filming exactly," announced Chip as he flipped open the computer's screen. "Here we go."

The video was only three minutes long, but it was the worst three minutes of Gabe and Sandy's life. Hearing Jacob scream, plead for mercy, and howl in pain while a circle of big men pounded, kicked, and sat on their son was off the scale horrible. On three separate occasions, Sandy had to turn away, tears streaming down her cheeks. Manny was quick with tissues and a reassuring touch on the shoulder.

Visions of Jay flashed through Gabe's mind, the day he first drew breath, his proud son beaming in a little league uniform, the look on the boy's glowing face when he made the 8th grade basketball team.

Another groan and screech of agony was emitted from the miniature speakers, recognizable immediately as sound coming from Jacob's distressed throat. Suddenly Gabe could smell Jacob as a newborn... could envision his engaging Christmas morning toddler smile... flashed back to his junior high trumpet solo... a lifetime of memories made even more bittersweet by the knowledge that his son had been violated, and he had been powerless to help. He had to just sit there and watch his own flesh and blood be sadistically tortured.

Gabe thought his chest was going to explode, his temple visibly pulsating with every beat of his broken heart... his anger turning into bile. For a bit, he had difficulty breathing. Watching those three minutes of footage constituted the worst experience of his entire life.

On and on, the video streamed, the parents unable to turn away, yet praying for it to end.

The room was silent after it finished, Sandy's sniffles and Gabe's heavy breathing the only sounds. Finally, the husband reached for his wife's hand and squeezed it tight.

Gabe's voice was ice cold when he finally spoke. "Thank you, Chip, for letting us come over. My attorney asked that we email him a copy of the video as soon as possible. Could I trouble you to send us both one?"

"Sure, be glad to. I don't know what happened out on that street, but it was wrong. It reminded me of those movies when the Nazi Brown Shirts burned and beat the Jews in Berlin back in the 30s. It was so... so... brutal and unnecessary. I hope you sue the pants off those cops."

After the goodbyes were completed, Gabe and Sandy drove off, the car filled with nothing but the hum of the tires. Several minutes passed before Gabe reached for his wife's hand, the gesture accepted with a warm smile. "For the first time in my life, I want to kill," Sandy confessed in a low voice. "I've never felt anything like this. If those policemen were in front of me right now, I would try to end their lives. What is happening to me, Gabe? What is going to happen to us?"

"We'll be fine," he answered calmly. "It's Jacob I'm worried about."

"District attorney's office," the lady answered.

"Hi, Susanna, this is Adam Barlow. I need to speak to whomever has been assigned the Jacob Chase file."

"One moment, Mr. Barlow, I'll see if it's been logged yet."

Adam could hear the indistinct click of keyboard buttons, the background noise generating a vision of the administrator checking her computer screen. "That would be Assistant DA Grossman. I'll connect you, sir."

The ADA actually picked up, the sound of his voice surprising the defense lawyer. "Grossman."

"Hey, Tony, this is Adam Barlow. I'm representing Jacob Chase, file number..."

"No need, Adam. I've got the folder right here in front of me. Looks like a pretty clear-cut case of evading, resisting, and obstructing to me. Do you want to plead it out?"

"The video we have tells a different story, Tony. I think we'll take this one all the way," Barlow replied, his voice growing icy cold.

There was a long pause, the word "video" causing the prosecutor to flip pages, giving him time to think. "I see here that the squad car's dash camera was inoperable the morning of the arrest. You have a third party video?"

Barlow's next statement sounded almost cheery. "Oh, yes, we do. And there isn't a judge in the county that's going to like what's on it. The reason for my call is to give your office a heads up. I'm filing for dismissal today, and I want charges pressed against these officers."

Again, the people's lawyer scanned the file, his mind racing with the ramifications of Barlow's words. *Not another one of those damn videos*, he was thinking. *Here we go again.*

Not spotting any proverbial smoking guns within the meager police report, Tony replied, "I'd like to see this video, Counselor. Perhaps we could meet a few minutes before the arraignment outside Judge Pearson's chambers."

"Fine by me, Tony. I'll show you the signed witness statements at the same time. I have a stack of them, and I intend to use them both to clear my client's name and as evidence against the officers. I'll bring you a set of copies."

As soon as the defense attorney disconnected, Tony dialed his boss's extension. "We've got a problem, and it's Officer Marwick again," he reported.

"What the hell has that gorilla done this time?" the perturbed District Attorney responded.

"Same as before, only this time the idiot did it in front of multiple witnesses... and a camera. Adam Barlow is on this like a pig on shit. He's filing for dismissal today at the arraignment, and he means to show the judge the video."

"Well, at least it isn't on the internet... yet. Let me know how bad it is, and I'll warn the chief what's coming. Oh, and break out some of that new level four body armor. One of these days, that man's going to shoot the messenger."

The two attorneys met in the county courthouse, outside of District Court 11, in an area reserved for just such assemblies.

Barlow started with the video, noting the other lawyer grimace several times during its three-minute length. After it was over, Tony regained his composure quickly. "That doesn't prove anything, Adam. Everybody knows that it never looks good when the cops have to use force to subdue a rowdy suspect."

"He didn't try to evade, Counselor. Just a few days prior to this incident, my client monopolized a basketball game in which the officer's son was the on-court opponent. That's the true reason why Marwick pulled Jacob Chase over. He saw the kid drive by and decided to get a little payback."

"Bullshit," Tony pushed back. "According to the officer, the kid didn't pull over for a significant distance. He was clearly trying to evade, buy time to dump his stash of dope, or something. Everybody knows the cops hate a runner more than anything."

"There was no evasion, sir. There was no high-speed chase. The kid pulled over in less than two blocks after the lights came on, and he kept the speedometer below the limit."

The prosecutor shook his head, "Again, Adam, you're barking up the wrong tree. It's the kid's word against a cop, and we both know that the judge is going to believe an officer of the law over any teenager, no matter how good his jump shot is."

Adam shook his head, pointing at the computer where a new video started playing.

The second recording was in black and white, depicting an image of a small parking lot, with a street beyond. Digital numbers displayed the time and date in the lower, right hand corner.

A car appeared in the scene, a police cruiser riding its bumper, but the roof-mounted lights were not flashing. "This is a video from the storage unit business at the corner, less than three blocks from where Jacob's car was stopped. You can clearly see the officer did not have his emergency lights engaged. He's lying… again."

Tony's head snapped up at that last word, but he didn't say anything.

"So, is the district attorney's office willing to drop the charges against my client, or are you going to tarnish that fine establishment's reputation even further by going in front of the judge?"

The less-experienced attorney didn't respond at first, his eyes darting back to the computer screen. Adam gave the man more than ample time to respond before frowning with disappointment and closing the laptop. "You're making a mistake, Tony. Instead of going after an innocent kid, your office should be out in front of this, dropping the charges against my client and filing a list of felony charges against those cops. That's about the only way this county is going to avoid a massive public outcry. Who knows, Houston might become a Ferguson on steroids."

The ADA shook his head. "Come on, Adam, be reasonable. You know there's an election coming up, and there hasn't been a district attorney elected in this city without the endorsement of the Police Officer's Union for over 40 years. If we go after Marwick, the union will come after us. My boss isn't going to go for that."

Barlow's eyes bored into the man across from him, a cloud of frost filling the room. He raised an accusing finger at the ADA and hissed, "That kid's world has been shattered, Tony. He had a full boat scholarship to play ball at a good school, and our abusive police department has killed that dream. Everything he's worked for... poof! Gone! That could have been my son... or yours... or anybody's. He doesn't come from a wealthy family. He's definitely not some privileged brat. The medical bills alone are probably going to send his folks into bankruptcy. This excessive force has to stop, and we both know it."

Tony didn't like be lectured. "Now aren't we just the high and mighty crusader for justice and morality?" the heated rebuttal began. "So we had a cop who stuck his toe over the line? It happens. These guys stick their asses up in the air like targets every single night. They see more shit in a week than most people see in a lifetime. They take risks to catch the bad guys, and then assholes like you and me let them go back on the streets to hurt more people. So yeah, they take a little retribution now and then, but overall, the system works. If we start hanging every cop who makes a mistake, that same system won't work. We need those men and women in blue. Without them, society would fall apart, and if that happens, it won't be a police officer roughing up your precious, fair-haired client – it will be a criminal who won't let him off with a few bumps and bruises."

Adam shook his head, having heard it all before. Reaching into a file folder, he produced a picture of Jacob's knee, and shoved it across the table. "This is a few bruises and bumps? This is a toe over the line? Marwick is going to kill somebody, Tony, and we both know it. Will that constitute sticking a toe over the line as well?'"

A complete dismissal of the charges against Jacob was beyond Tony's level of authority. "I'll have to take this back to my superiors and mull it over. How about we ask the judge to reschedule the arraignment for a few days out?"

"Fine by me, but no more than 48 hours. My client is scheduled to leave the hospital day after tomorrow, and I want him going home with his parents, not back to the county jail."

District Attorney Sanders grimaced as she scrutinized the video of Jacob Chase's arrest. Her reaction, however, wasn't due to the howling, misery-laced cries of the suspect, nor was she concerned about the officers' behavior.

No, what bothered the county's most powerful elected official was the potential public relations nightmare the video was sure to bring.

Barely 5'3" tall, thin framed, and often referred to as being "mousey" behind her back, the slender woman's outward appearance gave few clues to the furnace of aspiration that burned within.

She'd joined the Harris County office as an associate after serving one post-graduation year clerking for a federal judge. Her degree from the University of Texas School of Law, complete with the designation of "summa cum laude" on her sheepskin, meant the legal world was the young graduate's oyster. But she wasn't interested in contract law, teaching, or hanging her shingle in the corporate world.

Bypassing numerous offers from prestigious firms throughout the Lone Star State, she held fast to a seemingly insatiable desire to put criminals behind bars. She was passionate about defending the people.

Ferocious, unyielding, and deftly skilled in front of a jury, the young Ms. Sanders quickly made a name for herself throughout the legal community of the nation's fourth largest city. When she had been elected for the first time 12 years ago, Karen Sanders had campaigned as an aggressive, "no holds barred" crime fighter.

She'd seen so much during those years. One of the most striking developments affecting her profession being the advancement of technology. Everything from forensics to investigation tools had been touched by the developments.

So much of the digital age was a positive for law enforcement. Social media, for example, provided insight into many a criminal's mindset and was now commonly introduced at trials to prove a frame of reference or intent... sometimes even as evidence of a confession.

Innovations in communications interception made privacy a myth. Computer system forensics that could even retrieve the browsing history of the accused now played a role in the day-to-day prosecutions by her office. The police could track and retrace a suspect's travels via cell phone towers. Cameras could read license plate numbers, placing a specific automobile at the scene of the crime. The availability of this information created a swirling, ever-expanding toolbox to be used for the people's cause.

But, like most revolutions, there were negatives as well. Criminals had become skilled at manipulating technology at unprecedented levels, committing felonies ranging from identity theft to blocking critical police communications with portable radio jammers.

Of all the changes she'd seen impact her prosecutorial duties, the public distribution of citizens' recordings from smartphone cameras was one of the most significant developments of the last five years.

Most video was helpful. Police dash cameras had been used countless times to convict criminals or exonerate officers of bogus charges. These days, it seemed like every business, ATM, city bus, and citizen was now equipped to capture historical events. Heck, just about every 10-year-old kid in America owned the kind of phone that fueled documentary filmmaker fantasies. The law enforcement agenda had profited tremendously from the availability of the feed. In the vast majority of cases such evidence was beneficial in putting criminals behind bars.

But not always.

A wave of online video had invaded what was once a private, seldom witnessed aspect of society - the policing of America.

The spectacle of cops interacting with citizens was exciting stuff, often worthy of cell phone recording. For many, the act was merely a "one upping" of rubbernecking a freeway accident during rush hour. True opportunists realized that news outlets would pay for video of major crime scenes. So would defense lawyers and their experts.

Karen could remember watching the Rodney King video in law school, her professor predicting that the event would shift law enforcement tactics and procedures across the country... and within a matter of just a few years at most. In the end, the prophecy had been incorrect... or at least ambitious in its fulfillment. Despite millions of cell phones being on the street and each generation able to record significantly better quality images, the threat of being taped had done little to modify the average street cop's daily routine.

Two impediments to change stopped the movement in its tracks. At first outraged by the posted videos, savvy internet consumers soon became numb to the continuing onslaught of abuse. There were simply so many instances being recorded, the general public became immune.

Secondly, law enforcement administrators had adapted after the first wave of brutality videos were published online. Department spokespeople became well versed in dismissing and diverting questions about the apparent abusive practices of their officers as captured by amateur cameramen.

"We feel the video may have been edited so as not to show the entire episode," was a favorite snub, calling into question the motivation of the camera's owner. "You don't see the images of the suspect reaching for the officer's gun or when he is spitting at the police."

Oddly enough, the integrity of cell phone video was seldom challenged when it provided the police vital evidence in solving crimes or defending officers' actions.

"It's difficult to judge what was really occurring with only a two-dimensional view of fast-moving events," was another common dismissal. "From this angle, it's impossible to tell what was actually going down."

The rank and file lawmen also caught on very quickly. While she'd never observed it personally, Karen had heard whispers of informal training sessions where officers were taught how to surround a suspect, blocking the view of any prying cameras that may be lurking nearby. This technique became especially popular after so many departments began installing dash cameras.

Seizing cell phones that may contain "critical evidence" was in vogue for a while, but several court rulings had quelled such actions for the most part.

Not everyone believed the cops were brutal bullies hiding behind shields. Even when questionable video streamed on local news stations, the spin tactics deployed by law enforcement professionals were normally sufficient to convince the public to remain calm and to uphold the cops' positive image.

As more and more videos surfaced over time, the police became even more adept at diffusing outrage. Experts appeared on national networks, analyzing examples and defending the actions of their law enforcement brethren. "That's a commonly taught technique at the academy. The camera angle makes the procedure look a lot worse than what it really is." The public seemed to accept such accounts. After all, if the method were taught to everyone, effectively implementing it must be critical to police officer job performance. Right?

The men on the street weren't the only ones developing expertise in downplaying citizen-generated videos. Karen's professional circle, as well as most district attorneys' offices across the land, had developed several clever methods to counteract what appeared to be horrible acts by those paid to serve and protect.

One such method of manipulating public clamor, invented by her personally, involved the sitting members of the various grand juries, especially those that might be called upon to decide an officer's future.

Each member of the jury was taken to a police training simulator, where an assortment of scenarios was played out via video screen and laser-firing pistol. "Officers often have a few hundredths of a second to make a decision," the clean-cut, all American-looking instructor would caution.

He would then have each juror step into the emulator and face purpose built tests that served to drive home the reality of what our law enforcement officers face on the streets. Karen's favorite was the example of the man standing twenty feet away with a knife. In the simulation, he would charge, murder clearly in his eye. It was practically impossible for anyone to put a bullet into the suspect before the red lights flashed, signaling the officer had suffered a stab wound. Almost every citizen was amazed by how little time the officers had to make a lethal force decision. It was a lesson that would return to them while an officer was on the stand, testifying that he 'thought' the suspect was armed, and he was forced to make an instant judgment.

Another favorite was called "Hogan's Alley." This simulation had the juror standing in an office hallway, facing several closed doors. A surprise door would open, revealing either an armed suspect or a citizen merely carrying a cell phone.

The DA always made sure the grand jury was shown her favorite example, which over 99% of all trainees failed. A woman opens the door, partially turned away. The shadows and light make it look like she is holding some sort of shotgun. She begins to turn, and practically every cadet shoots. In reality, the shotgun is a folded up baby stroller, her odd motions due to the fact that she is holding the infant in the nook of her free arm. Everyone, no matter how tainted against the police, was touched by the lesson.

Her rolodex was now populated with a new category of expert, video analysts joining the ranks of forensics, DNA, and mental health professionals. It was just the way of a new world.

"We are not going to dismiss the charges against this young man," she finally pronounced. "To do so would bolster their civil case against Sergeant Marwick. As far as the complaint against the officer, we have an established procedure for that. They must fill out the necessary forms, which will then be assigned to Internal Affairs for investigation. If IA recommends further action, I'll take it in front of the grand jury. The criminal justice system will not be blackmailed or bullied by one screaming, young man who clearly has a low tolerance for pain or is just a crybaby."

Tony nodded his understanding, "You got it, boss," he replied and then bowed out of the room without further comment.

DA Sanders watched him go and then swiveled her chair to gaze out the window, quickly becoming lost in thought. "What a travesty," she eventually whispered. She knew the cops of today were no worse, no more violent or vigilante than at any time in America's past. If they didn't establish command and control of the streets, the criminal element would. Sometimes that meant playing rough. Sometimes that meant getting physical and letting the bad guys know who was in charge. "Some people only respect brute force and the willingness to use it. The police have little choice. Why can't everyone understand what we're dealing with?"

Judge Pearson's docket was full, as usual.

The harried jurist was well known for tugging on his salt and pepper beard while deliberating. If he stroked with a slow, smooth motion, his mood was cerebral and calm. If the distinguished facial hairs were pulled, his honor was growing impatient, or worse yet, frustrated with the proceedings.

As Adam and Tony watched from their respective positions facing the bench, both men were concerned that the judge wouldn't have any beard left by the end of the day. The dilemma? Neither attorney had any clue regarding which one of them was raising the judge's dander.

They sat silently watching Pearson's lips move as he read Adam's motion for dismissal. It was a lengthy document, an unusual submission for arraignment proceedings.

There had already been one recess, both of the attorneys being called to chambers so the judge could view the video recordings. Adam had presented them as evidence of the police report being false... then argued that charges based on a lie could not hold merit. Tony had countered, charging that neither piece of physical evidence, nor any of the witness depositions, was related to the primary charges of resisting and assault.

The situation was further complicated by the arrival of not one, but two local news crews, complete with cameras. Adam had sent copies of the video to both stations after hearing the DA showed every intent of prosecuting Jacob Chase to the fullest extent allowed by the law.

Pearson had grimaced when he noticed the cameras, tempted to order them out of his court. He then seemed to reconsider, staunchly returning to the business at hand.

Finally, the judge sighed and placed the thick set of papers on his bench. Glancing at each attorney, he rendered his decision. "I'm not going to dismiss the charges against Mr. Chase at this time. However," the judge continued, staring hard at Tony, "I find the evidence presented on behalf of Mr. Chase to be extremely troubling. In order to expedite a plea arrangement, I'm strongly suggesting the people dig deep and get very creative to settle this matter before trial. The defendant is hereby released on his own recognizance and should not leave the State of Texas without permission from this court."

The gavel tapping the bench signaled his honor was ready for the next docket case, but Adam was no longer paying attention. He'd achieved the bare minimum he'd come for, but nothing beyond that.

The defense counsel turned to see Gabe sitting in the first row, his eyes betraying no emotion. After gathering up his papers, Adam signaled for his client's father to follow him out into the hall.

The two men walked side by side, moving down the corridor until they eventually arrived in an isolated area. "I assume that didn't go well," Gabe stated.

"We avoided having to post bail," Adam responded. "But I was hoping for a complete dismissal. At least you can take Jacob straight home from the hospital."

"Thanks for that," Gabe nodded. "This isn't going to be easy; is it?"

"No, no it's not. But I'm confident we'll prevail in the end. Remember what I told you, Mr. Chase. We have three separate battles to wage before this war is over. We have to win Jacob's freedom first, then we have to see Officer Marwick and his cronies punished. Finally, we have sue the county to recover for your family's financial and emotional damages. All of this is going to drag out for some time, and we have to take it step by step."

Gabe considered his lawyer's prediction of the long road ahead of them, a path that would hopefully led to justice. He knew he was in for the fight, but then his thoughts turned to Sandy and Jacob. His wife was holding on, but just barely. His son was still difficult to peg, the pain medications and healing process masking the boy's true feelings behind a veil of narcotics and the sheer exertion of physical mending.

"Should we consider plea bargaining with the DA?" the troubled father asked.

"Ultimately, that decision is up to your family, but I recommend against it. Any offer made by the DA is going to result in Jacob carrying a criminal record for the rest of his life. It will influence every aspect of his future, from applying for a job to qualifying for a mortgage. Some colleges now run background checks as part of the entrance process. He'll be tainted forever if we follow that path."

It was all so permanent, Gabe thought. *Jacob will have to live with these decisions for the rest of his life.* "And if we choose to fight... and lose?"

Adam sighed, hating this part of the criminal justice system. "While it shouldn't be this way, the truth of the matter is that the district attorney's office is retaliatory and spiteful. Fighting them will raise the level of punishment they seek at a minimum, sometimes even increase the number and severity of the charges they bring. It doesn't seem right for a system based on the premise of innocent until proven guilty to operate this way, but that's just how it is."

"Sounds like there is a presumption of guilt, and if you try to prove innocence, you're even more guilty," observed Gabe.

"That's about it," nodded Adam. "But we have about the strongest case I've ever brought in front of a jury, and I'm not just saying that to increase my billable hours."

Frowning, Gabe felt a brief flash of guilt. He'd already considered the possibility that the smooth-tongued devil of a lawyer standing beside him was milking the old cash cow for all it was worth... or could borrow. Sandy and he had concluded they had no choice but to trust the only person in the entire process that had helped them so far.

Waving a hand to dismiss the notion, Gabe said, "I won't lie and say I hadn't thought about that, but Sandy and I trust you. How much money are we looking at if this goes to trial?"

"About $60,000 dollars, sir. Some of that amount represents my time and expertise. Some of it will be allocated for experts and specialists we'll have to bring in to help. There are court reporters during depositions, travel expenses, and all kinds of miscellaneous costs associated with the entire affair."

Again, Gabe had expected the amount, having done hours of research on the net. "I'll withdraw money from our retirement account. Thank God, the old 401K has been doing well in the markets lately. But then again, what choice do we have? I can't let my son go to jail and ruin his life while I still have a single dime left to my name."

Chapter 4

Peelian Principle

The basic mission for which the police exist is to prevent crime and disorder.

With injuries to multiple areas of his body, Jacob seemed to struggle with the crutches, breaking his father's heart even on the days when he managed to get around without stumbling. Just a few days ago, his son was a graceful athlete, soaring to unimaginable heights with his vertical leaping ability, moving at dizzying speeds on the court. Now he hobbled, his cut, muscular frame for naught, limited by the weakest link of his body-chain.

The worst of the knee's swelling had subsided – mostly. It was still an awful looking joint, shades of purple and green identifying the area aggravated from nerve and vessel damage. The first surgery would have to wait until the tissue surrounding the injury had healed.

Sandy didn't seem to be as melancholy as her husband. Her son was coming home where she could take care of him, see him without the restriction of narrow hours, exhausting drives, and pre-visit security screenings. For Jacob's sake, she had gone to the grocery store, stocking up on all of his favorite foods. The best television in the house had been moved to the teenager's room.

Gabe secretly smirked, his mind re-calculating the expected longevity of their home's flooring. *Probably saved ourselves from an $8,000 repair this year,* he sighed, relieved that the carpet's lifespan was no longer in immediate jeopardy from Sandy's troubled pacing. It had been a close call.

Jacob managed the backseat with only one minor groan and two grimaces of pain.

Blood clots were still a threat to his recovery, as were recurring effects from the concussion. The broken ribs were healing better than most of his other wounds. Gabe found it difficult to keep perspective regarding his son's situation, the father's rage welling up and then subsiding, his own regrets fighting an internal struggle with a dark need for justice. A victory by either would be bittersweet.

They exited Central Hospital's circular drive, never looking back at the nurse's aide returning to the building with the wheelchair. It was an episode of their family history that none of them wanted to remember, all of them secretly sure they'd never be able to forget.

Gabe pushed aside the negativity, partially bolstered by Sandy's steady stream of upbeat conversation and positive outlook. Mother was determined to cheer up their gloomy son. He was going home. It was all going to get better.

And it was for the first few miles.

A mere ten minutes into the ride, Jacob's anxious warning from the backseat shocked his parents, his words a revelation of the necessary emotional healing ahead of him. "Dad, there's a policeman behind you. Watch out!" the panic-laden voice cautioned. "Oh God, please don't pull us over… please leave us alone."

"It's okay, Jacob," Gabe reassured. "I'm not breaking any laws."

"That doesn't matter," the mumbled response sounded from the backseat.

The kid couldn't keep from turning around and staring in horror at the squad car following them, despite the pain his contortions were causing. Gabe noticed his son's breathing had accelerated, small beads of perspiration blooming on his forehead.

He's terrified, Gabe realized, trying to figure out how to help. *I suppose none of us will ever fully understand the hell he lives in since this happened.*

And then the trailing cop turned off, rolling away on a side street.

It was several minutes before Jacob's respirations returned to normal, but the threat remained present in the teen's mind. His eyes darted left and right, his head pivoting front and back in near panic.

The next random encounter with a police cruiser sent Jacob into a huddled ball, ducking low and turning sideways in the seat as if to hide. Jacob covered his face with both hands, slowly rocking back and forth while whispering, "No. No. No."

Gabe and Sandy exchanged a look, both parents suddenly realizing their son's injuries extended far beyond the physical damage to ligaments and tendons, muscle and flesh. A new urgency rose inside the Chase family sedan, a priority to get Jacob home and shield his injured mind from the world outside. It was a terrible recognition.

Sandy's motherly instincts surfaced. "Jacob, Manny promised to stop by this afternoon. She has been over a few times, helping me get your room ready. She can't wait to see you."

That single statement calmed the troubled teen instantly.

Mother and son were now connected, her gentle voice penetrating the wall of fear and distrust that existed just outside the sedan's glass and steel frame. Sandy kept up her side of the conversation, soothing Jacob with promises of his favorite flavor of ice cream, the arrival of his senior pictures in the mail, and Manny's promise of visiting as often as possible.

During the remainder of the drive, Gabe began to wonder about Manny's ongoing role in helping Jacob heal. His son's reaction to the mere mention of her name had been powerful, resulting in a nearly instant transformation. *They have a shared experience*, he realized. *The girl is the only person on earth who truly understands what happened that night. They're like two soldiers who shared a foxhole during battle. Only they know. Only they were there.*

Finally, they were pulling into the driveway, both parents watching their son's reaction closely in the rear view mirror. Jacob casually glanced at his childhood home and asked, "What time is Manny coming over?"

Big Jim's summons to the main headquarters wasn't all that unusual. His captain's tone was.

"I'm taking you off the roster today," his superior announced. "I have a feeling you're going to be downtown for the entire shift."

Marwick didn't like being called to the principal's office any more than a factory worker enjoyed being ordered to report to his manager. Still, he wasn't aware of anything he had done wrong. Maybe he was being promoted or had earned an award.

The big cop recognized the assistant district attorney as he ambled into the conference room, the man's presence dispelling any thought of reward or glory. When he saw the police union's lawyer sitting at the other end of the table, a sick feeling rose in the officer's gut. *Here we go again*, the sergeant said to himself.

"Thank you for coming," Tony began after everyone was seated.

As if I had a choice, Marwick thought.

"I took the liberty of asking Mr. Randolph from the Houston Police Officer's Union to join us in order to expedite the process," the ADA continued. "I hope you don't mind, Officer Marwick."

"Not at all, sir."

"We're here today to review the Jacob Chase incident. I assume you're familiar with that arrest, sir?"

It was rare for Jim to feel genuine surprise, and it showed on his face. The encounter with the basketball player hadn't been at the forefront of his thinking. "Vaguely," he responded. "That arrest wasn't any big deal as I recall. I've dealt with a lot more serious matters since."

Tony clearly didn't like the officer's answer, his response far more harsh than he intended. "Well, Officer Marwick, it's getting ready to be a big deal... a very big deal."

"Is my client being accused of wrongdoing?" asked the union lawyer.

"Not officially. Not yet. But I am reasonably sure that is coming down the pike, Counselor. That is why District Attorney Sanders recommended I request your presence here today."

Tony opened a thick folder resting on the table, shuffling through a few sheets of paper before pulling out the desired document. "What was your probable cause to initiate the traffic stop that night?" he fired.

"The suspect executed an improper stop, exceeding the designated zone with the front of his vehicle."

Tony wrote the officer's response in the margin of his paper and then continued. "Where was this improper stop? What intersection?"

"I don't recall exactly," Big Jim replied. "I was following the suspect's car because I found it suspicious that such a young operator was out on the streets at that hour. That, and the temporary tags prompted me to tail him for some distance, in an attempt to determine if there were any criminal activity in progress."

"And was there?"

"No, not until I decided to initiate the stop. When the driver failed to pull over, I believed he was stalling for some reason. I watched to see if the passenger threw anything out of the vehicle, such as narcotics or stolen merchandise, but I didn't witness any such act. There was a lot of movement inside, which made it appear as though the occupants were hiding something. By the time the driver curbed the car, I had already called in for backup due to the possible evasion."

The only noise in the room was the scratching of Tony's pen as he continued to note the officer's response. Finally, without looking up, he asked, "How far did Mr. Chase continue to drive after you turned on your emergency lights?"

"I don't recall exactly," Jim responded, trying to buy time and figure out exactly where this was all going.

"An estimate of the approximate distance will suffice, Officer."

The union lawyer sensed something was wrong and interjected, "Is there a problem, Tony?"

The assistant DA nodded, producing a laptop computer from his briefcase. He opened the device and clicked on a few keys. "This is a video discovered by Mr. Chase's defense attorney. It is from a storage business's surveillance system, located just three blocks away from where the arrest occurred. You'll notice that Officer Marwick's emergency lights are not engaged as the two cars passed through the camera's field of view."

Big Jim wanted to explode, his temper flashing hot before the grainy black and white image of his squad car showed in the frame. *How dare they question the word of a peace officer*, he thought. *I'm so sick of every fucking step we take being recorded by some obscure piece of shit camera.* It took all of his discipline to keep his emotions in check.

The sergeant took a deep breath to calm his voice, and then smiled when the right answer popped into his brain. "There is a reasonable explanation for that, sir. Several times during the pursuit I believed the suspect was about to stop his vehicle. I was in an unfamiliar patrol car that evening, having traded shifts for personal reasons. When I believed the suspect was pulling over, I tried to switch the light bar to the rear-only setting, and I remember having inadvertently hit the wrong button. That must have been right when we were passing in front of the camera."

Tony stared hard across the table, not believing a single word he'd just heard. But he held his tongue, recalling that the witness and he were on the same side – for now.

"Okay, that makes sense," the ADA lied. "I want to go back to a statement you made earlier. You stated that, and I quote, 'Such a young operator was out on the streets at that hour.' So you could see the driver clearly?"

Big Jim shrugged, "Clear enough to make a reasonable estimation of his age."

"Had you ever seen Mr. Chase before that night?"

"No. Not that I'm aware of," the cop lied again.

Tony moved back to the laptop, the sound of keystrokes sounding in the otherwise silent room. He spun the display around and said, "Do you recall this incident just three nights before Mr. Chase's arrest?"

The video this time was of Junior's basketball game, the clip shortened to show the blocked shot smacking Big Jim in the shoulder as he stood beside the court.

The union lawyer spoke before Big Jim had a chance, "This is ridiculous, Tony. Are you implying my client had it in for Mr. Chase because of a blocked jump shot? That's really a stretch."

Tony shook his head, "I spoke with the coach of Officer Marwick's son's team this morning. He stated that the shot blocked by Mr. Chase had been taken by the officer's son. Furthermore, he informed me that the young Mr. Marwick had been in the running for a potential scholarship, but that Jacob Chase's performance during the city championship game had put the officer's son out of contention. Furthermore, he confided in me that there had been an on-court incident between Officer Marwick, the officer's son, and the coach himself during halftime of the game. So no, Mr. Randolph, I don't think this is a stretch at all. My opinion, however, doesn't matter. It's the jury who will determine if the officer's frame of mind had any bearing on his actions that night."

The exchange gave Big Jim time to think. "I didn't recognize him before, during, or after the arrest," he stated firmly. "It is merely a coincidence. I don't even like basketball and can produce numerous witnesses, including several men in my precinct, who will testify to that fact."

The interview continued for three more hours, Tony doing his best to prepare Marwick for what he could expect once Adam got him on the stand. During the entire ebb and flow, Tony realized the man across the table from him was a well-practiced liar, and he was on the verge of erupting in anger at any moment.

Dishonesty wasn't a rare skill among law enforcement ranks. Most experienced cops developed the ability to maneuver the minefield of cross-examination with minor inaccuracies. They learned to fight off conniving, scumbag lawyers who were skilled at spinning the truth to free lawbreakers. It was a tool, in their minds, to keep criminals off the street and away from polite society.

As the afternoon dragged on, Tony began to sense that Officer Marwick's abilities exceeded far beyond justifiable white lies that had been conjured to thwart legal loopholes or crafty defense tactics. The assistant DA became convinced that Big Jim's creativity was fueled by some lopsided view of how the citizenry should be policed. The officer was clearly angry at being challenged at all, projecting an air of disdain that his word was being questioned.

He was a playground bully, Tony finally decided. *He stumbled into being a cop, and for the first time in his life, the undying need to control others was sanctioned and respected.* It was a common diagnosis, an occasional scoundrel in uniform relishing the gratification of being able to impose his will on the misbehaving examples of his fellow man. *A perfect job for the oppressor,* the ADA mused.

Driving back from the police station, Tony dialed his boss's cell. "He's a powder keg," he informed Karen bluntly. "If Adam gets a sense of that on cross examination, he'll press Officer Marwick, and the guy will blow sky high. And I don't have to remind you that any under-oath rant this guy spouts will result in exponentially greater sums being paid by the city if they win the civil suit."

"I understand," the DA responded. "Have they filed the formal complaint against the officer?"

"Yes, they did so this morning."

The pause that followed was so long that Tony had to check to make sure the call hadn't been dropped. His boss's voice finally came back, "Let's put a little reverse pressure on the kid. I have two specific detectives from Internal Affairs in mind. I'll call the chief and recommend that they're assigned to the investigation into the Chases' citizen complaint. We'll see how the other side holds up to a little heat."

After disconnecting, Tony continued to maneuver through the congested streets of downtown Houston. He couldn't help but feel the entire episode was spiraling out of control. "Where is this all going?" he whispered to the empty car. "How far are we going to take this?"

He knew enough of Karen to answer his own questions. "To the wall," he whispered. "Come hell or high water, she won't give in. That's why she's the DA."

Chip delivered Manny at the promised time, Gabe relieved that his son's greatest wish was going to go off without a hitch.

As the young girl rushed inside, the two fathers convened on the front stoop. Each had a dozen questions for the other.

"How's Jacob holding up?" Chip began, his concern genuine.

"I'm worried," came the honest reply. "His mother and I were so focused on his physical wellbeing; we didn't pay any attention to the mental trauma. He's not in a good place."

Chip signaled his understanding, his eyes betraying his dejected mood. "Manny hasn't been sleeping since this all went down, and quite frankly, neither have I. Like a needle stuck on a record player, I keep rerunning the events of that night in my mind, wishing I'd done things differently. Sometimes, I'd give anything to have it to do over; other times I tell myself I never want to experience anything like that again."

"I hear you," Gabe replied, "In a way, I'm glad I wasn't there. Who knows what I might have done to protect my child? As bad as things are right now, they certainly could have been worse."

"What I experienced was nothing compared to what Jacob endured," Chip added. "I tussled with that big cop for less than three seconds. Jacob was on the receiving end of their bullshit for several minutes. I can't imagine what is going through his mind."

"Sandy and I are thinking about trying to get him some professional help. He keeps claiming that he's just fine, but we know better. He has wanted to see Manny more than anything. Thanks for bringing her over."

Chip waved off the gratitude. "I'm sure it will do both of them some good. There is one thing I think you need to keep in mind. For me, at least, the lingering mental anguish doesn't have anything to do with the physical nature of the encounter. While getting pushed around sucked, that's not what has been troubling me – like most guys, I've been in a fight before. What is eating my insides is the betrayal. I've always taught my kids to go to a cop if they get lost. Find a policeman – they're there to help. You'll be safe with a cop. Now, all of that trust seems misplaced. All those years of believing what it says on the side of their vehicles... to serve and protect... now I feel like such a fool for believing that."

Gabe frowned, his thoughts having traveled the same road so many times in the last few days. "Do you really believe this isn't an isolated incident? You sound convinced that there is a systemic problem with law enforcement."

"Damned right I am. Since this all went down, I've been watching internet videos, perusing old newspaper reports, and generally paying more attention. So has Manny. I've read numerous studies, many by the government, others by law professors who monitor this sort of thing. After the events of September 11, law enforcement was granted a new status by the general public. Edicts like the Patriot Act served to embolden them even further. The American citizens let it slide, more worried about terrorist attacks than minor police overreach or any loss of civil liberty. Now, it's gotten out of hand, and we're all going to have hell to pay getting the genie back in the bottle."

Shuffling his feet, Gabe wasn't ready to agree wholeheartedly. "I still think the vast majority of cops are good men and women. I think there are a few bad eggs... and probably always have been. I've scrutinized the same videos as you, but I'm not ready to break out the torches and pitchforks just yet."

Chip reached to grasp Gabe's shoulder, squeezing gently to make sure his friend knew he was serious. "You might be right, but promise me one thing. Make sure that son-of-a-bitch that put your son in the hospital is taken off the streets. If we don't make the bad apples pay, the rot will spread through the entire barrel, and then we'll have no choice but revolution."

Gabe's smile was anything but a positive reaction. "Don't worry about that, my friend. Hell's fury has nothing on what's simmering inside my soul. My last dime and breath will be spent bringing those bastards to justice."

After a friendly exchange with Sandy, Manny found Jacob sitting up in his bed, staring blankly out the window.

"Some guys will do anything to get out of school," she greeted, making her smile as bright and wide as she could manage.

Jacob's face responded in kind, grinning widely and holding up his arms in an open invitation for a hug. The two teenagers embraced warmly, holding each other tight.

Manny sensed her boyfriend's tears a moment later, an initial sniffle soon followed by quick, rolling sobs that shook his entire body. She held on, some basic instinct telling her that keeping him close was the best comfort she could provide.

His outburst pushed her over the edge as well, overwhelming her resolve to be cheerful and upbeat during the reunion. She joined him, letting go of everything she'd kept bottled up, expelling it on his shoulder.

Eventually their storm of weeping subsided, the convulsions of emotion gradually dissipating. Both of their shirts were soaked through with hot tears; neither seemed to notice or care.

"I'm such a wimp," Jacob finally managed to croak. "I'm supposed to be so brave and resilient. I'm sorry about my outburst. I don't think I've cried so much since I was a little boy."

She waved him off, "Anybody would cry given what you've been through. It would be silly not to. Soldiers cry all the time, and nobody thinks they're wimpy…. You have no reason to be ashamed."

Her words drew a smile that did more to communicate the trust between them than anything he might have said aloud. "Thanks," he simply responded in kind.

They held hands, the platonic gesture coming naturally for two people who sincerely cared about each other. It was shelter for Jacob, therapy for Manny. Both seemed content to sit and do only that.

Neither knew how long it lasted, time not a factor in their minds. Jacob was content with merely sitting and peering at his girl, Manny satisfied with returning his gaze.

"How are things at school?" he finally ventured.

"Same old, same old. Everybody has been asking about you, wondering how you're doing and how bad you were hurt. You have a lot of friends, Jacob. Don't hesitate to be with them. The sooner you get back to your normal life, the better."

His reaction wasn't what Manny expected, a pained expression etching his face. He pointed toward the pair of crutches leaning in the corner and spoke with a harsh, hateful tone. "What life? That's my life now, standing over there in the corner. I can't play ball, I can't even walk and carry my own books at the same time. I'm never going back… I can't… I couldn't look anybody in the face."

The tears returned, but this time they were angry. "Why has everything changed, Manny? I didn't do anything wrong. I didn't hurt anybody, but I'm the brokenhearted one now. I didn't ruin anybody's life; yet mine has been trashed. Why? I just want God… or you… or my parents to explain why."

His pain was crushing, the deep questions of essential existence more than what the teenage girl could handle. Lacking any other viable response, she again fell back on her instincts and pulled him close in an embrace. It was another five minutes before they cried themselves out for the second time.

When they made eye contact again, Manny had regrouped, all of her thoughts from the past few days coming clear. "You have to get back on the horse, Jacob," she said sweetly, but firmly. "You are a winner, and winners don't let setbacks like this keep them down for long. In ten years, when we're married and having children of our own, we'll look back and draw strength from this. I know you. I know me. I know we both will."

He nodded, but something in his eyes told Manny he was still unsure.

She kept it up, trying to pace the conversation so as not to chase him back into the shadows of his memories. She wanted his thoughts moving forward and into the future. She chatted about tests and classes and who was dating whom these days. She brought him up to speed on the latest song just released by their favorite band.

Slowly he came out of the shell, responding to her comments and even once cracking a joke. That one small event proved uplifting to the uncertain, young girl. It was the only sign she'd seen that the Jacob from before still resided inside the body perched next to her on the bed.

Sandy announced her presence in the threshold by clearing her throat, happy to see both teenagers respecting the open door policy whenever they were together.

"I hate to break up the party," she smiled, "but I've got to help Jacob get ready. He's got a doctor's appointment this afternoon, and we can't be late."

"I understand, Mrs. Chase," Manny replied, leaning over to kiss Jacob's cheek. "If it's okay, I'll come back tomorrow after school. My parents said it would be fine."

"Of course, Manny. You're welcome in our home any time, sweetie."

This is going to take time, Manny thought, rising to leave Jacob's side. *I'll stay with him. I'll help him heal. He needs me more than anyone has ever needed me before. I'll be there.*

The week that followed was a whirlwind of never-ending doctors' visits, labs, and x-rays. The most welcome break in the medical regiment was Manny's daily appearance to help Jacob keep abreast of his schoolwork.

Jacob seemed to be taking it all in stride, but both Gabe and Sandy slowly began to realize that their son's demeanor was a façade, a calm surface cloaking the troubled waters below.

The first clue to his psychological disturbance was the change in his appetite. Normally a voracious eater, Jacob picked and poked at his favorite dishes. Slices of pepperoni pizzas were barely touched; bacon, lettuce, and tomato sandwiches often returned without a single bite mark scarring the bread.

At first, the couple wrote it off to the pain medications polluting their son's stomach and suppressing his desire for food. That excuse quickly faded as Jacob's need for the narcotics waned.

Already thin, with practically no body fat due to the demands of athletic conditioning, the weight loss began to show badly on his once impressive frame. Sandy noticed the sunken eyes first, Gabe commenting on his son's protruding ribs. He grew more and more lethargic, the light behind Jacob's eyes dimming a little more each day.

Finally, the time came for the psychologist's assessment, the renowned therapist recommended by Adam as a specialist in post-traumatic stress syndrome. Jacob protested vehemently, displeased that the scheduled appointment would delay his daily visit with Manny.

Trying to help her injured boyfriend through the riff, Manny had done her part to counter Jacob's grumbling. Inviting a select few of his friends, she organized an afternoon session of hanging out. The concept seemed to brighten the depressed, young man. Both Sandy and Gabe cursed themselves for not having thought of it earlier.

On the way back from the introductory session with the shrink, Jacob called Manny to let her know he was heading home and that she and their friends could come over.

In the front, Gabe and Sandy pretended not to be eavesdropping, but couldn't ignore the outburst that surged from the backseat.

"What do you mean you're the only one coming by?" Jacob asked, disappointment thick in his tone.

There was a long pause while Manny responded, and then Jacob's voice sounded deflated. "Oh. I see. Well, that's okay, I guess. Are you still coming by?"

A few moments later, Sandy noticed her son was crying. "Jacob? What's the matter sweetie? What's wrong?"

It took him a minute to answer, the teen obviously struggling to control himself. "The other kids aren't coming over. Manny didn't come right out and say it, but her meaning was pretty clear. Their parents don't want them associating with a criminal like me."

"What?" Gabe exploded, his fury bleeding through more than he intended. "What the hell are you talking about, son?"

Jacob cowered, his father's verbal eruption causing him to wilt. "It's just what she said, Dad," he responded meekly.

"I'm sure that's not what she meant," Sandy replied, her tone soft and filled with the honey of concern. "Are you sure you didn't misunderstand?"

"I'm not sure I understand anything," the whispered reply sounded from the backseat. "Nothing makes sense anymore."

They arrived home, no one daring to say another word during the remainder of the trip. Jacob entered the house and immediately hobbled for his room, ignoring the trays of snacks his mother had set out in anticipation of having a house full of teenagers. Gabe called Chip.

"Yes, that's exactly what has happened," Manny's father confirmed. "A bunch of kids were supposed to meet here, and then I was going to haul them over to your house in the minivan. I talked to several parents, and while most of them made up bullshit excuses, they finally admitted they were worried about their teens hanging out with Jacob. I'm sorry, Gabe, but that's the truth."

"That's bullshit!" Gabe fumed, not believing anyone could possibly think of Jacob as an undesirable influence. "That's not fair, Chip. How could they?"

"I'm sorry... I truly am. But I have to tell you, there's been more than one parent ask me why I am not worried about Manny still seeing Jacob. People talk, Gabe. Stories grow; rumors abound. It will settle down and get back to normal once the facts start coming out. This will all blow over."

"If Jacob makes it that long," he blurted before realizing what he'd said. "Thanks, Chip. I do appreciate your being up front with me."

Like a stormy sea crashing against the bulwark, the next blow to roll over the Chase home was delivered via the U.S. mail. Gabe had no doubt regarding the envelope's contents, hesitating to open the cover that surely conveyed even more bad news.

"Wow, I guess I had not expected this letter to be here so quickly," Gabe acknowledged, rubbing his temples to alleviate the budding tension headache. "Sandy and I will have to put on our parental thinking caps... somehow prepare him for this blow," he whispered. He tossed the letter on the kitchen counter alongside the weekly mailers, coupon bundles, and other paper-wasting junk, then headed to the bathroom for something to stop the pounding in his skull.

During his return trip to the kitchen, Gabe's cell rang, his phone's display verifying it was his office calling. The owners of the small engineering firm had been the most understanding employers anyone could hope for, trying their best to contact him only if there was a critical need. But Gabe was acutely aware that losing his job was not a luxury his middle-class family could afford right now. Luckily, this call was quick, only distracting him for a minute or so.

He completed the call, returning to open the letter. It had vanished. "Sandy, did you notice a letter from Jacob's college sitting here?" he asked.

"Yeah, I noticed it was addressed to Jacob, so I took it up to his room."

She realized the mistake instantly after the blood drained from her husband's face, wringing both of her hands as he rushed past toward the stairs. "Oh no... I didn't think..., Oh, good Lord, what have I done," she whispered.

Gabe took the steps two at time, but he was too late. Jacob was in his usual position, leg and head elevated by mountains of pillows. The letter rested on his stomach, tears streaming down his cheeks.

With urgency, Gabe rushed to his son, pushing the "*We regret to inform you,*" letter aside and cradling the distraught teenager's head. "I'm sorry Jacob, I didn't mean for you to open that alone. We both knew the college was going to cancel your scholarship, son. They really didn't have much choice."

"I know," he wept. "But I thought it would be because I couldn't play ball," he managed between sobs. "That letter says I was disqualified for admission because of my arrest. They think I am a criminal, Dad."

Gabe continued to hold his son, wondering when the world was going to give Jacob Chase a break.

Jacob had already amassed enough credits to graduate from high school, but state law required every student to earn a passing grade in certain prerequisite classes in order to walk the stage and collect his sheepskin.

The irony of their son having to pass a course in government and civics wasn't lost on the Chases.

He'd been doing okay working from home, but there were certain aspects of the mandatory class that required a face-to-face interaction with the instructor.

Mr. Ballymore had been kind and flexible on previous occasions, even coming by the house for an hour to make sure Jacob met the requirements. Today, however, the teacher's schedule only allowed the meeting to occur during the last period – at the school.

Sandy had been unsure about taking Jacob into the building, his mood unpredictable, his strength waning. After consulting with Manny, she decided to raise the topic and evaluate his reaction before committing to the course of action. Her son had agreed, noting it would be good to get out of his bedroom. "Don't be such a worrywart, Mom. Ya know, cabin fever can mess with a guy's head, too," Jacob teased. "Besides, it will be nice to see my old stomping grounds." A brief smile engaged the teen's lips, before his final remark. "Consider it therapy."

Since the canceled gathering at the house, Sandy knew Jacob had been avoiding social media. It was a tall order for a teenager, and a sure sign of her son's ever-deepening isolation. *Maybe he's right. Seeing the other kids could help break down the wall of ice he's building around himself*, she thought.

They arrived at the main entrance, Jacob taking it all in without comment. He was more skilled with his crutches now, able to keep up with her normal gait. They entered the building, proceeding to the attendance desk to sign in both student and parent.

Sandy harbored hope that they might run into one of her son's friends or teammates while they were there, and that the encounter would help Jacob come out of his self-imposed shell. However, their interaction with the receptionist had taken a little longer than planned. The bell rang, signaling the change in classes before mother and son could make their way down the hall.

Hundreds and hundreds of students poured simultaneously from the classrooms, rushing through the crowded space, slamming lockers while ongoing conversations filled the packed hallways. But all of that changed the moment the kids noticed Jacob. Sandy couldn't believe how rude the teens were, stopping all activity just to stare at her son as he passed. No one said a word, not one single person offering a greeting, smile, or even a nod.

At one point during the gauntlet, Jacob paused, staring longingly at another lanky lad sporting a basketball letterman's jacket. Sandy recognized the youth as the team's center, a friendly kid who was always hanging around with her son after practices and games.

"Hey Kip. What's up?" Jacob said nicely. "Been a while, dude."

The kid looked down with a frown, gave a curt nod, and then turned and walked away. Sandy couldn't believe it, but Jacob seemed to take it in stride.

They entered the empty classroom, Mr. Ballymore nowhere to be found. Jacob took a seat, ready to wait for the tardy teacher.

"I'm sorry, Jacob. I had no idea the kids would be so mean to you."

He managed a slight smile and said, "It's okay, Mom. I kind of expected it... Manny warned me. I've embarrassed the guys on the team, going from hero to zero after getting in trouble with the law. A lot of my friends stood up for me at first, but now that I'm going to be on trial, everybody assumes I'm guilty. I'll be fine."

"But that's not fair, Jacob. You're innocent until proven guilty, and people should know that."

"I always thought that, too," he sadly lamented. "But that's not the way the system works. Manny is taking a lot of heat over our relationship, too. Everybody is calling her 'Jailbait' and 'Prison bitch.' I'm surprised she's stayed with me this long. There's only so much a person can take."

Her son's words took Sandy aback, the depth of his understanding and analysis more advanced than his years would predict. She also found herself constantly astounded by the social complexities of high school. Things had seemed so much simpler back in her day.

Mr. Ballymore arrived just then, the hospitable man moving to shake their hands. Sandy drifted to the back of the room, keen on getting out of the way, and seeking some space to consider Jacob's state of mind.

We're in trouble, she decided. *And I'm beginning to wonder if there's a way out. Show me, Lord. I pray to you - guide us through these terrible times.*

The vehicle's left, rear taillight wasn't working, Big Jim's eye zeroing in on the malfunction from two cars back. No taillight and no brake light. *Oh, gawd,* he sighed. *Another asshole who won't spend fifty bucks to maintain his vehicle. Bet the inspection sticker dates back a few years on that piece of shit.*

Normally, the sergeant wouldn't bother with such a minor infraction. But when the traffic pattern placed his squad car directly behind the offender, the driver reacted with a hasty right turn into a residential area. Too quick.

Marwick followed. The response was instinctual.

A block later, Big Jim sensed something was wrong. The driver remained four to five miles under the posted speed limit and made an exaggerated stop at the next interchange.

For a moment, he hesitated. After the incident with the basketball player, he'd received a stern warning from his supervisors, the ass chewing including phrases like, "less aggressive," and "play by the book."

His bosses had made it clear he was under intense scrutiny, warning of the need to dot the "I's" and cross the "T's," and most importantly of all, "Keep your fucking nose out of trouble for a while."

It was maddening for a cop like Jimmy Marwick. Sure, things occasionally crossed the line, but the collateral damage was a small price to pay for aggressive police work that produced results. Accidents happened in every occupation.

Deciding he'd already invested the time, Jim flipped on the lights, blasting the siren for one short burst. He'd give the guy a warning and let him be on his way.

It was the driver's head that raised Jim's suspicions to a higher level. Traveling less than 30 mph, the visible portion of the operator's skull pivoted quickly right to left, as if he were in high volume traffic and was working the mirrors in an attempt to change lanes. The motion just didn't fit the situation.

The man pulled over soon enough, Marwick calling in the plates as both cars rolled to a stop. The dispatcher confirmed that there were no outstanding wants or warrants.

Exiting his unit, the officer kept his eye on the driver and approached from the recommended angle. *Be polite to the citizen*, he thought. *It's only a busted taillight. Be the nicest cop this guy has ever met.*

He found a middle-aged Hispanic man fumbling with his wallet. When Big Jim tapped on the window, the fellow behind the wheel nearly jumped out of his seat.

Experience taught every cop that many people became nervous when they were pulled over, regardless of the severity of their offense. Outright fear was less common, and more often than not, a sure sign of guilt.

"License and proof of insurance please," Jim stated with a neutral tone.

The driver provided his license quickly, having already started the process of removing it from his wallet. The insurance card took a bit longer to dig from the cluttered glove box. *He's scared shitless*, the officer observed. *His hands are trembling like crazy.*

If the driver had been Caucasian or of African-American descent, the reaction would have pegged the cop's internal suspicion meter. With Latinos, it was difficult to tell. Undocumented immigrants often behaved inexplicably when confronted by any official wearing a uniform, probably a reaction based on growing up in a place where the cops were corrupt… or worse.

"Do you know why I pulled you over, sir?"

"No, I don't. I know I wasn't speeding," the shaky voice replied, nearly cracking.

"You have a taillight out, sir. I also noticed the brake light on that side wasn't working."

Jim, once he'd explained the reason for the stop, had expected the driver to settle down. Instead, the opposite occurred. The man's eyes grew wide, small beads of perspiration burgeoning on his forehead. "You… you mean in the back… back there," the driver stammered, motioning with his head.

"Yes, sir. It could be a loose wire. Why don't you open the trunk, and let's take a look," Marwick stated, watching the driver's reaction closely.

It became instantly obvious there was something in the trunk the man didn't want the police sergeant to see. He motioned with his hands three times before speaking, and then his words didn't make any sense. "My cousin… looks at it. He's… he's a fixer… a mechanic."

Officer Marwick knew 99% of motorists in a similar position would jump at the chance to check for a loose wire as opposed to receiving a citation. "Please step out of the car, sir."

"No, no. I'm fine right here."

Louder this time, establishing command, "Please step out of the car, sir."

The response was just a blank stare, the driver's mind obviously in paralysis, trying to figure a way out. But Jim did not intend to allow time for that.

An important part of police training addressed what is called the "OODA" loop. An acronym for "observe, orient, decide, and act," the term was commonly used by both the military and private businesses alike. Created by Colonel John Boyd of the United States Air Force to establish a shared language and definition for fighter pilots, it described the sequence of events common in the human decision-making process.

Law enforcement training focused on instructing officers how to "get inside" of any suspect's OODA loop. Whether the situation involved an argument, interrogation, simple questioning, or a gunfight, it was commonly accepted that the guy with the shorter, faster loop would come out on top. If the cop could disrupt the other person's loop, the odds improved even more.

Jim leaned into the window, the appearance of the large cop's head intruding inside the car causing the driver to recoil. Marwick sniffed once, twice, and then pulled away quickly. "I smell marijuana. Are there illegal narcotics in your car, sir?"

"What? Huh? No! What are you talking about?" the pleading, confused man responded.

"Get out of the car! Now!" Jim shouted, reaching for his pistol. "Now! Exit the vehicle! Now!"

Without waiting for any response, Jim keyed the radio microphone on his shoulder, "Edward 41, send more units. Previous traffic now possible felony."

"Acknowledged Edward 41."

Jim drew his weapon and pointed it at the now obviously distressed driver. "Out of the car!" he screamed at the top of his lungs.

Finally, the driver's jittering hand reached for the handle, but then he froze. Jim decided to help him, moving a step closer, and pulling the door the rest of the way open.

"Why are you doing this?" the man questioned as Jim reached in to yank him out. But the seatbelt countered that action, keeping the suspect pinned inside.

"Get out of the car! Right now!"

Finally, the driver unhooked the strap and began exiting his vehicle. He wasn't quite to his feet when Jim holstered his piece and grabbed the smaller citizen by the arm, spinning him around to face the automobile. When he started to frisk the suspect for a weapon, the man shoved back with all of this strength and then reached for his waistline.

It all became a blur, Jim's OODA loop now the one being interrupted. Hesitating for a moment, trying to decide between pinning the suspect's arm and reaching for his own weapon, the decision process nearly cost the officer his life. He finally made his decision, his pistol clearing leather just as the small revolver in the driver's hand was whipping around.

Both men fired at the same instant, Big Jim's round striking the suspect in the chest. Somehow, the shot fired at the cop missed.

The stricken man staggered backwards, half-falling between the wide-open driver's door and the car's frame. But the gun was still cradled in the suspect's hand.

Jim fired again and again, the point-blank shots tearing flesh and crushing bone. He only stopped when the weapon that threatened his life fell to the pavement. In a flash, he scraped the pistol away with his boot, and then refocused on the suspect.

"Shots fired! Shots fired!" Jim broadcasted over the airwaves. "I need an ambulance and alternative supervisor to this location. Suspect is down. Repeat, suspect is down."

Once he was certain the now-prone driver wasn't a threat anymore, Jim holstered his piece.

The driver was still awake, but unmoving. There were three red spots now soaking through the guy's shirt, a growing pool of crimson spreading across the pavement. One of the chest wounds was bubbling blood.

"Why?" Jim barked at the dying man. "Why the hell would you try to kill me over a fucking taillight?" the bewildered cop demanded, his hands trembling slightly, his heart thumping wildly against his breastbone, a slight sweat beading on his brow as his adrenaline peaked.

But there was no answer, a pair of glassy eyes just staring up at the officer, no words uttered.

Other cops began rolling up, a line of uniforms rushing onto the scene. The blue brotherhood clamored for information about Big Jim, their concerns receiving only a dismissive wave of the sergeant's hand. "I'm good."

Then the ambulance arrived, but it was clearly too late. One of the other officers informed the EMTs that there was no rush. The gunman had stopped breathing a few minutes before.

Cameras appeared, pictures being snapped from all angles. All the while, Jim just wandered here and there, trying to burn off the adrenaline dump still surging through his system. The sergeant shook his head to clear the mental fog, trying to make sense of what had just happened.

When the captain finally arrived, he motioned Marwick to the side and said, "Let's have it, Jimmy. From the top. Right now, while it's still fresh in your mind."

Big Jim was a quarter of the way into his debrief when a thought interrupted his recounting. "Oh my God! The trunk," he said to the bewildered captain. "We need to open his trunk."

Without waiting for permission, Marwick hurried alongside the driver's door and reached in for the keys. Exchanging glances with several of the idling officers surrounding the car, the big cop hustled to the back and opened the lid. Even Big Jim inhaled sharply over what they found.

Two pairs of blinking, frightened eyes stared up at the gathering ring of police officers, both children squinting from the sudden rush of light. Grey, dirty, duct tape covered their mouths and bound their hands. The first thing the cops looked for was blood, scanning the tiny, cramped bodies for any sign of injury. The older of the two kids, a girl of no more than 10 years of age, had blood and small lacerations from just below her ankle down to her toes. She had kicked out the taillight's bulb with her foot sometime before succumbing to the effects of her growing dehydration.

"Holy shit," somebody muttered as all of the cops seemed to be reaching at the same time to help the kids out of the trunk compartment. "It's a hundred degrees outside. Get them out! Now!"

The two ambulance medics quickly abandoned the now dead driver turning their attention to the two children.

"I'm thirsty," the boy wheezed, as the tape was ripped from his mouth.

But the girl child had more important things on her mind. "You've got to go help my mom," she whispered. "Please… please go help my mom. He shot her," she said, pointing at the body lying on the ground. "She was bleeding on the kitchen floor. Please, Mister…. You gotta help her."

"Do you know this man? Who is he?" one of the cops asked, pointing toward the deceased.

"My mom married him, but he's not my dad," the girl croaked with a defiant tone. "They were arguing in the kitchen when he started hitting her. She was screaming, and then there was a loud bang. He's a very bad man."

Jim still had the driver's license, handing it over to another officer so he could call it in. Police cars would be on their way to the listed address seconds later.

"How did you know, Marwick?" the captain asked a short time later, watching as the EMTs checked the kids out.

"Like I've been trying to tell you, Captain, aggressive police work pays off. It was a righteous stop, but the dead guy just made all the wrong moves. *He* escalated the confrontation, sir. I just responded."

The senior officer nodded, having heard the same story a thousand times. Most felony arrests began as seemingly innocent traffic stops. Still with Big Jim's reputation, he had to be sure.

"Let's start again, Jim. From the beginning."

"We need to distract him," Gabe announced to his questioning wife. "We have to find something 'fun' the boy can enjoy. His entire life has just vanished into thin air... basketball... friends... school... even getting to drive a car. It's all been pulled out from underneath him. Just gone. Whoosh."

Sandy wasn't quite so sure. "He's still completing his schoolwork. He has graduation on the horizon, and there are all those social media thingies, like Facegram, and Tuber, or whatever they're called. And then there's Manny, of course."

"Yes, but think about that for a moment. It's all a pittance compared to what his life used to be, and none of it is much fun. It's as if he is watching his friends get on with their lives while he is trapped here until all this drama is resolved. Even then, he will have to make a new path for himself."

Knowing her husband and his unconditional love for Jacob, Sandy reluctantly agreed. "Go ahead. But I'm wondering if this plaything isn't as much for you as it is for him. A very expensive toy... I might add."

Pumping his fist, Gabe picked up the package and rushed for the stairs, eager to show Jacob his purchase. Taking the steps two at a time, the eager father announced himself before arriving at his son's threshold. "Jacob, you're not going to believe what I found at the hobby store! And on sale, too," he added for Sandy's benefit.

He found his son sitting up in bed, reaching for the ever-present crutches. "What's up, Dad?"

It was the first time since the incident that Gabe had seen a true flicker of light behind his son's eyes. "A drone! You bought a quad copter. Dad! How cool."

Setting the box at the end of the bed, he moved to help Jacob maneuver so that he could examine the new purchase. His son's obvious joy reminded the troubled father of Christmas mornings from long ago.

Jacob eagerly opened the packaging, pulling out the bright red flying machine. The frame was shaped like an "X" with four plastic propellers, one located at the end of each branch. The electronic brain was located in the center of the frame, including the camera lenses, flexible antenna, and a bracket that held the battery pack.

The drone weighed only a few pounds, its wingspan slightly wider than Jacob's lap. The teen was obviously enamored as he examined the device, flipping, turning, and inspecting every feature.

"Wow! It has a camera, point-of-view navigation, GPS…. It has everything, Dad! Where did you find it?"

"I went by Frank's Hobby Shop, and he'd just received this baby. He was having a special to introduce a new supplier, so I picked it up for $399."

Sandy appeared, leaning against the doorframe and observing the men of the Chase household. *Men? Right now, they're two boys,* she mused.

"Is this thing like that remote control airplane we bought a few years ago for your birthday, Jacob? I seem to remember long faces of disappointment after a few hours of trying to learn how to fly it, and then crashing it into the street," she asked innocently.

"Oh, no, Mom," Jacob exuberantly replied. "This model is equipped with an autopilot, gyro stabilization, and an app that allows you to control it from your smartphone." By now, the teen was grinning at the anticipation of the new adventure. "It practically flies itself. No pilot's license required for this model."

Not sure whether she was hearing pure male bravado or the substance of a genuine product review, Sandy flashed a mildly pessimistic expression, but covered it quickly so as not to put a damper on her son's excitement. Jacob wasn't going to let her rain on the new-toy parade anyway.

"The Hortons were playing with one of these things in the school parking lot after b-ball practice a few months ago. They let Jacob and me have a turn, and I was surprised by how really easy it was to control," Gabe confirmed for the questioning mom.

Jacob winked at his dad as if sharing a secret between men. "We even completed a clandestine op and got some close up footage of the cheerleading squad," he snickered, the tenor of his voice near that of his pre-arrest days.

Setting the drone aside, he reached to hug his father. "I want to fly it now," Jacob announced. "Let's test it out."

Gabe nodded his agreement, "I will start charging the batteries while you study the instructions. We can conduct our flight test out in the cul-de-sac. Should be a perfect day to learn all the moves; the wind is calm outside."

Passing Sandy in the door, he couldn't help but flash a smug, "I told you so" look.

"No spying on the neighbors," she cautioned, now smiling slightly herself. "We have to live here, you know."

It was almost an hour before the green LED of the charger indicated the battery was fully juiced. By then, Jacob had finished downloading the piloting app on his smartphone.

Gabe carried the drone outside, followed more slowly by Jacob as he managed his crutches.

"Ready for the maiden voyage?" Jacob asked, his thumbs working the smartphone's screen.

"All indicators are green," Gabe replied, doing his best imitation of a NASA launch controller.

The drone was sitting in the middle of a wide concrete expanse, looking like a cross between a giant insect and a miniature Transformer robot. With one last stroke of his thumb, Jacob peered up from the phone and beamed as the tiny propellers began buzzing in rotation.

"Taking her up," Jacob announced, his thumbs and attention returning to the control center in his cell.

The drone performed just as he expected, rising six feet into the air, and then hovering steadily.

"Going to make it spin around and catch you in the video, Dad. Smile!"

Again, the machine responded perfectly, rotating 90 degrees and stopping with its bug-eyed camera staring at a grinning Gabe Chase.

"That's fantastic, son. Is this one as easy as Horton's to fly?"

"Better. I can view what the camera is seeing on my phone. Here, let me show you. I'll turn around, and you hold up some fingers. I'll tell you how many."

Gabe waited on Jacob to hobble on his supports, holding up three fingers after his son had turned away.

"Three," Jacob announced with pride. "This is so cool. I'm going to take her up higher."

And without further ado, the red drone shot skyward like a rocket launching from the pad.

Gabe meandered toward his son, clearly wanting to join in on the action. Jacob positioned the phone so his father could see the screen, the two men enjoying an amazingly clear view of their neighborhood from 200 feet in the sky. Gabe waved his hand in the air, watching his miniature rendering on the phone mimic the motion in nearly real time. "That's amazing; there's practically no delay at all."

Sandy watched from the window, a smile spreading across her face. "Got to give it to you, Gabe. It's like the old Jacob is back."

The two played with the drone for several minutes, the machine hovering high above their subdivision, dipping and zipping up and down the street. At one point, Jacob brought it in low, wrapping an arm around his father, posing for the camera. The machine had the perfect angle, peering down upon the grinning pair and recording a quality, clear video.

Gabe noticed an odd look develop on his son's face as he stared at the small screen on his phone. "You okay?"

"Yeah," Jacob replied, a scowl crossing his brow. "I wish this drone had been hovering over my car that night. With video like this, there wouldn't be any doubt about what really happened."

Chapter 5

Peelian Principle
Police should always direct their action strictly towards their functions and never appear to usurp the powers of the judiciary.

Adam had done his best to warn them, had coached and reassured Jacob on how to handle the interview.

The two detectives met the Chase family in the Barlow Law Office, Adam convincing the concerned parents that the hassle of bringing Jacob to his complex would do far less damage than allowing the cops to enter their home. "Keep your house an island of tranquility, even if it is surrounded by the storm of legal proceedings. You both need it. Jacob needs it," he had advised.

By the time the Chase family arrived, the two detectives had already been shown into the well-appointed conference room. Neither of them was what Gabe had expected.

One was a short, balding man with a serious paunch that challenged the integrity of his leather belt. Hardly the television depiction of a senior crime fighter.

The other was dressed to the nines, including the most fashionable width tie and highly polished shoes. Not a single hair was out of place, the obvious result of significant quantities of glue-like man-spray.

After everyone was seated, Mr. Dapper fired the first question, "Why did you resist the officer that morning, Jacob?"

"I didn't, sir."

"So of all the people in Houston… of all the cars on the road that night, an entire group of Houston police officers decided to cull one Mr. Jacob Chase out of the herd and beat the shit out of him. Is that what you expect us to believe?"

Baldy didn't give the kid a chance to answer, adding, "I've read the service record of every one of those cops you claim used excessive force, son. There were over 50 years of law enforcement experience around your car that night. Four of the officers had received accommodations for valor above and beyond the call of duty. Two of them are up for promotion for their exemplary performance and leadership skills. Why should we believe they decided to risk their careers just to get in a few licks on a 17-year-old kid?"

Gabe threw Adam a harsh look, as if to ask why the lawyer wasn't coming to Jacob's rescue. But the attorney remained stoic, almost disinterested. The defensive parent then remembered the warning Sandy and he had received. "They'll be rough, probably downright mean to your son. This isn't testimony. It's an investigation, so I can't get involved unless they cross certain lines. Don't worry; Jacob will do fine."

"Because they did, sir. I don't know why, but they had no good reason to beat me that night. I didn't do anything. I swear," Jacob pleaded.

The two detectives glanced at each other, but it was impossible to read the nonverbal message they exchanged. "Okay, Mr. Chase, let's start from the beginning. Tell us about that morning."

Adam knew what the cops were doing – he'd used the same interrogation technique a thousand times. Their initial barrage of hardnosed questions had been designed to piss the kid off… or frighten him… whatever was necessary to burrow through the coached version of events. Emotion tended to make people tell their story at a different level of detail, speed of events, or perspective. The two investigators wanted only one deliverable from their interview – inconsistency.

If Jacob changed his story, even in the slightest detail, then he was lying in the eyes of the pessimistic officers. If he messed up the sequence of events, he was being dishonest. Later, the two gumshoes would compare their tape recording to the original complaint and highlight all of the divergences.

Watching the exchange, Barlow had to admit the other side had an asymmetric edge. Cops investigating their own seemed like a conflict of interest, and in reality, it was all that and more. The men questioning his client had to work with brother officers, in difficult conditions, every hour of every day. Who knew when their lives might depend on one of the men they were seeking to discredit or impeach? It was the same with the DA's office. The legal eagles needed law enforcement, depended on "Big Blue" to risk their lives while delivering the criminals and evidence. Going after one of their own co-workers was difficult at best.

Young Jacob Chase had a chance at justice, but it was slim. In the last year alone, 600 complaints of police brutality had been filed against the Houston Police Department, only four having ever made it to a grand jury. Even when cops reported on their fellow officers, something that occurred over 180 times per year, the fraction of policemen facing a judge was less than 1%.

But the advent of cell phone videos and cruiser dash cameras was changing the game. Adam thought they would at least get a judicious hearing, perhaps remove what he now considered a dangerous individual from his position of authority.

As he observed the proceedings, it was clear that Jacob was sticking to his original narrative. The lawyer watched as the two detectives became more frustrated, almost taking it as a personal challenge to cross the kid up. Gone was any desire to uncover the truth, honor being thrown out the window along with all of the moral implications of the story being told. The kid's consistency was a professional affront to their decades of experience and skill. Despite all of the tools in their significant bag of tricks, Jacob held true to his account of the event.

While on the surface it appeared as if information was flowing only in one direction, in reality Adam was gathering his own intelligence and evidence. The two officers were pressing hard – pulling out all the stops – going far beyond the call of duty. That told the attorney something, exposing the fact that important people were worried about Jacob's accusations. *Good,* he thought. *They should be.*

After two hours, Adam finally spoke up. "That's enough guys. I've sat here without saying a word for 120 minutes, listened to you rehash the same questions twelve ways from Sunday. My client has been hospitalized, is still suffering post-stress syndrome, and has been nothing but cooperative up until this point."

Detective Dapper's head snapped in Adam's direction. "Are you hindering our investigation, Counselor?" he challenged.

"Are *you* trying to put my client back in the hospital, Detective? I'm sure you two could eventually wear him down, trip him up after what – another 16-20 hours of non-stop interrogation? East Germany fell several years ago, gentlemen. We don't operate like that around here."

Both men bristled at the comparison, but neither replied.

"I have one last question for Mr. Chase," said Detective Paunch. "Do you really want me to ruin those officers' lives, young man? Do you really want us to take everything they've worked for and throw it away?"

Jacob reached into his pocket and pulled out the rejection letter from the college, sliding it across the table at the two interrogators. "No one seems to care that my life… everything I've worked for has been thrown away because of a bully hiding behind a badge. I've lost all my friends, my chance at an education, and I will probably be permanently disabled. So now it's my turn to ask a question - shouldn't someone pay for that?"

The two investigators packed up their briefcases shortly afterward, exiting the Barlow law firm without another word.

Jacob sat quietly in his chair, his gaze focused on some point in space above the conference table. His parents, regulated to watching the entire event from the back of the room, hurried to comfort him.

After ensuring Jacob was okay, Gabe approached Adam, naturally curious regarding the lawyer's opinion of how the session had gone for their side.

Sandy stayed with her son, congratulating him on being strong and sticking to his guns. No one seemed to notice his lack of enthusiasm, even the normally perceptive mother writing off his reaction to exhaustion from the effort.

Once in the car, Gabe and Sandy chatted non-stop as they struggled to process the influx of data obtained from the encounter. Neither of them had any experience with legal issues, and making sense of the afternoon's events put both of them on cognitive overload. Jacob dejectedly peered out the window as his dad navigated rush hour traffic. "They don't believe me," the teen whispered under his breath. "No one believes me."

Jacob excused himself after the Chases arrived home, seemingly unable to share the sense of progress his parents were feeling. "I've had enough for today. I'm gonna head to my room," the teen announced.

Kissing his mother on the cheek, he said, "I love you," and then hobbled to his father, extending his arms for a hug. Again, the young man muttered those same three words.

"Are you okay, son?" Gabe asked, detecting something odd in the teen's demeanor.

"I'm just tired, Dad. That whole thing just really wore me out today."

"Okay, buddy. Go upstairs and get some rest. I'll take Manny and you out later for ice cream to celebrate if you're up to it."

Nodding with a half-smile, Jacob made for the stairs, the effort of climbing to the second story seemingly more and more difficult with the crutches.

He closed his bedroom door, staring at his bed with disgust, dreading another afternoon on the once-comfortable mattress. He limped toward his desk instead, opening his laptop and bringing up the social media site Manny and he used to communicate.

"I'm tired from the interview today. Those guys were pretty rough, but everyone said I handled the questioning well," he typed. "I'm going to give you the day off," he added, ending the statement with a smiley face. "I love you, Manny, and no matter what happens, I want you to remember that. My parents and you are the only people who believe in me, and that means everything. I love you and always will."

He sent the message, aware that Manny wouldn't be able to see it until she was heading home – knowing it was against the rules for students to access their cell phones on school property.

Rising, he shuffled to his dresser and slid the top drawer open. In the back of the bin, he located a pair of rolled up socks, his lucky game pair from his last season. He turned the outer sock as if he were going to wear it, and a handful of pain tablets tumbled onto the dresser. He'd been collecting the powerful medication and hiding the unused pills from his parents.

At first, he'd stashed an occasional dosage because the medications hurt his stomach, and he didn't like how the narcotics made his head spin. The pain in his body was the lesser of the two evils. His mother made such a fuss if he tried to refuse the pills, so stashing them in his socks had been his chosen solution.

Later, when the mental pain began outstripping the agony of his physical injuries, he'd taken to putting the meds back for a rainy day – just in case.

After the lawyer had failed in getting the charges against him dismissed, Jacob had started looking at his now-significant pharmaceutical stash as a last ditch move to avoid going to jail. "I'll take them all before I go to prison," he'd vowed.

That pledge had directed the young man down a different path of reasoning. *What is so different about losing my freedom behind bars, and the future I now face?* Both options restricted his choices. Both meant a life where his once honorable reputation was tarnished beyond repair. Both were filled with day after day of nothingness.

And then there was the pain and suffering he was causing those around him. He'd limped downstairs a few nights before and overheard his parents while they were discussing the cost of his lawyers, medical bills, and the upcoming trial. They were being ruined financially, and the thought of his folks living in poverty or not being able to retire was a huge burden to bear.

Then there was Manny. He knew she was paying a heavy price for her loyalty to him. A perverted version of the truth was circulating all over social media. What kind of life could he promise her without college? What kind of provider could he be? With all of his mom and dad's funds earmarked toward keeping him out of jail – a higher education was out of the question.

And now, today, there were the policemen who might have their lives ruined because of him. Jacob realized they had just blindly followed the sergeant's lead. *They probably have kids, and some of them might even be my classmates,* he mused. *They might have sat across from me at the lunch table or have had my back on the court. Should those teens' lives be wrecked, too? How would those kids feel if their fathers lost their jobs or went to prison because of one mistake made in the early hours of a confusing morning? Where will all this pain and devastation end?*

No, everybody was better off if he just faded away - ceased to exist.

His resolve was bolstered by adolescent analysis, mental exercises that predicted years of surgeries, tons of pain, and months of being confined to a bed that was, in reality, nothing more than a prison bunk.

Jacob moved slowly to the display of trophies covering a specially mounted shelf. He gently touched a few of his favorites, the metal's cold surface unyielding under his fingertips. A grimace formed on his face, a wave of disgust welling up inside. Why had he wanted these useless trinkets so prominently displayed? Why had he felt a sense of pride and accomplishment over such meaningless symbols celebrating something so unimportant? So fleeting? So immaterial in the grand scale of life? He was embarrassed by how naïve he had once been.

He limped to the bed, managed to bend and sit without the ever-present crutches. Reaching for the bottle of water on the nightstand, he began swallowing three or four pills at a time, the handful of tablets taking several gulps to consume.

He lay on the pillows, the fresh smell of dryer sheets bringing a smile to his face. Mom was at it again, laundering his bedding while he'd taken a shower. "I'm doing this for you, Mom. I am doing this for you, Dad, and for you, too, Manny. You'll all be better off without me," he whispered. "I love you all."

Sleep came before any effect of the narcotic, Jacob's troubled mind finally finding comfort with the act of taking control of his own destiny. He had made a decision. He was in command, and it felt good. It had been so long since he'd experienced such a state, and now the pain would finally stop.

Manny cursed her stupidity, noting her phone's battery was dead after exiting the school's main entrance. Rushing for her bus, she was worried, knowing that Jacob would be upset when she didn't text him right away. Her stress doubled after remembering he was being interviewed by the cops early that afternoon.

She rushed into her house after the 30-minute bus ride, yelling a quick "I'm home, Mom," and heading directly for her room and the cell's charger.

Trying to decide which was faster, booting her computer, or getting enough charge on her phone, she chose to juice up the mobile's batteries.

Back down the stairs she galloped, making a beeline for the refrigerator, pausing momentarily to give her mother a hug. The two girls chitchatted about the day's events while Manny downed a large glass of orange juice.

"How's Jacob doing?" Amanda asked, bringing her sometimes scatterbrained daughter back to reality.

"Oh, crap. My phone. Be right back!"

It took a bit for the cell to boot, another few moments for Jacob's message to show up on the screen. "Now that's weird," she whispered, reading the odd text for the second time. "He must have had a really bad day."

Manny wasn't sure how to react to her boyfriend's unusual words and phrasing, something troubling about the finality of his last statement. "I better let mom look at this," she mumbled, bouncing back down the stairs with urgency.

Amanda took one look at the message and grew pale. "Call Gabe and Sandy, right now!" she barked, scaring her daughter with the outburst.

"Why? What's wrong?"

"Just call them. Tell them to go check on Jacob.... Never mind. I'll do it."

In a flash, Amanda pulled her own phone out of her purse, fingers flying through her contact list until Sandy's number appeared. It seemed like an eternity before Mrs. Chase answered.

"Hi, Amanda, how are you?" the cheerful greeting piped through the line.

"Manny got a really weird text from Jacob this afternoon. Sandy... you better go check on him... it sounded... well... troubling."

"Oh. No. Oh, Lord... thank you, Amanda," and then the call went dead.

Gabe saw a look of sheer terror cross his wife's face as she set down her phone. "What's the matter?" he tried to ask, but she was already darting for the stairs. He followed, some sixth sense telling him why his wife was in such a rush.

When Gabe crossed the threshold, Sandy was leaning over Jacob's bed aggressively shaking her son with the strength of desperation. "Is he breathing?" the boy's father managed.

"He's cold, Gabe. Oh my God.... Oh, my God. No, Jacob. Nooooooo!"

Gabe's phone was out of his pocket, his shaking fingers managing the 9-1-1 buttons. "Yes, this is an emergency! My son... I think he's tried to kill himself...."

Sandy's uncontrollable screams and hysterical sobbing made it difficult for Gabe to manage his own home address. "Okay, sir, I've got an ambulance on the way."

"What do I do?" he pleaded with the emergency operator. "Tell me what to do."

"Please be calm, sir, and be ready to let the EMTs in when they arrive," the hollow words echoed in Gabe's mind.

Officer Kirkpatrick walked into the restaurant, immediately spying the large table of cops at the back of the dimly lit dining area. *It's never difficult to find your party when in uniform*, he mused.

Zigzagging through the occupied tables of diners enjoying the locally well-known Tex-Mex fare, Dole was surprised to spot a few different faces at the table. His apprehension was further elevated when he noticed quite the assortment of "stripes and pipes," a reference to the rank insignias represented among the gathered throng.

The normal crew of "dawn patrol" cops had been supplemented this evening, some incident evidently holding the second shift boys over. After a few nods and hellos, the patrolman took the last, open seat and began perusing the expansive menu.

The table's in-process conversation consisted mainly of frustrated remarks by the second shifters, a semi-trailer full of hazardous material having overturned on I-45 just as rush hour was in full swing. It had been a mess, half a million angry commuters joining a dozen fire trucks and a small army of DOT cleanup experts in the gridlock.

The waitress appeared, stopping the in-progress rant dead cold. Policemen didn't like outsiders hearing their private conversations, no matter how innocent the interruption. It was a habit, born of hard lessons, and the never-ending isolation men wearing the badge experienced every day.

With all the separate-check orders taken, the attractive server hustled off toward the kitchen, apparently unfazed by the burden of tallying one ticket per diner.

After watching the gal sashay away, one of the two-stripers smirked and asked, "Hey, Big Jim, is that gal that just took our order the holster bunny you were telling me be about?"

Several heads at the table turned quickly to double check the waitress's backside as she disappeared around the corner, a few heads nodding in approval. All seated knew the reference, a "holster bunny," or sometimes "holster hugger," being a woman who sought sex with men in blue uniforms.

"So I hear," Jim answered. "According to a couple of the constables I know, she's damn friendly on occasion. One of them even went so far as to claim she intentionally kept a headlight out just so she'd get pulled over."

Everyone cackled at the remark, one of the third shift patrolmen pretending to pull his notebook out and scribble a reference. The banter and subsequent laughter continued.

Kirkpatrick didn't have any funny anecdotes or clever comments to add. Besides being the junior man at the table, he was a naturally quiet soul. Instead, he chose to study the older, more experienced cops around him. Especially those he hadn't worked with in the past.

Big Jim Marwick was there, the sergeant's attendance at any sort of social gathering both unusual and intimidating. Rumor had it that the large-framed cop was up for a promotion, which translated into most meals being taken with his superiors, not the precinct's lowly patrolmen.

"Hey, Jim, do you remember that kid that tried to evade you a few months back? You were working our shift on a swap," asked one of the owls.

"Yeah… I remember getting my ass chewed," growled the big man. "Internal Affairs is still looking at the cluster fuck, so I'm not out of the woods just yet."

"Well, I heard that kid committed suicide yesterday. Overdosed on pain meds."

The table grew quiet, many of the men seated having processed the scenes of teenage suicides. Such events never resulted in a pleasant day. About the only thing worse was when one of their own decided to end it all, which happened more often than any cop wanted to admit.

But Jim didn't seem to be concerned, waving off the foul air that had suddenly formed over the table. "Doesn't surprise me. He was weak. Most of those rich, white kids are a bunch of uppity, privileged little shits who think the world owes them a smooth sail. They grow up believing that mom and dad will bail their little, spoiled asses out when the occasional wave does rock their boats. When life introduces them to the real jungle, a lot of them crack up and go over the edge."

"Aren't the parents threatening a civil suit, Jim?"

"Yeah… just like everybody else we put cuffs on these days. You look at them funny, and they scream abuse. Fuck, what's this world coming to? I've gotten in trouble for supposedly beating up a couple of punks. Those pussies wouldn't have lasted a week in my old man's house… if you crossed him, you learned what a true ass whooping was all about." Marwick replied with a grimace. "Nowadays, my dad would probably get brought up on child abuse charges. Yet all my brothers and sisters have done well in life and managed to stay out of the prison system. Imagine that."

The discussion paused, many of the men sitting around the table unsure of what to say next. The long dissertation was unusual for any senior cop, especially on a topic such as pending litigation. Big Jim sensed the uneasiness, quickly deciding to move things along with a joke. "Do you guys think I should send flowers to the funeral?"

The attempt at humor fell flat, a few polite guffaws and grunts sounding around the table. Dole nearly choked on the mouthful of iced tea he'd just sipped.

Kirkpatrick was stunned, by both the news and the sergeant's reaction. He had been the one working the kid's hotfoot that night, a passing wave of guilt by association then replaced by an empty knot in his gut, all driven by the memory of that incident.

That wave of nausea was quickly surpassed, however. A surge of disgust began filling Dole's core, the revulsion fueled by Marwick's reaction. It was beyond cold and cynical – the man sitting at the end of the table was bigoted and tyrannical.

It was a blessing when the food came, the discussion, or lack thereof, interrupted as the waitress placed steaming dishes in front of each cop. Dole was no longer hungry, but welcomed the opportunity to stare down at his plate instead of into the faces of the men around him.

Using the childhood deception of pushing his food from side to side on his plate, complete with the charade of an empty fork occasionally traveling to his mouth, Kirkpatrick used the time to digest the words he'd just heard.

Here was Big Jim Marwick, field supervisor, veteran officer... well known for several high-profile felony arrests. He was a cop's cop, aggressive, unafraid, and always supporting the men and women of the department. When Kirkpatrick had first begun patrolling, Marwick was one of the names flaunted in front of the rookies. "You need to watch men like Big Jim – they know how to establish command of a situation."

Some role model, the young cop thought. *More like a megalomaniac. God, do I regret playing a role in that kid's arrest.*

But the sergeant wasn't finished.

With his dark, menacing eyes boring into Kirkpatrick, Marwick managed to degrade an already uncomfortable situation. "You guys want to know the real irony of that arrest? I wasn't in on what happened to the kid's leg.

Somebody muscled up that little shit's ankle without my consent. You'll never hear me saying that in court, or in front of the press, but I had nothing to do with it. They say it's lonely at the top, and I'll take my lumps like any good leader, but my life sure would be a hell of a lot easier if some of our guys could keep their shit under control."

Kirkpatrick was stunned.

Without thinking, the young officer's spine stiffened, his body coming upright at the accusation that had just been aired. Big Jim was spouting bullshit, trying to cover his own ass at the expense of others. A rebuttal formed in Dole's throat, all courtesy and respect for the ranking officer pushed aside. But he held it, some instinct telling him that the restaurant surrounded by a table full of cops wasn't the time or place.

Stewing quietly while he toyed with his food, it occurred to Dole that his repulsion went further than just the smug cop's attitude, or weak attempt to shift the blame. Marwick had lied.

The brotherhood of the badge didn't begrudge any officer for spinning the truth in front of the press, a lawyer, or even a judge and jury. After only a few months on the job, that word "truth" began to take on a new reality, somehow becoming distorted with right versus wrong, and "the way things really are."

But not to other cops. That wasn't done. The unspoken code of honor was absolute honesty with partners, supervisors, and other members of the department. You either spoke the truth, or didn't speak.

Kirkpatrick's mood remained foul as the meal continued, the cocktail of emotions filling his mouth with a bitter taste, completely overriding the flavors from his plate. Above all else, he felt betrayal. Jimmy Marwick was a traitor, violating the code by lying to his fellow officers. The duplicity was sickening.

Chapter 6

<u>Peelian Principle</u>
Police use physical force to the extent necessary to secure observance of the law or to restore order only when the exercise of persuasion, advice and warning is found to be insufficient.

The bile rose in Gabe's throat, a reaction born of both fear and of spying the man he loathed more than any other on earth.

During the few months that followed laying his son to rest, he'd become consumed with making Jacob's death count for some higher cause. And it had been frustrating. He studied police techniques, examined officer complaint statistics, and read every article and book relating to the subject he could get his hands on. He was a man on a mission, fueled by a seemingly empty home, growing divide with his spouse, and an unending carousel of mental images from Jacob's abruptly shortened life.

In the course of his research, he'd run across several references to a British politician named Sir Robert Peel.

Credited with having developed the foundation for all modern police forces back in the early 1800s, Peel had created what was now known as "The Peelian Principles," a simple list of nine items that were still held in high esteem today, hundreds of years after being penned.

The long-deceased man's work resonated with Gabe. Its timeless wisdom offered a guiding light as the desolate father struggled to define his own boundaries of what law enforcement should be and how the people should be policed.

The principles were simple, straightforward statements that reassured the grieving man that his outrage was warranted, his position reasonable and sane. In Jacob's case, the cops had violated practically every one of Peel's highly regarded guidelines.

Principle number one indicated, "The mission of police should be to prevent crime rather than suppress and punish crime," yet Jacob had been punished.

The next two rules specified that law enforcement required the support and cooperation of law-abiding citizens in order to accomplish this mission. Reiterating and expanding on the earlier tenets, Peel continued, "The more police are able to secure this cooperation, the less force and coercion will be needed."

By Gabe's way of thinking, the cops had done just the opposite. He no longer supported them, nor did Chip and Amanda. After eroding a strong base of public backing, apparently violence was the officers' only remaining pillar of authority. Jacob had found that out the hard way.

But it was the seventh principle that struck at the core of what needled Gabe the most. It included the words, "... the police are the public, and the public are the police...."

"How have we gotten away from this?" he asked aloud. "Any one of those cops would feel exactly the same way that I do if it had been their son being abused. Why can't they see that? Why can't they see we're all the same public? How can they perpetrate an 'us' versus 'them' attitude?"

Sir Peel had authored his principles at a time when the military was the primary enforcer of London's laws. The British Army acted like any other military unit of the era, policing the public as an occupational force, treating the citizens more like a battlefield enemy than fellow countrymen.

Upheaval and revolution were realistic possibilities in those days, and Peel's contemporaries knew it. The French Revolution had occurred not so long before, the ramifications of that uprising not lost on the British rulers.

Peel's epiphany was that every civilian instinctively desired rule of law, but concerned citizens didn't have the time or training to enforce rules and regulations. The police, in his view, were nothing more than common people who were paid a salary so they could be dedicated to the task. They weren't special, above the law, or granted excessive authority. Just plain, old, ordinary folks who maintained order for their livelihood, instead of running an inn or spending the day hammering on horseshoes.

Peel understood that force begat force, that resorting to violence was eventually answered with the same.

And it was violence that began to govern Gabe's thoughts. He joined a gym, visited a gun store, and had visions of leading an uprising against tyranny. But his internal voice of reason peppered him daily with logic, and reality soon overrode the violent rationale as a workable plan. After resolving his mental volley, he found himself exasperated and irritated with an undeniable revelation. The general public, with the exception of certain minority groups, didn't perceive the scale of the problem. Other than the occasional headline-making incident, he didn't sense a boiling rage just below the surface of the totality of America. Society was not uniting against what Gabe perceived as a common foe. There simply wasn't any revolutionary fire to ignite.

Those realizations served to deepen his anger and resolve, believing himself the lone, enlightened wolf on a campaign against injustice. It was new territory for a man with his background and views. He was a middle-aged engineer, never exceptional in physical pursuits, and far from fighting fit. His options were few, but more than zero.

He'd been stalking Officer Marwick for almost 10 days, listening to the now-familiar voice on the police scanner, waiting for just the right opportunity. It had finally come.

A domestic disturbance, shots fired, would surely bring the shift supervisor. It did.

The location was perfect, less than three miles from Gabe's home, the light fading into a clear dusk. Sandy was napping, the Remington 700 rifle and expensive scope sitting clean and ready in the closet. He'd practiced and drilled for weeks, finally able to strike a man-sized target at over 700 yards with a cold barrel.

A few quick buttons on his computer keyboard pulled up the satellite view of the crime scene's address. His printer was spitting out the remarkably detailed overhead image a few moments later.

Three more minutes passed before the rifle case and accessories were in the car, covered on the back floorboard with a blanket. He switched off his cell phone, removing the battery as an extra precaution. "I'm going to the market," his note to Sandy explained.

He'd had to orbit the apartment complex three times to identify a suitable spot. A drainage bayou ran alongside the main cluster of buildings, its parking lot packed with squad cars. A nature preserve, the dead end road of a never-finished development, and a backdrop of thick pine trees contributed to the perfect setting to implement his plot.

He exited the car, lugging out the large surveyor's case and tri-pod. The broken-down rifle laid discreetly inside what seemed to be an oversized briefcase. On the slim chance anyone happened to be watching, he didn't appear to be toting a weapon, but instead looked like some poor fellow trying to get his job done before capitulating to the Houston heat.

It was a 50-yard trek through the woods, his heart pounding harder with every step. Finally, at a great distance, he could identify the ant-like, cobalt blue uniforms scattered around the toy-sized police cars. He unfolded the tri-pod on the protected side of a thick bush and opened the case.

The bolt-action hunting rifle had been a bargain by all internet accounts. The middle-aged man walking around the gun show had fallen on hard times and was reluctantly selling his "baby."

"She's taken game in four states," the seller boasted. "I hate to see her go, but keeping the electricity on is more important than my annual hunting excursions."

Gabe had counted out a wad of hundred dollar bills and exited the convention center without anyone knowing his name.

Chambered in .308 Winchester, the rifle was a magnificent tool. Gabe had begun practice at 100 yards, not having fired a gun since hunting with an uncle as a teen. Within three days, he was striking targets at the 300 line. Another month and dozens of trips to a friend's farm later, he could ping a cast iron frying pan at 700 yards with practically every shot.

After glancing around to make sure no one was in the area, Gabe began pulling out the disassembled weapon. Although he'd practiced a hundred times, his shaking hands made snapping the components together difficult. "Taking another human life isn't a natural act," he whispered. "Settle down, old boy... you'll be fine."

And then the rifle was on the tri-pod, his fingers adjusting the scope. Officer Marwick appeared in the reticle less than a minute later.

Another mouthful of stomach acid came welling up as Gabe studied the overweight man. A walrus-like mustache, coal black hair, and a broad-shouldered girth left no doubt he had identified the desired target. Staring at the cop's pictures for countless hours no doubt had packed the father's heart with abhorrence, but it also insured accurate target acquisition of the scum.

The wind was calm, humidity average. Gabe adjusted the distance focus on the optic, bringing the man he loathed into a crisp, detailed view. "Only 590 yards," he whispered. "Cake."

Next, he attached the homemade noise cancelation device, the illegal tube of welded metal screwing onto the end of the rifle's barrel. He'd studied commercial designs on the internet and built his own model in the garage workshop.

Gabe pulled out a small notebook, scanning information about taking shots from this same distance. The table of numbers was written in his own hand, gleaned from his own Intel. The days at the ranch had provided his DOPE, or data on previous engagements. He knew exactly how much his bullet would drop.

The sub-sonic ammunition was specially made for hog hunters. It wouldn't provide a telltale crack as the bullet broke the sound barrier. He only needed a few minutes to escape, and his setup would make it extremely difficult for anyone to determine from whence the assassin's shot had come.

Marwick was still there, bent over the hood of his police cruiser, scribbling notes on some sort of form. Gabe clicked the scope's elevation knob, adjusting for the exact range and loft that would be required by his rapidly dropping projectile.

The image of the officer was perfectly centered in his field of view, the now-adjusted crosshairs residing directly on top of the man's head. Gabe waited patiently, giving some of the other policemen in the area a chance to clear out, hoping to catch his target alone.

The ideal situation finally presented itself, Marwick signaling one of his subordinates with a hand gesture, the other cop scurrying off to heed the command. "You're all alone," Gabe whispered, his finger moving to the trigger.

The metal felt icy against his digit, sending a slight shiver through Gabe's frame. He re-centered, and sent the command to squeeze. Gently, gradually, squeeze so that the shot would be a surprise.

But his finger wouldn't cooperate, his muscles seemingly too weak to manage the pull.

Gabe cursed himself, wiping the beads of sweat from his brow, forcing his breathing to slow down. "Kill the bastard!" he hissed. "Put that animal down. He tortured and murdered your son."

Again, his cheek welded against the rifle's stock, Marwick's despised image coming into focus, now leaning against the fender. "Kill him!" Gabe's mind screamed. "Think of Jacob."

But he couldn't... wouldn't pull the trigger.

Self-directed anger competed with embarrassment as he disassembled his weapon, Gabe calling himself every derogatory name he could muster on the walk back to his car. "You're a pussy... wimp... coward... gutless wrench," he continued, throwing the case in the backseat.

By the time he pulled back into his driveway, his mental state had deteriorated to the point where he was considering using the weapon on himself. "You can't even defend your own family," he chided. "You're not a real man. What use are you? You deserve to die."

Mulling over the decision to take his own life, Gabe decided to leave a note for Sandy, but there wasn't any pen or paper in the car, and he was afraid to enter the house, worried his wife would *know*.

It then occurred to him to make a recording of his last words. He found the cellphone, reinserted the battery, and rebooted the device.

He was searching for the recording app when the device rang, its unexpected, blaring tone causing his already stressed frame to nearly bounce off the seat. After recovering from the start, he glared down to see Adam's caller ID. "More bad karma, no doubt," he thought. "Might as well say goodbye to him as well."

"Good news!" Adam's cheery voice sounded across the airwaves. "The grand jury has concluded Marwick should stand trial on criminal charges. The DA doesn't have much option now... she has to bring him in front of a judge and jury."

After ending the call a short time later, the gravity of what he had almost done hit him. The weight was incredible, the sedan's glass and metal closing in on all sides. He threw open the door and rushed for the backyard where he wretched uncontrollably before collapsing on the manicured lawn, laying there until he regained his composure.

Gabe knelt beside Jacob's grave, noting the grass had finally concealed the raw patch of earth covering his son's final resting place. It was a sign. A harbinger of healing.

"Tomorrow it begins, son," he stated to the ground. "Tomorrow we begin the process of making your death count for something. The people who did this to you will pay; I swear it."

The words, mimicking what was left of Gabe's life, were hollow.

In the months following the funeral, Sandy and he had gone through the motions, waking up each morning and preparing for a day filled with an indescribable void of remorse and emptiness.

After the initial stages of mourning had begun to subside, Sandy had experienced a change of heart regarding the pending lawsuit. "Why don't we just let all this legal stuff go?" she'd suggested. "It's going to do nothing but cause us to relive the same horror over and over again. It feels like we're only out for revenge, and none of it will bring Jacob back to us. Let's just get on with our lives and be done with it."

But Gabe didn't see it that way. "We have to clear Jacob's name. Did you know there are folks out there who view his death as an acknowledgement of his guilt? Sandy, I can't, in good conscience, just walk away from that. And even more than that, I need to do what I can to make sure other parents don't experience what we did. No one should ever have to go through this again. That's why I'm pushing so hard… that's why I have to see it all the way through to the end."

For weeks, they had debated and discussed while Sandy did her best to restore her scarred and empty soul. She'd volunteered at church, joined a support group, and generally filled her days with honest attempts to let go of the pain and move on.

Her positive energy was the yin to his yang attempt at becoming a sniper and all of the negative time and effort he'd invested with firearms.

Gabe had never felt it necessary to mention the failed assassination attempt.

In addition to his lack of battle readiness, there were other reasons why violence wasn't the answer. Gabe's research found that most cops were actually stand-up individuals. For every documented case of abuse or brutality, there were a hundred acts of bravery, self-sacrifice, or service to the community above and beyond. Any solution had to be selective and target specific – carpet-bombing local law enforcement wasn't the rejoinder.

At one point, an organization called the Civilian Review Board had provided hope, at least for a while. He attended two of their public meetings, observing the proceedings quietly from the back, hoping he'd found an answer worthy of a strong commitment of his time and energy. Compared to the nightmare of shooting another human being, the monitoring institution appeared to be a proper, aboveboard alternative. But it wasn't… not even close.

He quickly discovered the board was powerless. The institution, as formed in Harris County, was a toothless old hound that couldn't even manage a mean growl, let alone implement the bite of change. Witnesses couldn't be called, case files weren't shared, and only meager "recommendations," were created. On the rare occasion when the mayor-appointed members did feel strongly about a case, their chain of command headed directly to the city's inspector general – an office that had zero authority over the police force. It was a dead end.

Gabe's search for a path to redemption led him to the chief of police. "Why not go straight to the top," he'd mentioned to Sandy. "The buck has to stop somewhere."

That effort quickly led to more frustration and anger. The chief had actually tried to fire a number of officers over the past five years, but a powerful police union and poorly negotiated contract with the city had resulted in a situation where it was nearly impossible to terminate any cop. Once an officer was deemed dangerous enough to justify termination, reinstatement via arbitration review boards occurred over 90% of the time. Even in the most heinous of cases, punishments, such as suspension or demotion, were almost always overturned.

Then there was the legal system – another avenue that had been gamed by law enforcement. On the rare occasion that Internal Affairs did recommend the district attorney pursue charges against an officer, the all-powerful, public-trusted grand jury was brandished as a powerful tool of justice. Gabe believed his cause had finally caught a break following Adam's news that Jacob's incident would be presented. It was an exception, however, with only a miniscule percentage of excessive force complaints ever heard by the esteemed body of jurors.

It only took a week's worth of research before Gabe discovered the grand jury system was a complete farce.

The grieving father's first hint had been the selection process. Of the 18 grand juries sitting at any one time in Harris County, only three had their members selected from the general public. The remaining 15 were pulled from a "special" pool of "volunteers."

It wasn't any surprise that most of these "volunteers" were retired government servants and wealthy, private individuals. Gabe found at least three former police officers on the rolls of one jury, another sporting a retired executive of the police union. But the rot went deeper than that.

According to the law in Harris County, the DA could pick which grand jury was to hear a specific case. At any one time, there were three choices available, one of which was almost certain to include a group that contained police sympathizers and insiders who were likely to give a peace officer an unfair tactical advantage in court.

He'd been stymied by the failure of every cerebrally proposed solution his creative and rational mind had considered. Once he clearly understood the structural flaws of the systems in place, Gabe had to wonder why police corruption wasn't even more prevalent. Law enforcement officers operated with very little likelihood of punishment. They were nearly immune from all of the systems that traditionally kept corruptive power from gaining the upper hand.

Even the federal government was hamstrung. Gabe had spent days studying the various "audits and investigations" generated by the Department of Justice. The powerful, federal organization had performed a deep dive into 23 different metropolitan police departments, and the results had been astonishing.

Gabe didn't understand all of the legal and constitutional boundaries, but it was clear that even the authoritative DOJ could only make recommendations to local mayors and chiefs. Arrests and prosecutions were extremely rare, and then only if the abuse could meet extremely high standards of racial prejudice and motivation. The FBI would investigate sexual and financial corruption, but excessive force seemed to dwell comfortably beyond the agency's scope.

As a result, the average cop operated on the streets practically impervious to the law, justified in his belief that even the most atrocious act would result in little to no punishment.

It was for these reasons that Adam and Gabe had decided to take the unusual step of filing the civil lawsuit before the incident had worked its way through the criminal system. The DA's presentation to the grand jury had stalled, apparently falling into the bottomless pit of bureaucratic silos and death by delay. But it didn't matter. Adam Barlow had pursued a civil remedy, filing a federal action against the city, the police department, and Officer Marwick, seeking $16 million in damages. The trial was scheduled to begin tomorrow.

At first, he'd been anxious to visit the gravesite and let Jacob know of the event. But the realities of the justice system, as it applied to cops, soon deflated that enthusiasm.

Gabe knew their likely victory wouldn't change a damn thing. He'd agreed to the lawyer's recommendations every step of the way, despite the full realization that even the most positive outcome probably wouldn't punish the cops or change the system.

All over the nation, an epidemic of successful civil law suits against police officers resulted in huge judgments. In 2010 alone, over $350 million had been awarded in excessive force cases. As a result, taxpayers had to dig deep to make restitution to the victims. Meanwhile, law enforcement officers were not responsible for doling out the lion's share of that money. Cops carried insurance, the expense often reimbursed by their departments. The premiums on such polices were in the hundreds of millions of dollars annually. Not a solitary dime of settlement came out of a officer's pocket.

He rose from the grave's side, brushing a few blades of the new grass from his knee, a tear from his watering eyes. No matter how hefty the future windfall, he'd give it all away to have Jacob back.

"I'll see you again in a few days, son," he mumbled to the earth. "I love you."

Gabe turned and began the long, lonely walk back to the parking lot, wondering if it would be easier to leave the next time. He pondered that question after every visit, and the answer was always the same. Reentering the world outside the neatly mowed rows of headstones and wispy cypress trees always flooded him with guilt. He could leave this place; his son never would.

While he'd returned to his job, the once satisfying occupation had become mundane, almost shallow. He performed well enough, but deep down inside, his heart was elsewhere. Somehow, the custom electronic circuits he designed for offshore oil platforms just didn't seem important any longer.

"Time to go home," he whispered to the empty car. "Time to face the music."

Sandy was in the kitchen, putting a final spread of mustard on a sandwich. Gabe pretended he didn't notice the packed suitcases stacked by the back door.

"I made your favorite," she announced in a monotone that did little to relay the depth of her mood. "Hot ham and Swiss with that fancy mustard."

"Thank you," he responded, kissing her softly on the cheek.

"I know you spotted my bags by the door. I meant to have them packed in the car before you got home, but you're a little early."

"I didn't have much to say to Jacob this afternoon," he confessed. "I guess I'm saving my powder for the results of the trial."

She nodded, finally shifting her gaze from the floor to her husband's face. "You know I love you," she began, a sheen of wetness showing in her eyes. "But I can not stay here while this trial is going on."

"I understand... and I love you too, Sandy."

"Stop this thing, Gabe. Please, don't drag yourself through all of it again. Time will heal; I swear it," she pleaded.

He looked down, shaking his head. "I promised Jacob," came the usual reply. "I gave my word as his father, and I'll see this through to the gates of hell."

She sighed deeply, tilting her head as if she was going to debate the issue all over again. But she didn't, instead rising on her tiptoes and kissing his cheek. "I'll be at my sister's house. Call if you need me."

And with that, she was gone, wheeling her two bags to the car.

He stood still, listening as her car backed out of the driveway and then motored down the street.

His resolve didn't waiver, no voices of second-guessing sounded in his mind. "I'm going to fix this little wrong in the world," his finally announced to the empty home. "It's all I have left to live for."

"Mr. Barlow, you may call your next witness," the judge stated from his bench on high.

"Your Honor, we call Dr. Sinto Okan to the stand."

A middle-aged Asian man rose from the gallery, striding confidently to be sworn in.

"Dr. Okan, could you please state your occupation and background for the record, please?"

"Certainly. In 1984, I was awarded my PhD from the University of California, Los Angeles, in Human Anatomy. In addition, I have five certified black belts in the martial arts, including Judo, Karate, Jujitsu, Kendo, and Tegumi. I have been an unarmed combat instructor for numerous police departments throughout California, as well as the federal law enforcement training academies in Maryland and Virginia. I have worked for the U.S. Department of Defense, the Central Intelligence Agency, and the Federal Bureau of Investigation."

Adam scanned the jury, noting their reaction to the impressive resume of his witness. "Could you please describe for the court what your primary responsibility was while employed at these esteemed government agencies?"

The witness nodded. "Yes. In all cases, I was hired to instruct trainees in the art of unarmed combat, pacification, arrest, grappling, striking, and general self-defense."

"So would it be an exaggeration to say that you, sir, are not a fellow to mess with in a dark alley?"

The courtroom erupted in laughter, Adam noting several of the jurors openly chuckling, despite the judge's gavel calling for order in his court.

"My apologies, Your Honor," Adam added before he was warned from a frowning bench. "I will rephrase my question."

After receiving a nod from the judge, Adam continued, "Dr. Okan, would it be an exaggeration to state you are one of the world's top experts in the countless methods and techniques used by police to restrain suspects and prisoners?"

"I don't believe that would be an exaggeration, sir," the witness responded in a flat, matter of fact tone.

Adam moved to a large projection screen mounted nearby. Peering up at the judge, he stated, "With your honor's permission, I would like to show the witness a videotape and have him answer questions as the images progress."

The judge had previously agreed to the defense's request in a lengthy session of pre-trial haggling. In addition, previous experts had stipulated that Chip's video was indeed taken during the night of the incident in question, and that Officer Marwick was the officer who starred in the recording.

Positioned where both the jury and witness could clearly view the images, the video began with Jacob on the ground, surrounded by several police officers. Marwick was standing at the prone suspect's side, screaming, "Stop resisting! Stop resisting!"

The operator running the computer-controlled projector froze the image, clicked a few keys, and a box appeared in the middle of the screen, magnifying a portion of the recording. It was a close-up of Jacob's already handcuffed arms, the silver metal of the restraints clearly visible on the boy's wrists.

"Doctor, in your expert opinion, is there any chance of this suspect harming any of the officers surrounding him?"

"No, even I would be unable to strike or harm if I were in the position of the handcuffed man. No question. His fight is over."

Adam nodded to his associate, who again tapped at the computer keyboard. This time the zoom focused on Marwick's upper body, a short duration of film showing the officer motioning to one of the other cops, making a lifting motion with his hand.

"I'm going to have the projectionist loop that last section of video, to make sure everyone on the jury can see."

After three repetitions, Adam said, "Now we will let the video continue."

The officer signaled by Marwick bent over, grabbed Jacob's bound wrists, and then began to lift, twisting the boy's arms up and back. Adam had to subdue a smile when two members of the jury winced at the display.

"Dr. Okan, does the technique being applied by the officer have some specific justification or purpose in subduing a suspect?"

"Yes. The human body will automatically react when reverse pressure is leveraged against the shoulder's joint. You can see the effect on the video as the suspect raises his hips to relieve the pain being inflicted on his shoulders. This method has been banned at most police training facilities, however, as it is very easy for an officer to dislocate both shoulders."

"So you are testifying that the man on the ground has no choice but to raise his hips."

"That is correct. If the officers believed the suspect was hiding a gun in the front of his person, they could employ this technique to force him to raise up off the ground."

"Thank you, Doctor. Please continue the video."

The next frames did indeed show Jacob raising his hips, but rather than check for any weapon, Marwick and another officer began screaming, "Stop resisting!" while repeatedly kicking the teen in the ribs.

"Doctor," Adam continued after giving the jury a chance to absorb the scene. "Can you see any justification for the officers' actions, specifically in kicking the suspect repeatedly?"

The martial arts expert responded in a clearly dejected voice, "No, I cannot, other than they are obviously trying to inflict pain on the suspect."

Adam signaled to resume the video, freezing the image just a few frames later. Marching to the large screen, he pointed to another officer who was placing his hands around Jacob's ankle. "I would like to identify this officer to the jury, his specific actions critical to our cause."

The video then began repeating less than five seconds of images, over and over, complete with sound. Big Jim could be seen nodding at the cop gripping Jacob's ankle, the man in charge clearly indicating he wanted some action performed.

"Doctor," Adam began, "Are you familiar with the maneuver being performed by the officer manipulating the suspect's ankle?"

"Yes, I am."

"And what purpose does it serve?"

"If the suspect was utilizing his knees in an attempt to rise off the ground, then pulling his legs back into a straight configuration eliminates any weight bearing capability. This forces the suspect back to a prone position, flat on his abdomen."

"And what about the twisting motion being employed by the officer on Jacob's ankle?"

"That is an unauthorized, extremely dangerous technique that can lead to excruciating pain and permanent damage to the knee."

The image on the big screen changed, the video now replaced with a still photograph showing Jacob's knee. The clearly tortured joint was inflamed, grotesquely swollen to three times its normal size. A murmur rose throughout the courtroom, including several gasps from the jury box. Adam timed it perfectly, "Damage like this, Doctor?"

"Yes, damage like that."

Adam didn't miss a beat, his pace perfect. "I'm going to let the video loop one last time and show the next few moments of the morning in question."

All eyes were fixated on the wide screen as the patrolman pulled and twisted on Jacob's leg, the computer operator letting the scene continue. Jacob's face showed in the foreground, a pale glow in the swirling background of blue police uniforms. The teen's whole body jerked as more torque was applied to his leg, then his spine rearing in protest just before a howl of pure agony sounded deep from his throat.

While it was impossible to see the manipulating officer's face, the policeman's reaction was clear. Both of the visible hands gripping Jacob's ankle sprang free, almost as if the cop had touched a stove's hot burner.

Seizures racked Jacob's still pinned body, his wailing of tortured distress so prevalent that the cops paused their attack.

Fortunately, for everyone in the courtroom, the playback ended.

Adam looked away from the screen and scanned the jury. Every single member was staring at Officer Marwick, the big man's expression apathetic and apparently unmoved.

The lawyer wanted to hammer the point home. "So, Doctor, in summary, what we see on this videotape is a purposeful, skilled manipulation of Jacob Chase's body that was intentionally performed to inflict pain and physical trauma. Is that an accurate statement?"

The witness nodded before catching himself and replying verbally. "Yes, that would be my expert opinion. The officers had Mr. Chase in what we call a 'deadly embrace,' a term describing the manipulation of one part of the body that causes an uncontrollable reaction by another limb or section of the anatomy. Pull a human's arms backwards, and the hips naturally rise. Place extreme pressure on the back of the head, and the neck will arch with an involuntary adjustment. The suspect's movements were not based on any effort to resist, but were in fact being orchestrated by the officer's actions."

After a pause to let the witness's last statement soak in, Adam closed, "No more questions, Your Honor."

The union lawyer rose from behind the defense's large table, strutting a few steps toward the witness. "Doctor, in your testimony, I heard you use the words 'unauthorized' and 'dangerous' when describing the techniques executed by the arresting officers on the video that we all just watched. Have you read the Houston Police Academy's Training Guide? Specifically the section on subduing potentially violent suspects?"

The witness nodded with a sly smile, "Yes, I'm quite familiar with that document. I wrote it."

"No more questions for this witness, Your Honor."

The mid-day recess was called shortly after the doctor's testimony had concluded. Gabe and Adam exited the courtroom, the attorney briefing his client on their options for a quick lunch. After passing through the heavy double doors, Adam glanced up to see the lead council for the defense waiting patiently in the corridor.

"Could I have a brief moment, Mr. Barlow?"

"Sure, Counselor," Adam replied, and then turned to Gabe. "I'll meet you downstairs in the lobby. Be thinking about what sounds good for a quick bite."

Nodding, Gabe wandered off, only slightly offended at being left out of the legal powwow.

"We would like to offer a settlement on behalf of the named defendants," the city attorney began. "We believe six million dollars is a fair amount."

Adam wanted to smile, but held a stern poker face. "That's ridiculous, Counselor. I can see the jury's faces, and I think we'll be awarded full damages."

The grizzled old lawyer didn't flinch, "Perhaps. Perhaps not. No one can ever be sure how a jury will find, sir. Be that as it may, what would you consider a fair award, Mr. Barlow?"

"I'm sure my client wouldn't agree to a penny less than 14 million, sir. He has lost his son forever."

Nodding, the older man responded, "See if your client will accept 14 million then. I can have the paperwork drawn up this afternoon. I'll be waiting on your call." Without another word, he pivoted, walking briskly toward the stairwell where Adam assumed the other members of his team were waiting eagerly for an answer.

Shaking his head, Barlow made for the elevators, wondering how Gabe would react.

He found his client waiting in the lobby, standing in a corner and watching the never-ending parade of people coming and going from the massive facility. Adam noted Gabe's reaction as a group of policemen walked by, a dark shadow of hatred crossing behind his eyes.

"Good news," he greeted. "They want to settle."

"What? Really? Already?"

"I thought that's what that old windbag wanted. They're offering 14 million, and I think you should give it serious consideration."

Gabe was dumbfounded, unsure of what to say or how to react.

"Come on, we can talk it over while savoring the best pastrami and rye in Texas," the lawyer suggested, placing a friendly, guiding hand on Gabe's shoulder. "And I'm buying."

Five days later, Gabe arrived home, copies of the settlement agreement resting in the passenger seat next to his cell. He wanted to call Sandy, wanted to let his wife know the lawsuit was over, ask her to come home. But he couldn't make the call, unsure exactly why his brain was rejecting the opportunity to deliver what should be extremely positive news.

He found the same, mysterious barrier impeding any celebration over their windfall.

While his disciplined, engineering mindset had never allowed such whimsical activities as playing the lottery, he had yielded to the occasional daydream, imagining what it would be like to hit a big jackpot. Even as he sat in his driveway, the city's insurance company was wiring such a life-changing payout to his attorney's bank. In no time at all, millions of dollars would land in the Chases' normally meager, joint checking account.

He should be happy, or content, or pleased, or something – but it just wasn't there. His core remained numb, a soulless void marked by emptiness, melancholy, and dissatisfaction. He had thought the win would breathe life back into his nearly departed humanity, but it hadn't.

"Maybe you were right, Sandy," he whispered, switching off the ignition. He decided to stay in the driveway for a bit, the prospect of entering the empty house an unpleasant notion. "You said the lawsuit wouldn't bring Jacob back, but I thought I would at least feel a sense of accomplishment... of closure."

Gabe forced his troubled mind into an avenue of analytical thinking, invoking the discipline of his trade. There was a problem, and he was a problem solver.

Over and over, his mind processed the events of the last few months, using every analytical technique his education and experience had engrained. The minutes passed, Mr. Chase sitting in his driveway, completely engrossed with his self-diagnosis.

It then dawned - a moment of eureka realization.

His anticipation of accomplishment hadn't occurred because he hadn't changed a damn thing. Officer Marwick, as of that moment, was still patrolling the streets, unaffected, unpunished, and untarnished.

To the city of Houston, the 14 million dollars was a drop in the bucket. Not one single public official – not the mayor, nor the chief of police, nor even a council member would be held accountable. He'd changed nothing. Ultimately, Jacob's death still didn't count for squat.

Gabe had held firm to the belief that the pain of reliving Jacob's episode would be worth the reward. A knot formed in the pit of his stomach when he finally admitted that his wife had been right. Perhaps he should've listened to her.

Not wanting to admit fault, he went on the defensive. All hope was not lost. There was still the upcoming presentation by the DA to the grand jury. With any luck, criminal charges would be brought against Marwick. While it was extremely rare for that supposedly esteemed body to recommend prosecuting an officer of the law, it could happen. Adam had expressed his doubts, begrudgingly admitting that there was still a chance, albeit a small one.

Gabe sighed, opening the door and stepping out onto the driveway. His thoughts moved on to a more pressing topic — what to do with his time.

Returning to the office no longer seemed reasonable. While his employer had been a saint of understanding and flexibility, Gabe had to admit he hadn't been on top of his game since burying his son. Even if he wanted to work, it didn't seem fair to not give his boss 110%. With the settlement money, employment was no longer a financial necessity. "Now I've got all the time in the world, son," he whispered, glancing toward the heavens. "I wish you were here to enjoy it with me."

Shuffling to the back door, Gabe draped his coat over a kitchen chair and stood silently, his gaze taking in the vacant home. A wave of despondency commandeered his emotions, some force inside of him generating a fountain of melancholy thoughts.

His mind traveled back to his father and the elder Chase's last years on earth. Gabe Chase, Sr. had worked his entire life in the West Virginia coalfields, raising two children on his own after losing his wife to cancer.

After college, Gabe and his sister had both moved on, seeking other regions of the U.S. where there was more opportunity. When his father announced his retirement, both children had begged Gabe, Sr. to sell the old house and move closer to enjoy a better life surrounded by family. The old man had refused.

During his many visits, Gabe had sat and talked with his dad, swaying back and forth in the old homestead's porch swing. The son could see the loneliness in his father, and yet the old man seemed anchored to rolling hills and the mine-scarred earth of his childhood.

"Why do you choose familiarity at the price of solitude?" he had once asked his pop.

"Loneliness isn't as bad as everyone says. Being at home, in familiar surroundings, is undervalued. Add those two facts together, and you'll have the answer. I love my children and their children. I look forward to every visit, phone call, and card in the mail. But this is my home. I know the hills, trees, birds, and people. Isolation is a small price to pay for living where you belong."

Gabe had watched his dad fade as the years passed, always hoping that the old man would change his mind, see the warmth family could provide, and realize the joy of exploring new scenery. The son had sworn he'd never make the same choice as his father, mentally barricading himself behind a wall of the familiar, treading only on comfortable ground. "We'll never be that way," he had promised Sandy. "We'll travel, explore, and seek new places, sights, and sounds."

Yet, here he stood... with enough money to go anywhere, do practically anything his mind could fathom. For the first time in his adult life, he had no responsibilities, no schedule, or agenda. "I could go eat a $300 steak," he whispered to the unoccupied house. "I could fly to Hawaii, book a room in Vegas, or cruise first class around the world. But here I stand, staring at these walls, somehow incomplete without my wife and son."

He eventually moved to the couch with a pen and paper, forcing a break from his current journey's destination of depression via introspection. It was an act of survival, as basic as eating or breathing.

Once seated, he began making a list of tasks that needed to be addressed – a long-term plan for successfully suppressing the reoccurring funk that now overshadowed his life. At first, the to-do's were logical and mundane, including such items as managing the windfall of cash, selling Jacob's Honda, hiring a housekeeper so that Sandy wouldn't return to a jungle of dust bunnies and cobwebs.

As more ink colored the blank page, the deliverables became less defined. A reoccurring theme began to emerge, his inner voice demanding he invoke actions that would make a difference. "Use the money to make sure no parent suffers such pain," he wrote. "Use your newfound wealth to force a change in how we are policed," the ink recorded as it spread across the paper.

But how would he operationalize his agenda? How would he turn the rhetoric of a heartbroken father into hope for an innovative and fair-minded system of justice?

Even with his share of the after-tax money, somewhere around seven million dollars, he felt powerless to implement his plans. He could support politicians who promised change – but that had never been effective on simple issues, let alone something as massive as forcing a shift in law enforcement's culture. Pile on the obstacles of a biased court system, corrupt jury appointments, the entwinement of powerful lawyers, a police force that felt it was under siege, and the problem quickly became overwhelming. It was too big, too widespread, and too engrained. The tragedy of Jacob's death was for naught, another statistic on the FBI's database that no one would remember in a few weeks.

Then it occurred to him that he didn't need to be a lone warrior in the fight to compel and implement improvements. After all, Sandy and he were reasonable, mainstream Americans. Weren't their values shared by the vast majority of their countrymen? Hadn't his son been an upstanding youth – a model teenager? Every other person who knew the facts of Jacob's horrendous journey had been infuriated, hurt, and touched. He needed others to know the story – a lot of others. Publicity. Exposure. Those were the weapons that could turn the tide and overcome the beast. *Shine light on evil, and it will die*, he thought.

Digging his cell phone from the hanging jacket, he hurriedly dialed Adam's number. "I would like a copy of the video presentation you made to the jury… the one that highlights those cops beating the shit out of Jacob," he informed the lawyer.

"Ummm… could I ask why?"

"Because I'm going to post that recording on social media with the hopes of churning public outrage. I'm going to use the settlement money to fire up a publicity campaign and pray it results in changes that will keep something like this from ever happening again. It's my new mission in life – a new calling."

There was a long pause, Adam trying to choose his next words carefully. "Gabe, you had better be careful with this. As your attorney and friend, I must advise caution. Can we get together tomorrow and talk it over?"

"I don't understand," Gabe pushed back. "I thought you of all people would be as excited as I am."

Adam was anything but enthusiastic at the concept. "You're dealing with the ultimate authority structure within our society. I'm afraid of a backlash if you go running off igniting some sort of firestorm against the system. Caution, my friend... you need to proceed with caution."

Something in the lawyer's tone communicated fear, and Gabe couldn't understand why. Adam had charged into the fight at his side, a full frontal assault via civil litigation. Why was he hesitating now?

"If you say so," Gabe finally replied. "But this time you're buying, Counselor."

The call was disconnected after the men settled on an early afternoon meeting at a popular barbecue restaurant. Gabe returned the phone to his pocket, now more depressed than before. "Why do rugs keep getting pulled out from beneath me?"

"If you go splashing that video all over the internet, it will accomplish nothing other than to piss the district attorney off," Adam stated clearly.

"So?" came Gabe's innocent reply. "Why do I care if the DA is honked off?"

"Because she's the person who is going to present the case against Marwick to the grand jury. How much energy, detail, and oomph she puts behind that little dog and pony show will make the difference between charges being filed or that goon walking free."

Gabe nibbled at his brisket, clearly not grasping the political nuances of the situation. "If the public is outraged over what that cop did, wouldn't that help the DA get that guy off the force? Wouldn't she look like a hero to her adoring public?"

Adam shook his head, the frustration bleeding through despite his patient attempt to explain. "First of all, the internet is full of videos of police brutality. There are so many that such acts are no longer shocking or noteworthy. Secondly, the cops have figured out how to deal with the occasional example that does go viral. They've become well versed in dismissing or downplaying even the most obvious examples of excessive force. They'll claim that Jacob's video doesn't show the entire encounter, and that your son was fighting with the police before the camera started recording."

"Go on," Gabe replied, still trying to comprehend what Adam was saying.

"I can just hear the HPD spokesman now," the lawyer continued. "He'll claim Jacob was fleeing the cops, became belligerent, resisted arrest, and continued to fight with the officers. It will be his fault that extreme measures were implemented to subdue. They'll tout his size, athletic accomplishments, and conditioning. Hell, they might even go so far as to open an investigation into you personally, Gabe."

"Me? What the hell excuse would they dream up to come after me?"

Adam grimaced, his expression indicating he felt Gabe was being naive. "Do you really have to ask that? After what they did to Jacob, would you put much past them?"

"Seriously?" Gabe questioned. "I'm having trouble believing what my ears are hearing. Everyone keeps saying that only a small percentage of these guys are bad cops, that the vast, overwhelming majority are disciplined servants of the public at large. Now, you expect me to switch gears and believe a punitive agenda is pervasive throughout the system. I just can't believe they would be so vindictive. They aren't an occupational army – they are supposed to protect and serve."

"Okay, let me give you an example," came the reply, the attorney's resolve to educate his client now renewed. "They open an investigation into you for editing the videotape, removing the parts that would prove Officer Marwick was within his legal rights to use that level of force. The potential charges would include tampering, obstruction, interference, and perhaps even perjury. Hell, they might even lump in some libel and slander."

"They wouldn't dare! Why... that would be so far off the reservation... they'd never get away with something like that."

"Probably not, at least not in the long run. But how many millions of that settlement do you want to give to guys like me fighting them in court? How much more mud do you want to drag your family through?"

Gabe was pissed, his anger barely restrained. Finally, he hissed, "I can't believe this could happen in America. I can't fathom this is the same country President Reagan described as 'The shining city on the hill.'"

His lunch partner only nodded, "I suppose you're right to be outraged. I used to be, but I work so closely with the system I guess I've gotten comfortable with the status quo. In reality, most of the cops are great guys. It's only the occasional bad actor who upsets the applecart."

Gabe scratched his chin, still mentally playing all the angles. "Why wouldn't the good guys want the thugs out of their departments? I don't understand this 'All for one, one for all' attitude."

"Because the guy we would call an overly-aggressive, domineering abuser of power is the same officer other cops want with them when things get rough or out of hand. He's the guy who kicks in the door and rescues the hostage, or the cop who throws the methamphetamine-crazed suspect with super-human strength to the ground. I know your son suffered, but often the attitude of a playground bully is exactly what the police need to do their jobs. You have to keep in mind that we expect them to deal with the absolute dredges of society. We pay them to hold the 5-year old girl who was just raped by her drug dealer uncle, and then expect them to smile 20 minutes later when they pull us over for speeding."

Gabe tilted his head, "It almost sounds as if you're on their side."

"There's a balance, Gabe," the attorney responded. "And I agree, Marwick shouldn't be on the streets. But if you go posting that video, you're going to hurt every cop, good and bad alike. Aren't they innocent until proven guilty as well? People only see the uniform, authority, and the capability to alter lives. Citizens lump them all together. The general public doesn't look at individual faces or badge numbers."

"If you were in my shoes, what would you do, Adam? I can't let Jacob's death become another meaningless statistic. I need to associate some meaning to his loss."

The attorney was normally the one asking questions, Gabe's turning things around catching Adam off guard. He toyed with his fork, pushing small bits of food around on the plate while he contemplated a response. He seemed almost embarrassed not to have a good answer to his client's query. With a hesitant voice, he ventured, "I suppose you could donate money to the police so they could buy body cameras and better dash cams."

"Marwick had a dash cam, and that didn't help. Besides, they all know how to defeat the cameras. You told me that they practice huddling and piling around suspects so any cameras can't see what's going on."

Adam sighed, "I can't really tell you how to change the system. But I do understand your need to do something. Post the raw video from an anonymous account if you must. Don't go near the modified version we used at the trial because they would know in a heartbeat who had access to that. For now, that's about the best advice I can give you."

Sandy answered the call on the second ring. "How are you, Gabe?" she said with a warm tone.

"I doing okay, I guess. I miss you terribly, you know."

"Is it over? I will come home the moment you tell me it's over," she said gently, a wisp of hope in her voice.

He didn't answer the question, choosing instead to ramble on about investments, the yard crew asking for a raise, and the neighbor's new car.

She listened politely, occasionally posing a question of clarification, letting her mate jabber as if she were just down the street or out shopping for the afternoon. Finally, when he'd exhausted the small talk, she gently submitted her question again. "Is it over, Gabe? Can we move on... together?"

Gabe hesitated, despite having known the question was coming. He had rehearsed the answer a dozen times in his mind. "No, my dearest, I won't lie," he finally managed. "Our victory in court... the money... it was hollow. Until that man is off the streets, it won't be over."

"That might be a long time," she answered sadly. "That might be forever."

"No, I won't let it go forever," he promised. "But it burns inside of me, Sandy. It is a fire I have to extinguish before I can have peace. I hope you still understand that. I pray you still love me."

"I'm afraid that fire is going to burn you up, Gabriel darling. It's a scorching, unbearable inferno too hot for me to stand beside, or I'll be consumed as well. I hope you understand that. I pray *you* still love *me*."

"I do, Sandy. I swear I do. I know this is hard for you to understand. I know you are healing your grief in an entirely different manner." Like a wordsmith considering his next query, he paused to ensure that every phrase was selected to perfectly convey his meaning. "I wonder... is it too much for me to ask if you will give me more time to work through this?"

Now, it was Sandy's time to reflect on her husband's words. She sighed and then responded, "Yes, of course I will wait. I have faith you'll come out the other side as the man I fell in love with. I know you need to quench this fire in your belly. But then I want you to come back to me as the man I love. I just wish I were strong enough to be there and help you. Understand I'm not that brave or strong just yet. But I hope you will never doubt my love, Gabriel William Chase."

His heart warmed at her understanding, his voice cracking slightly at the depth of affection and insight from her words. "Do you need anything? Money? Anything from the house?"

Her gentle chuckle was reassuring, the highlight of the call. "No, I don't need anything except my husband. I'll be waiting, Gabe."

DA Sanders saw Tony approaching, her first reaction being to duck into the ladies room in order to avoid the junior prosecutor. As tempting as the maneuver was, she resisted the urge. There was a long list of people she didn't want to see these days. So many in fact, there were days when relocating to a remote desert island seemed her only viable option. *Wonder if I could telecommute? I would avoid gridlock, and with what I saved on parking, I could afford a little seaside cabana*, she mused. Only when she contemplated the inaccessibility of Texas barbecue did she dismiss the passing thought.

"Good morning, ma'am," the young attorney greeted.

Karen merely nodded, her eyes sweeping the busy foot traffic moving through the courthouse hall to make sure no one was listening. "Morning."

"Is now a bad time? I hate to be a pest, but I've been trying to get with you for three days."

Karen frowned, "Really? Three days? I know I've been busy, but I didn't realize that much time had passed since we'd talked. Let's find someplace a little more quiet."

The duo continued on, strolling through a chorus of footfall echoes bouncing off the highly polished, marble floor. They smiled as they passed a judge's clerk scurrying with an armload of folders, subconsciously nodded at a pair of chatting pedestrians, and then dodged a crime reporter for the local paper. Both avoided making eye contact with the big league defense lawyer working a high-profile criminal case.

Tony wasn't stupid, immediately recognizing his boss's strong desire to avoid addressing his ever-growing list of needs. As they walked, he tried to prioritize and weed out the lesser demons. The tension grew thicker with every step. No way he could avoid the burgeoning elephant in the room.

Finally, they approached an empty courtroom, DA Sanders closing the double doors after they'd entered the vacant space.

"What's up?" she asked innocently enough.

He quickly ran through three items needing his boss's attention, receiving her agreement on a plea bargain, approval of a sentencing recommendation, and finally the reset of a pending hearing. It was the fourth topic that both of them dreaded. "Did you have a chance to look over my brief on the Marwick case?"

Karen's eyes dropped to the floor, but she still responded. "Yes, I've read it, and to be blunt, I keep shuffling it to the bottom of the stack."

Tony understood, his supervisor's response not totally unexpected. "Normally, I wouldn't press on a case like this, but somebody keeps agitating the local press and poking social media with a cattle prod. This one's not going to drift quietly away in the night. I received an email just this morning from the Houston Post, asking why the case had not been added to the grand jury's docket."

"I know, I know," she fumed, clearly frustrated. "But like most of these brutality incidents, we're between a rock and a hard place. I thought the civil settlement would tamp this down, but obviously it hasn't."

The problem the DA's office faced was well known by both of them. This was a no-win scenario, regardless of the outcome.

The DA depended on the police, worked with them every single day. In private, most cops would admit one of their own had crossed the line in this instance but wouldn't want Marwick prosecuted. They were dealing with an organization that saw repeat, violent, offenders released with a mere slap of the hand – why shouldn't the good guys wearing a badge receive the same altruism?

Every day, policemen watched the revolving door of "justice" as it returned hardened criminals to the streets for a variety of reasons. Technicalities, sleazy defense tactics, injudicious rules, or misled juries resulted in the more-jaded cops referring to themselves as fishermen. "We catch and release," the world-weary officers touted as their feeble battle cry. Karen understood the grievance of good men who risked their lives for the public welfare, only to watch robbers, rapists and murderers walk free. For the DA to drop the legal hammer on one of their own would classify her as someone who lacked the capacity to understand the frustrations and dangers involved in law enforcement. If the prosecution against an officer were successful, she would earn the title of "cop hater." And ultimately, her office's primary objective to represent the public would suffer from the black eye a media frenzy would prompt.

Not only would internal department morale be damaged, the public's interaction with street cops would be impacted as well. It had been well documented that once a cop had been convicted, the public became more aggressive and resistant to the local officers. Witnesses were hesitant to come forward. Informants dried up, and a more belligerent attitude prevailed toward the men and women in blue.

But merely slapping Marwick on the wrist could backfire as well. Public outrage could result in ever expanding rings of negative events. In previous, highly publicized cases, vigilantes had assassinated officers on the street. Demonstrations, some violent, others peaceful, had occurred in numerous metro areas, the cost to the taxpayers mounting into millions and millions of dollars in police overtime, lost business revenue, and frustrated citizens.

"I'm going to take the easy way out, for now," Karen finally declared. "We're going to use the tried and true tactic of stalling. Tell your curious reporters that the grand jury dockets are stuffed to the gills at the moment. Assure them that we are going to pursue this case to the full extent of our official capacity, and we want to make sure that a thorough presentation is made on behalf of our citizens. You know the public relations drill, Tony. Do me proud."

"Yes, ma'am."

Gabe's mornings were spent online, searching local new outlets for any sign of action against Officer Marwick. This morning produced the same result – disappointment. It had been the same, day after day.

He tried desperately not to become obsessed with the topic, but it was a difficult struggle, and he was losing. He'd resigned from his job months ago, the interest income from the settlement providing more revenue than his upper-middle class career had ever produced. The cleaning lady came once a week, even that frequency seemingly overkill as his bachelor lifestyle and tidy personal habits produced little in the way of filth. *At least she can keep the dust bunny population in check*, he mused.

He'd sold Jacob's Honda, sick of seeing the reminder in the driveway on the few occasions he did venture beyond the front door. Then there had been the random conversations on the phone with Sandy, his honesty and wife's perception leading her to believe he still wasn't "ready to let go of this."

The rest of his time was spent studying every aspect of law enforcement's use of force.

He monitored dozens of activists' websites, groups or individuals who reported, blogged, and opined on the topic. He subscribed to news feeds from every major national and regional outlet. He dedicated a significant portion of his day to internet voyeurism, lurking in forums designed specifically for law enforcement officers, online sites designed to allow cops a medium to share common experiences and frustrations.

At first, Gabe had delved into the dark side, convinced that there were fundamental flaws in America's system of criminal justice. While that notion proved to be true, his analytical mind also had to admit that several issues existed throughout the massive infrastructure, some of which worked against the cops.

Over time, a realization set in – most police officers were professional, even-handed servants to the public. They were asked to perform a nearly impossible job for little pay and even less respect by some segments of the population.

That admittance hadn't been easy for the still-grieving father to accept.

After three months of anxiously waiting for justice to be served against the man who he believed had ended his son's life, Gabe found himself as perplexed as Adam had been that day at lunch. He was struggling for an answer, determined to make a difference, committed to the cause of solving the problem. But how?

Glancing up from the computer screen, Gabe noted two squirrels chasing each other around the trunk of a front yard pine. Their movement held his attention, the distraction from web pages and streaming news video a welcome rest for his digital-weary brain.

The cause of the fur-commotion was unclear, each squirrel taking turns pursuing the other. The scuffle appeared pointless as well, neither animal seemingly capable of catching or besting the other. "Why are you guys wasting your time and energy?" he whispered.

On and on the contest continued, small streaks of brown fur and bushy tails flashing round and round the trunk, first this direction, and then in reverse. On the few occasions the two combatants did pause, they remained on high alert, eyeing each other with nervous suspicion.

It occurred to Gabe that he was doing the exact same thing, wasting his time and energy on what was proving to be a fruitless chase. He was circling the tree, just like his yard mates. He had to do something different. He wasn't a squirrel.

Wandering to the kitchen with thoughts of eggs and toast on his mind, a clarity of sorts entered his otherwise clouded mind. Somehow, that morning, he realized that to address his concerns, he must first find a solution to one simple dilemma. How to identify the bad cops while leaving the good guys alone? And furthermore, that identification process must provide proof – beyond any shadow of doubt when a white hat became corrupt.

"Brilliant!" he informed the cooking eggs. "I think I'm finally seeing the forest and not the squirrel-infested trees."

Gabe felt a sense of accomplishment with that epiphany, proud of himself for eliminating all of the clutter and rising above the many nuances and dichotomies that had plagued his rational mind for months.

Even that small amount of progress brought him relief. He decided to occupy his mind with something else for a time. He would give himself a break from months of swirling emotion and find another project for the time being.

He returned to his list, penned so many months ago. Most of the items had been crossed off, but a few remained. There, toward the bottom of the page, was the one task that had troubled him the most. "Clean out Jacob's room."

He sighed heavily, resigned that today was the day to accomplish this task. Enough time had passed. *Everyone keeps telling me that time heals all wounds. Guess I will test out that theory*, he contemplated. Anyway, Sandy would appreciate the gesture as a sign he was moving on.

It took more fortitude to climb the steps that he had anticipated; several folded, moving boxes cradled under one arm. His hand froze on the knob, uncertain if he really felt comfortable enough to do the job. "Maybe I should ask Manny to come over and help me?" he whispered.

But that wouldn't be fair. The young girl had suffered just as much, if not more, than anyone. Why drag her through the mourning process again?

For a moment, the father thought his heart might explode, the organ beating so hard that he could easily count the beats per minute. His skin was clammy and his knees weak. *Once your heart has been broken, I am pretty sure you can't be at risk for a massive coronary,* he consoled himself. Building the confidence necessary to engage the knob required pacing his breathing. After several deep, slow inhalations, he opened the door to the room where his son had taken his final air.

He lingered at the threshold for a few moments, taking in a scene he hadn't visited in months. His eye was immediately drawn to the wall opposite the doorway where the trophy shelf prominently displayed an assortment of cups, medals, plaques, awards, and certificates – miniature icons of Jacob's accomplishments still appearing shiny and new. The bed was made, the dresser and small desk neat and tidy. For a moment, he was jealous of the cleaning lady, envious of her ability to enter this part of his house without fear or remorse.

As he scanned the room's contents, his eyes paused on the drone. It was still sitting on Jacob's desk, the last material thing that had brought happiness to the tortured teenager.

Gabe thought back to that day... remembered his son's excited face and bright smile. He was glad he'd spent the money... happy that Sandy had finally understood the importance of the gift. Replaying those brief minutes in his head, Gabe took a step into the space, overcoming the sense of foreboding, lured by an aura of joy that still seemed to surround the bright red machine.

He lifted the toy from Jacob's desk, stepping back absentmindedly to perch on the edge of the bed, his eyes boring into the machine. His son's last words that afternoon echoed through his head, "I wish this drone had been hovering over my car that night. With video like this, there wouldn't be any doubt."

His thoughts soared as effortlessly as the tiny flyer had that afternoon, his reasoning as clear as the video images captured by its lenses. "With video like this," he kept repeating, "There wouldn't be any doubt."

He left Jacob's room, any desire to clean and pack left behind with the empty cardboard boxes discarded on the bed. Only the drone held his attention now, a toy... a plaything... a battery powered hobby with propellers. Yet, this odd machine was inspiring him in a way that nothing else had up to that point. It was a solution.

Chapter 7
Peelian Principle
Good appearance commands respect.

Finding the right office building had been easy. The Houston area was full of low-to-midrise commercial spaces. A recently completed, three-story tower sitting less than a mile outside of the city limits had provided the nearly perfect location. Just across the Harris County line on unincorporated land, it was evidence of the ever-expanding metropolitan sprawl taking advantage of cheaper real estate and lower development costs at the fringe of civilization.

The loftiest structure in the complex, it had been situated in an isolated area, surrounded by an impressive greenbelt. The grounds were impossible to view from the street, the entire space private and quite secure. The expansive parking area was a vacant, concrete slab, its perfectly striped spaces and unblemished curbs evidence of the newness of the facility. A key selling point had been the rooftop access via a metal fire door, only 10 concrete steps away from the "penthouse-type," executive suites. A new corporation owned by a foreign trust signed the lease.

Jacob Industries was described to the mildly curious landlord as a start-up, developing distribution management systems to be utilized by businesses operating fleets of delivery and maintenance vehicles. Implementing such a service would require expensive, sophisticated radio equipment, including rooftop antennas and secure rooms housing computer hardware. JI would do business around the clock, requiring the utmost in employee confidentiality and protection. The agent representing the building's management company just shrugged, replying, "They can turn it into Fort Knox for all I care, as long as they keep current on the association dues."

For several weeks, an army of carpenters, craftsmen, electricians, and laborers descended on the top floor, hammering, sawing, and unloading materials. The management company representative stopped by a few times, performing periodical walk-thru assessments. The inspector's only reaction was a smile, content that a stable, obviously well-funded entity was moving in.

While the build out was in progress, Gabe was busy elsewhere. Fueled by his newfound passion for drone technology, he began absorbing every possible detail regarding the unmanned flying machines. It came easy to him, a natural extension to his engineering education and background. Studying everything from aeronautics to radio frequency controllers, he consumed books, blogs, webpages, and university research projects like a man who had found his calling.

For the first time since his son's death, Gabe felt a purpose. His heart and soul had been seeking a cause, and now they had discovered it. Jacob Industries would make a difference – would ensure that other people would never suffer the same pain endured by his loved ones.

But he had to be careful.

If his plans worked, Gabe would be walloping a hornet's nest with a very big stick. He was absolutely certain that the authorities wouldn't appreciate his endeavors, but that wouldn't matter if they didn't realize who was behind it all. Operational security was the absolute top priority, but that wasn't easy.

It seemed like every step required some form of subversion, illusion, or borderline illegal activity. From setting up an untraceable corporation to acquiring equipment in such a way that there was no direct link to Gabe, establishing the cover business had required extra time.

His biggest single concern was purchasing the parts to assemble the flying machines. Many of the components were built overseas, but not all. Circuit boards, infrared cameras, carbon frames, and even spools of wire shipped from domestic suppliers. Gabe knew enough about law enforcement to know that if one of his "birds" fell into the authorities' hands, they would take the serial numbers from each manufacturer and trace them back as far as possible.

More than once during the execution of his complex scheme, Gabe had seriously pondered throwing in the towel. The closest had been during a conversation with Adam a few weeks before signing the lease. "You know if they catch you, you're in for a worse ride than Jacob experienced. Far worse."

"But I'm not doing anything illegal," Gabe had countered.

"And you think that matters? We're about to have the same conversation we did the day that you wanted to post that video. Illegal activity versus operating within the law is no longer black and white, my friend. If they dig hard enough, they can bring anybody up on charges. It's impossible to live, drive, own a business, or walk down the sidewalk without breaking one law or another. It could be taxes, import restrictions, zoning, or in your case, the federal aviation boys. Talk about regulations that contradict each other. There's an old saying amongst district attorneys – 'You can indict a ham sandwich.'"

Just like the day Officer Marwick had been in his rifle sights, Gabe had experienced second thoughts on several occasions throughout the process. The difference now was that he wasn't taking justice into his own hands, didn't feel as though he was committing any crime. He was on the moral high ground, and that gave him the strength to push on.

In fact, more so than any period in his life, Gabe was energized with the drive and desire of a worthy campaign. He suddenly found himself needing or wanting little sleep, the whirlwind of mental activity refusing to halt just because his head rested on a pillow. It was glorious work that would produce a cure for a disease-ridden system.

Gabe sat in JI's new parking lot, watching the movers unload a steady stream of boxes. He didn't want anyone to see him, wanted no witnesses to his association with the new entity. As Adam had put it, "You just never know whose brother-in-law is a cop."

And then the last man locked the door and climbed into the big moving van's cab. Gabe watched them drive away, feeling a sense of accomplishment and the beginning of a new stage in life. He was reborn with the religion, soon to sprout wings and avenge from the heavens.

He exited his new pickup truck, using the fob to lock the door. The security cameras had been carefully calibrated to allow a blind spot exactly where his reserved parking space was located. His path to the private entrance took him through a narrow, blind corridor, just outside of their field of view. No one would hack his system and find evidence of Mr. Gabe Chase entering the premises.

The heavy, steel door buzzed, unlocking via facial recognition software. He entered a small, unmarked room that contained nothing but an elevator door. The new-smelling car was open and waiting.

Moments later, he stepped out of the elevator and into the modest lobby. Cheap furniture was grouped here and there, the obvious indicators of a cash-strapped new business. While there was a small receptionist's bar at one end of the space, no young person would ever answer the phone or welcome guests there. JI wouldn't be receiving any calls, salesmen, or visitors.

A numeric keypad accessed a narrow hall; at the end were two heavy fire doors. One entry led to his personal apartment, the other to the inner workings of JI, Incorporated.

Deciding his own personal space was the lower priority, Gabe entered the company side of the suite, rolling up his sleeves in a symbolic gesture – ready to get to work.

The area was exactly what someone would expect from a start-up. Cheap cubicles were lined up in military formation as if readying for a parade. Each compartment was equipped with an inexpensive computer that Gabe doubted had been, or ever would be, turned on.

Just down the hall was the company break room, complete with fancy coffeemaker and miniature refrigerator. Everyone knew software companies ran on coffee – right?

A few short steps later and just beyond yet another secured doorway, he arrived at the nerve center of Jacob Industries, the location where the real agenda of the business would be addressed.

The server room contained a massive amount of computing power, more so than a firm with hundreds of employees would require. The rack-mounted, multi-core processors were connected with terabytes of solid-state memory storage and the absolute best fiber optic internet connections money could buy. It was a showcase of technology that would make even the most serious "geekdom" enthusiasts weak in the knees.

Sitting in one corner of the chilly, well air-conditioned room was the communications equipment. Again, no money had been spared on the receivers, trunk processors, and digital controllers. Only the antenna array was absent, that hardware being leased from a variety of third party providers scattered over the metropolitan area.

Gabe passed by, apathetic to the computing firepower he'd amassed, his gaze focused instead on the assembly room at the end of the hall.

Here, the movers and technicians had been instructed to simply unload several locked, hard-sided cases. Gabe immediately began lifting the containers onto a large conference room table and opening the combination locks.

An hour later, Gripen 1 was proudly on display, the drone's delighted master slowly circling his creation like a mad scientist admiring a newly breathing monster.

Named after the Swedish fighter jet, G-1 was itself a sleek machine. With a carbon and titanium x-frame, four 8-inch propellers, and an electronics basket equipped with the smallest, lightest, high definition cameras in the world, Gabe's design was the rival of any drone made, short of surreptitious, military grade technology.

The Gripen was equipped with infrared, zooming cameras that recorded video with an impressive level of clarity. *The term "high definition" has to be completely redefined,* the entrepreneur reflected while admiring her notable skill. Her observation platform included parabolic microphones, 48x zoom micro-cameras, and the most accurate GPS technology available. It was an impressive collection, all enclosed inside of a tiny flyer that occupied a space less than 80 inches square.

The airframe also sported an imposing array of computing power, resulting in a hybrid device that was as much robot as aircraft. She boasted four proximity sensors, stability algorithms, an autopilot, and emergency "Go home" programming.

The G-1 wasn't an overly fast bird, capable of only 35 mph with a full load of sensors. Nor was she long-legged, possessing a mere 120 minutes of flight time from her custom-developed battery pack having been repurposed from the latest model laptop computers.

While Gabe's $8,000 machine wouldn't compete with her Uncle Sam-sponsored, military cousins such as the Predator or Global Hawk, she was far and above the average hobbyist's equipment.

He flicked on the Gripen's inconspicuous power switch and then turned to a bank of computer monitors residing on a modern-looking glass and chrome desk. Here, he could view streaming video, GPS maps, satellite images, and the autopilot's display.

The real investment was located inside the software driving those displays. Gabe had contracted with offshore developers to code, test, and debug the brains that would allow the Gripen to perform his commands. Eventually, he hoped to manage a small fleet of drones from this location, and planning for that future expansion had mandated significant advancements over any existing systems available.

A look of satisfaction mixed with pride replaced his commonly downcast expression. Glancing toward the heavens, he whispered, "We're almost there, son. One day, the world will know our little secret, will understand how our cause can return justice to American society. Today is an important step. I love you, Jacob."

Gabe's attention was drawn away from the blueprint he was manipulating by the call coming in over the police scanner. After months of voyeuristic eavesdropping, he knew their radio-language by heart. The Houston police were involved in a pursuit.

Sliding to another of the many keyboards parked at the control cluster, he quickly replayed the looping digital recording, listening as the officer called for support and highlighting the location.

Within seconds, he'd entered the street address into the mapping system. "Good," he announced to the empty room. "That's within our range."

With nervous fingers flying over the keys, Gabe hungrily configured a flight path for the Gripen. A few moments later, the machine powered up and was prepared to launch from its hidden rooftop cradle.

Whispering a small prayer, Gabe hit the right sequence of buttons, and then directed his gaze to a nearby monitor.

There he watched the streaming video from the G-1 as the drone ascended above the office building, his pickup truck looking like an abandoned toy sitting alone in its reserved parking space.

Before the drone had even managed the parking lot, the police radio sounded again, the pursuing officer providing an update to the battalion of squad cars now rolling to join the chase. "Suspected carjacking, possible hostages, traveling past the 1500 block of Jones Road, heading north. Suspect is traveling at a high rate of speed."

Gabe had anticipated this, moving the mouse pointer to a new vector on the GPS map and then sending the modified destination to his flying robot. He watched with satisfaction as the blinking red dot indicating the Gripen's flightpath altered course.

The suspected carjacker was game for the chase, making several high-speed turns in a vain attempt to elude the converging fleet of HPD officers. For 14 minutes, the airwaves were filled with updates, responses, orders, and excited cops responding to the evasion.

All the while, Gabe's attention was divided between listening, updating the drone's course, and observing the lights of Houston pass beneath his drone's camera.

The Gripen was flying at 250 feet above ground, traveling at top speed. The altitude had been carefully selected for a variety of reasons, including the need to stay within the FAA's 400-foot ceiling for civilian drones.

Flying at that level would allow the G-1 to sashay over any building less than 24 stories tall, the north side of the city having few exceptions worthy of avoidance. He had identified five radio towers and two rows of high-voltage power lines that exceeded that height. And of course, the local airports were out-of-bounds.

The location of all known obstacles within the area had been programmed into the Gripen's avoidance software, but keeping that data current presented quite a challenge. Metro Houston was constantly expanding her highway infrastructure, creating towering, webs of intersecting asphalt that connected one side of the Bayou City to the other. Commercial construction projects abounded, the skies often littered with soaring cranes and other lofty impediments that were mobile, switching position from day to day.

The evolving nature of Harris County's landscape presented quite the challenge for Gabe's drone. As he watched the blinking illumination of suburban neighborhoods and corporate landscapes pass beneath G-1, Gabe recalled one such example that had drawn his attention just a few months before.

A car dealership was promoting a big sale, the center of its lot brandishing a huge display of colorful balloons to attract commuters driving on the nearby freeway. He'd estimated that impressive cluster of helium-filled advertisement was at least 200 feet above the earth. Never before had any structure or object exceeded 75 feet in that area. So, yes, accidents might happen.

Knowing this, he'd designed a redundancy, four pinhole-sized, proximity sensors, one on each side of the G-1. They were directly linked to the autopilot, working hand in hand with the collision avoidance algorithms pulsing through the Gripen's computer brain.

The transmission he'd been waiting for finally broadcast, the carjacker having discarded the idea of outrunning the cops in the stolen vehicle and instead deciding to imitate a track star. The armada of responding cruisers were now converging on a strip mall parking lot. "I've got a runner!" came the closest officer's voice. "He's heading around the south side of the building on foot."

Gabe's quick fingers reprogrammed the G-1, ordering it to the last known address and issuing instructions to hover at 200 feet just to the south. Without hesitation or protest, the drone responded. It would arrive at the destination in less than a minute.

Despite the aircraft's slow speed, its closure rate was impressive. The drone flew in a straight line, wasn't hindered by traffic signals or gridlock – didn't have to travel in right angles and never had to avoid one-way streets.

The monitor displaying the G-1's primary camera showed strings of rapidly passing, twinkling white and red lights as it flew steadily toward the designated coordinates. Having flown numerous test flights, Gabe realized he was looking at lines of headlights and taillights, all accented by street side fluorescent-topped utility poles.

A few moments later, the scene changed, a sea of blue and red strobes pulsing on the horizon. With his heart racing, Gabe watched as the outline of over a dozen police cars came into clear view. In a matter of seconds, he could spot officers scurrying about, positioning themselves to catch or block the running suspect.

The video was so clear that Gabe could read the strip mall's signage, noting the doughnut shop, dry cleaners, shoe repair, and mobile phone retail outlet – businesses that were now witnessing the massive police response.

"Doughnuts?" he smirked at the monitor. "One stop shopping for the cops tonight."

A quick command ordered the Gripen to switch to its infrared camera, another monitor now showing the multi-colored world of heat-spectrum energy translated into the human-visible light.

Gabe could spot the white-hot outlines of the police car engines surrounded by the black background of the cooler pavement. Cops were darting everywhere, giving chase to the suspect. Gabe's mechanical spy started scanning in the general direction the stampede seemed to be heading.

It was easy to pick out the officers in direct pursuit of the on-foot suspect, their movements and posture more rapid and alert. The G-1 spotted the man being chased well before any of the cops, identifying the lone individual sneaking behind a garage and then sprinting to the cover of two trashcans.

Gabe ordered the remote eye to adjust its position, the Gripen gliding less than 100 meters to the west where he could keep a lock on the concealed man.

Spying on the pursuit was drama of a sort, more entertaining than any television show Gabe had ever watched. He could zoom in and out, plot the participants, and even anticipate their next moves.

For a while, he thought the fleeing car thief was actually going to get away. Two patrolmen stalked right past the prone suspect, no more than 20 yards distant.

But then the game changed. A new shape appeared in the billowy, infrared world displayed on Gabe's monitors. The K-9 unit, complete with a German shepherd, was now on the scene. The dog found the crouching crook in less than five minutes.

For the first time since the launch, Gabe's blood pressure increased to an ear-ringing rate. Now was the test. Now it was time to prove that all of his money, time, and energy hadn't been tossed down a rabbit hole.

The cops were swarming the suspect, the heat of flashlight beams illuminating the culprit as the dog tugged ferociously on his leash. Gabe ordered the customized drone to hover directly over the crook, and then switched on its parabolic microphone.

He'd learned that the police were always conscious of cameras and witnesses. Like the night Jacob had been mauled, they formed a tight semi-circle around the captured carjacker. This ploy often resulted in questionable cellphone videos... the angle, view, and clarity allowing the cops to claim all sorts of justification for their actions. That tactic wouldn't work with the Gripen.

The lack of light didn't compromise the aerial vehicle's camera. In fact, the view was unequaled; the huddle of officers had not bothered to shield any activities from the skies. Gabe had the balcony seats at the opera.

He could see there was a brief struggle, five officers surrounding the prone man, forcing his hands behind his back. And then it was over. No beating, no kicking, no punches thrown.

In a way, Gabe was disappointed. "If you flee, we have an open license on your ass," one entry on a police forum had boasted. Adam had confirmed the same mentality existed among many cops. Yet, the handcuffed carjacker, now being led back to a patrol car, hadn't suffered any abuse.

He nudged the G-1's control, keeping a bird's eye view as the officers escorted their takedown back to the waiting armada of cruisers, but his mind was no longer centered on the scene playing out below the drone.

"Adam was right," he whispered. "Not all the cops are bullies. The guys I just watched were the ultimate professionals. Was Jacob's encountered really the ultra-rare exception?"

Shaking his head to dismiss the thought, Gabe told himself that his newfound doubt was unjustified. His research had shown that the Houston Police Department received over 650 complaints of excessive use of force a year. That statistic equated to almost two grievances per day, and a large percentage of those were submitted by fellow officers within the force.

Yet, he also knew HPD conducted hundreds of arrests daily. The accusations against the force were mathematically a tiny percentage. It only made sense that his first "observation" had been a clean arrest.

With faith in his mission reestablished, Gabe completed his scrutiny of the handcuffed suspect being guided into the backseat of a cruiser, and then ordered the G-1 home.

After verifying the flying robot was indeed plying the correct route, Gabe leaned back in his chair, finally content with the first experiment and already processing a list of improvements that needed to be implemented to ensure his project's realization.

The rain had finally let up, the stalled front hanging over southeastern Texas for the better part of two days. The Gripen couldn't fly in high winds or wet weather. It was a weakness in Gabe's grand scheme of aerial surveillance.

Clear skies and a calm atmosphere confined him to the assembly room, the nearly constant background noise of the police scanner filling the air while he worked on piecing together the G-2 unit.

This time, the call for additional backup units involved three individuals causing a disturbance at a convenience store. The on-scene officer had been assigned to a complaint that one of the individuals was harassing customers. Upon assessment of the situation, he was now requesting assistance.

Gabe turned on the voice to text translation that constantly monitored the police frequencies, converting the radio calls into searchable data. He highlighted the address, listened to make sure the software had it right, and issued the command string to the G-1 unit.

It was late afternoon, and the daylight posed additional risk. Gabe would have to be careful to keep his secret weapon close enough to provide meaningful video, but at a distance not to be noticed by anyone on the ground.

He modified the unit's programming to cruise at 380 feet, hoping the small profile and grey color exterior would avoid curious eyes. In reality, it was only the authorities or people at the crime scene that were a serious concern.

Less than 15 minutes later, the camera detected several police cars, the responding units parked haphazardly on the lot of a corner gas station and a convenience store. Gabe slowed down the G-1, keeping his distance, and hovering above a nearby empty lot. A quick sequence of buttons engaged the zoom, bringing the picture in close.

There were seven cops now, all of them gathered around three men alongside the building. Gabe could tell that things were getting tense, the body language and hand motions indicating the situation was escalating.

Without warning, one of the cops moved on the tallest suspect, spinning the civilian around and forcing him against the store's outer wall. In the blink of an eye, all three of the suspects were in a similar position.

Gabe wasn't listening, but knew the computers were recording both sound and video. He wanted to focus all of his attention on obtaining clear footage.

The largest man against the brick structure wasn't happy, his head half turned, bobbing up and down as he shouted at the cops. Gabe could see one officer frisking the gentleman while the other kept a close eye on the angry suspect.

When they started to pull the big guy's hands behind his back, he half turned to protest, and then the cops swarmed in.

Three of the officers tackled the suspect, throwing him to the ground and then piling on. They quickly formed their huddle, but Gabe had been anticipating the move.

Zooming in, he saw a cop manage to handcuff one hand and then the other. By the book, the guy on the ground was now subdued, helpless, and extremely unlikely to pose any threat to the surrounding police.

But they didn't stop. One policeman stepped forward, landing first one, then a second, and a final, third kick to the prisoner's ribs. Another officer knelt down, placing a knee onto the back of the man's head while yet a third pulled his nightstick and struck two blows into the prone fellow's leg.

Gabe had watched hundreds of internet videos, many of them more disturbing than what was flashing across the Gripen's monitors in real time. It was still sickening, a knot of bile forming in his stomach.

Evidently, the cops felt enough punishment had been delivered, the huddle breaking up and the now-grimacing suspect half-dragged by his upper arms to one of the police cruisers. The other two men were released.

After ordering the G-1 home, Gabe decided some fresh air was a necessity. Part of his brain was feeling the positive emotions of success, of a reward from all of his hard work and investment. But there was a dark side to the episode as well... the suspect's beating reminding him of Jacob's experience.

Stepping out onto the roof and half-watching for the G-1 to return, Gabe realized he was troubled by more than just memories of that horrible night with his son. The ass whooping he'd just witnessed was not the major factor in his funky mood either. The amount and duration of the violence captured by the Gripen's camera was insignificant as compared to a good bar brawl or gang fight. Most G-rated movies contained more grit.

No, what was eating at Gabe's soul was the fact that it was the police who had crossed the line. The men who were paid to protect and serve had become the judge and jury, and they had taken it upon themselves to issue the punishment. Public servants... peace officers... government authority... it was all so fundamentally wrong, and that was making him ill.

For the first time in his life, Gabe could relate to the feelings experienced by an abused child. He had just witnessed the trusted guardian, the authority figure charged with protection, suddenly become violent. And for no good reason.

Gabe didn't know what accusation had been leveled against the trampled man, had zero idea of what had been said during the pre-beating exchange with the cops. According to the law, the suspect's words didn't matter: foul language, insults, or calling the cops names should have no bearing on an officer's handling of the situation. Everyone was supposed to be innocent until proven guilty. What the Gripen had just recorded wasn't the American way.

As he mulled over what he'd just viewed, a slight buzzing noise sounded from the east. Gabe looked up to see the Gripen approaching, the steady drum of its propellers nearly inaudible until the machine was decreasing its altitude and making for the rooftop landing zone.

He watched the flying robot lower gently onto the pad, and then shut down its electric motors. The video and audio files had long since been transferred back to the main servers, two backup copies probably working their way through encrypted cloud storage even before the drone had flown away from the crime scene. Again, Gabe was proud of his accomplishment. "Now the game begins," he said to the silent robot. "Now things start getting serious."

Chapter 8

Peelian Principle

The securing and training of proper persons is at the root of police efficiency.

The squawk of Tony's cell phone roused the assistant DA from his dreams. With a scowl he snarled, "What now," reaching toward the nightstand, fumbling for the offending device.

"Tony," he answered, squinting at the small, but bright display.

"You better switch on the news," Karen's voice advised. "This is weird."

"Yes, ma'am… but… news? What time is it?"

Breathing hard, she answered, "It's 5:30 AM, Sleeping Beauty, and I am running on a treadmill at the gym. I'm watching the morning show on channel 17, but I'm sure all of the local networks are covering the same thing. Call me back when you are coherent."

He found the remote and flipped on the bedroom TV. It took a few more clicks before he found a news station.

"Channel 21 Eyewitness News received this video last night from an anonymous source. It shows an interaction between what appears to be Houston Police officers and an as of yet unidentified suspect. We want to warn you, the content of this clip is troubling."

Tony watched what appeared to be a standard police encounter, noting the number of officers and suspects. At first, he thought the footage was from just another cell phone video, snapped by some onlooker who happened to be in the area. He assumed the elevated angle of the recording was likely someone in a high-rise office building pointing a camera down at the incident.

But when the police started using force, the image gradually changed, obviously being adjusted to see inside the ring of officers surrounding the suspect.

The attorney had to admit it was excellent camera work, the image stable and clear. But how had it been done?

Standing in front of his television, barefoot and in boxer shorts, the attorney stood mesmerized by both the scene and the technology used to capture it. "How in the hell..." he started to question, watching the prone man take several blows from the cops.

The video ended with the suspect finally shoved into the back of a police car. But then something really odd happened. A solid white screen appeared, with the black words, "Citizens Observation Committee – Police Brutality Will Not Be Tolerated."

Tony was shocked, his thoughts interrupted by the anchor's voice returning to the air. "Again, Eyewitness News 21 received this video, in its entirety, via an anonymous email late last night. Our video engineers have verified its authenticity, but are unable to determine exactly how it was recorded. Joining me now in the studio, and making a rare on-camera appearance, is our executive producer, Carl Whitfield."

The broadcast changed to a scene of two men sitting behind the news desk. "Carl," the announcer continued, "you have over 30 years of experience with video technology. Before we went on the air, you told me this recording was an extremely interesting piece of work. Could you explain to our viewers exactly what is so intriguing about this example?"

"Sure," replied the obviously uncomfortable gent sitting beside the on-air personality. "The quality of this recording is far and beyond the capabilities of any cell phone or handheld movie camera I've ever seen. Its pixel density and sound characteristics are equal to Hollywood movie studio equipment, and yet it obviously was created on a mobile platform."

"So this wasn't recorded by someone just passing by the scene?"

Carl shook his head and then seemed to remember he was on the air. "No, I don't believe it was. If you watch the video frame by frame, there is no evidence of any editing or tampering. Whoever recorded this had access either to a crane or some other aerial device, in addition to some very expensive hardware."

The studio cameraman then focused back on the anchor's face. "Thank you, Carl. Our researchers here at Channel 21 have been unable to locate any information regarding the Citizens Observation Committee. Your Eyewitness News Team has, however, verified that HPD did respond to a call at the corner of West 34th and Baker Avenue at the exact time and date noted on the video. We are awaiting verification that the recording is from that incident, as well as further details of any arrests made at that time. Moving on to your morning weather forecast...."

Tony muted the television, his mind processing dozens of questions at once. Padding to the kitchen, he put on a pot of water to heat for instant coffee. The only thing he knew with certainty was that he wasn't going back to bed.

He'd spent the previous evening preparing the captured video for delivery to all of the local newshounds, a task that was complicated by the need to set up dead-end email accounts. Using an abundance of caution, he'd actually created and utilized the fictitious addresses while riding up and down the city's metro rail line, using an open laptop, just like the dozens of other passengers aboard the electric train. Access to the internet had been accomplished via a no-contract phone's WIFI hotspot. The cell had been wiped clean, crushed, and deposited in a dumpster after the last email was on its way across the digital landscape. It was the most expensive email package he'd ever distributed, but it was untraceable. The peace of mind he felt was well worth the extra expense.

It had seemed like an eternity passed while he waited for the morning news programs to splash his masterpiece. Far too keyed up to sleep, Gabe had occupied himself installing the latest upgrade to the system software. He had requested the modifications a few weeks ago, hoping the new code would allow even faster response times and more automatic transfers to and from the drone's computer brain.

After spending the morning flipping channels and relishing the results of his work, he'd finally grown tired of the same old news being repeated over and over again. He could finally sleep, confident that all of his time, expense, and effort were paying off. Jacob's death would have meaning after all.

He awoke several hours later, refreshed with a newfound purpose and reinforced vigor. After a quick meal, he returned to assembling the G-2's final components.

The hours passed, the next generation drone taking shape on the large worktable. Gabe, working with an expensive digital kitchen scale, was using the household hardware to weigh and log each component before attaching it to the new airframe. The goal was to reduce the drone's girth by nearly two ounces in order to extend its maximum flying time.

A beeping arose from the control panel.

The new software was working, he quickly surmised, abandoning what he termed "playing with the erector set," and moving to gaze at the bank of computer screens. The system was sounding an alarm beep, the electronic brain having recognized certain words streaming across the police radio. Gabe hustled to sit down, rapidly performing the now almost-routine actions required to launch G-1.

"At least it's nighttime," he whispered. "Maybe my little toy will get a chance to show off its real technological capability this time."

What had attracted the computer's attention was a call for a SWAT team, an armed suspect barricaded inside an apartment. Shots had been fired.

The Gripen performed flawlessly, zooming over the suburban landscape at 250 feet like a hawk chasing a mouse across the field. Again, the monitors displayed a large cluster of flashing emergency lights, announcing that the drone had indeed arrived at the correct location.

The G-1's microphone began eavesdropping, easily picking up the conversation and commands of the on-site supervisor. The suspect was currently barricaded in a second-story apartment. Apparently, when the cops had tried to serve an outstanding warrant, he had fired two shots.

It was some time later that Gabe discovered a major weakness in his system. SWAT teams specialized in negotiating with suspects, taking their time in order to accomplish their primary objective and "talk the suspect down." After hovering for close to an hour, it became evident that the Gripen didn't have enough battery power to wait out the lengthy arbitration process.

Gabe rotated the drone's camera, trying to identify a suitable location to land his flying machine until the action started. He wanted the drone's cameras to remain focused on the scene while stopping the electric motor's thirsty drain on the batteries. This minor adjustment to his plan morphed into quite the challenging task.

Pulling up a publicly available satellite photo of the area, he searched for just the right landing spot, but there wasn't one available. While he could detect plenty of flat, unobstructed rooftops in the vicinity, none of them provided an unobstructed view of the suspect's apartment.

Finally, he decided to touch down and trust the radio to handle the work. While he wouldn't be able to hear nearly as much information as the drone's on-scene microphones, he hoped he would have enough notice coming across the police scanner to get the G-1 re-launched and into position.

He spied an apparently abandoned gas station less than four blocks away from the standoff. Slowly maneuvering the G-1 over the structure's flat roof, he gently decreased the machine's altitude.

Implementing his scheme was far more difficult than he'd imagined. There was a slight delay between his commands and the Gripen's response. That time lag was further enhanced by the gap in video feedback displayed on the monitor. After a few white-knuckle moments, the drone was safe and sound, it's altimeter reading 4.6 meters and refusing to drop any lower. The camera confirmed it was resting safely on the metal pavilion that protected customers from the elements while they filled their tanks.

Gabe sat for what seemed like hours, trying to filter the multitude of police voices discussing the scene, waiting for something to change. He'd actually nodded off in the control station's chair when the tone of the scanner's broadcasts changed. "I think he's coming out," an excited voice reported.

"Does he still have the weapon?" a different voice asked.

"Unclear."

Bolting upright, Gabe's eyes zeroed in on the G-1's battery indicator, his foggy brain having no idea how long he'd been sleeping. A few quick mental calculations indicated the unit contained about 20 minutes of on-scene time before having to start for home.

It took a bit longer to reprogram the drone's flight path, this being the first time he'd had to override an existing set of instructions remotely. Finally, the Gripen was airborne and moving the short distance toward the apartment complex.

The infrared cameras made the scene below crystal clear. A ring of man-shapes surrounded a three-story building, their outlines bulging with helmets, body armor, and chests swollen by pouches. It was easy for Gabe to pick out the SWAT team, their AR15-style battle rifles glowing with a unique heat signature.

With a delicate touch on the controls, he managed an angle on the apartment's door. Again, it was easy to zoom in on the right threshold, two heavily equipped officers bracketing the opening and clearly on high alert. The image was crisp enough to see the exit splinters of two bullet holes on the door's surface.

Using the Gripen's parabolic microphones, Gabe could hear their negotiations with the holdout. "Come on, Benny," one of the SWAT cops was saying through the door. "For the hundredth time, there's no way out of that apartment but through this door. It's getting late, dude.

Everybody's tired and getting itchy. Come on out, and let's just call it a night."

"Fuck you!" a muffled voice from inside yelled. "I ain't tired, and I know the minute I come through that door one of you fuckers is going to plug my ass."

"Nobody is going to shoot you, Benny. That shit only happens on TV. Put down the pistol; put your hands on your head, and come out. There are 15 damn television stations out here filming away. Ain't nobody getting shot unless *you* get stupid."

There was a pause, Benny obviously weighing his options. Again, his voice rang thick with defiance, "Bullshit! I know damn well what happens when you shoot at a cop."

"Are we going to go through this again? You already told me you didn't know they were cops. I heard you loud and clear. It's okay…. Shit happens…. Accidents are a part of life. I give you my word, Benny. Come out the right way, and nobody's going to get hurt. If the cops serving the warrant didn't identify themselves like you say, then no harm, no foul. Convince the judge of that, and you'll not be charged for the shooting."

"I don't believe you," the voice from inside the apartment shouted. "I'm as good as dead anyway, so you're going to have to bust through that door, and I'm taking as many of you bitches out as I can. I ain't going to spend any more time behind bars…. No way, no how. So come on in, Gents, and let's dance."

Gabe watched as the SWAT negotiator bent his head to a shoulder-mounted radio. The video stream was like watching a badly translated movie, a slight delay between the officer's movements and his lowered voice rumbling over the scanner. "He's not going for it. Let's take this up a notch. Bring up the breaching team."

There was movement in the foreground, the rapid hustle and flash of more man-shapes. Before Gabe could zoom the camera back, the two officers bookending the apartment door were joined by several others, all of them hugging the outer wall of the structure.

"Stun grenade through the window?" whispered one of the new arrivals.

"No, he's got a mattress blocking the glass on the inside. The door is the only way," the tense responder advised.

Keeping low, two of the officers cut out of line, one of them wielding what appeared to be a heavy, round pipe with handles fused on the exterior. His partner was brandishing a shield. Gabe could see the team exchanging hand signals, and then the pipe was banging into the door, propelled with significant force by the burly cop.

The battering ram drew back for a second strike, but then the door flew inward, immediately followed by a man appearing in the doorway, his hand firing a pistol at the opening.

A nearby SWAT officer tossed something into the apartment.

The officer manning the battering ram ducked low behind the shield as twinkles of light continued to flash from inside the doorway. And then the entire interior of the apartment blinked bright white, as if a bolt of lightning had suddenly struck from the heavens. "A flash-bang grenade," Gabe whispered. "Damn."

The thunderous explosion was still echoing through the control room when the first cop entered the breach, his rifle high and sweeping. Gabe heard another shot, obviously the suspect's pistol, and then the officer's rifle ignited with a roar that sounded more like a buzz saw than a discharging weapon.

A few heartbeats later, it was over. The cops poured into the small dwelling, weapons on shoulders, sweeping right and left. Soon the interior was full of light, and the scene suddenly transformed to a cluster of armored-up men standing around, completely relaxed.

A blinking light on the monitor drew Gabe's attention back to his equipment. The G-1's battery was getting low. It was time to bring her home.

Gabe retired to his apartment after his flying-baby had returned to her crib. His mind was busy with engineering problems, mulling around such puzzles as extending the Gripen's air time and expanding its coverage of the city.

After making a BLT on sourdough bread, he plopped on the new-smelling couch and flipped on the television. The evening news, as expected, was filled with the SWAT team's deployment and eventual shootout with the police. Gabe found it ironic that both the police and the reporter got it right.

The camera then switched to the grieving widow, her sobbing pleads difficult to make out. "He didn't even own a gun," she claimed. "The police haven't shown me any gun. My husband was executed, just like all those videos we keep seeing on TV."

There were a bunch of neighbors and family surrounding the woman, all of them nodding their support, a few shouted out slogans of distrust and discontent toward the cops.

"You're right not to trust them," Gabe whispered to the boob tube. "But not this time. They called it straight."

The picture then turned to the HPD spokesman, who ran with the tried and true line that he couldn't comment on an ongoing investigation.

Gabe smirked, "There's not anything ongoing about it – the man shot at the cops, and they shot back. He's dead. End of story."

After finishing his sandwich, Gabe realized the irony of his defending the police. After what they'd done to his son... after all the pain they had caused his family, why did he feel compelled to stick up for the cops?

That line of thinking directed him down another mental corridor, and its substance was troubling to the core of Gabe's beliefs. This new logic dictated a new, perhaps unwelcome, philosophical epiphany. *Maybe the fault lies elsewhere,* the tormented father considered. *Maybe people like the man in the shootout were to blame for Jacob's death.* Gabe had only been monitoring the police for a few days, but already a vine of sympathy was sprouting in the forest of hatred that he felt towards the men in blue.

It wasn't that abuse was ever justified. Gabe could never go there. No, what he was beginning to sense was an understanding of what prompted the cops to perform such acts of brutality. They were dealing with everything from the mentally ill to the species' most vicious criminals. He wondered how the officers who were involved in today's shooting would cope when they ventured home to their own families. How would they interact with the wife and kids? Were they somehow able to just shake off the adrenaline rush of a combative citizen at will? Was that even possible? Did their jobs engender undue stress on their personal relationships?

Two days after the SWAT incident, Gabe was again taking a break and watching the local news. He was surprised to see the shooting was again dominating the headlines.

The victim's family had contacted a nationally known civil rights activist and requested his assistance in the effort to prove HPD's trigger finger had erred against an innocent man. One of the anguished family members was filmed, distraught and proclaiming, "Those cops just gunned Benny down in cold blood. The people have to take back this city."

The newscast displayed said activist, surrounded by several citizens, barking harsh accusations into the microphone. Gabe had to admit, the gentleman had all of his duck-facts in a row, spouting the same statistics and numbers he'd uncovered shortly after Jacob's death. *Wasn't the internet a wonderful thing*, he mused.

Again, he was plagued with indecision. The G-1 knew the truth, had it documented on both audio and video. The cops had played it fair and square, and his recordings would expose that reality beyond any shadow of a doubt. Should he reveal the facts?

While it was true that his recent experiences with stalking the police had rounded off a few of the sharper edges of his negative attitude toward law enforcement, Gabe still hated the authorities for what they had done to his son.

He now believed that the police, in conjunction with the governmental entities empowered to hold them accountable, were playing a statistical game... weighing the odds. As long as there was more "good" being accomplished than "bad," the scales of justice were balanced. Sure, occasional mistakes were made; people were hurt; lives were lost – but the overall numbers were positive for society. Those who were harmed, falsely imprisoned, or killed, could sue to acquire "monetary justice."

Adam Barlow had, in a way, seconded that very notion. The attorney, having functioned in the inner workings of the justice system for many years, couldn't understand why Gabe was so intent on pursuing a change. More than once, the legal eagle had advised his client, "Just take the money. Move away to some glorious paradise, and forget Houston ever existed. The cash can't bring Jacob back, but it can help with the healing."

Even Sandy, loving mother of a murdered child, had experienced a similar resolution. She had left him, more or less, over that single point of contention. "Let it go," she had begged him.

There was no simple explanation for how such a system composed of non-working checks and balances had come into being. Like organic matter creeping through excruciatingly slow, Darwinist changes, he was sure it had developed, morphed, and advanced in its complexity over time. Eventually, it was not only capable of survival; it had been ingrained with the skills necessary to dominate its sometimes weaker, nobler ancestor.

But the system was still wrong, clearly not the American way.

A justice system based on majorities wasn't what the founding fathers had in mind. Statistical means and averages weren't part of the law.

The principle was as old as society itself – restated and sanctioned generation upon generation. In the book of Genesis, the Christian Bible recounts the earliest example. Abraham was speaking with God about the destruction of Sodom, "Will you consume the righteous with the wicked?

What if there are fifty righteous within the city? Will you consume and not spare the place for the fifty righteous who are in it? What if ten are found there?"

God had endorsed the salvation of the innocent in the face of overwhelming wickedness, "I will not destroy it for the ten's sake."

Philosophers, lawmakers, and attorneys throughout the centuries have restated the same principle, now a cornerstone of our legal system – the presumption of innocence. The famous British jurist, William Blackstone touted its importance in 18th century England. His oft-quoted standard declared, "It is better that 10 guilty persons escape than one innocent suffer."

America's Benjamin Franklin echoed the same basic premise, which was expanded slightly by John Adams, asserting, "It is more important that innocence be protected than guilt be punished."

Yet, Jacob hadn't received any presumption of innocence, nor had some percentage of the citizens who encountered law enforcement. Gabe believed his son had been punished for some reason, known only to the mind of Officer James Marwick. And that violated everything he believed in, everything he had studied and adopted in this process of making Jacob's death count – from the Peelian Principles to the presumption of innocence.

The entire thought process drew Gabe back to the same starting point, the question of whether or not to divulge HPD's innocence in Benny's shooting. In the end, he cut through the rhetoric and examined the issue in its simplest terms. Certainly, one of Jacob Industry's goals was to protect the presumption of innocence. Secondly, the presumption of innocence in this case had to do with safeguarding HPD, who had acted professionally in this situation and had upheld the letter of the law. HPD was the blameless one here, and his video could prove that fact.

"I guess you'd better practice what you preach," he whispered to the television. "What's good for the goose is good for the gander. Presumption of innocence and the Peelian Principles are two-way streets."

Having made the decision to release his evidence regarding the SWAT team's breach, Gabe headed to the control room, finally comfortable with taking the high road. Right was right.

He was sitting down to prepare the files when the scanner software alerted to another HPD radio call. A man was walking through a park, supposedly carrying a gun.

The address was close, less than 20 minutes flight time for the Gripen. The weather was perfect, and in a matter of minutes, the G-1 was again soaring through the sky just as the sun was slipping over the evening's horizon.

With his attention divided between the monitor displaying the drone's flight and preparing the SWAT video for distribution, Gabe found himself again having more work than one man could handle. He wished he could bring someone else into the secret folds of the operation.

The city park proved to be a challenge for the G-1 and its array of optical cameras. Rather than a cluster of police focusing on a single location, this latest situation was more widespread and fluid.

The area in question was several blocks long and wide, with most of the cops converging on a wooded tract of land just south of a softball field. Initially, Gabe thought the solution was height, ordering his robot to 350 feet in order to provide a wider field of view and hopefully be able to follow the action.

But that didn't work, the heavy canopy of foliage blocking too much of the ground below.

He then zoomed in on the baseball diamond, finding the field vacant. Taking a huge risk, he ordered the Gripen to hover over the pitcher's mound at a height of 10 feet. "If any of the cops notice the drone, hopefully they'll think it is just a hobbyist taking advantage of the open spaces to play with his toy," he mumbled, trying to justify the bold move.

Such a low position required other modifications to the G-1's behavior as well. Gabe had to slowly spin the drone in order to scan the horizon and observe the greatest swath of territory. The tactic worked, but the change in protocol increased the diligence required by the operator to a nerve-racking level. For the first time, the Gripen's father was sweating as he manipulated his invention.

The radio helped Gabe coordinate his search as much as it did the swarm of cops moving through the area. When an officer reported, "I've got eyes on the suspect, 30 yards down the south hiking trail," Gabe knew where to position the G-1.

Before any of the police could approach, the Gripen was overhead. Gabe could clearly observe the suspect, casually strolling along the trail with what appeared to be a rifle case slung over his shoulder.

The pedestrian pulled up suddenly, no doubt hearing the shouted commands of two HPD officers hurrying up the path behind him. A moment later, the guy's hands were in the air.

Gabe turned on the microphone, listening with great interest to see how the exchange was taking place.

"Please set the case down on the ground, sir," one of the cops stated.

The fellow did as he was told without comment.

"What's inside?" the other policeman asked.

"None of your business, officer. Is there a problem?" the overwhelmed and startled hiker replied.

The cop didn't like the citizen's reply. "We had reports of a man walking through the park with a rifle. You're the only person we've seen matching the description. Is there a weapon inside that case?"

"No," the man reported confidently. "There is not a rifle inside that case."

More officers were arriving on the scene, the sole pedestrian now finding himself surrounded by a ring of pumped-up cops.

"Do you have identification, sir?" asked another of the recent arrivals.

"No, I don't carry my wallet when I walk these trails. I lost it some years ago while on a hike, and the hassle of getting all those cards and my driver's license replaced was major bullshit."

That answer didn't seem to please the police either. "You mean you don't have any ID on your person?" barked another officer, his voice dripping with disbelief.

"No, officer, I do not. I wasn't going to be driving a car or buying anything, so my billfold is at home on the dresser. Is it illegal to walk through the park without ID?"

"Yes, you are required to have identification in the state of Texas," replied the officer.

Gabe's attention piqued at that remark, knowing damn well that there was no such law. The cop was deliberately misleading the guy. Why?

"I don't believe that's accurate, officer," the confident fellow came back. "But if you're right, and I'm wrong, I guess you'll just have to arrest me."

"Let us verify you don't have a weapon inside that case, and I'm sure we can let it go," the mouthy cop countered.

Gabe shook his head, almost admiring the crafty policeman. They needed probable cause to search the case. Either that or the owner's permission. The lie about the ID law had been designed to obtain the suspect's permission, but he didn't fall for it.

"No, sir, I do not consent to my property being searched. Even if I did have a weapon inside, that isn't illegal either. Is there anything else? Am I free to go?"

The G-1's cameras clearly indicated the police didn't like the park-walker's question. Gabe could see two of the cops raise up on the balls of their feet, a third moving closer to the "suspect."

If he sensed it, the surrounded citizen didn't show any indication of hostility. He stood with his arms at his sides, calmly peering at the cop directly in front of him.

"How do we know you're not a felon?" the next questioner fired. "You're right in that carrying a long gun isn't illegal in Texas, unless you're a convicted felon. But you won't show us any ID, so there's no way to be sure."

"Do you naturally assume everybody you approach is a criminal, officer?"

Now the cop was getting mad, his elevated emotion bleeding through in his voice. "I do when they won't show me any fucking ID and act like an asshole. Please turn around and spread your arms. I'm going to frisk you to make sure you're not carrying a weapon."

"Why? Why are you doing this?" the guy asked, now getting upset.

"Officer safety," came the harsh response. "We have the right to frisk you in order to verify you're not carrying any sort of weapon while we are conducting an investigation."

The citizen actually laughed, pivoting his head to the gang of officers that had him surrounded. "There are seven of you and one of me. I don't think you're in much danger, sir. Am I free to go?"

The answer to the question came in the form of a physical assault, a policemen coming up from behind the walker and throwing him violently to the ground. Less than a second later, the huddle had formed.

Gabe couldn't believe what he was seeing, the encounter surfacing a cruel realization that Jacob had most likely suffered in a similar way. Sure, the guy hadn't just exactly kissed the cop's ass, but he had every right to refuse the search. It didn't matter what he said or how he acted, the police had no authority to act as judge, jury, and executioner.

Just like on the recording of Jacob's encounter, the cops played it to the hilt, shouting for the suspect to "Stop resisting," and they pummeled and kicked the now-screaming citizen.

Gabe could see one officer stepping on the man's elbow, intentionally pinning it down while his comrade continued shouting, "Put your hands behind your back! Stop resisting!" The unfolding drama was sickening.

Another cop was already looking inside the rifle case, pulling out a long, black-colored tube that Gabe immediately identified as a pool cue. There were other accessories inside, including a nice looking table-brush, a set of billiard balls, and various chalks.

Thankfully, the beating ceased as soon as the non-weapon had been exposed. Still, Gabe could see the moaning, handcuffed victim lying on the ground, a huge patrolman with his knee resting on the fellow's skull.

Gabe's attention was then drawn to two officers who moved off to the side, a confidential conversation now taking place.

"We have got to rack something up on this guy now," the one officers began, his muted tone still audible to the G-1's sensitive microphone.

"Resisting, obstruction, and trespassing should do the trick. He's going to raise a stink, but the DA's offer to drop the charges should keep his mouth shut. He'll probably lick his wounds and fade away."

"I would have sworn he had a weapon in that case. Why the hell wouldn't he let us look?"

The older of the two officers shook his head, "Who knows? All I can say is if you act guilty, you are gonna be treated as if you're guilty. Besides, this guy's attitude sucked. Maybe he'll think twice about getting shitty with the cops the next time. Let's haul him back to the cruiser and take him in. I'll call the DA on the way."

After watching the handcuffed walker being escorted back to a waiting patrol car, Gabe ordered the G-1 home. He was having second thoughts about helping out the SWAT officers, the display of brutality and abuse he'd just witnessed influencing his mood more so than he'd ever thought possible. He could hear the citizen's cries of agony echoing through his head - could substitute Jacob's voice without using much imagination.

Despite only a few minutes of actual clock time passing, it seemed to Gabe like it took the drone forever to return home. Like a kid on Christmas morning, he was anxious to start packaging the new recordings. Once again, his faith in the mission of JI was refueled. Feeling like the cause was indeed righteous, he was again confident that he was traveling down an honorable path.

"I'll expose both incidents," he surmised. "The park's bad news will bury the SWAT team's good, and from what I just saw, that's the way it should be."

Chapter 9

Peelian Principle

No quality is more indispensable to a policeman than command of temper. A quiet, determined manner has more effect than violent action.

Karen's phone had exploded with activity, the mayor, council members, and patrolmen's union all demanding both her wisdom and a course of action. In fact, her personal and office lines were so inundated, the police commissioner hadn't been able to get through, finally resorting to summoning her via messenger. It was an all-hands-on-deck emergency meeting at city hall.

The dust had quickly settled after the first video of the convenience store incident, most of the city's upper management too busy to let an isolated occurrence divert their busy schedules. But now there were three recordings being shown over and over again, prompting everyone from the press corps to the civil rights organizations to whip up outrage in the Houston community.

Even the national networks were calling every extension in her office, begging for some sort of official comment or reaction. Fox News had left no less than 30 messages on her voice mail, CNN and the other cable outlets not far behind.

But there was nothing she could say, and that didn't set well with the powerful woman. DA Sanders wasn't fond of ignorance, nor did she appreciate the outside interference burdening her already over-taxed staff.

The conference room was filled with uniforms and elected officials, most gathered in small cliques here and there, whispering in hushed conversations.

Evidently, she'd been the last to report, as the mayor brightened upon her entry and immediately called the meeting to order. "Let's get started, people," she said. "We've got a lot to cover."

After a quick flock to the table, Houston's first lady nodded toward the police commissioner and said, "Charlie, I understand you have new information, please open the meeting."

"Yes, Madam Mayor, one of our technical staff informed me just a few minutes ago that the video images being messaged to the local news stations were created with a drone."

"A drone?" everyone seemed to ask at once, and then several conversations started simultaneously, all the attendees trying to ask questions or discuss the revelation at the same time.

"Please! Everyone! Please let the commissioner continue," the mayor shouted, settling down the room.

Nodding toward the large screen at the one end of the conference table, the city's top cop stood and strolled purposefully toward the newly appearing projection. The image was a still shot, displaying an overhead view of a park-like setting. All of the attendees knew exactly which recording produced the frame, the local news stations cycling the clip to the point of nausea.

"You can spot its shadow, right here," the commissioner stated, pointing toward a small dark space on the ground that 99.9% of the population would never notice. "My experts are certain that's the drone's shadow."

"That would make sense," the chief interjected. "The angle, clarity, and stability of the three videos had been a mystery. Somebody has a very sophisticated toy, and that stalker is following my men around making home movies. Wonderful."

The mayor peered at Karen, as did most of the room. "What can be done about this, Ms. Sanders?"

"Off the top of my head, without any research, I can't think of a single law that is being broken," the DA replied. "Flying a drone isn't illegal. There are no city ordinances prohibiting such activity and no state or federal laws that I'm aware of."

"Doesn't the Federal Aviation Administration have restrictions or rules regarding such activities?" someone asked from the end of the mahogany table. "I keep reading about drones causing near-misses with commercial aircraft."

Karen nodded, "Yes, they do, but those restrictions are fairly loose and as of right now, badly defined. I've not seen any video taken near an airport, nor have we seen any examples where the public has been in danger."

"It's no different than an illegal wiretap," the chief pushed back, his voice sounding near desperation. "Whoever is behind this has been listening to my men conduct their operations without a warrant. Surely we can do something about that?"

Again, Karen had to disagree. "No, it's not illegal as long as the recordings are taken in a public place. Having the drone camera is no different from having a cell phone camera with a microphone. The quality, or capability doesn't make any difference, and we all know of the court rulings that have clearly stated the police, when in public, have no right to an expectation of privacy."

Sighing loudly, the commissioner groaned, "We've got to do something. My officers are already suffering morale issues from having a hundred cell phones stuck in their faces on every arrest. Now they have to be aware of the skies, too? We're going to end up with a police force that is scared to make a move for fear that some jerk with a vendetta is going to chop up a video to make the cops look bad, and then share it with the world."

"Are you saying these videos were tampered with, Commissioner?" Karen asked.

"No... we have no evidence of that at the moment."

"Didn't one of the recordings actually support your men?" came a question from further down the table.

"Yes, it did," answered the chief. "But we all know bad news makes it around the world before good news has breakfast. I have not heard one single newscast or read any articles that point out the positive in this story."

"Then I'd tell your men to stop beating the shit out of our citizens," the smug voice of one of the councilmen interjected, a man known to be at odds with the chief regarding several incidents of police brutality. Then, without waiting for any response, he glared at the mayor and said, "And if you're thinking of passing some half-assed city ordinance prohibiting the use of drones, you can forget about it. I know I've got enough votes on the council to block any such move."

Tempers, on both sides of the issue flared, the room erupting with voices debating the harsh, but true statement.

"People!" the mayor shouted. "Settle down! Order!"

It took a few moments for sentences to be finished and final statements to be made, but the group of movers and shakers finally quieted. It was Karen who broke the silence, "Look, we all know I can indict a ham sandwich if I want to. We clearly have an overzealous citizen who has taken a bold step. My concern and duty is for the public safety, first and foremost. I think we should investigate this matter, under the guise that this activity could lead to potential risks for the public at large. What if this drone crashes into a moving school bus of children? What if an officer is distracted and is harmed? I need someone to knock on my door with a name and address of an individual, and then I can take action. In the meantime, my hands are pretty much tied."

The mayor smiled, pleased that someone had finally made a positive suggestion. Both the police commissioner and the chief looked happier than before.

"But how do we go about finding the drone's operator?" the city attorney asked. "Do we bring in the military with some sort of radar? How do we track down the owner?"

The chief shook his head, "When I heard it was a drone, I stepped outside and made a quick call to an old friend who is a recently retired Air Force General. He told me a small, most likely plastic flying machine like a drone would be nearly impossible to track on radar, even utilizing a ground-based unit like the one the Army uses to protect its troops. They're pretty stealthy."

"What about finding out who sells such equipment and tracking down who made a purchase in our area?"

The commissioner responded, "My technical guys think this specific unit is homemade. They're unaware of any commercially available drone that has the same capabilities. We've seen image stabilization, infrared, zoom-capable cameras, and very fast response times. This isn't a machine someone ordered from 'Drones Are Us.'"

The mayor, riding Karen's coattails and furthering her agenda, sounded from the head of the table. "I suggest our esteemed law enforcement begin an immediate investigation into the matter. Since I've been elected to this office, there have been many times I've been advised, 'Things will turn up; they always do.' While I never know the details of how that occurs, somehow... someone seems to make it happen. All I can say is let's hope this is another example."

"I don't think there is any need for cloak and dagger here. We should go public with this," the chief decided. "Maybe someone has seen the drone's handler or can provide a tip. I suggest we open up to the press and see what kinds of responses we get."

No one seemed to have an issue with the idea, so the mayor gave her blessing. "I'll have our PR people provide a statement, Chief. You'll have it by this afternoon."

The meeting adjourned a short time later, Karen neither pleased nor disappointed in the outcome. On one hand, she had more information than before, and that knowledge reflected a positive light on her mood. On the other, she was going to have to begin prosecuting cops, and that was a huge negative hanging over her head.

Gabe knew they would be coming. The public outcry over his videos was dictating the news cycle, with everyone from the ACLU to an assortment of police unions joining the fray.

It was amazing to watch the lines being drawn, the list of those supporting his endeavor as surprising as those who opposed. One thing was consistent and predictable, however – the cops weren't happy campers.

While he'd taken every step to ensure secrecy, Gabe was sure they'd eventually find him. Everyone makes mistakes, and the creation of Jacob Industries had been a complex gauntlet to navigate. While he was sure Adam wouldn't violate the sacred attorney-client privilege, somewhere, somehow, they'd track him down.

The trick was to delay the inevitable until he'd garnered enough support to fight off the onslaught of a pissed-off justice system. If he could get the people behind him, his chances of surviving the attack were greatly improved.

And so far, the results had been positive.

National commentators were going on the record in support of the "Houston Archangel," as one nightly journalist had dubbed Gabe's alter ego. But support wasn't unanimous. More than a few noted newscasters and legislators had expressed concern about personal liberties and raised the now common debate about intrusion into the privacy of all Americans. The military had been using drones for years, as had the U.S. Border Patrol. Those activities, combined with the NSA's notorious spying, had raised all kinds of concerns. The Gripen had merely marshalled the argument into a new phase of reality.

Fear of copycats was something Gabe hadn't anticipated. Police departments all over the nation were on high alert, voicing their concerns that the public would be at risk if every cop hater in the country began filling the urban skies with machines that could target law enforcement. *Today, these machines are only carrying cameras, but tomorrow it could dive bomb a hostage negotiator,* one top ranking police chief grumbled.

Even the feds got involved, the head of the FAA holding a news conference warning of harsh penalties and jail time if that agency's regulations were violated. Gabe had to smirk when the bloated Washington bureaucrat warned of the dangers involved, even going so far as to state, "When one of these hobby machines drops an airliner full of innocent people, the operator will be charged with capital murder."

"Oh, yeah," Gabe had snapped back at his television, "the cops are killing far more people per year than are riding on any one airplane. We'd have to drop an entire fleet of airliners to equal the death toll, so just shove it, buddy."

Now that the authorities had figured out his operation, it was time to take the next step, and that meant mobility.

There was one event that could potentially tie Gabe directly to the drones, and that was someone spotting the G-1 returning to its home base. If a random witness reported such an observation to the authorities, his strategy to rebalance the scales of justice would be blocked in a matter of hours.

Jacob Industries' new office complex was the perfect solution in all regards, with one exception – JI was the building's only tenant. Even the dumbest detective could figure out that a multi-level, commercial building should command more than one vehicle in the parking lot.

The only solution Gabe could envision was varying his base of operations – going mobile. He'd considered having multiple locations to launch and land his flying robots, but in the end decided that would only increase the odds of discovery. No, the smart money was on mobile launch and retrieval.

Fortunately, the Gripen was a slight machine that didn't require massive landing facilities. Its battery charger plugged into any wall socket.

With all that in mind, he'd arrived at a simple, effective solution – the pickup truck.

The drone would easily fit inside the bed, the flying machine's amazing stability more than capable of touching down in the confined area. The truck was obviously mobile and hardly noticeable given the number of similar vehicles that plied Houston's roadways on any given day.

Having settled on a strategy, Gabe soon found himself at the truck accessory store, shopping for some sort of cover for his pickup's bed. The number of options was dizzying.

He could buy soft covers, hard covers, electric covers, and folding covers. There were models from a variety of manufacturers, some even providing matching paint jobs. Who knew?

Finally picking an electrically operated roll-up model, Gabe perused a popular hunting magazine while he sat waiting for the installation to be completed. He glanced up from the page when a familiar voice sounded from the door.

"I thought that was you," Chip announced, moving over to shake Gabe's hand. "How the hell are you, stranger?"

After recovering from the mild shock, Gabe stood and returned the greeting. "Chip, it's so good to see you. Oh my God, what's it been? Seven, eight months?"

"At least," replied Manny's father. "I've started to pick up the phone and call you a dozen times, but you know how it goes. Amanda and I were so upset after Jacob's funeral… and it took months before Manny got over her grief."

Gabe nodded his understanding, "I feel the same way, Chip. I'm a little embarrassed that I've let so much time pass by without at least calling to say hello. So what's going on? How is everybody?"

A sad expression flickered across Chip's face, but only for a moment. "Things were a little rough there for a while," he stated in a low tone, moving closer to keep the conversation private. "I lost my job after being arrested, you know. Amanda and I had depended on my income to keep our heads above water. For several months, I thought we were going to lose the house and everything."

Puzzled, Gabe frowned. "I thought all the charges against you were dropped? You lost your job?"

Nodding in disgust, Chip snarled, "Yeah. Our company had a policy about arrests. Can you imagine that? And then there was all the time off fighting city hall. Who knew – right? Anyway, by the time I cleared my name and paid for a blood-sucking lawyer, Amanda and I were broke. I took a job here, installing truck covers just to make ends meet. It was the only thing I could find, the only place that would even talk to me after finding out I had an arrest record for assaulting a police officer."

Gabe was shocked and embarrassed that he hadn't checked up on his friend. "I'm so sorry, Chip. I wish I had known. I might have been able to help."

"When I heard about your settlement, I thought about asking you for a loan, but then I remembered about all those stories you read... the ones about people winning the lottery and every half-baked relative and former acquaintance appearing out of nowhere with their hands extended. I just couldn't do that."

Again, Gabe felt terrible. Chip was an honorable guy who had done the right thing. Without his help, Jacob Industries and the drones would still be a dream.

"Didn't you file your own suit?" Gabe asked, trying to salvage some of his own personal dignity.

"Yeah, we did. It's still pending, but I don't have much hope. There wasn't any video showing what the cops did to me, and that weakens my case considerably. The city is stalling, filing motions to reschedule, and all kinds of legal mumbo-jumbo. I don't hold out much hope, and the expense is killing us."

"How's Manny doing?" Gabe asked, wanting to change the subject.

"She's doing well in school, making some inroads to try and live a normal life. Jacob's death tore her up pretty good, Gabe. There for a while, her mother and I were worried she might try and follow him... if you know what I mean."

Before Gabe could say anything, a voice sounded from back inside the shop's garage area. "Hey, Chip, the truck in bay number two is ready for ya."

"Gotta run," Chip said. "I can't afford to lose this job. It was great talking to you, Gabe. I'm glad you hurt those son of a bitches... glad you hurt 'em bad. Give me a call sometime, would ya?"

"Sure, Chip. I promise."

And then he was gone, leaving Gabe in the waiting area, alone with his thoughts.

Retaking a seat, he ignored the magazine that had previously held his attention, so angry with himself that he could only stare at the floor. "What a self-centered piece of shit you are, Gabriel Chase. How uncaring and selfish can a man be?"

He'd been so wrapped up in revenge, so consumed with his own problems and issues. Any idiot would've realized that his family wasn't the only one being wrecked by the events of that night. Even the most antisocial fool would have at least called and checked up on the other victims.

For a moment, he tried to displace the anger and remorse, making a vain attempt to transfer part of the blame to Chip and Amanda. But it wasn't righteous or fair. If nothing else, the Dentons had shown unbelievable honor and respect by keeping their problems to themselves. "Now that's a true friend and a big man," Gabe whispered to the empty lobby. "What a stand-up kind of guy."

It then occurred to Gabe that perhaps fortune was on his side, yet again.

Chip would be the perfect employee for JI. The man was obviously motivated against ruthless law enforcement, having direct knowledge, and firsthand experience of the problem.

Not only was the man honest and upstanding, his actions that night had shown guts and a capability to handle pressure.

But would he be interested in such a dangerous endeavor?

"It won't hurt to ask," Gabe finally mumbled.

Before long, the shop announced that his truck was finished, the new bed cover installed and tested. As he sauntered out to the parking lot, Gabe spied Chip working on another vehicle in the bay. He strolled over and said, "Hey, Buddy, what time do you get off today?"

"Around five, unless a job holds me over."

"Can I pick you up at quitting time this afternoon? I have a business proposition for you... one I think you'll like. Let's get together over coffee and talk it over."

Taking a step forward with a smile, Chip said, "Oh, Gabe, I didn't mean to lay a guilt trip on you. You don't owe me a thing. I appreciate the thought, but you've got your own troubles."

Gabe shook his head, "No, this isn't a guilt trip. Seriously, I've been looking for someone to help me with my new business venture, and after we just talked, I realized you might be the perfect fit. Please, sit and talk with me for a few minutes. If you don't think it's a good match, then no harm, no foul."

It didn't take Chip long to think it over. "You buying?" he asked with a grin.

"Sure am. Wouldn't have it any other way."

"Okay, cool. I'm not in a position to pass up a free cup of coffee. I'll see you around five."

Gabe exited the shop after verifying he could operate the new, electric bed cover. Glancing at his watch, he decided there was enough time to test his theory on mobile launch and recovery.

The first stop was back at JI's office, the heavy cases containing the G-2 unit loaded in short order. Next came the long drive out to the farm.

He drove around for a while, circling the remote property to ensure there weren't any prying eyes or nosey neighbors. Finally, parking well off the road on one of the many lanes crisscrossing the property, he began to assemble the next generation of his design.

The G-2 had extended range and a more advanced computer brain. With a high-speed, wireless link, Gabe could control the unit via a laptop computer sitting inside the truck's cab. While the resolution and capabilities weren't as sophisticated as the main control center back at the office, he thought it was good enough to do the job.

After assembling the Gripen-2, he set the ultra-light bird in the bed of the truck and then pressed the button to close the rollaway top. There was plenty of clearance.

Next, he reopened the mini launch bay and ordered the second generation, airborne spy to lift off.

Skyward it climbed, soaring toward the clouds just as he'd expected. After completing a quick aerial tour of the grounds, he ordered the drone home.

It was an amazing sight, watching the new Gripen glide in and hover above the truck's bed. Missing dead center by only a few inches, the G-2 touched down a few moments later, sheltered and secreted by the pickup's sheet metal walls.

With that test completed, Gabe again launched his flying robot, sending it on a preprogrammed course around the farm. After ensuring it was following the waypoints, he started up the truck and drove a half mile further down the lane.

"Come home," he commanded toward the heavens, fingers rapidly typing on the laptop's keyboard.

Just like before, the machine responded, appearing over the nearby patch of pine trees and sailing toward the back of the truck.

The unit's internal GPS was accurate to within 10 feet if the military wasn't scrambling the signal. Gabe noticed the autopilot was slightly off, but that wasn't a serious concern. He quickly disengaged the automatic control and took over manually. A few adjustments later, the Gripen landed gently in the bed of the pickup.

"Too easy," Gabe smiled. "Now let's go recruit a new employee. Together, we'll really give the cops something to think about."

The national reaction to the Archangel story coming out of Houston was widespread and intense. The media couldn't get enough. Sensing blood in the water, they swarmed like a school of hungry sharks. Voices from social media across all platforms from the White House to a plethora of police unions felt the need to chime in. Congressmen and Senators began calling press conferences; some for, some against the notion of private citizens monitoring the police.

Cable news commentators enjoyed a field day, many coming out in support of whoever was behind the airborne surveillance. Others were trying desperately to "shoot down," the concept.

As the day wore on, one overriding trend became clear. Those opposed to the Archangel were having trouble justifying their position.

"The police don't need to be distracted by some clown buzzing their heads with drones when they should be concentrating on catching the bad guys," spouted one retired police captain. "When one of our brave officers gets killed because he was ducking a flyby instead of watching the felon with the gun, I believe the Archangel should be brought up on murder charges."

The show's host didn't buy it. "In the three examples out of Texas, did the police even know the drone was there?" he asked coyly.

"I don't know. I wasn't there," the captain gruffly responded, taking the easy way out.

"Well, evidently the officers on the scene didn't know the drone was above them. I doubt they would have used such excessive force if they had realized they were under surveillance. And isn't that really the Archangel's goal?"

On and on the debate raged across the internet's blogs, radio talk shows, and television news programs.

By the time America was driving home from the office, two incidents of copycats were being reported. A drone operator in New Mexico had taunted the police as they made a traffic stop. Hovering in the distance, the machine monitored a rather annoyed looking state trooper as he wrote a speeding ticket. A crowd of onlookers had gathered nearby, breaking out in applause when the tiny robot had buzzed off.

One of the most telling stories to hit the national stage was a caller on a Houston radio program. "I was pulled over about a month ago," the man began. "The cop wanted to search my car. I refused. He got mad, saying that if I didn't have anything to hide, why did I care if he looked inside my car? So now, I want to ask the same question back to all the police bitching about the Archangel – if you don't have anything to hide, why do you care if the drone is watching you?"

It was the essence of a nationwide argument. *Why should the police be bothered if they weren't doing anything wrong?*

"Two-dimensional video always looks bad," responded one commentator. "Any time force is required by law enforcement, it is upsetting to the general public who may not know the suspect's criminal history. You may see the cops get a little rough with a guy and think it's excessive, but what you may not know is that the last time the officer approached that individual, the guy pulled a gun and started shooting."

Polling showed America was split on the topic, almost half of the people for, half against the monitoring of police officers as they performed their duties.

"We already have a system in place," pushed back one expert on an afternoon cable news show.

"It doesn't seem to be working," replied the host. "Only a small percentage of officers who receive complaints ever face criminal charges. As far as internal department disciplinary actions, the average penalty is three days without pay. Hardly a deterrent given the frequency of excessive force claims filed across the nation on a daily basis."

"If Americans truly believe the system isn't working, then they should fix it with their vote in the traditional way. Having some unregulated and uncontrolled outsider policing the police is just opening a can of worms and adding additional complexities to an already difficult problem."

Bringing democracy into the argument intensified the debate. Several people pointed out a nationwide trend – the correlation between the police unions' endorsements and the candidates who became district attorneys. One activist in New York City even went so far as to claim that there had not been a single DA elected in his lifetime who did not first win the highly coveted nod from the union. It did make folks wonder if the deck were stacked against a system of checks and balances.

And then there were the privacy advocates. In recent years, America had been racked by numerous reports of NSA and government spying. Much of the citizenry was already weary of Big Brother watching their every move, analyzing their emails, and eavesdropping on their phone calls. The concept of private individuals being able to perform the same intrusive acts sparked outrage by some.

Others, however, took a different position. If the government was spying on everyday citizens, why couldn't those common folk return the favor and spy right back? A few outliers even went so far as to advocate drones monitoring all branches of government, keeping an eye out for corruption, graft, and other abuses.

"The FBI could have 300 million informants if this trend continues," remarked one Senator who supported the Archangel's existence. "If every elected official, police officer, federal employee, and lobbyist thought a drone was keeping an eye on their activities, you might have a more affective government for the people. Fill the skies with eyes and ears, I say. Bring on the drones."

Of course, the predictable comparisons to George Orwell's famous novel, *1984*, filled the airwaves. Where would it end? Were Americans' bedrooms safe from prying eyes? Would any conversation ever be private again? Some argued that privacy was already an illusion in America.

Gabe, as he drove back from the country, was completely unaware of the commotion his machines were generating. Country and Western music filled the truck's passenger compartment, assisting the driver's elevated mood as he managed an easy pace through the winding, pastoral setting.

The passing greenery, combined with the day's technical successes, marked a welcome relief to the stressful, work-filled days of late.

As he approached the Houston metropolitan area, he considered switching to a more informative station, but decided against it. The headlines had grown mundane, and he didn't want anything to dampen his enthusiasm for the upcoming interview with Chip.

"That's you?" Chip spouted, almost spitting a mouthful of coffee. "*You're* the Archangel?"

Gabe merely nodded, concentrating on reading his friend's reaction. Would Chip be able to keep a confidence? Was he merely surprised? Or was Manny's father convinced his old friend had gone insane and couldn't wait to call the cops?

Shaking his head in disbelief, Chip continued, "I guess I should've known. Amanda and I thought you'd be off traveling the world, spending your money in an effort to forget what happened. I'm just stunned over this little revelation."

"I probably never seemed like the type to embark on something like this," Gabe admitted. "But letting Jacob's life end without meaning was simply unacceptable. Creating the drones was the only option I could come up with that was non-violent and might accomplish some good for the country. If nothing else, we might give other parents some level of peace over their teens' interactions with law enforcement."

Chip grunted, "I'm not so sure that I wouldn't have turned into an active shooter if I'd been in your shoes. But I've got to admit, your way is the better option."

"I need help, Chip. Are you interested?"

"Seriously? I thought you just wanted to get that dark secret off your chest. There's really a job?"

Gabe smiled, "Yes, I've got my hands full and could use another pair. Finding someone I could trust, as you might imagine, has proven to be difficult."

"What do you need me to do?"

"Assemble drones, drive them around for launch and recovery, keep an eye on the office, learn how to program them to run the missions…. You name it; I can use some assistance. How much were you making at your old job before that night with the cops?"

With a shy look, Chip divulged, "I was at 92K with pretty good insurance. Now, I'll be lucky to make 36 this year. Amanda found some part-time work at the school, but we're still pretty strapped."

"This job pays 110K per year, but no bennies as of yet," Gabe announced with a serious expression.

"What? Are you pulling my leg? That's an awful lot of money for a job that I'd be happy to do for free. You can count me in on anything that messes with those fucking cops."

Gabe smiled at the response, Chip's willingness to take on the authorities an important qualification. "No, I'm not pulling your leg. The hours will be a little strange, and I guarantee you'll earn your money. What do you say?"

It was easy to tell Chip was mulling it over. "I can't think of any drawbacks or negatives, other than probably getting the shit kicked out of me again if the cops catch us. Will this job require committing any felonies?"

"No, that's the best part," Gabe laughed. "As far as my attorney has been able to determine, we're not breaking a single law. Now you and I both know that doesn't mean shit these days, but for the record, we're legal beagles."

"And what would I tell Amanda?" came the most important question.

"Anything but the whole truth… for her own protection. I'm sorry to lay that job requirement on you, but we can't let anybody in on this. I would suggest you feed her the same line of crap that I gave the building's management office."

Gabe continued, explaining the little, white lie.

"Okay, I'm in. When do I start?"

Smiling and extending his hand, Gabe said, "As soon as possible. If you have to turn in a notice, I understand. If not, I'll see you tomorrow."

"Notice," Chip stated, waving his hand through the air, "I don't have to give those guys any notice. What time do we get started?"

After giving his new employee directions, Gabe asked Chip to be there around 8AM. "I'll give you the nickel tour," the entrepreneur mad scientist promised.

Chapter 10

Peelian Principle

Police must secure the willing cooperation of the public in voluntary observance of the law to be able to secure and maintain the respect of the public.

"We're going to hit that drug store on the corner right before they close," announced Tito. "It's the day after social security checks, and all of those old people go in to get their scripts filled. Most of them pay with cash, and that old fucker running the place gets too busy to run to the bank."

"Sounds like a plan," answered Jackson. "I could use a cash fix about now, and it sounds like an easy mark."

"I used to go in there for smokes before I got ratted out last time. There were always a lot of dollar bills stuffed in the drawer. We'll just wave our heat around, and they'll hand over the green. If anybody gets frisky, fire off a shot, and things will go our way."

"Where we going to hole up afterwards?" came the logical question.

"Now that's why I like working with you, Jackson. You're a man who thinks ahead... who has some experience under his belt. We'll exit out the back door... where there are no windows... and bust it over to Marco's. He's cool."

"Does he know we're coming?"

Laughing, Tito spun a finger around his ear. "Marco? Marco don't know shit. He's high as a fucking kite or crashed on that smelly-ass mattress of his. Attila the Hun could be holed up in his living room, and that crack head wouldn't know or care."

The two crooks remained parked on Tito's couch, watching an old movie and smoking cigarettes. Only occasionally did they glance out the dirty window to gauge how much light was left in the day.

At 8:45 PM, Jackson pointed to the revolver stuck in his belt and announced it was time to go. "Don't that store close at 9?"

"Let's roll," Tito responded, sticking a small, nickel plated automatic in his pocket.

It was only a few blocks to their mark, both men glancing all around to make sure there was no sign of any HPD cruisers rolling up on their heist. They entered the front door, only slightly annoyed by the old-fashioned bell that signaled their presence.

"May I help you?" greeted the ancient shopkeeper behind the counter.

Tito's weapon was drawn in a flash, Jackson showing his piece a split second later. "Empty the drawer, old man, and there won't be no trouble."

The pharmacy's proprietor had been robbed before, the appearance of the two pistols having little effect on his demeanor. "The kitty's empty, boys," he stated calmly. "I installed a new time activated safe after some punks cleaned me out last month."

To prove his point, the man behind the counter hit a button on the cash register and pointed to the empty drawer.

Tito's famous temper flashed, "Bullshit!" he snapped. "How were you going to make change if I wanted a pack of smokes or something? Where's the cash, you old fool? Tell me before I blow your fucking head off."

Instead of answering, the store's owner pulled out a small wad of one-dollar bills from his pocket. "This is all I got on me; take it if you want. Otherwise, I'd be hightailing it out of here if I were you. The kid working the back has already hit the alarm button. The cops will be here any minute."

Being a man who didn't handle failure well, Tito's anger flashed into an intense, uncontrollable rage. All humanity and reason abandoned his mind, all self-control evaporating in an instant. He pumped two shots into the old man's chest.

A moment later, the two empty-handed crooks tore out the front door, both of them hightailing it down the sidewalk toward Marco's dilapidated apartment. Everyone in the vicinity had heard the gunshots, everyone having a pretty good idea what had just happened. Robberies were common, assaults and muggings not unheard of.

Officer Kirkpatrick had just signed in when the call broke the radio's silence. A robbery, two armed suspects on foot, shots fired, and an ambulance requested.

Dole knew the address and neighborhood. He could visualize old man Roberson, the pharmacy's friendly owner who offered cops and their families a small discount whenever they stopped in. The family owned business was right in the middle of the precinct's worst neighborhood.

He and the other patrolmen would pop in now and then, mostly to buy some chips or an occasional caffeine-laced drink to make sure they stayed alert. Areas in decline, like the one surrounding the drug store, needed small businesses in order to recover and improve. If the cops could show their support, others in the area might take notice. It was a small thing, but every little bit helped.

Gabe heard the broadcast as well. While he was unfamiliar with the address and had no awareness of the area's deterioration, he had noted a higher than average number of calls in the general vicinity.

Chip was mobile, cruising around in the pickup, the G-2 charged and ready under the bed cover. He jumped when his cell rang.

"What's up?" Chip answered, already looking for a spot to hide the launch after spotting Gabe's caller ID flash on his phone.

"Are you ready? We've got our first one, and it's happening less than a mile from where you are."

"Give it to me – I'm ready," Chip responded with confidence, eyeing a carwash less than a block away.

"I just sent the package. It should show up in your inbox any second now. You know what to do…. Good luck."

Chip was turning into the currently unoccupied carwash when the laptop riding in the passenger seat chimed with the new message. Ignoring the computer for a few moments, he maneuvered the truck behind the empty stalls and into an area where islands of vacuum cleaners stood like robotic sentries guarding the empty lot.

Double-checking that he wasn't visible from the main road, Chip then opened the small computer and began the sequence he had practiced a dozen times under Gabe's watchful eye.

It took less than a minute for the course and coordinates to transfer into the G-2's memory, another few seconds to open the electric cover, exposing the Gripen. A series of keystrokes later the electric motors began to spin the propellers with an insect-like hum.

And then the machine launched, shooting heavenward at a rapid pace.

Chip closed the truck's bed, scanning around for any potential witnesses. It was chilly outside, the drop in temperature and the late hour making it unlikely anyone would be stopping in to wash a car.

His first instinct was to ease the pickup into the evening traffic, Gabe and he discussing the need to always keep moving if there were any chance someone had spied the launch or landing. But there was also the wisdom of staying put in a good hiding place. It was impossible to tell when or where the next workable concealment would be available.

Despite his survival instincts screaming to leave the scene of his "crime," Chip decided to stay put and wait for the drone to return.

In the meantime, he dug a few quarters out of his pockets and placed a couple of the floor mats on the concrete nearby. If someone did pass by, he would look like any other customer, using the vacuums to clean out a messy cab.

As soon as the G-2 was airborne, Gabe took over control from the command center. In reality, either Chip or he could pilot the drone, but the boss didn't want to overwhelm the new employee.

The machine performed just like its older, slightly less-sophisticated sister, buzzing along at 250 feet toward the address that was now attracting a significant police response. Armed robbery was serious enough. An attempted homicide and escaping shooters meant that HPD would be pulling out all the stops.

Gabe switched to infrared immediately, the urban sprawl beneath the Gripen now displayed as glowing, fluorescent colors as the flying machine sped towards it destination. He sat back, happy for once that he wasn't one of the men that had to respond and chase armed villains.

Officer Kirkpatrick was manning the fourth car on the scene, the ranking officer ordering him to move two blocks north and search the back side of a residential neighborhood.

It was a poorly lit area, one of those tracts of land that wasn't wide enough to be developed, but was too small to accommodate swings, a slide and picnic tables. Parking his cruiser, Dole exited and began stomping through knee high weeds. The ground was littered with windblown trash and small piles of debris abandoned by the locals.

He made his way down a long row of privacy fences bordering one side of the unused property, hoping that the criminals hadn't climbed the barrier and entered the backyards on the other side. If the crooks managed that neighborhood, it would be nearly impossible to root them out.

With his flashlight scanning the brush, grass, and occasional sapling, Kirkpatrick continued searching, weapon drawn and coiled for violence. "If I were trying to evade the cops, this is where I'd hide," he whispered, pining for a K-9 unit to help him flush the crooks.

The Gripen arrived over the scene less than a minute later, pulling into a high hover directly over the just-robbed pharmacy. For the first time since JI had become operational, Gabe wasn't sure where to focus the drone's high-powered cameras.

There were a couple of police cars in front of the business, but no visible officers. Radio traffic confirmed that the thieves were no longer inside.

Ordering the Gripen to pivot, Gabe began studying the surrounding terrain, finding the expected mixture of homes and businesses filling the monitor's display. He guessed the cops would be patrolling in their cars, circling the immediate area in search of the suspects. Until the radio or visual indicated they had put eyes on the wanted men, there really wasn't much for the G-2 to record.

And then the bright, white, outline of a man with a gun came into view. A man on foot, walking along what appeared to be some sort of nature reserve. Gabe assumed it was a cop, the body language and posture giving no indication of flight. He ordered the Gripen closer for a better view.

Kenny and his brother had been playing in their backyard, waiting for their mom to come home after her shift at the grocery store. Having responsibility for his younger sibling was a big hassle for the 12-year- old boy, but a single, working mother didn't have many after-school entertainment options for the struggling family.

When the two boys had heard the sirens, it had inspired a game of cops and robbers. Mom wouldn't be home for a while, and Kenny knew his pesky, little brother was afraid of the woods at night. The older sibling wasted no time suggesting they move out of the yard and into the open area behind their home.

With toy guns in hand, the two boys squeezed through the loose boards that marked the boundary of their normal play space, neither giving much thought to how fuming mad their mother would be if they were caught leaving the property. In a way, sneaking off only served to raise the excitement of the clandestine endeavor.

Kenny, begrudgingly, had accepted the role of the robber. It was his turn to play the less desirable part in the childhood game, and besides, it was the only way he could convince his younger bro to exit the known confines of their yard and enter the scary world beyond the fence.

Moving off to hide and wait for his brother to flush him out and engage in the inevitable gunfight, the lad ambled his way down the privacy fence, thinking of a large bush up ahead that he was sure would disguise his location long enough to ambush and scare his little brother.

As he progressed, Kenny slowed his pace. It was dark, the trees and brush casting weird shadows from the ambient, city light surrounding the overgrown area. The boy remembered occasionally spotting homeless people wandering through the area, his mother actually calling the real police after finding one old man huddled in a makeshift tent near their back fence.

Those memories engaged automatic precautions, the pre-teen now making his footfalls with extreme caution, his ears perked for any sign of people or worse yet, animal predators that might be lurking nearby. He held out his gun, hoping the toy would spook anyone… or anything… that might jump out at him.

Gabe was having trouble getting a good angle on the roving cop, the combination of trees, buildings, and homes making a clear view of the ground difficult.

He inhaled sharply when he spotted the second image presented on the display. Another person with a gun was on a collision course with the cop. They were going to meet where the two fences formed a corner.

Switching quickly to the regular cameras, Gabe realized it had gotten very dark outside. He could see the policeman's flashlight working the underbrush and weeds, the cop making his way slowly toward what would surely be a surprise encounter at the corner.

Gabe then ordered the G-2 back to infrared, finding the scene more clearly defined. He zoomed in on the other armed individual, his mind wondering who was going to win the inevitable shootout.

Something odd caught Gabe's attention, the weapon held by the stalking suspect showing up a different color than the policeman's drawn pistol.

That observation increased Gabe's scrutiny, his fingers flying over the keyboard as he adjusted the Gripen's sensors. Infrared still provided the most detailed view; the gun looked just plain weird.

It then occurred to him that the guy getting ready to run right into the cop was very small. Using the cedar privacy fence as a guide, Gabe took a haphazard measurement of the unknown person, and then moved the G-

2 slightly in order to compare it to the height of the still advancing policeman.

The non-cop was either a midget or a child. Gabe's logical mind immediately calculated the statistical probability of each option and assumed the person was probably very young. From there, his mind leapt to an assumption about the weapon directed at the officer. Its plastic surface would perfectly explain why this pistol appeared so different from the cop's metal firearm in the infrared setting.

"Holy shit!" Gabe exclaimed, "That cop has no way of knowing that 'firearm' is a toy. It's dark. Both figures are moving like they're scared. That officer is going to kill that kid."

For a brief moment, Gabe pined for some sort of speaker on his robot. If he could speak to the officer, he could warn him of the quickly approaching encounter. But the Gripen was mute by design.

Five steps separated the two outlines on his monitor.

He considered buzzing the cop, distracting him in hope of avoiding an encounter that was sure to result in another child's death. But that maneuver, in the dark, over unknown terrain, would be difficult at best. Would the cop pay any attention?

Four steps.

Gabe sat urgently trying to figure out a solution, watching in horror as the two human images on his screen continued toward the fence lines' intersection, each second bringing them closer and closer together at the corner.

Three steps.

When both of their outlines filled his screen, Gabe was even more convinced the smaller figure was a kid. The movements matched, the body motions more juvenile than adult. And just like Jacob, Gabe felt powerless to do anything.

Two steps.

The Gripen's controller stopped breathing when the two shapes were mere feet apart, still unable to anticipate each other due to the tall planks of the fence. The cop clearly heard something, his pistol moving to point directly at the corner.

Gabe had a fleeting idea. "I could kamikaze the cop," he suggested to the lonely control room. "I could ram the Gripen into his gun. I'd lose the drone, might even give the cops some hint as to who's been spying on their asses, but I would save the kid."

One step.

Kirkpatrick heard a twig snap, most likely due to someone's footfall. The undergrowth was thicker here, saplings and thorny bushes making his sweep even slower than before. And now he was sure someone was lurking around the corner.

Not wanting to make himself an illuminated target, he switched off his flashlight and halted. There was another footfall... somebody was definitely around the corner.

He clicked off his safety, ready to drop the hammer if one of the crooks came into view.

Dole spied movement, the dim outline of a shape appearing just beyond where the fence switched direction. He flicked on his flashlight, the warning, "Police officer! Freeze!" forming in his throat. In the torch's blink, he spotted the outline of the gun and the extended hand that was wielding it.

His trigger finger began to squeeze, his brain calculating where the target's body would be in proportion to the weapon and arm, adjusting his own aim for a center-mass shot.

The officer felt the trigger break just as something slammed into his wrist. His weapon discharged, the bright muzzle flash and roar of the .40 caliber weapon illuminating the landscape.

His training called for a follow-on shot, but harsh bolts of pain throbbing through his limb made controlling his muscles difficult. Somebody screamed; the flashlight hit the ground, and there were blurs of movement throughout his confused field of vision.

It took a few moments before his stunned, aching arm would respond, another second before he got control of the flashlight's beam. Assuming an armed criminal was surely taking aim at his chest, Dole pointed his torch where he'd spotted the offending weapon.

"Holy shit!" he barked, the scared, wide-eyed image of a young boy squinting from the flashlight's glare. "Get on the ground! Now!" the cop ordered, still not sure of what was going on, his bewildered mind resorting to the most basic training stored within its memory cells.

"Get on the ground!" he shouted, control of his pistol arm finally returning.

Finally, the kid did as he was ordered to do, hot tears streaming down his cheeks from fear and the shock of a gunshot that had blasted right by his head.

Dole then spied the toy gun, lying on the ground where the freaked out kid had dropped it. He picked it up to double check, a thunderstorm of emotions erupting when he realized he'd almost killed a child.

"Shots fired due to misidentification," he breathed into his shoulder mounted radio, not sure what the proper terminology or code words were... and really not caring. "I'm okay, but I could use some backup over here," he finished.

"What the hell were you doing out here, kid?" he snapped at the weeping child at his feet. "You damn near got us both in hot water. Jesus Henry Milton Roosevelt Christ – that was close."

In the distance, Dole could see other squad cars pulling up beside his still idling cruiser. Two new flashlight beams began bouncing along the terrain, brother officers on their way in support.

When the field supervisor arrived, he listened intently to Kirkpatrick's explanation, watching as the young patrolman reenacted what had just occurred.

The kid was still there, sitting against the fence, hugging his knees, and watching the cops go about their routine with frightened, darting eyes.

When Dole had finally finished his report, the older officer shook his head. "How in God's name did you miss him?" he asked. "You must have had an angel on your shoulder, Kirkpatrick. That's all I've got to say."

"He did have an angel," sounded another officer's nearby voice, his beam searching the weeds around the area. "He had an Archangel, and here it is," he proclaimed, lifting the now bent and useless body of the Gripen from the ground.

"Do we run?" Chip asked, looking at the video playback of the kamikaze drone-strike over Gabe's shoulder.

"No, I'm not sure they can trace the Gripen back to us. I've tried to be very, very careful. Even if they did, running wouldn't do any good. I've got plenty of money, but they would instantly freeze my accounts. Any place I'd care to live has a pretty tight extradition treaty."

"What do you think they'll charge us with?"

Gabe shook his head, his eyes never leaving the last frame of the now-ended recording. "I don't think they can legitimately charge us with anything. Oh, they'll try to cook up something; I'm sure. My attorney says in the long run, after significant expense, they'll have to drop any bogus charges. At least that's what he thinks would happen."

Chip groaned at the last part of the dialogue, hating that his future was dependent on what someone "thought," especially an ambulance chaser.

Gabe understood his friend's reaction, his low voice saying, "I'm sorry I got you into this, Chip. You know I didn't have any choice. I'd be as guilty as Marwick if I had let that kid die."

Patting his new boss on the shoulder, Chip nodded. "I would have done the same thing. I'm not upset with you, just pissed this had to happen on the first good job I've had."

The two men sat in silence for a bit, both minds speeding rapidly, but down different tracks. Chip was trying to figure out how he was going to explain his deception to Amanda, uttering the occasional small prayer that she would understand, and not take Manny… and his life… away from him.

Gabe was trying to figure out technically what the cops could determine once they'd dissected his drone.

He'd been careful, filing off the serial number from any component. But that wasn't foolproof. He hadn't, for example, disassembled the tiny electric motor to see if it were stamped with any sort of internal identification.

The police would now know what frequency he was using to communicate with his robots. That again wasn't particularly damning, the bandwidth of the Gripen's receiver within a commonly used range of airwaves. Besides, he'd leased antenna time through JI, as did hundreds of corporations throughout the Houston area.

He wouldn't put it past the authorities to start monitoring the G-2's programmed frequency, but that wasn't a showstopper either. It was a few minutes work to switch to another band.

He wondered about fingerprints. He'd assembled the drone personally, never wearing gloves or taking any precautions. Yes, the drones were kept very clean in order to maximize their battery time, but Gabe was sure that somewhere his unique digit-marks still soiled the robot's surface.

What did that mean? He thought hard, trying to remember ever being fingerprinted. Sandy had gone through the experience some years ago, her volunteering at Jacob's elementary school requiring the intrusive process before they'd let her step foot inside the door. No, he concluded, his fingerprints shouldn't be in any database. If he were arrested, then the proof would be evident, but until then, the coppers wouldn't be able to hunt him down. At least not from fingerprints.

"I don't think we have to change anything but the radio frequencies," he announced to the still-worried looking Chip. "Unless you touched the drone before you launched it, they shouldn't have anything to go on."

"No, I didn't touch it. But what about the autopilot's coordinates to return home?"

Gabe had already considered that. "Didn't you launch it from the car wash? It would automatically return there unless overridden. I'll reprogram the frequencies, and we'll watch our backs for a couple of days. I think we should concentrate our efforts on Officer Marwick's precinct and shifts. If they are going to shut us down, I'd feel a whole lot better if we had taken care of that asshole first."

Nodding his agreement, Chip added, "Any news on the DA pressing charges?"

"No. They're obviously stalling, which I've found out isn't unusual. Stupid me, I thought when the grand jury recommended prosecution, that was that. Who the hell knew they could keep playing games until the cows came home? If we can catch Marwick red-handed, then they won't have much choice. We'll lay low with the exception of his beat, and hope he fucks up before they figure out who we are."

"You're the boss," Chip stated with a sly grin. "By the way, can I have the bottom bunk in our prison cell, Mr. Boss-man, sir?"

"So whoever was operating the drone saved that child's life?" Karen asked the police technician.

"Yes, ma'am. It looks like the remote operator deliberately ordered the machine to hit Officer Kirkpatrick's weapon. From what we recovered from the unit's video memory card, it was clear from the infrared that the boy had a toy weapon."

"Are you sure this wasn't a deliberate attack against a police officer?" the chief asked from the other side of the table. "Why would someone who's been trying to destroy my department want to help a cop? It doesn't make any sense."

Karen looked at the chief and frowned. "Obviously, they're not trying to destroy your force. At least it doesn't seem like it to me. The video of the SWAT team's breach has probably saved the city a significant lawsuit, and bought your department a ton of positive public relations. If we were dealing with pure cop-haters, they would have kept that recording to themselves."

The top-cop waved a dismissing hand through the air, "That was just a head fake... a false gesture to establish credibility on their part. Believe me, if they wanted to help us, they wouldn't be broadcasting every little mistake we make."

After waiting to make sure the discussion was over, the mayor continued. "Has the recovered drone provided any clues regarding who we are dealing with?"

The chief nodded at his technical expert, granting permission for the man to answer. "Very little," came the shy response. "We found three different partial prints, none of which drew a hit from any agency database. The serial numbers from most of the parts have been ground off. We did discover two SKU codes, but both components were manufactured in Asia. We've asked the FBI to follow up, but our experience has shown cooperation from foreign manufacturers in such matters is unlikely."

"You mean you've recovered one of their units, basically intact, and we're still no closer to finding out who's behind this?" asked one of the city councilmen.

"That's not entirely correct, sir," the chief interrupted. "We've filled in several blanks. For example, we know the range of the device, how it receives its commands, and we can now confirm it is a custom-built unit. Those facts, while appearing scanty, help us in building a profile of the owner-operator."

"Go on," the mayor stated, clearly intrigued.

"One thing we know is that the launch and apparent recovery isn't from a fixed position. The memory core we recovered indicated the drone had been programmed to land at a car wash less than two miles from the incident. We believe someone would have been there with a car or truck, ready to load the unit after it landed. We know our suspects are well funded, technically capable, and extremely cautious."

"So what's the next step, Chief?" Karen asked, finally rejoining the conversation.

"We are running down a list of people who have filed grievances or complaints against the department, trying to narrow down the list of those who match the criteria I just stated."

Karen grunted, "That's got to be a long list, Chief. What? A couple of thousand names?"

"What the hell is that supposed to mean?" the old cop snapped, his fiery stare burning in Karen's direction.

DA Sanders just smiled, apparently unaffected by the gruff challenge. "Nothing, Chief, nothing at all. I was just stating that a department the size of HPD would naturally have hundreds of such incidents per year, and that would equate to quite an extensive list of potential suspects."

Dole hadn't been able to eat since the night he'd almost slaughtered the kid. Despite his commander insisting on his taking a couple of days off, Kirkpatrick just couldn't clear the images out of his head.

He didn't have any problem with using extreme tactics on hardcore criminals or the terminally stupid. Those examples of humanity often received exactly what they were asking for.

But kids? Young people? That was an entirely different ballgame. One he'd never anticipated when he'd pinned on a badge.

And the young man a few nights ago wasn't his first aberration.

Jacob Chase. He now knew the name by heart, could recite the case number from memory. He'd read the file no less than ten times – and knew without a doubt Sergeant James Marwick was a liar.

After that night in the restaurant, Dole had begun to wonder just how far into the pits of treachery Big Jim was willing to go.

Dole had the uploaded video file from Marwick's cruiser that night. Big Jim had been crafty enough to erase the memory card before returning the vehicle the next day, but the older cop wasn't technically up to speed with how the newer video systems operated. That recording, salvaged from the department's cloud storage cache, clearly showed there hadn't been any evasion or resistance on the part of the teenage driver. Big Jim was not only a liar, but a self-promoting, malicious individual who was damaging the entire force with his antics.

For a while, Dole had pondered calling his father and seeking the more experienced cop's advice. But he didn't, well aware of exactly what his conservative parent would spout. "You never, never, ever turn on another cop. Doing so will ostracize you from the family, and the next time a bad man has a gun to your head, those ex-family members might just be a little slow to react."

Kirkpatrick was sure his grandfather would share the same point of view. He could just hear the patriarch's gravelly voice instructing, "Always go through the chain of command if you've got a problem. Never go public. Never go to the press, or take matters into your own hands. Use the established channels in your department."

But that option was suicide, if only via a different poison. Dole knew what happened to those officers who reported on other cops. Overtime disappeared, promotions were bypassed, and the brotherhood became hostile. Besides, he was almost as guilty as Marwick. While the big sergeant had given him the visual command to implement the hotfoot, it had been Dole's own hands that had used excessive force.

Was it really his fault? Was he really to blame?

The radio call that night had indicated a suspect was fleeing. Dole and the other officers had responded in kind, adrenaline-charged and determined to make sure the chase ended before anyone got hurt. If they had all known the truth, had been aware that there really wasn't any pursuit or indication of guilt, then the entire encounter would have turned out differently. Another child might still be alive. The sergeant had misled his brothers. He was a dishonest piece of shit, hardly better than half the scum they sent to prison every day.

Thoughts of resignation circulated through the young cop's troubled mind. Maybe his dad had been right... maybe he wasn't cut out to be a police officer.

For a while, the option of turning in his badge and gun provided a relief of sorts. Dole's thoughts wandered to other occupations, speculating on which ones couldn't involve shooting children and ruining lives.

But then he rebelled at the concept. Police work was supposed to be honorable, driven to better the community and improve lives. "To protect and serve," he whispered. "If all the guys who think like me leave the force, who is going to protect and serve?"

He had a vision of sorts, a mental image that actually made him laugh aloud. A muster had been called, all the officers at the local substation ordered to gather in one room. Dole could see Big Jim's face atop every uniform, the entire force populated with Marwick clones. It was funny, then sad, and finally frightening.

There was another way out. A move that carried much risk, but the potential of a huge reward. He could release the videotape from Marwick's dash cam.

"Why not?" he asked his empty apartment. "It seems to be all the rage these days. Everybody's doing it."

Again, he chuckled, wishing he could see the huge sergeant's face when the recording was aired on the local news.

But what if his fellow officers found out? What if Marwick put two and two together?

"You'll be assassinated," he said. "There will be a call… a prowler or open door or alarm. Someone with a gun and knowledge will be waiting. The shot will be to the head, well away from the protection of your body armor. Is it worth it?"

Dole took another sip of his beer, pondering the fork in the road that life had presented. Finally, he reached a conclusion, deciding to release the video. "You're just a walking dead man if you don't. The guilt of inaction will eventually eat out your core, and you'll be no more than a zombie behind a badge - uncaring, numb, and lifeless. It doesn't make any difference if it's the assassin's bullet that ends it all or withholding the truth that does you in. The story has the same ending."

Big Jim was preparing for his shift, running down the nightly roster and scanning the day shift's blotter. "Nothing special here," he noted. "Just another evening fighting crime for little fame, no glory, and less pay."

The sound of someone clearing his voice caused him to glance up, a lieutenant he didn't know and his captain standing nearby, each wearing their best, "You'd better believe this is serious shit," expression all over their faces.

"Marwick, this is Lieutenant Cranfield from Internal Affairs. He'd like to have a word with you," the captain announced, pivoting to exit the room without another word.

"I assume you've seen the video released this morning, Sergeant Marwick. I was ordered to come here and take your statement regarding this new evidence."

"Huh? I've seen all of the Archangel videos, but I didn't know about any new ones this morning," Jim replied honestly.

The senior officer shook his head, "This wasn't an Archangel piece. Channel 14 news is playing what appears to be a recording made from your dash cam the night of Jacob Chase's arrest. Normally, my boss wouldn't be so concerned about such a release, but with a potential prosecution in the works, he sent me over here to listen to your side of the story."

Marwick experienced genuine fear, the pit of his gut suddenly knotted, the back of his knees cold and damp. "I can't comment, LT.... I haven't seen it."

Pulling a laptop from under his arm, Cranfield said, "I can fix that, Sergeant. Let's go into one of the interrogation rooms and enjoy the show."

Big Jim didn't like the idea, but he couldn't think of any excuse not to. Weapons weren't allowed in the interrogation rooms, and he knew that every word would be videotaped.

For a moment, Marwick thought he should ask for his lawyer, but decided against it. He hadn't seen the recording, and it might not be that big of deal. This young IA guy might just be playing head games to see if the accused would make a mistake. More than once he'd used a similar technique, approaching a person of interest while pretending to have uncovered some blockbuster piece of evidence. More often than not, the suspect had started singing like a bird.

After checking their weapons, the two cops entered the closet-like, stark room. Inside there was only a small table and three plastic chairs. The drywall was bruised, dented, dinged, and scraped, evidence of previous occupants' violent outbursts.

The door closed with an electric hum and pop, the heavy lock engaging to secure the room. Marwick knew there would be at least two cops witnessing the encounter. He also was fully aware that the only way out of that room was to be "buzzed" out by one of the observing cops.

Without any prelude, Cranfield opened his department-issued computer, punched a couple of buttons, and flipped the screen around to allow Marwick an unobstructed view.

Big Jim sat and watched the nine minutes of black and white images, a wave of relief flushing through his core when he realized the recording didn't show anything new. In fact, it wasn't as revealing as the private cell phone video shown at the civil trial.

Once it had finished, Marwick looked up at the LT and shrugged.

"Do you have any reason to believe this recording has been tampered with or falsified in any way?"

"No, but I'm not an engineer or expert on such things. I wouldn't have any way of knowing," Jim replied coldly.

"Does this recording match your recall of that evening's events, Sergeant Marwick?"

Again, Jim shrugged. "That was a long time ago, LT. I've made half a dozen felony arrests and worked hundreds of shifts since that night. Even if it is 100% genuine, I don't see what the fuss is about, sir. There's nothing new on that video."

Cranfield pulled a small bundle of papers from his jacket pocket, unfolding the documents and flattening them with his hands on the table. "This is your official report from the incident, Sergeant. You claim that the suspect attempted to elude your attempts to execute a legitimate traffic stop for, and I quote, 'some distance.' Yet the video indicates the vehicle's operator, Jacob Chase, pulled to the curb less than two blocks after your squad's lights were engaged. Do you consider two blocks to be the same as some distance?"

A scowl manipulated Jim's bushy eyebrows, his forehead wrinkling in disdain. "Did you come all the way down here to split hairs, sir? If so, then I think it's time for me to call my lawyer. If the boys down at Internal Affairs are looking for a scapegoat... or playing some sort of political game, then I'm through cooperating."

"That is your right, Officer Marwick," came the calm reply. "But, as I'm sure you're aware, filing a falsified report, perjury, misappropriation of department resources, and assault are all serious charges. I'd hardly call our activities splitting hairs."

"Call it what you will, sir. I won't be answering any more questions without representation."

Cranfield tried a few more interrogation angles, working on the timeline before Chip's video had begun. It was obvious the Honda's operator hadn't resisted, let alone displayed any sort of threat to the arresting officer.

Several times during the video's replay, the IA man asked Jim the same question. "Why didn't you stop the arrest right there? Why didn't you hold the other responding officer back? Why did you let this go on and on and on, Sergeant?"

But Jim's mouth was as good as sewed shut, the savvy cop knowing not to say a word. The two men finally left the room, Marwick's captain waiting in the hall. "You're on temporary suspension with pay until further notice, Jim. Go home. Call your lawyer, and wait until you hear from the DA."

Somehow, Jim managed his cubicle without blowing his top. Thankfully, word had spread around the substation, the news allowing Marwick to maneuver the halls without anyone saying a word.

He called his wife, keeping his tone even and smooth despite the growing pressure of a volcanic-like dome of rage that was building inside. "I need for you to pick me up at the station," he informed Mrs. Marwick. "I've been suspended with pay, but I can't use my cruiser."

His mate of 19 years knew better than to seek details. "I'll be right down, Jim," she promptly and simply replied.

While he waited, Marwick pretended to be tidying up paperwork, his eyes remaining down and seemingly focused on the task at hand. But it was an act.

Inside, a fury that began as a light breeze was reaching Category 5 hurricane status, his mind contemplating how he could discover the Benedict Arnold who had released the video, and what would become of the turncoat once he was uncovered.

In the 20 minutes it took for his ride to arrive, Jim made several assumptions. The Archangel had shocked and awed the department with his video expertise and willingness to attack the police department. The release of his dash cam video had been the same modus operandi. He was convinced that the same person was responsible for both outings.

In spite of the gale force anger that clouded his thinking, Jim managed to arrive at another astute conclusion. Someone had it in for him personally.

He mentally inventoried the other videos that had been released, noting that none of them had targeted any specific officer. That fact, combined with the operator's profile that had been circulated throughout the department, led Jim to believe that he had been specifically targeted.

All of the videos to date had been recorded on the north or west side of Houston, the area where he commonly patrolled. The detectives had calculated that the individual responsible for the drones was technically savvy and well versed in police procedures and communications.

It made sense to Marwick that such a person could somehow manage to come up with the video of his dash camera, absolutely logical dots to connect.

But who?

Who would have a vendetta against him personally?

Jacob Chase was the fulcrum, his name a constant that spanned seemingly unrelated events. It had to be one of the other officers who responded that night... some pussy who didn't have the guts to walk the line required for aggressive police work.

For a moment, Jim had doubts about his hypothesis, considering the alternative of an inter-department rival, waiting to pass him in the law enforcement hierarchy. That option was quickly dismissed. He recognized that as of late, he'd been the black sheep of the precinct. Big Jim's current, civil lawsuit and several past missteps already removed his name from consideration for job advancement. *No,* he decided. *Nobody is gunning for my position right now.*

Furthermore, there couldn't be any cops walking around with a disciplinary chip on their shoulders. He hadn't had to take such action in years, the latest crops of rookie officers from the academy having been a competent crew.

No, it had to be related to the kid's case from so long ago, and that narrowed down the list of suspects.

Jim's cell rang, the caller ID indicating his wife had arrived. After informing his spouse he'd be right out, Jim cleared out a few personal items and headed for the parking lot. He paused after stepping outside, turning back to peer at the place that defined so much of his life. "I'll be back," he stated with confidence.

"Did you hear what happened to Marwick?" Chip's excited voice came over the cell call.

"No. Did someone finally shoot the SOB?" Gabe speculated.

"I just saw a little news blurb…. He's been suspended. No doubt, it has to do with that fresh video that magically appeared. How did you do that, by the way?"

Gabe was puzzled, and it bled through in his voice, "Huh? What video? I've had my head down trying to build the G-3 unit. What have I been missing?"

It only took a few minutes before Chip had brought his boss up to speed.

"No shit? That's fantastic! While I wish I could take credit for hacking into the police video management system, honestly, I had nothing to do with it."

"Damn. And here I was thinking I worked for the smartest guy on the planet," Chip teased.

"Nope. You work for only the second smartest guy on the planet," Gabe mused. "Obviously, we have a new ally. Someone with real connections."

"We have started a movement, man," the excited protégé beamed. "Any idea who our co-conspirator could be?" Gabe inquired, now moving back to the new mystery.

"No. None. But it has to be somebody on the inside, and he surely has a big pair of 'nads. It would take some guts to go poking around in the law enforcement system," Gabe speculated.

"So Marwick finally pissed off the wrong dude. Cool. Can't think of a nicer guy to get his ass handed to him. Wonder what happens now? Maybe this means somebody has to admit what he did to both of our families," Chip concluded.

"Obviously that new video is going to put some additional pressure on the DA to follow up on filing the criminal charges against him. I'd just about given up hope. In the meantime, I think I would try to avoid running into Officer Marwick. That guy was a ticking time bomb before, now I'm sure he's about ready to split atoms."

"Should we be watching him? I mean with the drones?"

Gabe had to admit, Chip had an interesting idea. "God… I'd love to, but I'm pretty sure Adam would advise us that such activities would be considered stalking. He'd probably throw in a few dozen FAA violations as well."

"Shit," Chip responded, disappointment thick in his tone. "That sounded like fun. We could park a drone on his ass and dare him to do something about it. That would send our friend Big Jim over the edge for sure."

Gabe's chuckle drifted through the phone, but then he became serious. "Marwick deserves the benefit of the doubt, just like Jacob did. We have to assume he's innocent until proven guilty… treat him the same as we would want someone to handle Jacob or Manny. While I'm just as convinced as you are that the guy is a danger to society, until he's convicted in a court of law, he's just another badge."

The response was a grunt, followed by, "Oh yeah? Clearly, you haven't wrestled with that 'badge' in your driveway like I have. I got all the proof I needed, right there. Guilty as charged, asshole. But I suppose you're right… as usual. Still, I'd love to post an internet video of Marwick trimming his nose hairs or drooling on his pillow at night. Something gross and offensive as hell."

"Maybe we can hover one of our units outside his prison cell window and record video of his jail house lover and him? Now that would go viral in a heartbeat."

Chip laughed hard at that one, so deeply in fact, Gabe made a note to keep an eye on all of their drones if Marwick actually ended up behind bars. Finally, after a few moments, Chip was back to business. "Anything you want me to take care of while you're creating the next airborne Frankenstein?"

"Yes. I want you to take Amanda and Manny out for a nice dinner, and get ready to work some long hours. I think we need to press our advantage while the momentum is on our side. I'll have the G-3 assembled and tested in another few days."

"You got it, boss. Call me if you need anything."

Kirkpatrick pulled into the diner's parking area, subconsciously scanning the cars scattered around the lot. It didn't surprise him to find he was the only cop this evening, the rest of the guys having eaten over an hour before while he'd been delayed waiting on a wayward tow truck.

Shrugging, he pulled into a close-in spot and pulled the cruiser out of gear, then radioed the dispatcher with the proper code indicating he was taking his "lunch" break.

He opened the door and stood, some sixth sense making him spin, only to find Sergeant Marwick standing directly behind him. "Shit!" he inhaled sharply. "You scared the crap out of me."

"You should be more aware of your surroundings," the hefty cop replied. "I just walked straight up…. It's not as if I were stalking you or anything. You extra jumpy for some reason tonight?"

For a moment, he thought Marwick might have figured out who had turned in the video, but then immediately reconsidered. There just wasn't any way that could have happened so quickly. Deciding their meeting was purely coincidence, Dole answered honestly. "I've been jumpy as hell since I almost shot that kid. This is the first night the captain has let me back on duty."

"I heard about that," Big Jim replied. "Weird. Just plain weird. But that kind of fits in with what I want to talk to you about. Can I buy you a cup of coffee?"

Kirkpatrick shook his head, "I should buy your coffee. You've had a rough couple of days, too... probably worse than mine."

"Fine by me," Marwick answered, nodding toward the greasy spoon.

As Dole followed the other officer into the late night establishment, he returned to worrying about Marwick having figured it out after all. The entire encounter was just bizarre, completely out of character.

After the two officers were seated and had ordered, Big Jim wasted no time. "I'm well aware that you don't know me that well, but I've kind of got my back up against a wall and thought you might be able to help me out without anyone down at the precinct knowing about our conversation."

"Sure, Sergeant. You've always played square by me," Dole lied.

"Somebody managed to download, or copy, or steal the dash camera recording from that night I had your cruiser. I checked around with a few old friends of mine, and they're like me... a bunch of old-fashioned shits who don't understand all this technical gobbledygook. I figured a young guy like you would have a better handle on it and might do an old law dog a favor and explain it all in plain English."

Dole nodded, still not quite sure Marwick wasn't laying some sort of tiger trap. "I'll do my best, sir, but I'm no expert. What is it you want to know?"

"First things first, where would they have gotten a copy of the recording? I know the card I gave you back was erased. I accidently wiped it clean when I was creating my report. So where did this new version come from?"

It occurred to Dole that the older cop was playing dumb. After all, cloud-based storage wasn't rocket science. He decided to answer honestly, just in case it was a test. "The camera system in the patrol car you were assigned that night has an automatic backup to what is called cloud storage. Basically, every so many hours, a copy of all recordings is sent wirelessly to an internet server somewhere. I don't know where."

Tilting his head, Marwick seemed to ponder the response for a long time. "So why is there a memory card like all the other cameras? Kind of seems redundant."

"In case the wireless signal can't get through, I suppose. Hell, I'm not a computer engineer."

That answer seemed to satisfy the beefy officer. Marwick started nodding his head, indicating he now understood. "So if the video was out on the internet, practically any hacker could have broken in and downloaded a copy."

Dole decided to play dumb himself. "I suppose so. Again, I couldn't write a computer program to save my ass. I only know about the cloud storage because the tech that installed it in my cruiser about drove me nuts. The guy was so excited about that particular feature that his behavior was memorable. I was a rookie at the time and thought I had to pay strict attention to anything anybody said."

Marwick grunted, having witnessed years of stupid rookie tricks. After a brief pause, the big man's expression became serious again. Glancing over his shoulder to make sure no one could overhear, he said, "I'm convinced that the Archangel is the guy who hacked into the department's video vault and copied that recording."

If his co-diner hadn't been so large, and so very dangerous, Dole would have busted out laughing in the man's face. Using extreme levels of self-discipline, he managed to keep his expression "conspiracy theory" serious, replying, "Really? You think so?"

"Who else could it be?" Jim replied. "Some asshole has a vendetta against me and the department and has either hired professionals to smear our good name or is doing it all himself. I intend on finding the guy, and…."

Dole didn't ask, "And what?" He didn't need to. Instead, the younger officer tried to appear accommodating and said, "What can I do to help?"

"I'm not sure just yet. Even now, I have enough friends scattered throughout the force to keep me in the loop, so I won't ask you to get involved just yet. Still, it's good to know a man has friends. Thanks."

Kirkpatrick wanted to grab the thickheaded cop and shake some sense into his malfunctioning grey matter. Didn't Marwick realize he'd already involved another man simply by showing up at the diner? Was this buffoon not taking the charges against him seriously? Surely, even Big Jim wasn't *that* stupid or naïve.

Poking another fork of hash browns into his pie hole, Dole pretended to be busy chewing while trying to think of something to say next. As if he were reading the younger man's mind, Marwick glanced at his watch and announced, "Shit… it's late. I got to be running."

Again, the younger officer was shocked when the sergeant stretched out his hand. After a quick shake, Jim muttered a hasty farewell. "Thanks for the java," the sergeant offered as he was headed toward the door.

After finishing his meal, Dole worked on his coffee and tried to clear his head so he could be alert for the rest of his shift. It was an extremely complex situation, very difficult to read. As he threw back the bottom of the cup, he settled on having handled the peculiar encounter reasonably well, giving himself a mental pat on the back.

"Keep your friends close and your enemies closer," he whispered, strolling out the door.

Chapter 11

Peelian Principle
The ability of the police to perform their duties is dependent upon public approval of police actions.

There were 14 people on Big Jim's list of potentials. While he'd had far more official complaints filed against his badge number over the years, many of those citizens were no longer in the picture. Some had died. Some were still in prison. Some had moved away from Houston.

To whittle that number down to three had taken a few days, half a dozen phone calls, and more computer time than Marwick could ever remember investing. A few suspects had been eliminated after the big cop had assessed them as too stupid to be the Archangel. Another number scratched off because they barely had a pot to piss in, let alone the finances to shop the internet for sophisticated drones and their custom parts.

He organized the remaining candidates, determined to utilize his paid time off in a productive manner by performing some undercover surveillance. Gabriel Chase was first on the list.

He had parked down the street from the Chase residence for an entire day, waiting for someone to return home after a long day at the office. Eleven hours, four cups of coffee, and a to-go burger later, Jim began to wonder if anyone still resided at the address in the older, middle-class neighborhood.

Given the late hour, darkness, and lack of local traffic, he decided to take a chance and get a closer look. It was risky, the captain and DA sure to blow a fuse if he were caught snooping around a still active case and potential witness.

He knew the suicide kid's father had settled with a ton of cash, the police union representative and city manager making their displeasure clear to the chief. Shit rolled downhill in the police force hierarchy, the avalanche of manure soon passing through the captain and landing directly on Jim's head.

"Did you take your millions and move to Hawaii, Mr. Chase? Or did you invest those ill-gotten gains in drone technology and night school computer classes?" Jim asked the apparently empty house.

With flashlight in hand, he exited his private vehicle and made for the modest but dark home.

He entered the backyard via the side gate, a strategy designed to prevent nosey neighbors from spying a strange man peeking in their friend's windows... and calling the cops.

He found the lawn well maintained, the bushes trimmed, and the back windows closed and locked. But the drapes were open.

Jim flashed his light inside, finding a humbly appointed home that was particularly neat and tidy. He could see in the kitchen, noting no dirty dishes resided in the sink, no loaf of bread or bowl of fruit on the laminated countertop, no coffeepot on the stove. The only sign of life consisted of a series of small mounds of mail. Piled in several neat, short stacks, the system seeming to indicate some nice person next door was checking the box while the homeowner was out of town.

"I bet you're spending your dirty money traveling the world, Mr. Chase," Jim whispered to the manicured backyard. "Wherever you are, it sure doesn't look like you're living here. One down, two to go."

It was almost midnight as he drove out of the Chase's subdivision. The next name on his list lived not far away, and the benched cop was still too keyed up from his backyard invasion for home or sleep. "Can't hurt to scout it out before tomorrow's detective work," he convinced himself.

Chip and Amanda's home was still clearly occupied. Driving to the unassuming abode surfaced old memories of that night. Marwick didn't feel any regrets or guilt. His only emotion was a curiosity regarding why his instinct had failed him on that occasion. He would have sworn the basketball star was up to no good. "It happens. No one is right 100% of the time," he reconciled. Self-confidence had never been an issue for Big Jim.

Pulling his car off at the end of the street, he sat and scanned the residence, the blue flashes of light visible through the curtain a sure sign someone was home and up late watching the TV.

Satisfied he had work to do tomorrow, Jim put his car in gear and proceeded home. "I'm going to find you Mister Archangel, and when I do, I'm going to pluck those wings off your body nice and slow and painful like. You are going to regret the day you fucked with Jimmy Marwick and the Houston Police Department."

Sunrise saw Chip and Amanda's sleepy street was again blessed with the presence of one James Marwick. Sitting with two sandwiches, a thermos of coffee, and a reasonable quality camera, Big Jim was ready for a day of observation.

He'd arrived early and prepared, having no idea where his suspects worked or what time they normally left for the daily grind. Houston's traffic was notoriously nasty for those commuting to work or school, some suburban drivers leaving hours before the normal workday began. Jim didn't want to miss anything.

He remembered the teenage girl from the incident, watching her bound to the curb and smile at the approaching bus. She hadn't changed much.

The wife was next, backing out of the driveway in an apparent rush for the office… or store… or wherever she worked. Jim didn't remember her from that night, had no background information on her whatsoever.

And then there was nothing. His primary target was either off today, unemployed, or working from home. A little disappointed, but not discouraged, Jim refilled his coffee cup. He watched the steam rise from the Styrofoam container and dissipate into nothingness. "That's just like all the bullshit that Mr. Goody Two Shoes Archangel is throwing at me," he whispered. "It all seems hot and important at first, but soon it will disappear without leaving a trace."

Chip had helped Amanda get Manny off to school, the two parents fussing about the lack of frontal lobe development being displayed by their absentminded daughter.

After both of the girls had finally made it out of the house, he was clearing away the breakfast dishes when Gabe's caller ID flashed with his cell's display.

"Good morning, boss," he answered cheerfully.

Gabe was excited. "Hey, Chip. Sorry to call so early, but I'm kind of pumped up and anxious to run a test. I finished the G-3 a few hours ago, and I think it's ready for an extended flight."

Smiling at his friend's enthusiasm, he replied, "Very cool! I am at your beck and call, sir. When and where do you want me?"

"Are you home right now?"

"Yes, sir."

"Just stay there, and keep an eye out over your backyard. I'm going to send our newest Gripen over to visit. We can run a few tests then."

"Should I make it an extra cup of coffee? How does it like its eggs?" Chip teased.

After chuckling for a bit, Gabe said, "It likes 115 volt AC, black... no sugar or crème."

"I'll brew up a fresh jolt. Talk to you in a bit."

Chip continued about his morning routine, mentally calculating the G-3's flight time. Two pieces of toast and a quick load of the dishwasher later, he was sitting on his back stoop, scanning the heavens.

It was amazing how close to his home the drone managed before he saw it. Gabe had modeled the grey and blue paintjob after the camouflage used on WWII fighters. It blended well with the background sky.

In fact, he heard the machine before he saw it, gazing upwards as the flying robot slowed into a hover, about 50 feet above his lawn, closer to the tree line. Chip smiled when the Gripen waggled its greeting, an obvious "hello" from Gabe at the controls.

Smiling, Chip waved back, using a middle finger. His phone rang a moment later. "I saw that," the laughing voice scolded.

"I just wanted to make sure the camera was in focus," he teased in return. "How many fingers was I holding up?"

"The flight went off without a hitch, but that's not really what I wanted to test. I've installed a new capability in this model. It's called, 'Follow me.'"

"Huh? I don't get it."

Gabe continued to explain the upgrade, expanding gradually in simple terms. "You can select a target, like a person or a car or even a horse. Once you do that, the drone will track it no matter where it moves. Unless it can outrun the Gripen, it should stick like glue."

"You should call it 'Shadow mode,'" Chip mused. "That name sounds more spy-like than 'Follow me.'"

"I didn't name it," Gabe answered, snickering at his friend's observation. "The option is becoming a standard with drone technology. Guys want their little flying buddies to follow them as they mountain bike or downhill ski or whatever. From what I've seen on the internet, it allows for some really impressive video recording and unique action shots."

"So how do we test this hound dog's nose?" Chip asked.

"I'm going to scan your neighborhood real quick and make sure no one is out and about. If the coast is clear, then I want you to take a walk for a few blocks and see if the Gripen will follow you around."

It was Chip's turn to laugh. "I'm going to ask for a raise. Manual labor? This job is too rough. You're a slave driver."

Gabe didn't respond, his focus now on the Gripen's controls. He elevated the machine to 250 feet and began scouting the vicinity of Chip's house.

Caught up in the jovial mood and pumped with the excitement of his new model, Gabe couldn't help but throw out a little of his own cornball humor. "Hey, Chip," he stated, as if something important was to follow. "I hate to tell you this, but you're going to need a new roof soon. Your shingles are looking pretty thin."

"Really? Shit! I just put that on about 11 years ago," his comrade replied with a serious tone.

Shaking his head, Gabe decided he should leave the comedy up to his friend. "Nah. I can't tell a good shingle from a bad one. I was just messing with ya."

Now curious about what the infrared camera would show, Gabe flipped the control, watching as the image on his monitor turned into the lava light colored display. He was trying to determine if he could judge the thermal integrity of Chip's roof when something caught his eye.

There was a hotspot just down the block from Chip's home, the car's engine nice and cool, but the interior glowing bright with heat.

The visual didn't make sense to Gabe's logical, engineering brain. If someone had just arrived and parked, then the car's motor would be very hot. If someone had just entered the car and was preparing to drive off, then the interior wouldn't be saturated in heat.

"Everything okay?" Chip's voice sounded over the cell.

"I don't know. There's a strange vehicle two blocks north of your house. Is there any way you can take a peek without raising their suspicions? I know someone is sitting in it."

"Sure, I'll go upstairs and spy from behind the curtains. Can I have a secret designation, like 007 or something cool like that?"

Gabe didn't bother to answer, his attention now back on controlling the Gripen. Something about the vehicle was troubling him.

He took the G-3 high, ordering the autopilot to 390 feet above the ground. He then commanded his machine to slowly move at an angle so he could view inside the car. Gabe knew motion attracted the human eye, and he didn't want some nosey neighbor calling the cops with claims of alien invaders getting ready to destroy her neighborhood.

Chip's voice came back, "I see the car, but can't tell who's inside. I've never seen it around here before, but that doesn't mean shit. I'm not the type of guy who logs every Ford or Chevy that rolls past on the street."

"Hold on a second. I'm positioning the Gripen to get a view."

The thermal was useless, as it lacked the ability to peer through the glass windows of the suspicious car. The regular-light camera worked just fine, however, Gabe keeping the drone at a great distance and using the zoom.

It took a few moments, the outline of the driver finally visible. "It's Marwick," Gabe announced with a chill running down his spine.

"No shit? Are you sure?"

"I'm sure," Gabe replied, his tone cold and tight. "I'd know that son of a bitch anywhere," he continued, just for a moment pondering a confession of his rifle-stalking stint. But he didn't, instead choosing to close the thought with only a strongly stated, "Believe me."

"What do we do now?"

"I don't know," Gabe sputtered, trying to work it all out. "I guess we need to make sure he's watching you."

"Okay. I don't think I'm going to like this," Chip stated.

"Why don't you run down to the corner store and get some milk," Gabe started. "I'll fly the Gripen along and see if he follows you."

"And if he stalks me into the parking lot and then crushes me under his car as I'm walking in, what then?"

Gabe had to laugh, even though he wasn't sure if Chip was joking or not. "Don't worry, I'll have it all on video, and I vow to avenge your demise."

"Thanks for that," he answered curtly. In a moment, he quipped, "Give me a minute. I've got to make sure my 'tightie whities' are clean. Mom always drilled me to wear clean underwear in case I got hit by a car and had to go to the hospital."

"Smart woman."

A short time later, Gabe caught Chip's silhouette on the corner of the monitor, the bait casually sauntering out to his car. Flicking to the thermal, he realized Marwick's engine was now running, the white-hot exhaust and bright spots under the fenders making the identification a no-brainer.

Chip backed out, heading in the opposite direction from where his stalker was parked. Sure enough, Marwick followed. The Gripen's master redialed his friend.

"He's behind you. So now we know," Gabe informed the prey. "Been nice knowing you."

"Seriously, what do I do now?"

"Just park; go in; buy milk. Then pray and go back home as normal. Don't act any differently. Don't look around or try to be sneaky or do anything stupid. If he realizes you're on to him, he'll be more cautious, and we'll have a harder time finding him."

"Okay, but if he kills me at the store, I'll never speak to you again."

"Fair enough. Oh, and don't do too much shopping. The Gripen's battery is running low."

"Thanks. I'm soooo happy to hear that. Bye."

Gabe watched Marwick follow Chip into the strip mall's lot and park some distance away. He was relieved that the burly officer never exited his car.

Ten minutes later, Chip was back safe and sound in his home, and dialing his boss. "How do I explain the extra milk in the fridge to Amanda, Mr. Know-it-all?"

"A craving? I am bringing the Gripen back home. If I have a headwind, it's going to be close."

"Where's our friend right now?"

"He's down the street. Not in the same spot, but close."

"Manny will be home soon. He wouldn't…."

Gabe thought about that, sure Marwick was only trying to find the Archangel. Still, there was no way to predict the crazy cop's intentions. "He's just looking for the Citizen Observation Committee, not school girls. I wouldn't worry about it too much."

"I've got my skeet gun in the closet. I think it's time to get it out… just in case."

Again, Gabe had to pause, his friend's reaction a bit of a surprise. "Up to you, I guess. I'd probably do the same. Just keep in mind, he's looking for someone related to the drones and the video. He's suspended, pissed, and desperate. If you don't give him anything to make you a suspect, then pretty soon he'll move on."

"Great. Just what I need. A pissed, desperate, frustrated Goliath parked right down the street. Nice."

"Just go about your business as normal. I bet he's gone after two or three days."

Indeed, Gabe's prediction had been correct. After watching Chip's home all of the following day, Big Jim decided to move on.

But the third candidate on his short list proved a non-starter. The guy had succumbed to cancer two months before.

Now the exasperated, suspended officer found himself in a quandary. He was still convinced the Archangel was at the root of his problems, but didn't have any good leads.

After placing a round of calls to everyone on the force he still counted as a "friend," an internal rage started fueling Marwick's impatient perspective.

The DA was making noise about a trial, his attorney receiving the preliminary requests for depositions just a few days ago. It took longer and longer for his representative from the patrolman's union to return his calls.

Paranoia became a frequent visitor to the exasperated cop. Once he thought someone was following him, backtracking the offending sedan and accosting the driver, accusing the shocked civilian of being "a blood sucking, internal affairs cocksucker."

He nearly shot a pizza delivery boy, unaware that Junior had ordered a pie.

With that mindset, Jim easily convinced himself that he needed to revisit every fact, including the people he was sure were involved. Chip was at the top of his list.

"He's back," the call came to Gabe. "I can see his car sitting just across the street. He's getting bold."

After pondering the new information, Gabe responded, "He's just trying to pressure you into making a mistake. I wish there was a way to keep a Gripen hovering over your place – just in case he got frisky. But we can't. The batteries just don't provide that kind of air time."

"I'm sick of this," Chip replied. "There has to be some way to turn the heat around and chase him off. He's suspended, so why don't we call the cops and report a suspicious vehicle? I bet he's violating some cop rule by stalking me."

"I suppose you could. Wouldn't hurt. At least he'll know someone's on to him and maybe that will be enough."

The call to 9-1-1 proved difficult for Chip to dial. He now found himself trying to maneuver through a waist-deep current of stress, every step seemingly life-altering important and irreversible. He procrastinated over making the call, idling around the house, watching TV, and peeking out the drapes every few minutes.

It was madding.

Yet every time he picked up the phone to punch the numbers, he hesitated. "Maybe he'll give up and go home," he moaned, inventing any excuse to avoid escalation.

After several hours and the impending nightfall, Marwick's presence outside his home became intolerable, overriding any worry over provoking the husky cop.

He texted Gabe, "He is still there. Can't take it anymore. Calling 9-1-1. Been nice knowing you."

Next came the actual call to emergency services. With a cracking voice, he reported the address, telling the female voice on the other end that a suspicious man had been sitting outside of his home all day. The dispatcher promised to send a car.

Officer Kirkpatrick received the call, including the address and description of the vehicle. He didn't connect the dots with the incident at the same location until he rolled onto the street. "Shit," he mumbled. "What the hell is Marwick up to now?"

He pulled up behind Big Jim's private car, skipping the normal procedure of using his spotlight to illuminate the suspicious vehicle. "What's up, Sergeant?" he greeted after approaching the window.

"Hey, Kirkpatrick. Did someone call me in?"

"Yup. Got a call a few minutes ago about a suspicious man sitting here all day. You doing a little surveillance work?"

Marwick nodded and then shook his head in regret. "Sorry about that. I'm a little frustrated and opted for a new tactic to get different results. I guess somebody called it in. It won't happen again."

The responding officer nodded his acceptance of the apology, despite finding such words completely out of character for a man like Big Jim. It made the younger cop curious. "So if you don't mind my asking, who's the mouse you're hoping will take the cheese?"

Jim nodded toward Chip's house, "You remember the guy who lives there. He and I danced in the driveway when we saw him trying to record our takedown. I did some deductive reasoning and decided he was one of the few people that carried a grudge against me and the department and possessed the resources to fund something like the Archangel. I watched him for a couple of days, but he must work from home, because the guy never leaves the house. So I decided to be a little more visible... see if I could force his hand... flush him out."

"I see," Dole responded, not liking the explanation at all.

It wasn't lost on the young officer that his decision to release the Marwick video was now putting others at risk. While he'd half expected Big Jim to come after him personally, the fact that other innocents might now be in the unstable man's crosshairs made Dole very uneasy. *Oh what a tangled web we weave,* he thought.

"Look... Sergeant.... It's none of my business, but I think you should be more careful. I'm not going to say a word, but what if another squad had gotten this call tonight? Someone who didn't know you? If IA found out about your conducting police work while you're on suspension, I don't think the boys downtown would appreciate that much."

Jim scowled, anger mixed with a hefty dose of impatience coloring his face. "I'm not doing police work. I'm researching my own defense against pending charges. And if any cop from our precinct wants to hassle me over that, then so be it. I'll hand them their fucking heads."

"I understand and sympathize," Dole lied. "But you're walking a real fine line. I don't know much about your case, but I can't believe stalking witnesses is going to play well."

It was obvious from his expression that Jim hadn't thought about that. It took several moments before he came up with the next justification. "No witnesses have been named as of yet, so I'm not tampering or intimidating anybody. But, I'll give you my word... I'll be a little more discreet going forward. I wouldn't want to distract the precinct from more important work."

Kirkpatrick made the decision to accept Marwick's reasoning. Closing the conversation with a half-hearted reply, "Good night, sir. Be careful out there," he made for his squad car, wondering if he'd have been so easy on someone he didn't know.

"Probably not," he muttered as he watched Marwick drive off.

Putting his own vehicle in gear, the young cop followed, intent on continuing his regular patrol. *I've created a monster*, he speculated. *That guy is going to hurt somebody, and the whole thing will unravel.*

He made a mental note to keep an eye on the address that held Big Jim's fascination, hoping the DA would put the man away before things spiraled out of control.

Twelve miles away, Gabe was having similar thoughts as he reviewed the Gripen's audio and video recording of the encounter between the two cops. Marwick was a powder keg, and it wasn't going to take much of a spark to set him off.

His mind wandered to the firestorm of events surrounding his actions. The Gripens were causing quite the stir across the nation, some of the unintended consequences casting doubt on the wisdom of his acts. *Was it all too much? Had his campaign to make the police accountable for their deeds gotten out of hand?*

He'd just read an internet news piece about a New Jersey cop who had pulled his shotgun and blasted a drone out of the sky. The cop had been sure it was spying on an undercover drug sting taking place nearby. After rushing to investigate the downed flyer, he found a distraught father and son standing over the kid's destroyed birthday present. The gunshot, convergence of multiple police cars, and overall commotion had spooked the drug dealer, and no arrests were made. It was the first such incident that provided the cops with a valid argument on their side of the anti-drone ledger.

Then there was the drone manufacturer who had launched a new marketing campaign that was taking the internet by storm. The "Weed Angel," was a diminutive, fold-up model that could carry up to a quarter pound of cargo. The company claimed that anyone in possession of marijuana could load, power up, and launch a small bag of weed skyward and out of law enforcement's reach, accomplishing such a feat in less than the amount of time it took to be stopped by a police officer. "Fly your weed to safety, and keep your ass out of jail," the advertisement touted, complete with video reenactment of two young men panicking at the sight of flashing blue strobes in the rear view mirror.

After spotting the police car's lights behind them, the two actors had quickly unfolded and stashed their small bag of contraband inside of the drone's tiny cargo hold. As they rolled to a stop, the passenger sent the drone buzzing out the sunroof, preprogramed to travel home. The commercial ended with the duo of dopers arriving back at their house, finding the illegal pot resting safely in the backyard, and sharing high-fives all around. According to one news report, the product had sold out on Amazon in less than 20 minutes.

Gabe had laughed at the clever marketing, despite thinking marijuana was dangerous. "Now I need to develop a product that delivers Doritos via drone," he mused. "Maybe I can partner with White Castle, and fly sliders around to cure the munchies."

All over the country, drones were a primary topic of conversation.

Police departments from coast to coast were in outrage. A few mid-sized organizations staging sick-strikes until their city councils outlawed the flying threats. One mid-western town had already passed an ordinance making it illegal to observe or record the police via an airborne vehicle. The ACLU, despite having been anti-drone where the government was concerned, found itself all twisted up in the throes of hypocrisy. It was every American's right to observe and record public settings, including police proceedings. What platform was being used was beside the point, or so argued the federal injunction filed to overturn the town's new law.

Gabe was also shocked to learn that people were trying to contact him personally. It seemed the man behind the Texas Archangel was in high demand.

There were internet postings everywhere from Craigslist to conspiracy and militia blogs, most requesting for the Archangel's master to contact an interested party. Some were from news departments, requesting an interview, others from private companies that wanted to do business, most seeking some sort of endorsement for their products.

Some people judged the entire uproar as nothing more than a mountain being made over a molehill. One late night talk show host loosed a drone to fly around his studio audience, making sure no one was guilty of excessive laughter over his monologue jokes.

A college professor made the front page when his students arrived in the classroom, only to find a small drone hovering over the lectern. The machine was carrying a petite voice recorder and began replaying the taped lecture after the bell. On the chalkboard directly behind the flying-teacher was a handwritten message; "This drone is videotaping your attention levels during the lecture. Students caught napping in class will find their images pasted all over the nightly news and the internet, drool and all."

Gabe had found many of the various twists and turns humorous – or at least mildly entertaining. There was some aspect of human creativity that always made him feel warm inside. *It was hope*, he determined. *As long as we are thinking and creating, there is hope for us.*

But none of the ancillary uses sprouting from his creativity seemed to help with the current Marwick situation. Or did they?

Of all the brouhaha arising from his actions, there had been one position that had resonated well with the Archangel's inventor. If it was okay for the government to use technology to watch the citizens, why wasn't it fair for the people to turn the tide on their representatives? Gabe liked it, thinking that little nugget of wisdom summed up the entire debate. He felt like the creator of a watch-dog poster boy.

So how could he utilize the Gripens to protect Chip from the out of control Marwick?

There was also another factor in play. Despite the fact that the country was divided over the topic, Gabe was bolstered by the group that believed in his cause. No longer did he feel alone, fully conscious of the millions of like-minded people from all walks of life that were adding their voices to the chorus of support. It emboldened his thinking and expanded the options.

Despite countless mental cycles seeking a solution, Gabe could not conceive of a strategy to help Chip. While he was sure Marwick's desperation would eventually lead to the man crossing the line, Gabe had no idea how to run interference for his friend in the interim or anticipate damage control needs in the near future.

"Keep working on it," he muttered, staring at the now fully functional G-3. It will come.

Needing a distraction, he settled on beginning a full diagnostic of the new Gripen. The effort was interrupted by Chip's cell call.

"He's left my street, I think, but there's no way to be sure what that jerk is up to," the troubled voice stated. "The cops came, but they didn't do shit. Now I bet Marwick is driving around, plotting how to kill me slowly."

"I know," Gabe responded calmly. "I was watching the meet with one of the G-1 units. I overhead the entire conversation."

"And?"

"And you're right; the cops aren't going to do shit about him. He's too well connected. We're on our own."

Chip paused before responding, his voice growling low and mean. "If he comes into my yard, I'm going to cut the son of a bitch in half with this 12-

gauge. If he bothers Manny or Amanda, I'll give him a bus ticket to hell via buckshot."

Gabe was a bit taken aback by his friend's tone, never having heard Chip so upset. What was worse – he believed his buddy would follow through on the threat. "I'm working on it," he promised, his words ringing hollow. "There's always a solution."

"Any ideas so far?"

"What if you and the girls just packed up and headed out on a little vacation? You know, take a trip out of town until things cool off. I hear there are some very affordable cruises leaving out of Galveston all the time."

"I thought about that," the concerned family man replied. "Even if I could think up some white lie to get Amanda on the boat, there's just no way. Manny has finals coming up, and she has already missed a few days with the flu. Amanda's still not sure about my new job and paycheck being the real deal, so she's still working part time. We can't just pull up and sail off into the sunset…. There's just no way."

"I was afraid of that," Gabe admitted, "but I had to ask."

"Look," Chip's agitated voice resonated on the line, "I have zero issue with confronting that asshat. Mr. Marwick and I already had a little chat once in my driveway, and I wouldn't hesitate a second time. What's eating me alive is the potential of surprise. Right now, he has every advantage over the time and place of an encounter. He can ambush my ass while I'm sitting on the toilet or snoring away in dreamland. I strolled out to get the mail today, paranoid as shit, worried that fucker was hiding in my bushes. When you throw in my wife and daughter, their schedules and their vulnerability, it's enough to drive a guy mad."

Gabe rubbed his chin, staring at the cell phone as if his friend were standing there in person. "So we're thinking the same thing. We need to come up with some way to take the initiative away from Marwick and shift it to our side. I'm all in with that strategy. It's the 'how' that currently eludes me."

"Well, we've got to come up with something. I'm getting jittery from toting this shotgun around as I go about my routine. I don't want Manny or the cat to surprise me… if you know what I mean. That could lead to a disaster."

"Do me a favor while we're thinking this through," came Gabe's less than confident reply. "Don't leave the house without letting me know first. Just send me a text, or make a quick call. I can have a drone there in less than 20 minutes and at least be able to help a little."

"Okay, boss. You got it. And thanks, Gabe. Thank you for being there."

"No need to thank me, buddy. I'm the one who got your ass into this mess in the first place. Marwick wouldn't even remember your name if it hadn't been for the drones."

There was a short, insincere chuckle across the connection. "Now we both know that's just bullshit. You didn't cause all this. That fat ass bully who is now parked on my street fired the first shot when he chose to pick on Jacob. No matter how this nightmare concludes, you remember that, Gabe. Never forget. You didn't start this fight, but if God in Heaven will allow it, you and I will damn sure finish it."

Gabe ended the call, amazed at Chip's last proclamation. The loyalty was uplifting, the man's no quit attitude inspirational. "I've got to make sure he comes out of this unharmed," he announced to the resting G-3. "Your sisters and you need to help me."

As his nemesis predicted, Big Jim's simmering anxiety was expanding beyond containment. It seemed like all four walls were closing in around the suspended officer, hemming him in while sucking the oxygen out of his environment. His lawyer was now in the process of trying to delay the initial hearings and actions in the criminal case being brought by the DA. But an earlier call from his counsel had advised of a sudden urgency to set a trial date from the once supportive authority. Fewer of his "friends" on the force were returning his calls, and the incompetent detectives downtown seemed to be making no progress on identifying the Archangel.

Time was running out. He couldn't depend on anyone but himself.

Whether it resulted from paranoia, apprehension, or just plain, old pigheadedness, Jim couldn't let go of Chip. He was convinced the man had something to do with the avalanche of undeserved shit that seemed to be raining down on his head.

Yet, his surveillance hadn't produced anything other than a warning from a near-rookie cop, several harsh looks from the suspect's neighbors, and a roaring case of hemorrhoids from sitting so long in the car.

Desperate, running out of options, and absolutely confident he was barking up the right tree, Marwick made the decision to approach Chip face to face and determine if he could shake some fruit off the reclusive man's branches.

The only problem was the where and the when.

Walking up to the front door wasn't an option. Humans, like all animals, are territorial. It was well understood by all cops that most people would resist twice as hard if confronted on their home turf as compared to out in the streets, away from their residence. It was a predictable reaction, resulting in both physical and mental escalation.

Jim wanted his approach to elicit fear, not defense. That meant he would have to catch Chip while he was out and about. Not an easy task, considering the guy had only showed his face once in three days.

It then occurred to Jim that he probably wasn't the only one tiring of hide and seek. Completely unaware that his inability to see the world from someone else's perspective, to put himself in any opposing role was his biggest single weakness as a police officer, Jim just couldn't accept that any person could view things differently. He was tired of the game; therefore, Chip must be tired as well.

With that line of reasoning engrained in his thoughts and championing his movements, Jim drove back to Chip's neighborhood. This time, he parked in a new spot, but was still within easy view of the suspect's dwelling. "Come on out and play, Mister Archangel," he whispered, turning off the car that had been his home as of late.

Chip spied the vehicle five minutes later, his habit of randomly checking the street now entrenched in his daily routine.

"He's back," the text to Gabe disclosed.

"Launching the G-1," the response reassured a few minutes later.

Shaking his head at the self-imposed imprisonment, Chip tried to busy himself with mundane tasks around the house. The shotgun was never far from his side.

The flight to Chip's subdivision passed quickly, the Gripen enjoying the benefit of a tailwind. Gabe was ready, manning the control desk as the now familiar rows of suburbia came into view. It only took a moment to spot Marwick's tan colored Impala.

He maintained the drone high and out of sight, positioning the flyer in the general area of the sun just to secure the robot from curious eyes. He could observe Marwick's outline through the open driver's side window. A small geyser of hatred welled up inside Gabe's throat, the image of the man who had beaten his son causing the hostile reaction.

The G-1 hovered for several minutes, all three of the men on the stage unsure what to do next. It was a showdown of inactivity.

Chip finally called his boss, unable to occupy his time with make-work chores. "I'm so sick of this. It's driving me batty. I don't care what we do, but let's do something."

"You're just playing into his hand if you go out and confront him," Gabe cautioned. "If I were in his shoes, that's the move I'd be hoping for."

"Okay, how about I go drive around? He'll follow, and we can see how aggressive his mindset has become."

"Where would you go?"

Chip was clearly getting agitated. "Just around. You know… a pleasant drive through North Houston. Hell… how am I supposed to know?"

Gabe realized that logic and rational behavior were quickly falling from favor. Both men fully aware that Marwick would like nothing more than to catch his prize out in the open, yet both of them were considering just such a move. It was the exhaustion that was making them rash, they were weary of the siege and demanding closure. No wonder people were constantly making stupid mistakes under pressure.

"No," Gabe finally stated with a firm voice, unwilling to submit to stupidity. "We are not going to be the ones who fuck up. You are going to sit tight and wait him out, come hell or high water. It's the smart thing to do. It's tactically sound. Don't let him win."

Chip's reply was interrupted by a tone indicating another call was coming in. "Hold on a second," he informed Gabe, "Someone else is trying to call."

After finding the right button to switch calls, Chip answered, "Hello."

"Hello, this is Richard Sullivan from Central High School. I need to speak with Chip Denton, Manny's father."

The hairs instantly rose up on Chip's neck, a call from his daughter's school extremely rare. "This is he."

"Mr. Denton, I'm a substitute gym teacher, and Manny has hurt her ankle," the deep male voice advised. "She is on her way to the nurse's office to have it checked out, but I wanted to give you a call and let you know of the injury. She may need to come home a little early today."

Something didn't mesh about the call. It took Chip a moment to figure out what the nagging, little voice inside him was saying. Manny wasn't taking gym this year.

"I see, Mister… Or is it Coach? I'm sorry, what did you say your name was?"

"Sullivan," came the unhesitating response.

The hairs on the back of Chip's neck were standing on end, his mind racing with suspicious thoughts. "I almost didn't pick up your call, sir. The caller ID was blocked."

"I'm calling from my personal cell. The rest of the class is still outside right now, but I wanted to give you a heads up as soon as possible."

"Mr. Sullivan, thank you. I was on another call, could I dial you right back?"

After the extended pause, Chip was certain whoever was on the other end had nothing to do with his kid's education. "We're going back inside shortly. I don't think my phone works in the building. Besides, the nurse should be calling soon. From the looks of it, you might want to get her ankle x-rayed. Perhaps make plans for a quick ER visit."

"I will do so, sir. Again, thanks for calling."

Chip switched back to his boss, the urgency bleeding through in his voice. "You still there?"

"Yeah... I was beginning to think you'd forgotten about..."

Chip interrupted, "Is the G-1 still watching Marwick?"

"Sure, why?"

"Did he just make a phone call?"

Gabe got it immediately. "Hold on, let me rewind the video. I wasn't paying attention."

The sound of keyboard clacking came through the cell connection, Gabe obviously manipulating the buttons in quick succession. "Yes, he did. How did you know?"

Chip exhaled, relieved that Manny wasn't hurt, pissed that Marwick would try such a stunt. "Because that son of a bitch just called me."

After a quick recounting of the conversation, Gabe was amazed. "He is getting desperate. What do you want to do?"

"How much battery is left in the G-1?"

"Maybe 30 more minutes, give or take. The wind has picked up a little."

"Is the G-3 ready?"

Gabe glanced over at the worktable and shook his head. "No. Not really. In an emergency, I might risk it."

"Shit. That asshole just pretended to be a substitute teacher at the high school. He claimed that Manny injured herself and needs emergency care. He is forcing my hand, Gabe. I need a guardian angel on my shoulder…. I was going to drive to the school, pretending as if I wanted to check if Manny were okay. I wanted to find out what he was up to."

"You don't think 30 minutes is enough?" Gabe responded, redoing the math in his head.

"Who knows? If he runs me off the road, then maybe not."

"The company pickup is still at your place. Why don't you drive it? His sedan couldn't do much against that heavier truck."

"Now there's an idea. It's in the garage. Follow me."

"Got it. Good luck," Gabe said, the concern coming over the line.

A few moments later, Chip hit the electric garage door opener and then backed the pickup into the street. He hadn't made it to the first stop sign before Gabe's text buzzed on his phone. "He's started his car. The G-1 is right with you."

The school was only a few miles away, the route entirely comprised of surface streets with 40 mph limits. Chip wasn't worried about the Gripen being able to keep up.

Twice he caught a glimpse of Marwick's tail, the tan Impala hanging back a reasonable distance, weaving carefully through the snarled afternoon traffic. After a few stoplights, Chip turned into the massive, suburban high school's parking lot, not surprised to find the visitor spaces completely full.

Big Jim was pleased, his scheme working perfectly. To begin with, he now knew who Chip Denton worked for, the license plate on the truck registered to one Jacob Industries, Incorporated. He didn't think it was a coincidence that the suicide kid and the company employing his primary suspect shared the same name.

Secondly, he'd not only managed to flush the recluse out of his house, he'd convinced the guy to drive right into his trap.

Like most big city high schools, Central had its own police force. Consisting mostly of retired constables and HPD officers, the massive number of campuses and students had required the creation of an independent law enforcement department some years ago.

There were over 80 cops on Central's roster, all of them deputized, registered peace officers with the same authority as a deputy sheriff.

Two of the officers were close friends of Marwick's, both men owing their easy duty, high paying, semi-retired positions to the sergeant's connections on the school board. Both were tough as nails, old school cops.

While planning this new initiative, Jim recalled the night he'd pulled over the president of the school board, the man obviously driving under the influence, blowing well above the legal limit.

The poor fellow had been desperate, a common reaction by individuals whose jobs depended on public reputations. Big Jim had let the powerful man go, even going so far as to escort the gentleman to his driveway.

Brimming with gratitude and relieved to be off the hook, the elected official had no idea he'd just made a deal with the devil.

But Jim knew better than to press it. Influential men didn't like a blackmailer constantly knocking on their doors. Only occasionally did Jim make a phone call, asking a small favor for a fellow officer who was retiring, but hadn't managed his finances well and could use a part-time job. Most were hired the same day. Most owed Marwick their livelihood.

Big Jim watched his prey turn into the big campus, a smirk of satisfaction on his face. Even if Mr. Denton called 9-1-1, the city would only transfer the call to the school's force. And they were already on the job.

Chip managed a parking spot at the far end of the student lot, a considerable jaunt to the main entrance. Before exiting the truck, he scanned the area, looking for Marwick's sedan. The dirty cop was nowhere to be seen.

He did spot one of the school's police cruisers patrolling the area, but that wasn't any big deal. During Manny's tenure, he had spotted several of the district's cops on the job, most of them older guys who were always posted around basketball and football games. Friendly gents. Always smiling and waving.

They even had their own on-campus police station, Chip having taken a tour during one of Manny's orientations. He'd thought it was overkill at the time, complaining to Amanda about the waste of taxpayer dollars. The tour guide had overheard the remark, responding with the retort, "Most parents would prefer to have disciplinary issues handled here, rather than at the main county jail downtown."

Taking one last glance around the horizon, Chip tried to locate the G-1, but couldn't. He had no idea where Gabe had directed the robot to hover. He hoped it was close.

He'd only crossed three rows of parked cars before the first cop pulled up. Chip casually waved, understanding why the officer would be curious about a pedestrian crossing the lot while classes were in session. When the second squad car appeared, he began to get nervous.

"Excuse me, sir," the first officer shouted as he exited the car, stopping Chip's progress. "Could I see some ID, please?"

Chip realized he was screwed immediately. Not only were the two school cops huge fellows, they had him cornered in a remote section of the parking lot where other foot traffic was extremely unlikely. Their aggressive posturing was just short of open hostility.

"Sure, officer," he replied, reaching for his wallet.

No sooner than Chip's hand had made it to his back pocket, the officer in front of him went for his holster and barked, "Real slow now, buddy. Pull out that ID real slow."

I am so fucked, Chip thought, doing exactly as the officer requested and presenting his driver's license.

With one big guy in front and another staying directly behind him, Chip felt a wave of helplessness deep inside. It was a somewhat disconcerting sensation, and were it not for the G-1 somewhere overhead, he would be sweating bullets already.

"What is your purpose at the school today?" asked the officer who was examining Chip's license.

"A teacher called and said my daughter had been injured during gym class," he responded honestly. "I was on my way to see if she was okay."

"And who was this teacher?"

"Richard Sullivan, I believe," Chip responded, again telling the truth, but not believing it mattered one iota.

Front-cop peered over Chip's shoulder at back-cop. "Do you know of a teacher named Sullivan?"

"Nope. Never heard of him," came the immediate answer.

"He said he was a substitute," Chip added.

Front-cop tilted his head to the microphone pinned to his shoulder. "Dispatch, this is 31. Can you call the main office and see if a there is a substitute teacher by the name of Sullivan working today?"

"Roger, 31," sounded a female voice.

"And Ginger, could you also see if there is a student, last name Denton, in the nurse's office?"

"Will do, 31."

The three men stood silently on the hot pavement, Chip knowing full well there wasn't any teacher named Sullivan and no student named Denton receiving medical treatment. Regardless, there wasn't anything he could do but pray the G-1 was doing a good job of recording the entire scene.

The policeman's radio broke the troubled man's concentration, "31; No record of any Sullivan. No student by the name of Denton."

"Dispatch, 31, roger that."

Now the cop's stare was boring into Chip, his posture becoming stiff and threatening. "So, Mr. Denton, want to tell me again why you're in the student parking lot, walking around like you're looking for a backseat to hide in, perhaps to surprise an underage female victim?"

Before Chip could respond, the back-cop spoke for the first time. "He looks like the kind of sicko who'd get off on raping a child, doesn't he?" the voice sneered.

Chip snorted, unable to help himself, despite the implied threat. "I'm telling you the truth, officer. I received the call not less than 30 minutes ago. I'm not quite sure what's going on."

"And I suppose you have a call log on your cell phone with a Central High School number listed as the caller?"

Nodding, Chip held out his phone, which was immediately snapped away by the cop. While he couldn't be positive, he thought the guy mumbled something like, "Can't record without this," but he wasn't sure given the nervous-blood pounding in his ears.

The cop didn't even bother to look at the call log, instead motioning Chip toward his parked cruiser. "Please step over to the patrol car, sir."

Chip hesitated, knowing that the G-1 wouldn't do him a bit of good if the two guys transported him to their little, private, on-campus police station. Once inside that building, he would be completely at their mercy. His mind started racing, trying to figure a way out.

"Officer, perhaps I've been the victim of a prank. If we could go inside, I'm sure the ladies working the main office would vouch for me and the fact that my wife and I are very active, responsible parents."

"That's what they all say," chuckled the back-cop.

"Please place your hands on the hood of the car, sir," ordered front-cop. When Chip tried to comply by placing his palms directly over the emblem, the cop pointed to a spot on the side, slightly behind the wheel well.

Gabe had told Chip about the police knowing how to avoid their dash cameras, and now he was seeing evidence of it up close and personal.

Moving to the indicated spot, Chip did as he was told, suffering the indignant process of being frisked. When no weapons were found, the almost disappointed officer barked, "Please place your hands behind your back, sir."

Again, Chip complied without protest, the cold steel closing around his wrists reminding him of that night in front of his house.

"Please step to the back of the car, sir. We are taking you to the campus police facility on the other side of the property to continue our investigation. Our sergeant will meet us there."

Chip started to turn as commanded, not noticing the back-cop's duty boot hovering over his own foot. The combination of cuffs and tripping-obstacle caused the prisoner to lose his balance, his shoulder brushing against front-cop.

The next thing Chip saw was the pavement rushing up at his face, back-cop lifting him by the belt and throwing the helpless man forward.

The impact with the blacktop surface sent white lines of vibrating pain through Chip's field of vision. And then the cop began screaming, "Why did you just assault that officer? What the hell is wrong with you, attacking a police officer? Are you on drugs?"

Just as Chip's head was starting to clear the pain, a sharp, stabbing ache racked his ribcage. "Stop resisting!" screamed the cop as he kicked Chip in the side. "Stop resisting!"

I'm going to die, right here, Chip thought. *These fuckers are going to kill me right here in the school parking lot. Manny will find my dead corpse lying in a pool of blood.*

But then the beating suddenly stopped.

Trying to regroup, Chip couldn't see anything from his facedown position. For a moment, he thought the two cops had let up because someone was passing by.

Then a buzzing sound filled the air, one of the cops saying, "What the fuck is that?"

Chip managed to turn his head and see the Gripen hovering at eye-level, its electronic lenses pointing directly at the police officers. For such a small machine, its profile was indeed threatening.

The closest cop actually reached for his weapon, pulling his service pistol halfway out of its holster before his partner reached across and blocked the draw. "It's only a drone. What are you going to do if your shot misses and hits the school building behind it?"

Realizing his error, the officer returned his iron, his eyes never leaving the menacing robot. The calmer of the two officers spoke again, "I believe we're the first to actually lay eyes on the Archangel."

"You mean that thing's been recording us this whole time?" asked the more flustered of the two.

Before any answer came, another voice rang out across the parking lot. "What's going on over here, guys?"

Chip, recovering from his face plant, recognized the coach's profile as the muscular, ex-athlete approached across the massive asphalt rectangle. Manny was hurrying alongside the high-ranking school official. The G-1 accelerated away, rising quickly into the air and zooming into the distance.

"Police business, sir. Please move on," tried the older cop. But it was clear the coach wasn't having any of it. It was about then that Manny spied her father on the ground, handcuffed and bleeding. "Dad!" she shouted, running toward her father.

One of the officers stepped in front of the rushing girl, grabbing her by the shoulders and stopping her cold. "Police business, young lady, please stay back."

Chip detected other people in the parking lot, the sound of footsteps coming from all directions. It seemed the basketball team was joining their coach.

"Why were you hitting that man when he's handcuffed and on the ground?" the coach asked. "What is he accused of?"

"That's none of your affair," barked one of the cops.

"It's *my* affair," came another voice, the school principal now joining the ever-larger throng gathered around the two police cars.

When the cops didn't answer, the schoolmaster circumvented them, bending down to closely examine the prone suspect. "Chip? What in the world is going on, Chip?"

"I have no idea," he managed, spitting blood from his bleeding mouth. "I was walking toward the entrance when these two thugs stopped me. Next thing I know, I'm getting the shit kicked out of me for no reason."

The principal turned to look at the officers, who sounded their own defense. "He was acting in a suspicious manner," stated the front-cop. "When we tried to restrain him, he began resisting, so we had to use force to subdue the suspect."

"My dad would never do that!" Manny protested, tears streaming down her face, her mind locked in a déjà vu loop, viciously cycling between her memory of the beating months before and the image of her dad bleeding in the high school parking lot.

The coach glared at the principal and explained, "I was in the gym when I got a phone call saying someone was getting beat up in the parking lot. I rushed out to see these guys kicking the man on the ground."

"And you, young lady?" the principal asked Manny. "I got a text saying my dad was in the parking lot. I saw the message between classes and ran out to see him."

Everyone stood around for a while, a standoff in progress as neither side appeared willing to back down. The coach's cell phone dinged, announcing the delivery of a new multi-media message.

Chip was pulled upright, one of the cops begrudgingly retrieving a first aid kit from his car and letting Manny attend to her father's cuts.

While the principal was talking quietly with the two officers, the coach continued watching the video attached to the recently arrived message. "Sir," he eventually said, getting the school administrator's attention. "I think you'd better watch this. It's a video I just received from the Citizen Observation Committee, and it shows these two officers aren't exactly telling us the whole story. I am pretty sure our institution doesn't want to be a part of this kind of publicity on the evening news."

Chapter 12

Peelian Principle
*The test of police efficiency is the absence of crime and disorder, not the
visible evidence of police action in dealing with it.*

Marwick could care less about the trouble befallen his two friends on the
school's force. Nor did he mind Chip Denton escaping the interrogation
planned for him at the campus jail. Big Jim had what he was after, and
now he was running open-field.

With a confidence derived from having correctly pegged Chip Denton as
being associated with the Archangel, the suspended cop was pursuing his
prey with a renewed vigor and determination.

It took longer than anticipated to find any information on Jacob
Industries, even longer still to obtain the address. Despite the delay, one
large, happy cop rolled into the empty parking lot and began to study the
mysterious corporation's facilities.

At first, he thought he'd arrived in the wrong location. From the front
gate, it was clear that the small office complex was of recent construction,
the unfilled lot and still-fresh landscaping indicative of a recently
completed project. He'd used the fire department's emergency access
code to open the drive's barrier. *Yet another benefit of being on the right
side of the law*, he mused, pulling up to park across from the front door.

A quick jaunt around the exterior, combined with his flashlight beam
piercing the tinted windows, showed the bottom level was completely
void of occupants. In fact, it had never been built out, the raw concrete
floors and ceiling appearing new and unmodified.

The sophisticated security cameras provided the first hint that the
premises weren't entirely void of habitation. When he spied Gabe's lone
vehicle sitting in a reserved space at the rear, he knew he'd discovered
the Archangel's headquarters.

For a moment, Big Jim considered calling the authorities and trying to cut a deal. He'd exchange the information now in his possession for immunity from prosecution and reinstatement at his old job.

The idea was quickly dismissed, Marwick realizing the animal he was about to snare was far, far more valuable on a national level. He began inventorying the federal officials he'd met and worked with over his years in law enforcement. Surely, one of them would be very interested in getting the credit for capturing the now infamous Archangel.

He knew a couple of the local FBI agents, mid-level guys at best. He'd been to the DEA's Christmas party a few years ago, invited to the affair after playing a minor role helping the local agents with a significant drug bust.

After careful consideration, the head of the Houston ATF office finally surfaced as his best option. While he couldn't truthfully call the head man a friend, Jim had worked with his group more than once, the outcome always positive. More than any established relationship, Marwick's profile on the ATF's honcho was that of an ambitious fellow, always looking at the proper career moves to achieve advancement or promotion.

The boys down at Alcohol, Tobacco, and Firearms worked inside a powerful organization that enjoyed extensive authority, few oversights, and even fewer constraints. They operated at a level of freedom that was the envy of many other agencies, including the FBI, Federal Marshals, and local law enforcement.

Jim started to dial the number, but then stopped. What would he say? "I'm sitting outside of an apparently empty office building, sure that the Archangel is inside?"

There was only one shot at this, and he couldn't fuck it up. Any failure at this point would look like a desperate, half-crazed cop trying to avoid prosecution. No, he had to be sure.

That meant catching one Mr. Gabriel Chase inside, red-handed, fondling one of his little drones.

Big Jim exited his car for the second time, deciding to circle the building in hopes of finding a way in. He scoured the Impala's trunk for tools first, pulling out a mid-sized crowbar and hefting the weighty iron instrument with a gleam in his eye. The pistol on his belt added to his reassurance, his success so far merely icing on the ego that fueled the big man's confident swagger.

Gabe, three floors above, inhaled sharply when Marwick produced the pry bar, noting the intent to break and enter displayed all over the deranged cop's face.

He had no idea how his nemesis had tracked him down so quickly, writing it off as unimportant and probably due to some minor detail Adam Barlow and he had overlooked.

The only thing that mattered now was the burly, unstable barbarian at the gate.

Gabe considered calling the cops, a report of a strange, husky man with a crowbar and a scowl of ill intent was surely a legitimate complaint. But he quickly dismissed the idea – Marwick knew all the cops and would talk his way out of it, just as he had in front of Chip's home.

He watched the security monitors as the potential invader circled the perimeter, hoping that his fortress would dissuade the man. For a bit, he actually thought his optimistic thought would come true, Marwick skulking back to his car after examining the strong steel doors at both the front and back of the facility.

"I've got a week's worth of food and water in here," Gabe advised the monitor. "How many bologna sandwiches do you have in your car, big man?"

But even if his enemy did leave, Gabe was still in a pickle. He had his sniper rifle and a few shells, but the previous experience with trying to pull the trigger was still sour in his gut. However, now he was facing a life and death situation…. Could he shoot another human being?

The police scanner sounded in the background, the sudden noise startling Gabe. He recognized a familiar voice as it came over the speaker, and it gave him an idea. Taking one last glance to make sure the beefy cop was still sitting in his Impala, Gabe rose from the console and hurried for the roof.

Officer Kirkpatrick was just exiting the all-night breakfast chain when an odd noise sounded over his head. Looking up, half expecting to see a beehive or similar gathering of buzzing insects, he scanned the area and then shrugged. Nothing seemed out of place.

He wandered through the nearly empty lot, occupied with the patrol route that would consume the remainder of his shift. He entered his cruiser and started the engine, taking a moment to glance at the mounted computer protruding from the dash.

He was just reaching for the radio's microphone, ready to sign back in from his meal break when movement caught his eye. He froze, a rare bolt of fear rushing through the officer's veins like ice water.

There, hovering over the hood of his cruiser, was a machine. It took the stunned man a few moments to realize it was nearly identical to the one that had saved him from shooting a child just a few weeks ago.

Fascinated by its sudden appearance and not sure what to make of the social call, Dole had to remind himself that there was a human being controlling the device. "What do you want?" he whispered.

It was then that he noticed a white piece of paper rolled into a tube that was hanging beneath the drone's midsection. As if on cue, the machine changed its attitude slightly, making the note even more visible. It was an invitation of sorts, almost as if the machine were asking him to remove the cargo.

Slowly, his eyes never leaving the four spinning propellers, Dole exited his car. With even more caution, he took a step forward, extending his hand as if he were about to pet a snarling, muscular dog.

The plastic tube containing the paper came off easily with barely a tug. With its message delivered, the drone rose 25 feet into the air, and then paused as if watching to make sure the note was read.

Kirkpatrick unrolled the small communiqué, finding neat block lettering done by hand. It read, "Marwick is here with murder in his eye. I helped you with the child's plastic gun. Please help me. Come to…," followed by an address.

"Shit," Dole hissed, unsure of what to make of the strange encounter. He glanced back at the hovering machine, not knowing what to do.

In a flash of self-preservation, the young officer decided to help the Archangel. His choice wasn't born of nobility or honor due to the debt he owed the operator for saving an innocent child… nor was his decision motivated by a sense of civic responsibility.

No, Dole realized that if Marwick made the Archangel's owner talk and learned that the man had nothing to do with the release of the dash cam video, the unstable cop would continue to hunt for the person who had betrayed him. That trail would eventually lead back to one Officer Kirkpatrick.

Peering back up at the still staring drone, Kirkpatrick announced, "Okay, I'm on my way. I owe you one."

The small machine dropped down lower, coming to a stop not more than four feet away from Dole's face. Its front tilted up and down, as if the machine were nodding its head in thanks. And then it was gone, whisking off in a flash, disappearing into the night sky.

An idea occurred to Big Jim. Cursing himself for not having thought of it earlier, he again exited his vehicle and popped the trunk. This time, he reappeared brandishing the tire jack in his meaty hand.

He'd assessed that the steel doors protecting the building's entrance were too stout, even for the crowbar. Rather than stand around like an idiot, he'd returned to sit and think.

He was about to drive away, pondering some of the more potent options he had stored at home. Those would produce a considerable explosion, but he didn't give a rat's ass about collateral damage.

But then, he remembered a rather crafty thief they'd collared some years ago. The man had used a hydraulic jack to open even the most fortified doors. The felon had gained a certain notoriety over the years, only to be captured after one of his "cracked," doors broke all the way off its hinges, pinning the hapless burglar under its considerable weight.

Big Jim had just such a tire jack in his trunk.

It took a few tries before he identified the proper approach, bracing the jack's piston against the door with its angled base anchored against the concrete stoop.

His first attempt had resulted in the jack just tipping over as he pumped up the piston.

The second try was even less effective, the powerful tool merely scraping the paint as it slid up the smooth surface, unable to gain traction.

After an adjustment and the discovery of an expansion crack in just the right spot, Jim smiled when the piston wedged firm and started bending the door inward, its hinges groaning under the strain.

On and on he pumped, the metal door giving way, unable to withstand the tons of force being applied by the hydraulics. Soon there was a loud pop, followed by the scream of surrendering metal.

Now there was an opening perfect for his crowbar. After inserting the tip, Big Jim pressed both hands on the handle and dedicated his significant weight to the effort. The barricade began to give way.

A voice from the darkness startled the husky cop, causing him to drop the crowbar and reach for his pistol. "What are you doing, Sergeant," Dole said calmly, staying back in the shadows.

"Kirkpatrick? Is that you? What the fuck are you doing here?"

Dole stepped into the clear, responding with a smirk. "Funny. I was just wondering the same about you."

"Get your ass over here and help me, son," Marwick commanded. "I'm 100% certain the Archangel is inside this building, and I'm going in after him."

"No, you're not, Marwick," came Dole's surprisingly strong voice. "You've caused enough damage for one bad cop. Now take that pistol out of your belt very slowly, and lay it on the ground. You're going to go back to your car, drive straight home, and wait there for the DA to throw your ass in jail."

"What?" Big Jim barked, spinning to face the younger man. "What the hell are you talking about?"

"I know you lied about that night Jacob Chase was arrested. I'm the one who leaked the tape because you violated the code…. You are a liar and have no honor. You deserve to be behind bars."

"Why, you little shit," Marwick spouted, taking a step toward the smaller officer. "I'm going to kick your…" but then he stopped, seeing Dole's pistol pointed directly at his head.

"Lay that tool down, and go back to your car. I'm not going to fuck around with this. You're out of control, Marwick, a mad dog. And tonight, I'm the dogcatcher."

Jim's demeanor changed, lifting his hands in surrender. "Whatever, punk. I'll go, but you've not heard the last of me."

Making to pick up his tire jack, Big Jim managed to half bend when Dole's command came loud and strong, "Don't even think about it. Now drop that piece, and get the fuck out of here before I accidently blow your fat head off. Do it!"

With his off hand, Jim reached for his pistol, holding it out by the barrel so Dole could see. He bent deeply, making of show of gently placing the weapon on the sidewalk at his feet.

With a surprisingly swift motion for such a burly man, Jim's hand scooped and flung the crowbar all in one move.

Dole ducked the whizzing metal projectile, but didn't recover in time to stop Marwick from gripping his firearm and getting off a shot. The .40 caliber bullet struck the young officer in the chest, the impact to his armor still enough to stagger Kirkpatrick. The second shot hit him in an unprotected shoulder, the third shattering his knee.

The pain surging through Dole's body was unbelievable, his brain nearly shutting down from the shock and agony. He spotted an image appear above his head, the sneering face of Big Jim Marwick glaring down with hatred and disgust flaming in his eyes.

Dole spied the burly cop's pistol come up, the round muzzle appearing as big as a dinner plate. "You fucking, punk-ass piece of shit. How dare you question a superior officer's motives? Who the hell made you the God of police morality? You deserve this for ruining a better man's life."

Lying helplessly, Dole thought to close his eyes as Jim's finger tightened on the trigger, but he couldn't force himself to look away. For a hundredth of a second, he believed his wounds were causing a ringing in his ears, the distraction quickly dismissed as he watched Marwick lower the barrel so that the weapon lingered just above his forehead, aimed at the fallen officer's pulsing temple.

"You want to work with angels? Fine. I'm going to send you to them," hissed the big man.

But he didn't. The buzzing noise was back, breaking Marwick's concentration.

Jim looked around, quickly raising the pistol from Dole's face. There was the G-3, hovering a short distance away from his head.

Kirkpatrick saw the machine as well. Despite the pain resonating through his body, something different about the drone's configuration drew the wounded man's attention.

There was a tube... no, a pipe under the main airframe. A plain, grey piece of lead, plumbing pipe. He knew instantly what the gizmo was, and he summoned all his available energy in an effort to turn his body away.

Marwick tilted his head, seeming to forget about the man at his feet, studying the hovering robot with vengeance in his eyes.

Despite outweighing the drone by nearly 300 pounds, the hefty cop seemed to hesitate. There, suspended in mid-air, was the supreme icon of all of society's problems.

In Big Jim's mind, the drone represented all that was wrong with the world. *Eyewitnesses aren't shit*, he considered. *Any good lawyer could trip one up*. Even an occasional camera wasn't a serious threat. But then came the cell phones, carried by far too many onlookers, their video often leveraged as weapons against those in authority. They hampered law enforcement, restrained those wearing the white hats, and required extra effort to neutralize.

But this... this flying monstrosity of technology... this was the apocalypse of proper policing.

"You're the epitome of evil," Jim whispered. "A demon, released from the depths of hell to trouble good men like me."

Lifting his pistol to point at the drone, Big Jim added, "I'm going to kill you *and* your master tonight."

A ball of fire and whizzing lead shrapnel replaced the drone, the tiny pipe bomb attached to the undercarriage exploding with significant force. Only Big Jim's body prevented Dole from acquiring additional injury.

After the thunderous roar and smoke had cleared, Kirkpatrick managed to open, and then focus his eyes. He found himself looking at Marwick's lifeless, nearly decapitated body lying just a few feet away.

And then there was a pair of hands checking the wounded cop's body. "I'll get you some help," a voice echoed, its volume made distant and weak by the ringing in Dole's ears. He couldn't keep his eyes open any longer, finally giving way to his brain's desperate desire to shut down and avoid the pain.

Epilogue

Karen left the DA's offices at her usual late hour, crossing the elevated people-bridge to the parking garage on the other side of the street.

Her Mercedes was in its assigned spot, the secure, well-guarded facility eliminating any safety concerns normally experienced by a single lady working late hours.

She unlocked the expensive sedan with the remote, its plush interior and solid luxury of leather and wood enabling her to temporarily set aside the day's pressing matters. She sighed in relief after starting the engine, the surroundings reminding her of a comfortable pair of well-worn jeans or a soft spot on the sofa.

Taking a moment to stare across the Houston skyline, she waited for the GPS mapping system to display the least gridlocked route home. The half-height concrete wall bordering the parking garage's exterior exposed a number of skyscraper office lights, the view making her feel less alone with the burden of her extensive office hours.

The drone appeared out of nowhere, hovering just outside the garage's outer wall, less than 15 feet from the hood of her car.

She froze for a moment, the unusual sight taking her breath away. Eventually recovering, she studied the machine, trying to determine any hostile intent. The German sedan's glass and steel provided a barrier of safety. Despite the device's aggressive shape and unblinking lense-eye, she didn't feel threatened.

Inhaling a calming breath, she opened the car door, gradually exiting to stand beside her fortress on wheels. She was ready to dive back inside if the buzzing menace displayed the slightest ill will.

"Hello, DA Sanders," the computer-generated voice attempted to engage in social amenities. "I saw on television where you expressed a desire to speak with me, and thought I would introduce myself."

Something in the mechanical voice's statement struck Karen as funny. Notwithstanding the circumstances, late hour, and totally startling encounter, she blurted out a chuckle and then smiled.

"You could have called my assistant and made an appointment like most people," she grinned. "But I understand why that might be a bit uncomfortable, given the situation."

"You'll have to forgive me, I didn't mean to startle you, but the concept of walking into the DA's office and introducing myself didn't seem wise. I have similar aversions to phone calls and emails, if you know what I mean."

"I understand," Karen nodded, relieved the Archangel seemed to be of a reasonable intellect. Still, she didn't move from behind her open car door.

"So how can I help you, Ms. Sanders?"

"I think you can help the people of Harris County," she replied. "I think your drones might be the answer to a systemic problem that has plagued our city for decades, and I would like to work with you. Cooperate. Join forces, if you will."

"Go on, please. I'm intrigued. This is unexpected."

"Your activities over the past few months have given my office a much needed out. Before you got started, I couldn't pursue bad cops without significant risk to both the police and my office's effectiveness. I'm sure you appreciate why."

There was a pause, Karen unsure if the drone's connection had been dropped, or if the device was malfunctioning. "Are you there? Can you hear me?"

"Sorry, Ms. Sanders, I was thinking. At times, I'm not very quick on my feet, as it were. So what do you have in mind?"

"At first, I believe it best that we take baby steps and operate on a clandestine basis. Correct me if I'm wrong, but I get the sense that your motivation isn't to destroy our police force, but simply to improve a system that is failing the people. If my analysis is accurate, then couldn't we do a better job if we worked in concert to accomplish the same goal?"

"Yes, I suppose so," the machine conceded. "If I trusted you, it could be an effective partnership."

Again, Karen had to smile. She was beginning to like the Archangel, finding the honesty refreshing. "Trust is earned, sir. It is a two-way street that requires the repetition of honorable responses over a period of time. I'm at risk as well, given that a significant portion of the electorate hasn't decided if your drones are good or evil. Folks might not vote for a district attorney who harbors the devil."

Again, another long pause. Then she remembered another question. "By the way, what should I call you?"

The response was immediate, but initially unclear. It took the DA a moment to realize the computer was struggling to translate laughter. "I guess Archangel is as good as anything. Batman has already been taken."

"And this is not Gotham City, for sure," Karen replied, joining in the humor. "Okay, Mr. Archangel, is there a chance we can work together?"

"There is always a chance, Ms. Sanders. And if it helps, please call me Gabriel… it's the only Archangel's name I know. What do you propose?"

Karen hadn't really thought that part though, the meeting completely unforeseen. She decided to just blurt out an honest first thought. "I would appreciate seeing any videos recorded by your devices before you released them to the general public. I promise you I will use the evidence appropriately, regardless if it incriminates or supports the police. You've got the entire department paranoid as hell now, looking over their shoulders at shadows and frightened of every mid-sized bird flying overhead. If I use your recordings to take care of business quietly, behind the scenes, it will help all involved."

"And if I give you the recordings, and you don't take action?"

"Then by all means do what you've been doing and release them to the media," she countered.

"I don't hate the cops, Ms. Sanders. As a matter of fact, I've gained more respect and understanding of the issues facing law enforcement than I had before I started flying little robots all over the city."

Nodding, Karen acknowledged, "I realized that a short time ago as well. But you've caused their department no small amount of controversy and bad blood. A lot of people are convinced that you're anti-law enforcement."

The drone-voice didn't respond right away, the background hum of the propellers and motors the only sound in the empty garage. "I wasn't the cause of the police department's grief. No more so than a news reporter can be blamed for covering a natural disaster. I only exposed what was happening. In the end, transparency will put the public on law enforcement's side. They've been a secretive, isolated entity for so long, and now that has to change. I'll admit that when I started this enterprise, I despised all cops. I'll also confess to having a single-minded purpose to expose and discredit the police. All cops... every stinking one. Over time, I learned the truth. From above, I watched and learned. Policing doesn't have to oppose or shun the average citizen; it should embrace and integrate the public. We have to get back to Peel's Principles, and as long as you are moving in that direction, I will cooperate."

Karen nodded, the statements coinciding with her beliefs on multiple levels. Before she could respond, the digital voice continued. "I have to ask, ma'am, why don't you just build and deploy your own drones? They're not that expensive or difficult to operate. I am sure the city of Houston can afford them."

The District Attorney was ready for that question, having already explored the possibility. "Because after a time they would simply be absorbed and corrupted by the system. The genius of your actions has been the neutrality of a private citizen controlling the oversight committee. It's been more potent than citizen review boards, or outside audits. It is simply a high-tech form of what the founders set up as checks and balances... a way to keep any one branch of government from becoming too powerful. We lost those safeguards in law enforcement a long time ago, and now you are providing a chance to get them back into working order."

"Okay, Ms. Sanders," Gabe replied through the computer interface. "How do you want me to deliver the product?"

"To my private email. I give you my word I will keep our confidence. I hope to receive the same in kind."

"Oh, don't worry, ma'am. My friends wouldn't appreciate my socializing with lawyer-types. I won't say a word. Now if you'll excuse me, I have to take my wife out for a night on the town. It's our anniversary."

"Nice to finally meet... errr... talk to you, Gabriel. I look forward to our confidential partnership."

And then in a flash, the drone was gone.

Karen stepped to the wall, peering out across the lights of Houston while deep in thought. "Maybe together we *can* make things better for all involved. But first, I'm going to go home, pour a glass of wine, and take a hot bath. Dealing with these robot drones is tough work."

THE END

Made in the USA
Lexington, KY
15 October 2016